Sign up for our newsletter to hear
about new and upcoming releases.

www.ylva-publishing.com

Other Books by A. L. Brooks

Write Your Own Script

A.L. Brooks

Acknowledgements

Big thanks to Ylva Publishing for continuing to support me and my writing. This one was special to me, and I'm glad we could bring it to the f/f world.

Thanks to Alissa for an awesome editing experience once again. To my beta readers, Erin, Amy, and Katja, who wowed me with their comments – you gave me all the feels on this one!

And last, but by no means least, to Dobby, for inspiring Gizmo, and to Melanie, Dobby's partner in crime, for letting me use that little dynamo as the inspiration.

Dedication

Tanja, my love, this one's for you. You're my superstar, every day

Part One

Chapter 1

"YOU LOOK TIRED, DARLING."

The words were delivered in a tone oozing with false concern, and Tamsyn instantly tensed. Melinda, the young actress who had spoken, leaned forward and stared at her in the large mirror before them, cool blue eyes seeming to bore into every pore. Tamsyn resisted the urge to squirm under the scrutiny.

Pulling gently at her own face, the skin soft and pliable, Melinda grinned and sat back in her chair. Marie, the make-up artist, glanced quickly from one to the other, then picked up a brush and feigned disinterest.

"Have you ever thought of getting any work done?"

It took every ounce of professionalism Tamsyn had not to retort with the venom she wished she could really exude.

"I was amazed when someone told me you're still all natural. As soon as this fades," Melinda pointed at her soft cheek, "I'm getting everything possible done."

She really was crass and—Tamsyn hesitated over the phrase but decided it fit—as common as muck. Melinda seemed to revel in hitting the front pages of the trashiest magazines. With her brassy blonde hair—clearly from a bottle—large but apparently totally natural breasts, tiny waist, and long legs, she was the tabloids' favourite, and played up to that fact with alarming skill.

"How many scenes do you have today?" Tamsyn asked, a poor attempt at diverting the conversation, such as it was, away from their disparate looks and age. She raised her chin when Marie gently pushed it upwards, and closed her eyes as the soft brush skittered over her cheeks.

"Just two. I'll be done by lunchtime, so I'm heading back to the hotel for an afternoon in the spa."

Lucky you. I'll be filming a fake rainstorm and it'll be amazing if I don't come down with the flu afterwards.

Marie started on Tamsyn's eyes while Melinda sipped at her coffee, her narrowed eyes watching Marie work. Tamsyn tried—but failed on a number of occasions—to avoid that gaze.

"Marie, you're a genius," Melinda said smoothly, a few minutes later. "You'd never know Tammy had all those little wrinkles now."

Tamsyn gripped the armrests of her chair, willing her anger to subside. These little digs had been going on all week, ever since Melinda turned up on set. Twenty-five years younger than Tamsyn and obviously the director's favourite, she seemed to feel the need to make that point every five minutes of every day. She had been pushing all of Tamsyn's buttons, sapping her energy in the battle to resist rising to the bait. Tamsyn was already tired, and dealing with this little bitch really wasn't helping.

Marie, thankfully, ignored Melinda as she finished Tamsyn's make-up. It probably helped that Marie wasn't that much younger than Tamsyn and could probably empathise with her discomfort.

"There," she said, squinting at Tamsyn in the mirror. "All done."

Tamsyn turned her head left and right, then nodded. "Thank you, Marie. It's perfect."

Marie smiled, turned Tamsyn's chair around so that she could exit gracefully, and stepped back to let her do so.

"See you on set, Tammy!" Melinda called.

Tammy. Who the fuck does she think she is? No one has ever called me Tammy.

Marie's soft touch on the small of her back helped ground her, and knowing she had an ally kept her walking forward rather than turning around and slapping the younger woman.

She rolled her shoulders as she exited the room. *God, I'm so tired.* She knew it was all self-inflicted, but she couldn't seem to stop the momentum of what she'd started two years previously. Turning fifty had affected her in more ways than she'd anticipated, and none of them good. A fear of what the future could entail for an actress her age had suddenly consumed her, and she'd been battling against it ever since, taking on more and more, insisting on doing ever more physically demanding roles, and trying to prove to herself and the rest of the world—which was extraordinarily fickle when it came to its love of celebrities—that she was still a viable force.

It had worn her down, and she knew that deep down inside, but she couldn't seem to admit it openly. Carmen had expressed concern only a few weeks ago, and Tamsyn had brushed her off. Today, however, facing the rainstorm scene, her arms already aching from the multiple re-takes they'd done of the canyon scene the day before, Tamsyn wondered if she shouldn't actually listen to her agent once in a while.

She smiled at the crew as she passed them. She had always made a point of being approachable, remembering her early days in the business when she'd seen some of the top stars treat the crew like something less than human, and had vowed never to stoop that low. The smiles she received in return always made her feel good.

"You're late," Don snapped, his voice loud across the enclosed set. He wasn't even looking at her, just standing with his arms folded across his broad chest, his gaze on a cameraman moving his rig into position.

Don Speed was one of those young, hotshot, everyone's-talking-about-me directors who thought he was God's gift to everything. He was tall, good looking, and exuded an air of haughty disdain for everyone and everything. Tamsyn had disliked him from minute one, although she could begrudgingly admit that he had a fantastic eye for a scene. It was such a shame he had to be a total asshole as well. He'd made it perfectly clear he didn't think an actress of her age was suitable for the role, but he'd been outgunned by the producers, who had wanted to work with Tamsyn for some time now. Everyone on set had picked up on the tension and tiptoed around them both.

"Sorry," she replied, breezily professional over the subsurface tension. "I was in make-up."

"Trust me," Don snipped, finally looking over, then looking her up and down, "there isn't enough make-up in the world to hide how old you are. But don't worry, love, we'll use a soft-focus lens."

Tamsyn's brain went into a deep freeze: her mouth wouldn't function. Her simmering anger suddenly threatened to boil over. Melinda giggled as she strolled over to where Don stood. That was the flame, along with the satisfied smirk on Don's face as he realised how much his comment had hit home, which was the touch paper.

A large cup of orange juice sat on a high table behind the sound boom, close to where she was standing. Her arm moved almost without thought to grab it and, in one smooth motion, fling its contents straight into his face.

"Fuck you," she snarled, before turning on her heel and walking serenely off set.

Chapter 2

"WHERE THE HELL ARE WE?"

Tamsyn pushed her sunglasses up into her hair and stared out of the window. The scenery that was trundling by as the car humped and bumped its way down the country lane was pretty, that much she could begrudgingly admit.

Carmen exhaled loudly. "North Norfolk. You know that."

Slouching back into the comfort of the plush leather seat, Tamsyn glared at Carmen but said nothing. Their driver, Heather, the consummate professional, also said nothing, but Tamsyn couldn't help wondering what she must think. She'd driven Tamsyn before, of course, but not to anywhere like this.

The Mercedes lurched as it ran through what must have been a crater of a pothole. The suspension on the expensive car was good, but not *that* good.

Tamsyn winced. She'd need a good yoga session after this to ease out the kinks and creaks in her spine. Thank God she'd remembered to bring her mat.

They rounded a bend in the lane and swept through a pristine white wooden gate onto a gravel driveway which curved around a wide lawn filled with trees. Beyond that stood a large house, its flint walls gleaming in the bright April sunshine. The woodwork surrounding the door and windows was painted a beautiful sage green, contrasting nicely with the two elegant bay trees flanking the front door.

To her consternation, however, at a murmured word from Carmen, Heather took them past the beautiful house and down yet another narrow track to the side of it. This one was closed in by trees; their thin branches swished and scraped at the sides and roof of the car as they passed. Tamsyn stared longingly back over her shoulder as the house receded out of sight. When she turned back to the front window, she swallowed back her nerves. The lane was dark, and a little creepy, and although she knew she was being irrational, she suddenly wondered just what Carmen had meant when she'd said Tamsyn needed to hide away from the world for a while.

She was about to speak, to put on her best haughty tone and confront Carmen about whatever this insane plan was that she'd cooked up, when the car rounded yet another bend and her words died in her throat. The lane opened out from the gloom of the enclosing trees into what she could only describe as a picture-perfect scene. Immediately in front of them was a lake, partially ringed by reeds and rushes, with a deck on the far side that led perhaps twenty metres out into the water. Tied up to that were four single-person kayaks with their oars laid on the boards of the deck. Beyond the deck, sitting about a hundred metres on either side of it, and therefore a good distance apart, were two cottages. Backed by a line of woodland that stretched as far as Tamsyn could see, the cottages were symmetrical, each having a single door flanked by two windows. A curl of smoke rose from the chimney of the cottage on the right, and a small red car was parked in the gravel driveway.

The lane split at the edge of the lake; Heather took the left branch and a minute later pulled the Mercedes up alongside the unoccupied cottage. She hastened out to open Tamsyn's door.

"Thank you," Tamsyn murmured, pulling her sunglasses back down onto her nose even as she stared around her at the gorgeous scenery. Of course, only one thing marred that view, which was evidence of another human close by. Before she could speak, Carmen held up a hand.

"Yes, I know. It isn't the total privacy I wanted to get you." She glanced over at the other cottage then back to Tamsyn. "But at this short notice it was the best I could do."

"I thought the idea was I would be alone." Tamsyn tried to hold back the acidity in deference to the presence of Heather, who could more than likely hear every word even as she busied herself unloading suitcases and boxes from the boot of the car.

From the look on Carmen's face, she failed.

"Tamsyn," Carmen said, her exasperation evident, "I am your agent, not Wonder Woman. Besides, in the UK today, there are very few places where you can truly be in solitude and yet still have many of the comforts you are used to." She walked over to Tamsyn and placed a gentle hand on her forearm. "This will give you the time you need. And my aunt has assured me that the other tenant is after just as much peace and quiet as you are. I doubt you'll even see her."

Relief swamped Tamsyn at the mention of the other person's gender. At least she wouldn't have to deal with the unwanted advances of some middle-aged man who'd *"always been a fan and always wanted to meet you in person"*. She received enough of that any time she walked into a restaurant or café, even when trying to be incognito.

Knowing she was being unreasonable, and knowing just how hard Carmen had worked to set up this retreat for her, Tamsyn let out a slow breath and smiled.

"Thank you. I know you've done wonders in making this happen. You are *my* Wonder Woman. Always."

Carmen blushed and dipped her head, scuffing her shoe against the gravel at their feet. "Shut up."

Tamsyn smirked. "Come on, let's get me settled in, shall we?"

She leaned into the car to retrieve her handbag and coat, coming upright just as Carmen attempted to lift one of the suitcases and yelped as the weight of it nearly brought her to her knees.

"Shit, this weighs a ton! What have you got in it?"

"Your next bonus payment," Tamsyn purred. "So keep quiet and carry it."

Carmen huffed and lugged the suitcase over to the cottage's front door. Heather, who was exiting as Carmen approached, took one look at her struggling and held out a hand.

"Careful, it's heavy," Carmen said, passing it over.

Heather, much to Tamsyn's merriment, grasped the case in one very competent hand and carried it into the house as if it weighed no more than a bag of feathers.

Carmen glared at her. "Shut up."

Tamsyn laughed out loud.

"Right," Carmen said, rubbing her hands together. "I think that is you sorted."

Tamsyn matched her in looking around the cottage. The living area and kitchen had been combined into one big room, warmed by a larger-than-expected fireplace set in the end wall. They'd lit the fire as soon as they'd finished bringing in all the luggage. Then, while Heather waited out in the car, Tamsyn and Carmen had inspected the kitchen, checked that the fridge and pantry had been stocked with everything Tamsyn had requested, and taken a cursory look at the bedroom and bathroom. Everything was appointed with enough luxury to keep Tamsyn in the lifestyle to which she'd become accustomed, and she'd witnessed Carmen's barely-disguised sigh of relief when she'd announced she was very happy with the place.

"Yes, everything else I can do myself after you've gone. And please, you must thank your aunt for me," Tamsyn said, as they strolled towards the front door. "She has done an amazing job at such short notice. You've spent my money well."

Carmen laughed. "Oh yes, trust me, she's been very well reimbursed for this. I'm sure she thought I was joking when I asked for a case of champagne along with everything else. You certainly are like no other guest she's had here."

"Are you sure we can rely on her not to go to the press?" Panic fluttered in Tamsyn's stomach.

"Of course!" Carmen was wide-eyed. "Really Tamsyn, you do need to trust my judgement on things like this. Have I ever let you down?"

Tamsyn's panic transmuted to shame. "No." She pulled Carmen into a hug. "You never have and I seriously doubt you ever will. Sorry."

Carmen gave her a squeeze before pulling away. "Forgiven." She looked around once more. "Sure you're going to be okay?"

Tamsyn took a deep breath. No, she wasn't sure, not at all, but that wasn't what Carmen needed to hear.

"I'll be fine. This is, as you said, just what I need. And I will do that thinking you suggested. I promise I won't just wallow in champagne for two weeks."

Carmen chuckled. "That's good to hear. Okay, mobile reception can be a little patchy up here, but you've got Wi-Fi in the cottage, so you can always email, okay?"

Tamsyn saluted. "Understood, ma'am." She laughed as Carmen rolled her eyes. "Don't worry, I'll be fine. I'm a grown-up."

Carmen's expression turned serious, her forehead creasing into a frown. "I really hope so, Tam. I… We can't have a repeat of what happened with Don. I know you know that," she raised her hands as Tamsyn started to object, "but I'm serious. Get this sorted out in your head. I understand, you know I do. But this is the industry we work in, and this is the way it is. Baby steps, Tam. You're not the only one wanting to change it, but there are ways and means. Right?"

Tamsyn's frustration came from knowing both that Carmen was right and that it was ridiculous *she* was the one who'd had to run and hide with her tail between her legs. It should be Don having to "think things over" not her. She gritted her teeth and smiled.

"Right. Got it. I'll be a new woman when you come back to collect me. Trust me." She crossed her fingers behind her back, hoping Carmen couldn't see.

With a shake of her head and a rueful smile, Carmen walked out the front door. Moments later, Tamsyn heard the car pulling away and flopped down onto the small, red leather sofa, facing the fire. The flames mesmerised her, and soothed her, banishing the troubled thoughts from her mind.

She woke sometime later, an awful crook in her neck from falling asleep sitting up. A quick glance at her watch told her she'd only snoozed for about an hour. Her rumbling stomach told her she had missed lunch.

Well, that's easily remedied, and at least it will get me up and moving. God knows I can't sit here for two weeks doing nothing.

She found a carton of organic tomato soup in the fridge and heated it up while she organised the food she'd requested. It would be so tempting to ignore her healthy diet while on this retreat, but she knew she'd only regret it. So, into the cupboard went her organic granola, seed mixes and dried fruit, her Asian ingredients, and her vitamins. In the fridge there was already plenty of low-fat yoghurt, vegetables, fruit, organic chicken, organic soups, and fresh juices. And champagne. It was her one concession to being forced—as she saw it—into this position.

After pouring the hot soup into a bowl and placing that on a tray, she ate in front of the fire. It was more soothing than she would have imagined not to be surrounded by the noise of the radio or TV, her usual accompaniments at home. There was a TV in the cottage, and probably a radio somewhere, but somehow she didn't need them. The crackling of the fire kept her company, and she was surprised at how calm she already felt. She knew there was only so long a person could maintain anger, but she hadn't expected it to dissipate quite this quickly.

She smiled. Maybe, like Carmen had said, this place *would* do her good after all.

Why the hell did I pack so many?

Tamsyn swore loudly for the third time as she lugged the case into the bedroom, cursing herself for being old school. All of this would have been so much easier if she'd ever invested in an e-reader. But no, she had to go all traditional and buy paperbacks.

Stupid.

Giving up on even the idea of lifting the thing onto the bed, she opened it on the floor. The sight of all the books that awaited her instantly wiped the scowl off her face.

Hello, my beauties.

Slowly, almost reverently, she lifted each book from its resting place and laid them out on the bed. Spreading them into two long rows widened her smile. So much joy to be had in the coming few weeks. Her secret pleasure, to be indulged at a rate of a book a day with any luck. She probably could have brought more, but knew it would better for her health if she made sure she actually left the cottage each day, so she'd planned to split her time between reading, yoga, and long walks around the estate. Carmen's aunt owned fifty acres, all of it encircled by private woodland with walking paths woven throughout. Tamsyn couldn't remember the last time she'd actually taken a solo walk. Back in London, or any of the cities where she was usually based around the world, she was too recognisable to risk it, always ensuring she had someone with her to fend off her wide-eyed fans or offer a quick escape from the more persistent ones. Here though, she had every hope that some quiet time would be hers. Time amongst the trees, the birds, and the sounds of the wind.

But first, finish the unpacking, then some yoga to ease out the kinks.

In the end she decided to leave the books in their suitcase. While there was a small bookcase on the wall facing the bed, it was already filled with a pitiful collection of trashy novels supplied by the owner and she couldn't be bothered rearranging it all.

After changing into soft yoga pants and a loose T-shirt, she unrolled her mat on the polished wood floor of the bedroom. The area at the end of the walnut-framed bed, between it and the bookcase, was plenty wide enough, and it meant she almost faced the window. She cracked it open, delighting in the swell of birdsong and cool, fresh air that immediately filtered into the room. At each standing pose she only had to swivel her eyes a fraction to see the trees and the weak afternoon sunshine casting a golden glow across the sky.

Dropping into Downward Dog, she revelled in the slight pull of her spinal muscles, the easing out of her hips and hamstrings. At fifty-two, her body was in better shape than she might have anticipated in her late teens, when she had still been trying to lose the last of her puppy fat, feeling awkward and gangly in her still-developing body. Now, after years of being in the public eye, and the adoration and abuse—in equal parts—that exposure bestowed on her, the yoga she'd practised all that time had enabled her to maintain the slimness that was expected of her, as well as a suppleness that, for her, was far more important.

Easing back into Child's Pose, she moaned with pleasure as her spine stretched, her arms held out in front of her on the floor. Damn, that felt good. She held it for a little longer than usual, then came upright to sit on her feet; finished with her breathing exercises, she let her shoulders roll and lower as the glow of her workout warmed every inch of her skin. Almost better than sex.

Almost.

She smiled to herself, stood up, and walked to the bathroom to pat down her warm body with a small towel. Once she'd changed back into sweatpants and a hoodie, she hauled her big slippers from under the bed and wriggled her feet into them. Tonight was all about making a delicious dinner, drinking a couple of glasses of champagne, and curling up on the sofa with a good book. She shivered in anticipation and turned to the suitcase holding her books.

Okay, which one of you is first?

Two minutes later, her choice in hand, she wandered through to the kitchen, dropping the book on the sofa as she passed by. She stoked the fire and added another large log; that would see her through the evening, she suspected. After pulling some vegetables and chicken from the fridge, she went in search of a chopping board and a knife. She had just grabbed both implements when a sharp bark out back had her gasping and almost dropping the knife.

She crept over to the door. Not being a huge fan of dogs, she hoped this one wasn't right on her doorstep. A quick peek out of the glass that formed the top third of the door gave her a sense of relief; the dog—a small, brown, wiry thing—was in her garden but not that close to the door. How had it gained access to her garden? She glanced around. Oh, there—an open gate where the garden adjoined the path that led to the woods. So where was the dog's owner? Oh well, not her problem. Not unless the little mutt came any closer.

She stepped back and continued with her chopping. A minute later a woman's voice called, "Gizmo! Gizmo! Where the hell are you, you little shit?"

Tamsyn snorted. Gizmo, what a name. Although, on reflection, perfectly suited to the scrawny little beast. And at least the voice confirmed that the neighbour was indeed female.

"Gizmo! Get back here!"

A couple of quick yelps, their volume receding as the dog clearly scampered away, signalled that peace was restored to Tamsyn's corner of the world.

Perfect. Just me and the latest Maddie Jones. She glanced over at the book where it lay, enticing her, on the sofa.

Soon, sweetheart. Soon.

Chapter 3

MAGGIE STARED DOWN AT GIZMO, her scolding face on. "You, young man, are in a heap of trouble."

Gizmo blinked, then licked his chops. Was he actually grinning at her? Little git.

She shook her head, then laughed. Gizmo barked and jumped up a couple of times.

"All right, all right. God, why can't I resist you?"

She crouched down and accepted his licks and snuffles all over her face. Stroking his head and back, she sighed. He was a cheeky little sod, but his love for her always made her feel better.

"Come on, that's enough fresh air for today. Time for snuggles by the fire."

Strolling through the trees had become her new favourite thing this past week. Usually they were confined to the local park near her house in Putney. Having such an expanse to play in had sent her beloved Border terrier into paroxysms of delight, and his enthusiasm was infectious. So what if she hadn't written a single word since she'd arrived here?

They reached the gravel driveway of her cottage and shimmied past the car to get to the front door. She glanced back at the other cottage, the single light coming from what she knew was the kitchen, and hoped that whoever was staying there hadn't been too disturbed by Gizmo's antics.

Gizmo squeezed through the door before she'd even got it fully open, and ran straight to his water bowl where he lapped noisily for a couple of minutes while she removed her coat and shoes. It was nicely nippy out, and her face was tingling now that she was back in the warmth of the cottage.

She walked over to the fire and added some more wood, noting that her pile was diminishing but it would at least last her through to tomorrow morning.

The bottle of red wine she'd opened the night before was standing on the kitchen counter, and moments later she was sipping a large glass by the fire. She'd taken to sitting in the single armchair. The sofa was comfy enough, but there was something even more comforting about being embraced completely by the chair—Gizmo usually either laying on the floor by the fire or wedged between her folded legs and one arm of the chair.

She stared at the flames as they danced in the grate. Her eyes felt tired. Hell, the whole of her felt tired. The burnout had hit her hard and fast, and although she knew her recovery would happen at its own good pace, she couldn't help but will it to go faster. She had deadlines to meet, fans to keep happy.

Yes, but you also need to keep yourself happy.

She could almost hear her sister's voice, her gentle yet firm pleas for Maggie to slow down, stop working so hard, to find some time for herself.

She snorted and Gizmo, who had passed out in front of the fire after guzzling down his water, twitched in his slumber.

Well, now she was realising Ruth had been right all along. Writing under two pseudonyms, in two entirely different genres and markets, had seemed like such a good idea when it first started. And the money it earned, and the plaudits and awards she'd garnered in both markets, had only spurred her on. She'd been churning out three books a year, on average, for the last four years. Of course, in doing so she had barely seen her family, or friends, and her last girlfriend had disappeared six months into that first year, claiming—quite rightly—that she never saw Maggie so they could hardly call it a relationship, could they?

She'd convinced herself none of that mattered. It was the acclaim that fed her soul, fired her up. Finally she was something. Someone. From being nothing at school, and not much else in her twenties, when she'd first started dabbling with writing—having always felt it was in her—her early successes in short story competitions and submissions to magazines had lit a fire beneath her for something more. That first novel, in her early thirties—*God, was that fifteen years ago already?*—had only made her burn faster and harder. It had sold reasonably well, and although it took her another three years to write the sequel, she'd found her audience from the first book desperate for that follow-up, and a new audience had discovered her thanks to a new agent and the change of personnel at her publisher. Suddenly, she was a name. The new face of historical romance.

Then she'd had the bright idea of switching personas. Of keeping her original pen name, Jessica Stewart, for that genre, and inventing a new name to explore a market more true to herself. The historical work had almost been a fluke, utilising elements of her studies from her time at university. But the other, the romantic lesbian fiction, *that* came from her heart. Her soul. And much to her own surprise, she'd been an instant hit there as well. Maddie Jones was a big name in the lesfic market these days.

But now, bizarrely, all of that had dried up. She hadn't written a word in three months. Both publishers were clamouring for new titles, but she didn't have it in her. The ideas weren't there, and sitting in front of a blank screen wasn't conjuring up any inspiration.

So, here she was. On retreat, as she was calling it. She'd agreed with her agent that she would take a month off, see if she could free the block. She had no idea what would happen if it didn't work.

The warmth of the wine and the fire were making her drowsy, and her head dipped. This was the other thing she couldn't quite get used to—she was tired. Constantly tired.

Of course you're tired. You're burned out. You have nothing left in the tank.

Burned out. She'd thought that only happened to city workers, the people making all the big deals in the financial market. It had never occurred to her that it could happen to a writer. A writer of romances, for crying out loud.

She chuckled and Gizmo raised his head, his liquid brown eyes blinking at her.

"Relax," she said, and took another sip of her wine. "It's just me, going slightly bonkers."

No, not bonkers. Not really. Just a bit…lost.

—⸙—

"Stand still, you little bugger." Maggie grabbed Gizmo by his collar and hauled him back towards her. "I thought you loved walks. Why are you fighting me on this?"

She finally managed to clip the lead into place and stood upright again. As soon as she did, Gizmo strained the leather leash in his eagerness to reach the front door.

"Good God you're fickle."

Stumbling after the little dynamo, she grabbed the keys from the small table in the entranceway and locked the door behind them once they were on the front step. The cold pricked at her ears, and she smiled. Another beautiful morning in this small piece of paradise. And to her, it *was* paradise—nothing but nature all around.

After yet another restless night, she knew the fresh air would do her good. It was crazy, she thought, as she let Gizmo lead them towards the path that squirmed through an opening in the trees about a minute from the back of their cottage, that for someone so worn out she couldn't get a decent night's sleep. She hadn't done since the first night here; the speed with which she'd booked the trip, packed, and closed up her house had worn her down to the point where not sleeping was impossible once she'd arrived at the cottage. But since then, all of the doubts about her writing had plagued her brain, and so far none of the remedies she'd tried for easing her mind before sleep had worked.

They were in the trees now, and the change in the sounds around them, and in the very air itself, soothed her. Maybe she should try sleeping out here one night. She snorted. *Yeah, so not going to happen. Imagine all the wildlife skittering around!* She'd give herself a heart attack before daybreak wondering if she was going to be eaten by wild animals. Even though she knew it was ridiculous—there were no carnivorous predators in Norfolk— the thought of exposing herself to the rawness of nature that way did not appeal.

A yelp from Gizmo brought her sharply out of her reverie and she looked around to see what had him so worked up. Then she stopped, and stared, because standing on the path ahead of them, looking concerned at the noise and the rather agitated little hops Gizmo was making, was Tamsyn Harris.

Maggie shook her head. No, there was no way that could possibly be Tamsyn Harris standing in a Norfolk woodland, all alone, only twenty paces or so in front of her. Tamsyn Harris was a world-famous actress who split her time between London and Los Angeles, eating out at all the best restaurants and being seen in all the most fashionable places when she wasn't working on a film or TV series. This woman, whoever she was, just bore a remarkable likeness to her, that's all.

Mind you, it's extraordinary how much her double she is...

"Good morning," Maggie called, yanking Gizmo back on his lead and pointing a finger at him that said "Behave!" when he turned reproachful eyes on her.

"Is your dog safe?" the woman replied.

Maggie was affronted. Safe? Of course Gizmo was safe, what a ridiculous thing to sugg—

"Only I'm not exactly a fan of dogs."

She *sounded* like Tamsyn Harris too, with that hint of huskiness in the posh-but-not-too-posh tone that Tamsyn Harris used. Maggie stared at her again, taking in all her features. The chestnut brown hair was mostly hidden by a stylish woollen cap, but it was the right shade. She wasn't close enough for Maggie to see her eyes, but the height seemed about right, even in the flat walking boots she wore, and the body shape was too, although many women were as slim as Tamsyn so that wasn't much of a clue.

When Maggie let her gaze drift back to the woman's face, Maggie realised she was still waiting for a response.

"Oh. Sorry. Gizmo's fine, don't worry. All bark and no trousers this one."

Gizmo whimpered, as if offended.

Finally the woman smiled. It was weak, but even so it transformed her face and suddenly, right then, Maggie knew. That smile was unmistakable.

Holy. Crap.

The actress walked slowly towards her, then gestured to the path. "I'm just going to pass by, okay?"

"O-Of course." Maggie's heart was thundering beneath her ribs. *Tamsyn bloody Harris!* Maggie's celebrity crush since she was eighteen years old, only yards away from her and about to walk within inches of her—how was that even possible?

Tamsyn approached, gave Maggie a half-smile, then side-stepped around Gizmo with caution. He stared up at her, his mouth open, tongue lolling, and for a brief moment Maggie wondered if she was standing in the middle of the pathway in much the same manner. A quick check confirmed that, to her relief, her tongue was still contained within her closed mouth. She knew, however, that her eyes were as wide as saucers.

She should say something. Ask her—are you *really* Tamsyn Harris? But her brain wouldn't engage properly and when it did, her overwhelming sense was, much to her surprise, to protect this woman. To keep her secret. Because, clearly, Tamsyn was here incognito—there was no entourage, no sign of any companion. And for someone as famous as Tamsyn Harris to do that, there must be a significant reason behind it. As someone who was in Norfolk dealing with her own demons, Maggie could respect that.

No matter how desperate she was to run after her and ask for an autograph.

Shit. She recognised me.

Tamsyn kicked at the path with her boot and grunted. *Damn it!* She risked a quick glance back over her shoulder, and was relieved to see the woman and her dog had moved on; they were now mere specks in the distance, only visible by the scarlet red of the woman's coat.

Well, it had probably been naive of her to think she'd avoid her neighbour the entire time she was here. They did occupy the only two holiday cottages on the property, after all. And braving a walk had seemed like such a great idea when she'd thrown back the curtains and seen the cold, bright day that she'd forgotten all about the woman and the dog across the lake.

She huffed out a breath, and listened to the birds tweeting somewhere high above her. At least the woman hadn't pounced—her eyes had been so wide Tamsyn feared they were going to pop out of the poor thing's head, but she'd kept her distance, and kept her mouth shut. Tamsyn smiled. It had been a long, long time since that had happened, and it felt good.

I wonder if she walks that dog at the same time every day. I could always make sure I walk in the afternoons, if that's the case.

As soon as she thought it, she felt a bit daft. It was only one woman, and they were sharing this space for however long their breaks overlapped. Trying to avoid her was ridiculous. Not that she'd be inviting her over for dinner or anything crazy, but perhaps to say hello to on the path, especially if the woman didn't go all fangirl on her, wouldn't be that bad. Besides, if there was one thing Tamsyn had noticed, it was that the woman was delicious to look at. She grinned. Oh yeah—honey-blonde hair that dropped just past her shoulders, hazel eyes with just a hint of crow's feet at the corners, pitching her age within a few years of Tamsyn's own, and a face of simple beauty, made even more so by the lack of make-up. She was the same height as Tamsyn, and although she'd been bundled up in that red coat and jeans, appeared to have a similar build.

Tamsyn breathed in a deep lungful of the woodsy air. It had been quite a while since she'd looked at a woman. Properly looked. Most of her assignations over the years had required the utmost discretion, meeting in dim hotel rooms, arrangements made by Carmen through her extensive channels. Some lovers had lasted more than a week or so, but rarely. Tamsyn was too public, and too much in need of protecting her image to be seen with a woman on her arm. She made sure she was photographed regularly enough with a beard, usually some other actor, or a musician—always younger than her, of course, and grateful enough for the publicity to keep his mouth shut.

It was the most bizarre Catch-22 these days—just when more and more celebrities were embracing the new dawn and coming out left, right, and centre, Tamsyn was having to do even more to stay in the closet. Roles for a fifty-two-year-old were hard enough to come by without being the fifty-two-year-old lesbian. She was already sick of directors telling her she couldn't play a love interest anymore—imagine how they'd react if she attempted to read for such roles having just announced her sexuality to the world? She'd never work again, she knew that—at least, not in the roles she wanted. God knew she wasn't anywhere near ready to be the new Miss Marple.

Unbidden, thoughts of her friend, Lesley, came to mind. Lesley had taken a different path and come out when they were in their early thirties, nearly twenty years ago. She was just beginning to make a name for herself on British TV dramas and had seemed completely taken by surprise when those roles began to dry up. After working the off-West End theatre scene for a few years, and even trying her hand at hosting a reality TV show for a couple of seasons, in the end she'd admitted defeat and walked away from acting entirely.

Tamsyn had tried to support her through every step—their friendship stretching back to their late teens and their first breakthroughs in the cut-throat world of acting—but she'd never been in agreement with Lesley's need to come out. Lesley always maintained that she wasn't bitter about what had happened, but there was a tightness in her eyes whenever she said it and Tamsyn didn't believe her for one minute. She wouldn't say "I told you so", but Lesley's experience had only strengthened her decision to stay closeted.

She spotted a fallen tree trunk just off the path and wandered over to it, perching on it at first to make sure it was steady, then relaxing back fully when she realised it would hold her.

Now that she was at the top, winning awards and able to cherry-pick her roles, it only made the current situation all the more infuriating. That little shit of a director had no right to treat her the way he did. But he was the upcoming star, never mind her reputation, or the glittering list of roles on her résumé. '*A short illness*' was the excuse fed to the press to explain her sudden departure.

Bullshit, all of it. Don was threatening to have her axed completely, and Tamsyn knew Carmen was doing everything she could to make sure that didn't happen, calling in favours from all over the place. If Tamsyn didn't care so much about the film, and the story it was telling, she'd have told Don to shove it even harder. Still, throwing that orange juice into his face *had* been rather satisfying.

She smirked as the image of him with orange bits dripping off his nose came back to her. The snorts and sniggers around set had also been rather pleasing, although they'd been cut short by his threatening, steely-eyed glare.

A blackbird landed almost at her feet, sticking its beak into the undergrowth to search out a snack. *What a simple life.* No egos to deal with, no tantrums to throw. She heard a bark, somewhere in the distance, and her smirk, much to her own surprise, transformed into a smile. That dog was pretty cute, she had to admit.

And then, of course, there was its owner…

Chapter 4

TAMSYN BLOODY HARRIS IS STAYING in the cottage across the lake! Be still, my beating heart.

Maggie chuckled, knowing darn well who she'd be thinking of as she snuggled under her duvet later that night. She had followed Tamsyn's career through the years, seen pretty much every movie she'd made—except for that dodgy period in the early nineties when she'd done those two sci-fi ones—and drooled over her incessantly in her role as the head of the Met Police in the TV drama Blue Lights, which had won her two BAFTAs.

Gizmo gave one of his short yelps that meant he was up to no good and she shook herself out of her haze. She stepped through the undergrowth to see what had him snuffling so excitedly, his tail twitching and his ears pinned back. She peered over his head and snorted.

"Gizmo, it's a bloody frog. Or toad. Whatever. It's not something you need to bother anymore." The amphibian was frozen in place, its head hunkered down into its stubby neck as Gizmo sniffed all around it without touching it, clearly very uncertain as to just what sort of creature this was.

"Come on." She pulled on his lead. "Leave the poor thing alone."

Miraculously, Gizmo obeyed, and Maggie smiled, knowing that for all his boldness, in meeting something he didn't recognise there was a little bit of fear in him that meant he'd easily give in to her command. He perked his ears up, and trotted off, tail held high, as if continuing on their walk was all his own idea. She laughed.

God, I love that dog.

They stayed out in the woods for another hour. The trail between the trees was easy walking—leaves and chipped bark covered the rough path, and very few sections required much more than a scramble past the lowest of branches. Gizmo was in his element, and Maggie knew she was too. She'd often thought about selling up the Putney flat and finding a place like this, somewhere secluded and away from the hustle and bustle. Maybe she should be thinking about that again, given how pressured her life felt these days.

Gizmo barked, and somehow Maggie wasn't surprised to see Tamsyn on the path in front of them again. They'd been going in opposite directions before, so it made sense that if they both stayed on the trail they'd meet back up eventually.

"Hello, again," Maggie called, amazed that she not only found her voice but that it came out cheery and strong, rather than weak and star-struck.

Tamsyn raised her hand in a half wave and then, much to Maggie's shock, stopped and waited for them. Gizmo, of course, immediately ran up to the new person and began sniffing around her feet and ankles. Tamsyn flinched but held her ground, and Maggie tugged Gizmo back. If the world-famous actress was scared of dogs, Maggie wasn't going to make it worse.

"Sorry," she said, as she reined him in to her side and stepped to within three or four paces of Tamsyn. "He's just very excitable. He doesn't mean anything by it."

Tamsyn smiled. "Actually, he's okay. I guess it helps that he's cute."

Tamsyn Harris thinks my dog is cute! Maggie held back the beam of delight, but only just.

"Oh yeah, but he knows it and uses it to his full advantage," she said, grinning.

"Listen," Tamsyn said, her voice suddenly a little croaky. "I... So, I'm guessing you know who I am, yes?"

Maggie nodded. "Tamsyn Harris. Or her stunt double, maybe."

Tamsyn's laugh was like a bell chiming in the woods. "Unfortunately, I'm the real one."

Maggie cocked her head. "Unfortunately?"

Tamsyn's face fell. "Sorry, ignore me. Look, I just wanted to say, firstly, thank you for not saying anything earlier. I can't tell you how refreshing it was to be left alone."

Maggie shrugged. "You're here on your own, as far as I can tell, and that spoke volumes. I...I just wanted to respect that. Even though I am, I have to admit, a huge fan."

Tamsyn tipped her head in acknowledgement. "Then I appreciate it even more." She inhaled deeply. "I need some peace and quiet, for a couple of weeks. But I'm aware we're now sharing this space, so I didn't want to come over all diva and ignore you. I suppose I just wanted to say, meeting like this, saying hello, checking out your cute dog—all of that would be okay. I don't want you to think you have to steer clear." She shook her head. "God, even that sounds diva-esque."

Maggie chuckled. "No, it doesn't. I get it. I'm here for some quiet too, and I understand where you might be at." She shrugged again. "I guess we all have things we have to deal with, don't we? No matter how famous or not we are."

"Thank you." Her eyes went wide. "God, I haven't even asked you your name. Sorry, that's so rude—"

"It's Maggie." She smiled at Tamsyn. "It's nice to meet you." Quite how she was remaining so calm in this surreal situation she couldn't say.

Tamsyn smiled. "Nice to meet you too, Maggie." She blinked a couple of times, then glanced up at the sky, where clouds were starting to scud across above the trees. "Looks like the weather's turning. I'm going to head back now."

"Yes, us too. This one's hungry and needs his food." At the mention of the F-word, Gizmo turned circles and whimpered.

Tamsyn laughed. "Clever dog."

"Hmm," Maggie replied, "I'm not so sure about that. Trust me, he can do some pretty stupid things too."

"But I bet you forgive him because he's so cute?"

Maggie laughed. "Oh, yeah. Trouble is, he knows it."

"One can always forgive the cute ones anything," Tamsyn said in that smoky voice, and an exquisite shiver ran down Maggie's spine. Tamsyn was smiling, and her eyes—those famous deep brown eyes—were sparkling, and Maggie, for one brief moment, saw something else in them. Something very much like hunger of a different kind.

The moment passed, and Tamsyn's eyes shut down. "Right, I'll be off then." She smiled tightly and walked past Maggie, who was left standing in the path, a hungry dog whimpering at her feet, in a state of confused shock.

***

Tamsyn was shaking as she hurried back into her cottage, but it wasn't from the cold. *It's been way too long since I got laid. That's the only explanation.*

She hadn't been able to stop it. That lowering of her voice, the want—no, *need*, crawling over her skin. Standing in the middle of the woods, face glowing as she smiled in the weak sunshine, Maggie had looked…edible. Tamsyn had almost twitched. Almost stepped forward and done something so ludicrous she still couldn't get over how even the thought of it had entered her brain.

I wanted to kiss her. To run my hands over that beautiful face, pull her in close, and kiss her.

She slumped down on the small armchair that flanked the fireplace. What the hell was going on with her? Yes, she had short flings, but they were with women she at least spent an evening getting to know before taking them to her bed. Maggie was a complete stranger, someone she'd only had a five-minute conversation with.

Yes, but a gorgeous stranger. *And God knows you haven't had anyone gorgeous to spend time with in a long while, stranger or otherwise.*

Yoga. Its calming rhythm would quiet her soul and snap her out of this strange head space. She hauled herself out of the chair with a grunt, and set up in the bedroom for her usual routine.

An hour later she felt physically revived, but mentally…not so much. Maggie's hazel eyes haunted her. That smile tugged at somewhere deep down inside. Damn it! She didn't need any stupid distractions. She needed calm, and tranquillity, and an escape from stress.

A book. That was what she needed. Another good book and a glass—or two—of champagne in front of the fire. She'd finished that Maddie Jones book in one sitting the night before, and hadn't been disappointed. Tamsyn had read nearly all of hers now, and every single one touched something in a place she thought couldn't be touched. Sometimes she allowed herself to dream about falling in love the way the women did in Jones's books. In her stories, they always found each other at their hour of deepest need, and pulled each other through while having lots of lovely, steamy sex. *Yeah, if only.*

She pondered the remaining selection and picked up something different, a historical romance by Jae. She'd tried reading historical fiction years ago at the recommendation of a friend, but although the author, Jessica Stewart, was the biggest seller in the genre, all those heaving bosoms and over-the-top macho men did nothing for her. But surely historical *lesbian* fiction would be something very different, and this one had garnered rave reviews on Amazon, so she was willing to give it a try.

After pouring herself a glass of fizz, she went to stoke the fire. It was then she realised she'd already run out of kindling. She had logs, yes, but something to start the damn thing with, no. She hunted around the cottage for a newspaper or anything else that would serve as an alternative. Her gaze fell on the trashy novels on the bookshelf in the bedroom. Could she? No, that would be rather rude—and possibly drop her into hot water with Carmen. After another minute or so, she gave up. There was nothing she could use.

How had this got missed? She was on the verge of getting angry, and even considered marching over to the main house to complain, when she realised just how ridiculous she was being. So one small thing was missed in the rush to get her set up in this cottage, so what? She should be grateful that so much of what she needed and wanted *had* been taken care of by Carmen's aunt. A lack of kindling was not the end of the world—she'd just turn up the regular heating.

Oh, but sitting by the fire is so nice…

She sighed. There was, of course, one person she could ask without having to traipse all the way over to the main house. Maggie might have a bit to spare. Just for one night. It was the sort of thing neighbours did for each other in remote places like this, wasn't it? It would be a quick trip over there, a little bit of small talk, grab some kindling and back home. Nothing to it.

No ulterior motive.

Not at all.

The loudness of her snort surprised her. *Yeah, right. Who are you kidding, Harris?*

27

Before she could change her mind, she strode over to the front door and pulled on her boots. A quick glance outside confirmed her suspicions. Those clouds had decided this little bit of Norfolk was exactly where they wanted to dump their rain. It wasn't heavy yet, but it looked like it would be soon, so that meant coat and umbrella too. The sky, while gloomy with clouds, still allowed enough light through for her to easily see her way, but she decided the path that skirted the lake would be better than going through the woods, where it looked much darker and, if she was honest, creepy.

She hadn't really looked at the lake since she'd first arrived, but as she walked along its edge now, she knew she'd need to spend some time here when the weather was clearer. Reeds and rushes moved in the wind with a swishing sound that was soothing and almost musical. Somewhere off in the middle, a small squadron of ducks swam in formation, unfazed by the raindrops that splattered the surface of the lake around them. It made her smile, to see creatures so small carrying on oblivious to the weather while she, the big human, was scurrying along under an umbrella as fast as her legs would take her without breaking into a jog.

She slowed down. If the ducks could handle it, so could she.

Two minutes later, she reached Maggie's cottage. Soft lights lit each of the windows and a drift of smoke escaped the chimney.

All right. I just need some kindling, that's all. Quick visit in, grab what I need, then get out just as quick.

She took a deep breath, and veered off the lake path onto the gravel driveway.

———— ❦ ————

Maggie switched on the lamps that were dotted around the living room and switched off the main light. Much better. The warm glow of the lamps competed with the small flames from the fire she'd only just lit.

She was feeling down and couldn't quite put her finger on why. When she'd first returned to the empty, cool cottage she'd thought it was just the gloomy weather. After the last few days of perfect blue skies and thin but cheery sunshine, the change was disheartening.

But it wasn't that, not really. So maybe it was the fact that she'd been here a week and still not written a word? If this trip was supposed to unblock her, it was failing dismally so far. But she knew that wasn't the reason either.

Maggie had always been a woman who was happy in her own skin, and being on her own. Not that she didn't want to be in a relationship, or be loved, but she'd never out-and-out looked for it or felt she needed something like that to complete her life. She'd had a few relationships over the years, some that lasted years, some only a few months. She'd been in love, truly and completely in love, twice, and while she didn't imagine, at her age, that there was much likelihood of achieving that again, she'd be happy to meet someone rather lovely and see what they could make of things.

And that cut to the crux of the matter and her current mood. She was lonely, and she missed having that special someone in her life. It was ridiculous but when she allowed herself to think of being with someone again, a woman just like Tamsyn would be perfect. Smart, funny, and more than easy on the eye, but also with her own career and independence so they wouldn't live in each other's pockets. As much as Maggie was blocked at the moment, if she was going to be with someone again, she needed that person to give her the room to write. It was her full-time job, after all, not simply a hobby to while away her free hours. Her last girlfriend hadn't understood what the writer's life was like.

And perhaps I didn't understand either, and blithely assumed I could have it all.

That wonderful few minutes with Tamsyn Harris had, much to Maggie's surprise, opened up something else she'd been in denial of for quite some time. When she wrote lesbian romances, she poured every ounce of her inner desires and dreams into those characters, but she'd been doing it almost without realising. She felt empty after finishing each one, and she'd never understood why, until now.

It was still only three in the afternoon, but she poured herself a glass of wine in defiance of the time. *To hell with it, I'm on retreat. I can do whatever I like.* She was walking back to the armchair with the glass in her hand when Gizmo let out a short bark and scrabbled towards the front door, his claws unable to gain any purchase on the polished wood floor in his haste. Moments later, the door knocker rapped three times. Gizmo barked twice more until Maggie said, "Quiet down, Gizmo," as she strode across the room to see who was calling.

Her heart leaped as she swung the door open and saw Tamsyn Harris on her covered doorstep, a wet umbrella folded by her side. Gizmo seemed equally as giddy, hopping and leaping around the actress's feet. To her credit, she stood her ground, but a frown marred her otherwise perfect features and Maggie reacted quickly, reaching down to grab Gizmo by the collar and pull him away.

"Calm down, you little bugger." She looked him in the eye. "Go to your basket."

He whined, but did as he was told, looking back over his shoulder occasionally as he walked slowly to the kitchen.

Tamsyn laughed. "Wow, that's a sulk if ever I've seen one."

Maggie turned back to her, heart still beating wildly. "He'll get over it."

They stared at each other for a moment.

What the hell is she doing here?

"So, I'm sorry to disturb you," Tamsyn said, breaking the silence. "But I don't seem to have any kindling and was wondering if you could spare some until I can get over to the main house tomorrow morning."

"Of course. Yes. Come in. I have plenty." Maggie's mouth was running away with itself, but she couldn't seem to stop. If Tamsyn noticed, she was good at hiding it.

Maggie stepped back to allow Tamsyn to enter the cottage, where she lingered on the doormat.

"Please, come in." She gestured to the living room.

"I'm wet," Tamsyn said. Even in the low light, Maggie could see the blush that spread across both of Tamsyn's cheeks, and her brain struggled to comprehend why. "From the rain. I… My coat is going to drip all over your floor."

Maggie waved a hand. "Don't worry, it'll dry up in the warmth from the fire."

Tamsyn smiled, but it lacked its usual radiance. "Well, okay. I don't want to keep you from whatever it is you're doing."

The snort was out before she could stop it, and now her own cheeks warmed. "Um, yeah, I'm not really doing anything." She swallowed, her nerves now threatening to derail her completely. It was one thing meeting the famous actress on a woodland path, quite another to have her standing in Maggie's living room, her skin glowing from the remnants of her blush coupled with the warmth of the fire. *Bloody hell, she's as gorgeous in real life as she is on the screen. More, actually.*

With the last strand of common sense she had left, Maggie stepped away from the entranceway and marched over to the kitchen, talking over her shoulder as she did so. "I'll just grab a bag from the cupboard to put some kindling in for you."

"Thanks. That's...great."

As she reached the kitchen, Gizmo looked up at her from his basket, his eyes wide. She ruffled his ears for a moment, then turned to the pantry where she knew she had stored some empty plastic bags from the groceries she'd brought with her. With one in hand, she returned to the living room. Tamsyn had moved to the fire and was holding out her hands towards its heat.

"It's getting cold outside," she said, her voice soft, "now that the clouds are moving on."

"I bet. Here, let me just shove some of this in here." Maggie knelt beside her and began pushing handfuls of the kindling into the bag. In her haste, her nerves jangling at the mere presence of the woman beside her, she was careless, and the sharp jab of something digging into her thumb made her yelp and yank her hand back from the kindling pail. The bag she'd been stuffing fell to the floor.

"Are you okay?" Tamsyn knelt beside her.

Maggie looked down at her hand. The splinter was, thankfully, large, and would therefore be easy to extract. "I'm fine. Just wasn't really looking at what I was doing." She blushed again. *Great, now she'll wonder just what you were looking at instead.* "It's a splinter but it's easily—"

"Let me see."

And suddenly Tamsyn was holding Maggie's hand in both of hers, turning the palm up so she could see the damage. Her hand was cool, but beautifully soft, her fingers long and slender, and Maggie's temperature rocketed. Tamsyn bloody Harris was holding her hand. *I might actually faint.*

"Ah, yes. You're right, that's easily retrieved. Just give...me...a... second." She used her perfectly manicured nails, deep burgundy in colour but not overly long, to pinch hold of the splinter and carefully extract it from Maggie's skin. A bead of blood followed its departure, and before Maggie could do anything about it, Tamsyn let go with one hand, dipped into her coat pocket, and came up with a tissue, which she pressed gently against the bloodied spot. "There," she said, her voice only just above a whisper, "that should do it."

Maggie looked up then, and it was her final undoing. Tamsyn's face was mere inches away, her brown eyes a deeper colour than Maggie remembered from all the times she'd gazed at them in magazines and on the internet, her rich hair framing her features as the firelight played across them.

Tamsyn stared back at her.

The room was quiet except for the occasional pop and crackle from the fire. Maggie held her breath, not wanting the moment to end. She could look at that face for days and never be bored. This close up, she could see the small crow's feet at the corners of Tamsyn's eyes, the slight pull of the skin around Tamsyn's lips, and somehow that pleased her. That underneath the gloss and glamour there was a real, live, fifty-two-year-old woman, only three years older and going through the same changes in skin and body as Maggie herself.

"You," Tamsyn whispered, "are a very beautiful woman, Maggie."

Maggie blinked as her heart pounded, but just as she started to form a response, Tamsyn's eyes went wide, and she stood with such speed that Maggie almost fell back on her ass.

"Sorry," Tamsyn said, her voice tight. "I need to go."

"Tamsyn, wait!" Maggie pushed herself upright as fast as she could, then had to pause a moment as she was swayed by a head rush.

But Tamsyn didn't wait—she was gone before Maggie could say another word, and by the time Maggie reached the door, Tamsyn was merely a shadow in the distant gloom.

Chapter 5

YOU IDIOT! WHAT WERE YOU thinking?

Tamsyn slammed the door behind her, clumsily wrestled herself out of her coat, and threw it towards the hook on the wall, oblivious as to whether it landed correctly or not. She kicked off her boots, pushed her feet into her slippers, and slapped her way across the wooden floor to the kitchen. Last night's bottle of champagne was still half-full. She pulled it out of the fridge and poured a glass, chucking back two big gulps before topping up the glass once more.

She *hadn't* been thinking, that was the trouble. She had been mesmerised. Maggie had looked incredible by the light of the fire, and the feel of her hand, the warmth of her skin against the cool of Tamsyn's own, had addled her brain and allowed her mouth to open without censorship. The words had been the truth, but they were a truth that should never have seen the light of day. Her only hope now was that Maggie, who had seemed so respectful of her need for secrecy and distance, would maintain that and not run straight to the tabloids.

Oh, God, what if she *did* go to the press? Tamsyn's stomach dropped. Maybe some damage control was needed here. Should she call Carmen? Or maybe Tony, from her PR firm, would be better? But then, of course, in order to explain why damage control was needed, she'd have to face their scrutiny and leading questions. Bizarrely, both of them had quietly tried to encourage her out of the closet in the last couple of years, but she'd dug her heels in. They didn't really get it, didn't understand what life was like on set, even though they insisted times had changed and theorised she'd be no worse off with the opportunities that came her way.

Shit, what a mess.

Completely lost, and bewildered, and still so angry at herself, she chugged back two more mouthfuls of champagne. She was swilling it like beer. Willing herself to calm down, but actually having no idea how to do that, she paced across the living room.

The knock on her door, though not loud, shocked her. She stood, rooted to the spot, willing the visitor—who, she knew, could only be Maggie—to depart.

"Tamsyn. Ms Harris. I know you're in there. You...you forgot the kindling." Maggie's voice held a tremble.

Tamsyn's head dropped until her chin nearly hit her chest. It would be easiest to ignore her, to wait for her to go away, but Tamsyn couldn't be that woman. This was all her own doing, and just as with the situation with Don Speed, she had to face up to it.

She placed her half-empty glass on the coffee table, sucked in a deep breath, and walked over to the door. As she opened it, Maggie's wide-eyed face came into view. There were raindrops clinging to her honey-blonde hair, and on her nose and cheeks, which were rosy red.

"Hi," Tamsyn said, which was all she could manage. Maggie was looking at her with something akin to fear, and it broke her heart.

Maggie held up the bag of kindling. "I...I didn't want you to get cold," she said, her gaze averted.

Tamsyn took the bag from her. "Thank you. That's very kind of you."

"You're welcome." Maggie turned and hopped off the front step onto the driveway.

"Wait!" Tamsyn called, shocking herself. "Please... I... I'm sorry. For what I said. It was...inappropriate."

Maggie had frozen on the spot but not turned around. She did look back over her shoulder, however, at the word "inappropriate".

"Did...did you mean it, though?" Her voice was nearly snatched away by the wind, but Tamsyn heard the words clearly enough.

Lying would be easiest. Safest.

"Yes."

Maggie smiled a slow, small smile, and Tamsyn felt the corners of her own mouth lift in response.

"Then it wasn't inappropriate."

Tamsyn laughed, and the release of tension that came with it flooded her with warmth. "Good line," she said, doffing an imaginary hat.

Maggie shrugged. "I'm a writer, I'm supposed to have good lines."

Her eyes widened again, and Tamsyn would have bet a lot of money that Maggie had not meant to reveal that little snippet of information.

"Want a drink?" Tamsyn asked, gesturing back into the cottage. The invite came easily and she didn't regret it. "I have a bottle open. You can stay and warm up a bit before your journey home."

Maggie smirked. "Well, it is such a long way, after all." She paused, looked at the ground, then back up. "Are you sure? I don't want to intrude. I know you need your privacy."

"I'm sure. I want to…thank you. For…everything."

Maggie turned to face her, finally, and took a step nearer. "There's nothing to thank me for, Ms Harris."

Tamsyn shuddered. That level of formality sounded all wrong coming from this woman. "Please, call me Tamsyn. Here, especially, I'm just Tamsyn, okay?"

Maggie's smile was a beacon of light in the darkness around them. "Okay. Tamsyn. I'd love a drink."

She came back up the step, staring at Tamsyn for a moment before stepping into the house. That look stirred a heat that Tamsyn tried desperately to tamp down. What was it about this woman, about her presence, her refreshing calmness that affected Tamsyn so?

Come on, get a hold of yourself. For starters, she's probably straight, so just rein yourself in.

"Here, let me start the fire," Maggie said, reaching for the bag of kindling.

"Thank you. I'll get you a glass of champagne in return."

Maggie chuckled. "Wow, that hardly seems a fair trade, but sure, I'll take one."

Tamsyn laughed as she headed towards the kitchen. "You're going to think it's terribly pretentious of me, a true sign of the diva I must be, if I tell you it's all I drink."

"All day?" Maggie asked, her tone full of mirth.

"Ha ha." God, when was the last time she'd had this kind of light-hearted conversation with a woman? With anyone? "What I meant was," she continued, pulling the bottle out of the fridge again, "it's the only alcohol I drink. Far less calories than things like wine or spirits."

Tamsyn poured Maggie a glass, then turned to watch her set the fire. She moved with assurance, her hair falling around her face in a sensuous curtain. Tamsyn wanted to run her fingers through that hair, tug on handfuls of it as she pulled Maggie round to face her.

Oh, my God, stop!

Maybe she should switch to reading that erotica collection she'd brought with her tonight.

Maggie turned then, and smiled, and Tamsyn nearly dropped the glass she was holding.

Beautiful.

It was the only word that kept coming to mind.

"Oh, is that for me?" Maggie gestured to the glass, saving Tamsyn from herself.

"Yes, of course. Here." Tamsyn thrust the drink forward and Maggie walked over to take it.

Tamsyn retrieved her own glass from the coffee table, then turned to touch it to Maggie's.

"Thank you for the kindling," she said. "And thank you for being okay about earlier."

"You're welcome." Maggie sipped at her drink, then rolled her eyes. "Oh, wow. That's *nice.*"

Tamsyn laughed. "Yes, it is, isn't it? One of the perks of being me."

"I'm sure there are lots of perks, aren't there?"

Tamsyn's smile dropped; she couldn't help it.

"Oh, sorry," Maggie said in a rush, "you don't have to talk about that part of your life if you don't want to. I know you're here to escape all that."

Tamsyn stared at her. "You…you do?"

Maggie blushed and moved away towards the fire. "Well, I mean, I just assumed… You're on your own, no entourage, and this place is pretty much in the middle of nowhere. Sorry, maybe that was rather presumptuous of me."

Tamsyn stepped quickly to her side. "No, it wasn't. It was spot on." She was grateful when Maggie finally met her eyes. "Very astute." She grinned and Maggie smiled. "I had a bit of trouble on a film set, and we all decided

I needed a break. That's pretty hush-hush, by the way, so I'm trusting you'll keep it to yourself."

"I will." Maggie's tone was so earnest that Tamsyn wanted to weep.

"Thank you," she whispered.

Maggie took another sip of her drink, then snorted. "I have to tell you, though, this is pretty surreal for me, right now."

"What?"

"I'm standing next to Tamsyn Harris in a cottage in the middle of nowhere, sipping her champagne. As someone who has watched your career for many years, and loved pretty much everything you've done, I kind of feel like I'm dreaming right now." She shook her head. "Sorry, that's probably the last thing you needed to hear, me going all fangirl on you."

Maggie's words seemed sincere, and honest, and—unlike many, many other situations where she'd met fans—didn't set her on edge.

"You know, it really didn't sound like that anyway. I'm flattered by what you said, but not in the usual superficial way I feel whenever I meet a fan. Somehow, you're different to that. It's nice."

"You're very different to how I thought you'd be if I ever met you."

"I'll take that as a good thing."

"Do. Maybe it's because we met here," Maggie mused. "Somewhere so unexpected."

"Away from any glitz and glamour, you mean?"

"Yeah. Out of your usual zone, I'm sure, and I'm a city girl, mostly, so it's out of mine too."

Tamsyn sipped her fizz, mind whirling. Maggie was delighting her more by the second, and it was getting way beyond the physical now.

"Okay, I can't quite believe I'm going to say this, but would you like to have dinner with me? You mentioned you're a writer, and I'd love to hear about that, and, well, I'd quite like an evening where I could just be me, talking to another human being, if that makes sense."

"Are you sure? I mean, you don't even know me."

"Trust me, I'm qualified in 'Stalker 101' and you have none of the trademark signs. I think I'm safe."

Maggie threw back her head and laughed. "Then my cunning disguise has worked. Hurrah."

Tamsyn sniggered, a sound she wouldn't have known she was capable of making. "Damn, you're good. I'm doomed."

"Nah, you're right. You're safe with me." Maggie smiled over the top of her glass.

They shared a look then, a look that contained warmth, and understanding, and...something else. Affection? Maybe. But maybe something already deeper than that. Whatever it was, it shook Tamsyn, but not enough for her to turn away.

"But," Maggie continued, "as much as I would like to accept your offer, I have to get back to Gizmo. I didn't leave him any food out because I only thought I'd be a few minutes over here." She sipped the last of her champagne. "But, um, if you really would like to spend an evening together, you could always come over to our place tomorrow, if you like. I mean, if that's not too—"

"That sounds wonderful." Tamsyn beamed at Maggie, a sense of excitement coursing through her. "Shall I bring a bottle?"

"Of this?" Maggie tipped her empty glass. "Certainly!"

Chapter 6

I'M COOKING DINNER FOR TAMSYN Harris tonight. I must be bloody mad.

Maggie skittered around the cottage trying to do eighteen things at once to make the place presentable for a BAFTA-winning actress to dine in. The panic in her belly made her hands tremble every time she attempted to pick something up. Gizmo sat in his bed, licking his chops after eating his dinner, and staring at her.

"Yes, I know. Your mum's turned into a crazy woman. Blame her!" She pointed in the vague direction of the other cottage.

"*'You could always come over to our place tomorrow, if you like'*," she muttered. "Jesus H Christ, what was I thinking?"

She slumped down on the sofa, cleaning temporarily forgotten. "I wasn't thinking. That was the whole bloody problem. She was standing there, looking so gorgeous and a little bit vulnerable, and I'd had a glass of champagne, and then bleugh, out vomited the invite." Maggie hung her head in her hands. "Oh, my God. What the hell am I going to talk to her about all evening?"

Gizmo padded over and laid his chin on her knee. It barely reached, but she appreciated the gesture. She stroked his snout and his whiskers, and he made that cute little snuffling noise that meant he was enjoying it. She'd figured out long ago it was his equivalent to a cat's purr.

"And you have to help me, okay? You need to be charming, and quiet, and just all round cute. Keep distracting her, okay?"

He gazed up at her, those big brown eyes melting her heart, as always, and she chuckled and pulled him onto her lap for a proper snuggle.

"God, Gizmo. This is crazy," she said into his fur as she nuzzled his neck. He licked her cheek, the soft rasp of his tongue feeling strangely soothing, when normally she would push him away and wipe her face with a loud "Yuk!"

After a few minutes of cuddling, she felt better. It was amazing how therapeutic a doggy hug could be.

Okay, let's do this, but let's do it properly, and methodically.

She inhaled and exhaled nice and slow, then popped Gizmo back on the floor and stood up. Glancing round the room, she took stock. Fire already lit, and plenty of wood to last through the night. The living room itself was reasonably tidy and a few minutes' work would sort out what was left. She wandered over to the bathroom on the other side of the entranceway. This took only a minute of hanging towels properly and tidying her toiletries to make it presentable before she moved to the kitchen-cum-dining area.

"Well, this needs a bit of work."

Rolling up her sleeves, she got on with it, all the while thinking about what she'd cook. She had some salmon in the fridge, and a selection of vegetables, and decided that would make a decent meal for a famous actress.

After cleaning and preparing veg, she remembered to get cleaned up herself and changed into the nicest pair of jeans she'd brought with her, as well as a soft, long-sleeved shirt. It was about the most presentable outfit she could put together, but even if she'd brought something 'posher', she wouldn't have worn it. As much as it was freaking her out that Tamsyn Harris was coming to dinner, this *was* Maggie's home, albeit a temporary one, and she had every right to feel comfortable in it. And, she reasoned, Tamsyn had said she wanted to have an evening where she could just be herself, and not the famous actress. So jeans, plain old salmon and veg, and an ordinary chat was what she'd get.

Satisfied at last with all she'd done, Maggie returned to the kitchen and poured herself a small, fortifying glass of white wine. She eased into the armchair and sat watching the fire as she sipped, smiling to herself—no one she knew would believe her if she told them who she was having dinner with. Not that she *would* tell anyone. She was determined to protect Tamsyn's privacy. Still, it would make a great story over dinner one night with her sister, or her friend Sally, both of whom were also big fans.

She sat bolt upright in her chair.

To hell with telling her sister or Sally. This whole situation would make a great story, period. Her mind exploded. *Yes!* Imagine, the scene—famous lesbian actress in hiding from the press meets lonely writer on retreat. Sparks fly, romance blossoms, they return to 'real life' as partners and face the world together.

Scrambling out of her chair, nearly spilling the wine in her haste to place her glass on the coffee table, she looked around the room for her notebook and pen. The brown leather Moleskine went everywhere with her for exactly this purpose. When inspiration struck, she wanted some means of recording it before it was lost. Finally spotting it on the bookshelf across the room, she strode over to retrieve it. Not even bothering to sit down again, she scribbled frantically as the outline of the story spilled out onto the pages. She couldn't write the words down fast enough, and her handwriting turned into an ugly scrawl within moments, but who the hell cared? It was the first concrete idea she'd had for a new book in months and her blood was almost fizzing in her excitement.

When Gizmo scurried towards the front door moments before the knocker rattled against it, she almost groaned aloud in frustration—the ideas were still coming, and she didn't want to be interrupted, not now! Then she remembered who was on the other side of the door and her heart thumped. This was where reality stepped in and took over from her imagination. The famous actress, who was very obviously straight, was only here for dinner and some conversation. But that was okay—Maggie could let her imagination run riot later. The thrill of sitting down to write a new story brought a lightness to her steps as she crossed to the door, and she smiled. God, when was the last time she'd had that buzz?

When she swung open the door, Gizmo weaving around her legs to greet their visitor first, the smile was still plastered on her face.

"Hi," Tamsyn said, and held out an ice-cold bottle of champagne. Then she tilted her head as she studied Maggie. "You're beaming. Had some good news?"

Maggie chuckled and stepped aside to let Tamsyn into the house, watching her walk carefully around the excited Gizmo, who was doing that quirky little half-jump step he did when he sensed a special occasion.

"Sort of. I...I've been experiencing writer's block for a while, and suddenly had...an inspiration...for a story." She willed her cheeks not to blush, given the inspiration was standing only three feet away. "It's quite exciting to have that feeling again."

Tamsyn peeled off her coat and hung it on a hook beside the door. "I can imagine. Good for you!" She bent down to unlace her boots.

"Oh, I'd keep those on if I was you," Maggie said quickly. "The floors are freezing and I don't have spare slippers."

"Ah!" Tamsyn continued with the unlacing. "I came prepared." She slipped off the boots and dipped a hand into her large handbag. "Ta-da!"

Maggie laughed as Tamsyn pulled out a pair of fluffy slippers that looked very well worn.

"Perfect. I'm impressed."

Tamsyn smiled. "I told you, I wanted an evening where I could just be me, and *me* wears these slippers all the time when I'm actually able to be at home. I even have a slightly more serious pair for when I'm travelling or on set. Standing around all day in the heels they usually make me wear is so hard on the feet."

"I can imagine. So, please come in, and sit down—rest those feet."

Tamsyn grinned. "I like your thinking. But first, let me open the champagne. It's nicely chilled, as you can probably tell."

Maggie handed it back and led Tamsyn into the kitchen. Her nerves had dissipated rapidly under the warmth of their initial interaction. Tamsyn—if she could just get used to thinking of her as that, and not as Tamsyn-Harris-famous-actress—was lovely company.

After pulling two glasses down from the cupboard and placing them on the small dining table which she'd already set for their meal, Maggie moved to switch on the oven.

"I'm baking some salmon and steaming a mix of vegetables for supper. Is that okay?"

"Oh, sounds lovely. And no carbs, which is brilliant."

"Yes, I knew you didn't eat them so—" Maggie stopped, her face flushing crimson. She didn't dare turn round.

Tamsyn walked up behind her and leaned round to look at her. "Please don't be embarrassed that you knew that about me. I know things like that are in the public domain, and easy for you to find out. I think it's very thoughtful that you made the effort to check."

Oh, lordy, if only it were that simple. There was no way she was going to tell Tamsyn that she knew about her diet because she'd followed her career and life so closely she knew pretty much *everything* that was in the public domain and had no need to check in advance of the evening.

Instead she shrugged, and smiled, and said nothing. She also wasn't comfortable lying outright to Tamsyn, so silence was the best path.

"Right," Tamsyn said briskly, stepping back. "Champagne."

"Yes," Maggie said, glad for the save. "Lovely!"

When Tamsyn had poured, they chinked glasses and sipped.

"Thank you for this," Tamsyn said over the rim of her glass.

"Wait until you taste the food before you say that." Maggie smirked, amazed at how relaxed she felt around Tamsyn—and at how it was already getting easier to think of her as just Tamsyn.

Tamsyn laughed. "Okay, now I'm worried."

Maggie gestured towards the living room. "Want to sit by the fire before I cook? Unless you're hungry right now?"

Walking over to the sofa, Tamsyn shook her head. "No, I'm fine for now." She sat on the sofa, crossed one leg over the other and wriggled back into the cushions. "That's better."

Maggie didn't feel so comfortable that she'd sit next to her on the sofa, so she opted for her usual armchair. Gizmo padded into the space between the two pieces of furniture, his favourite soft toy—a long, snake-like shape made with tiger stripe material—between his jaws, and stopped at Tamsyn's feet, gazing up at her.

Tamsyn stared at him and Maggie tutted. "Oh, Gizmo, really? I told you to be charming and you bring her Snakey?"

"Snakey?" Tamsyn had one eyebrow arched in a way that simultaneously made Maggie's breath catch and caused her severe eyebrow envy.

"Well, you know, given he's a dog it doesn't have a proper name—he couldn't pronounce it, not with the shape of his jaw."

Tamsyn snorted. Actually snorted, and Maggie chuckled.

"He's had that toy for two years," Maggie continued, gazing fondly at Gizmo. "Prior to that most toys were ripped to shreds within months, or even weeks, of being in his possession. But there's something about Snakey, apparently."

As if aware he was being watched, Gizmo marched across the room, Snakey clamped tightly in his jaws, and settled down in front of the fire. He stretched out so it looked like he was cuddling the toy.

"Oh, my God, that is beyond cute." Tamsyn was staring at Gizmo with an awestruck expression on her face. "I said yesterday I'm not too fond of dogs but this one might persuade me otherwise."

Maggie gave a little fist pump, which made Tamsyn laugh again. Maggie loved that she could do that because every time it happened, Tamsyn looked a little less worried about the world.

"So," Tamsyn said, after another sip of her champagne, "you're a writer. Published?"

You could say that.

"Um, yes, actually."

Tamsyn made a rolling motion with her free hand. "And...? Details please?"

Maggie half grimaced, half smiled. "Er, well. I write under a pen name, publishing historical fiction."

"And how many books have you published?"

"Six, so far." *And eight lesbian ones, but we're not talking about those.*

Tamsyn's eyes went wide. "Six? Wow. I'm impressed." She paused to take another sip of her drink. "Um, I've read a bit of historical fiction, but not much. Well, just one author actually. Wasn't really my cup of tea, I'm afraid—all those heaving bosoms and macho men riding about the countryside."

Maggie dipped her head in acknowledgement. "Well, that's okay. At least you tried. A lot of people can be quite snobbish about the genres they read, as if only certain ones have value."

"Oh, yes, I'm sure. A little like moviegoers."

"Of course! Yes, I imagine we have quite similar experiences of that."

"So, is that the only genre you've ever written in? Don't fancy trying something else?"

"Well... I have dabbled in some other things, yes. But those six have been my money makers. And I do really enjoy the research side of things, which you get to do more of than in most other genres."

"So, are you famous?" Tamsyn waggled her eyebrows. It was extraordinary how many nuances she could generate just with her face. All that acting, Maggie assumed.

She chuckled and blushed. "I am quite well known, yes."

"Go on then, tell me your published name."

There was no harm, was there? After all, she knew exactly who Tamsyn was.

"I write as Jessica Stewart. I doubt you've—" Tamsyn's rich blush had the words dying on her lips. "Oh. It was one of my books you read, wasn't it?"

"Oh, God," Tamsyn said in a whisper, "I'm so sorry. It wasn't the writing, let me say that straight away. It was just the storylines and, well..." She shook her head. "Good grief, this is embarrassing."

It did sting, Maggie could admit that much. She knew that not everyone loved her books. She'd always known that. But she'd rarely come face-to-face with someone who had made it so clear that they didn't like what she wrote. And for it to be Tamsyn Harris was just the sour icing on the bitter cake.

Tamsyn put her glass down and shuffled forward to the edge of her seat. "Maggie, I'm so sorry. The words I used earlier were careless and thoughtless. If I had known who—"

Maggie raised a hand. "Honestly, it's fine. I've heard worse, believe me." Her voice sounded flat even to her own ears.

"Should I go?" Tamsyn was already half standing.

"What? No!" Maggie was aghast—did Tamsyn really think her that shallow? "Seriously, it's fine. You are perfectly entitled to your opinion." She sighed. "I can't lie though, having someone I admire so much not like what I do.... I mean, there's no rule that says you should, but it just... Do you get what I mean?"

Tamsyn nodded and sat back down again. "I do," she said softly. "I'm sorry I hurt your feelings."

"Apology accepted. Let's just forget it, shall we?"

"We shall." Tamsyn grinned suddenly. "Of course, you could get your own back, if you wish."

Maggie was puzzled, and her face clearly reflected this, as Tamsyn's grin became a laugh.

"Well, I'm pretty sure you haven't loved *everything* I've done, have you? Go on, score one for your side—tell me which of my films or programmes you hated."

"Oh, no, I couldn't! And I don't need to. We're fine, honestly."

Tamsyn shrugged. "Okay. But I still think I might want to worm that out of you sometime this evening. Maybe after another glass of champagne, hmm?"

Maggie laughed. "You're crazy, has anyone ever told you that?"

Tamsyn rolled her eyes. "Frequently."

They prepared dinner together. Not that there was much to prepare—Maggie had taken care of most of it before Tamsyn arrived. As she watched Maggie work, Tamsyn berated herself for the umpteenth time for the gaffe over Maggie's writing. It was the strangeness of their situation, she knew that. She'd never have said anything so artless at any other kind of social occasion. As famous as she was, she always had to watch what she said; one never knew who was bloody listening. She'd let her guard down, which was testament to the warm welcome Maggie had given her this evening.

And I paid her back by insulting her.

She wanted to groan out loud but bit it back. Maggie seemed fine, after all, laughing with her as they tried their best to Julienne the vegetables—as per some of the upscale restaurants they'd both dined at—and failed to produce anything more than lopsided straws of carrots and pepper. Like her, Maggie was used to a modicum of fame, and they had already swapped stories of the best places they'd eaten in London thanks to various events in each of their own entertainment worlds. It had levelled things between them a little, and Tamsyn was glad, because relaxed Maggie was even more delightful to be around than quietly star-struck Maggie. And a heck of a lot more attractive, if that were possible...

It was difficult yet wonderful to be in such close proximity to her as they worked. While they were both obviously being careful in moving around each other, not touching or brushing, Tamsyn found herself wishing that once, just once, Maggie would lean in a little closer as she reached for that salt cellar. There was a hint of an enticing scent coming from her, and Tamsyn wanted to know if it was perfume, or shampoo, or perhaps simply body lotion. The urge to sniff her like some kind of lesbian bloodhound in heat was becoming stronger by the minute.

"Are you okay?" Maggie's voice snapped Tamsyn out of her daydreaming.

"Fine. I'm fine. Sorry. I think it's the champagne, and the warmth in here—I seem to be falling into a semi-comatose state already." *Nothing to do with how intoxicating it is being around you.*

Maggie smiled. "You need food. If you open the fridge, there's some olives on one of the shelves. They'll tide us over until this is cooked."

"Great idea." To be honest, anything would have been a suitable distraction at that point. Hell, she'd have even petted the dog if it provided a few minutes of not looking at Maggie. It was rather strange, in a way. Maggie wasn't glamorous, or dressed to the nines, not like any of the women Tamsyn usually dated. Although she wore simple attire, it suited her and showed off the beautiful curves of her body in all the right ways. But it was more than the looks and the clothes. It was her entire demeanour. Calm, down to earth, humorous. Not standing on ceremony, or trying too hard to impress. She was just being Maggie. Tamsyn envied her the ability to be that way while still being a relatively public face.

Ducking her head into the fridge, she cast her gaze around for the olives. They weren't obvious, and she started to move containers and bags of ingredients around in her search.

"Any luck?" Maggie's voice came from beside Tamsyn's right ear; she must have walked up so quietly that Tamsyn hadn't heard her.

She turned her head to respond and only just held back a gasp. Maggie was standing so close, in the small gap between Tamsyn's body and the open door of the fridge, that Tamsyn could count the lashes that framed each beautiful hazel eye. She stared, bewitched, as those eyes widened slightly, then softened, then turned a shade darker. Out of the corner of her eye she saw Maggie's tongue dart out to lick her lips, and the action sent a shiver of desire straight down to set off a low throbbing between her legs. Maggie's gaze travelled slowly over her face, as if drinking in every detail of Tamsyn to store up for later. It was as sensuous as a caress and it took a moment for Tamsyn to register that, and to instinctively know what it meant. How had she not seen it before? Was Maggie that good at hiding her feelings?

"Tamsyn," Maggie breathed, the warmth of her breath stroking across Tamsyn's lips.

How had they got so close? Who had moved first?

Even though a part of her mind was warning her of the danger, she couldn't listen to it. She raised a hand and ran a thumb across Maggie's lower lip. Maggie let out a soft moan. Meeting her gaze, Tamsyn swallowed hard at the heat she saw there. Heat that only reflected her own, she knew. The throb between her legs climbed in intensity. Good God, how she wanted to kiss those lips, to pull Maggie close and know what it would feel like to run her fingers through her hair.

Maggie's hand landed gently on Tamsyn's hip, and while the motion itself wasn't so startling, the connection was. Tamsyn abruptly took a step back. Her left side was cool from the open fridge but the rest of her was burning with a heat she both wanted and feared.

"Sorry," Maggie said, flushing a crimson red and stepping back, bumping her head on the fridge door as she did so. "*Shit.*"

Before Tamsyn could make any move to keep her there, to explain or mollify, Maggie was gone, out of the kitchen and into one of the other rooms where she loudly shut the door.

Tamsyn hung her head. *Damn it.*

She closed the fridge door and rubbed her left cheek to bring some heat back into it. Gizmo wandered into the room, his head cocked to one side as he tried to figure out what was going on and why a stranger was standing in his kitchen, not his mum.

"Sorry, boy, I upset her. And I need to fix it, so stay right there." She pointed a stern finger at him. He blinked and sat down.

Well, holy shit. Tamsyn Harris, dog trainer. Who knew?

Using her amazing powers of deduction—the bathroom door was open—she knew Maggie was in the bedroom. Taking a deep breath, she walked to the door and knocked once, firmly. No answer. Tamsyn sighed; she couldn't force Maggie to talk to her, but she had to ensure Maggie knew she'd done nothing wrong.

Knocking again, she listened as hard as she could, her ear pressed to the door.

"Maggie, come on, I know you're in there. Please, I would like to talk to you, to explain what just happened."

"There's nothing to explain. Please, I'm embarrassed enough as it is. Can you just go?" Maggie's tremulous voice broke Tamsyn's heart.

"No, I'm afraid I can't." Not knowing or understanding why she was doing this, pressing the point so hard when Maggie had given her an out, she turned the handle and opened the door.

Maggie was sitting on the bed, hands under her legs, knees pulled up to her chin. She groaned at the sight of Tamsyn walking into the room and turned her head away.

"Please, just leave me alone." Her voice was muffled, but the anguish in it was clear.

A strange calmness had descended on Tamsyn, something she couldn't explain then or later. She pushed the door closed behind her and walked across the room, her pace even and gentle. The bed dipped as she added her weight to it, and Maggie's head snapped round as Tamsyn shuffled up alongside her and laid a hand on her hip.

"Maggie, please listen to me. That, in there, was not all you. It was me too."

The confession felt wonderful, freeing. Damn the consequences, though somehow she knew there wouldn't be any she couldn't handle—she trusted Maggie with this. She had no idea why, but she did.

Maggie stared at her. "W-What?"

"I wanted that kiss just as much as you did." Tamsyn was almost whispering as thoughts of how much she *still* wanted it coursed through her.

Maggie blinked, and her mouth dropped open in a small 'O'. Tamsyn smiled. God, she looked adorable.

"A-Are you...*gay?*"

Tamsyn took a deep breath. "I'm a lesbian, yes."

"Holy shit," Maggie said, then clapped a hand over her mouth.

Tamsyn chuckled. "Indeed. Not something I've ever advertised, and never will, probably. It's a hard enough life without... Well, you know."

"I...I guess." Maggie lowered her legs and shimmied around a little to face Tamsyn more easily. "You... We... In there..."

"Maggie." Tamsyn was swamped with a need she couldn't control, and didn't want to, not now. "I... I told you yesterday how beautiful you are. I wasn't lying. You're... You take my breath away."

"Oh." Maggie's eyes were shining.

"Can I ask? Are...you?"

Maggie smiled. "Lesbian? Oh, yeah. Duh."

Tamsyn snorted softly. "Well, that's the trouble with being so far in the closet. No working gaydar."

Her tone was wry, but underneath she heard her own bitterness and squashed it down before it ruined the moment. Maggie was smiling, and it lit up her face.

Tamsyn couldn't hold it back any longer, couldn't deny it anymore.

Moving slowly, but with intent pounding through her veins, she leaned forward. Maggie inhaled sharply but in the next moment rose up on her hands to meet her, and a moment after that, Tamsyn did what she'd been wanting to do since the beginning. She kissed Maggie. Their lips met, and it was every kind of softness and warmth she had missed for so long. And yet it was also more than that. This was *Maggie* she was kissing, and that held its own value, and a high one at that.

Maggie's lips moved under hers, sampling, savouring, it seemed, and the touch reignited that throbbing from earlier and sent it to fever pitch. Tamsyn opened her mouth, tentatively let her tongue dip between Maggie's lips, and was rewarded with a moan, and a meeting of tongues that wrenched a sound from her throat that was part torture, part ecstasy. She pressed closer, Maggie's heat searing her body in the few places where they touched and making her crave more. They were both diving deeper now, both adding a delicious force to the movement of their lips, their tongues. Maggie was emitting the most incredible sounds from somewhere deep in her throat, and every one set off another spark of arousal that skittered down Tamsyn's spine to her thighs, her belly, and her clit.

They came up gasping for air and stared at each other.

"That was…" Maggie managed to mumble, shaking her head slightly.

"Uh-huh." Tamsyn traced a line around Maggie's mouth with a fingertip.

Maggie shifted, bringing herself more upright, her body closer to Tamsyn's. "So," she said, her gaze flickering away and back again. "We, um, kissed. W-What happens now? I mean, um, what does that mean?"

Chapter 7

MAGGIE STARED AT TAMSYN WHILE she waited for a response.

Oh, my good God, I just kissed Tamsyn fucking Harris. But the minute she thought the words, she admonished herself. *No, I didn't. I kissed Tamsyn, just Tamsyn.*

It was an important distinction. When she'd peered into the open fridge alongside Tamsyn, she hadn't been thinking, "Oooh, I'm snuggled up to the famous actress here." She'd only been aware of the warm presence of a gorgeous woman in such close proximity. A woman whose eyes drew Maggie in, whose lips looked like they'd be perfect to kiss, and whose hint of vulnerability triggered a level of affection that seemed out of proportion to the time they had actually spent together.

Tamsyn shuffled where she sat. Maggie could feel the aftermath of that kiss sizzling between them, and on every point in her skin where Tamsyn's body heat touched her. Tamsyn's face was still flushed, and her weight pressed against Maggie made her want to pull Tamsyn down and carry on where they'd left off a minute ago. It had been a very long time since a woman had fired her up so completely, so quickly.

Tamsyn swallowed, and a half-smile crossed her lips. "Well, that's the sixty-four-million-dollar question, isn't it?"

Maggie blinked, her mind in a daze as she stared at those luscious lips again. "What question?" she murmured.

A husky chuckle left Tamsyn's throat. "Your question. About what happens now."

"Oh, yeah. That." Maggie tried to pull her mind back, but it was a losing battle. "Well, I vote for more kissing."

Tamsyn held up a finger. She was smiling, but it was one of those smiles that lacked conviction, and Maggie's fog faded in the face of its blandness. Pushing herself up a little more, easing Tamsyn away from her slightly in the process, she stared at her.

"I just need to make something clear. If that's the way we're going to go. The more kissing way." Tamsyn looked...haunted, and Maggie wondered at the cause.

"Um, okay."

"I can't..." Tamsyn looked towards the ceiling and exhaled before returning her gaze to Maggie's. "This can only be something brief, and passing. No strings. I can't do strings. If that's not something you can respect then we should stop now, have a nice meal, and that'll be the end of it. I also need to ask that you keep this to yourself—no going to the press. I don't think you would, but I've learned it's best to make things very clear from the start so that my...partners understand the situation." She shrugged, but her eyes stayed locked on Maggie's. "I have a career to protect."

The words were cold, but Maggie picked up on a layer of something behind them, underneath them, running so deep she wondered if Tamsyn was even aware of it: regret. She stared at Tamsyn, who looked resolute, almost stern. Was she trying to convince Maggie, or herself? Either way, it was as if they were negotiating a business agreement, and the impersonal nature of that had her flopping back onto the bed, her gaze on the ceiling.

"Maggie?"

She turned her head to look at Tamsyn. "Talk about mood killer," she said, not bothering to hide her irritation. "Is there some contract you need me to sign too? An NDA, perhaps?" Anger rumbled up, and she sat upright before pushing herself off the bed. Tamsyn watched her every move, her eyes narrowed. "Do you know what's so funny about all of this?" Maggie strode to the window, looking out into the darkness between curtains that weren't quite pulled across the glass.

"What?" Tamsyn's voice, even in that one word, was tight and on edge.

Maggie turned back to face her. "I didn't kiss you because you're Tamsyn Harris, world-famous actress. I kissed you because you're Tamsyn, a gorgeous woman I met out on a walk yesterday and was enjoying a lovely evening with, and who I'm wildly attracted to." She sighed. "You wanted to be yourself this evening, and for me, setting one or two little blips aside, you were. You were Tamsyn, and I liked kissing Tamsyn."

When Tamsyn didn't respond, other than to blink a few times, Maggie threw up her hands and stomped out of the room. What was the point? The woman was so fixated on protecting her damn career she wouldn't even allow herself to relax for one evening. Which was such a shame because for a few minutes there, more than a few minutes, she had, and she'd been a wonderful person to be around. And to kiss.

When Maggie walked into the kitchen, Gizmo leaped up from his place by the fire, leaving his beloved Snakey behind, to follow her. He'd always been good at judging her moods, and the tilt of his head told her he knew she was ruffled and in need of some doggy attention. She knelt and hugged him close.

"I'm sorry." Tamsyn's words were quiet, but in the stillness of the cottage carried easily from where she stood in the doorway.

Maggie stared at her, her chin on Gizmo's head.

Tamsyn shrugged, then folded her arms around herself. "What you said in there, you're...you're right. I was me, tonight. Mostly. And it's been a long time since I've been able to do that and it...unsettled me. It was way too easy to fall back on being that other Tamsyn. I'm more used to being her. Even though she stops me from being who I really want to be. Who I really am." She leaned against the door frame and sighed. "The trouble is, I have to be her, don't you see? That's my life. It's everything. So although I perhaps handled our situation badly, and my words could have been chosen better, the underlying facts are still true. I can't offer you anything more than a holiday fling."

Maggie let go of Gizmo and stood up. "I don't remember asking you for anything, fling or otherwise. What I really resent about all that you said is the implication that I am only in this so that I can tick 'famous actress' off my list of accomplishments or something. That I am, or was, only doing this because of your name. It never crossed my mind to look beyond this evening, and it never crossed my mind to wake up in the morning and call the tabloids with all the juicy gossip. I thought I was kissing the real Tamsyn in there, but who were you kissing? Because it certainly wasn't the real me if that's what you thought of me."

Tamsyn stared at her, cheeks flushing. "Maggie, wait, that's not true! I…" She pushed off the door frame, unfolded her arms, and took a couple of tentative steps forward. "Please believe me, when I was kissing you, I wasn't thinking any of those things. I was only thinking about how incredible you felt, how bloody amazing it was to kiss such a beautiful woman, a woman I was spending such a wonderful evening with. It was only afterwards that famous Tamsyn took over and fucked it all up."

In spite everything, Maggie couldn't help snorting at Tamsyn's use of the F-word. It sounded so incongruous coming from such a well-spoken woman, even though she'd used the word many times on screen.

"What?" Tamsyn asked, a hesitant smile forming on her lips.

"You used the F-word." Maggie shrugged, chuckling. "Somehow it tickled me in amongst all the drama."

Tamsyn's smile this time was wry. "Well, I am an actress, *darling*. We do like a bit of drama."

"I'll say."

Tamsyn stepped nearer still. "I really am sorry," she said quietly. "I never meant to ruin what was becoming one of the best evenings I've had in quite a while."

Maggie could hear the sincerity in her tone and see it in her eyes. "I know you didn't." She glanced at the clock on the wall. "Look, it's getting on for dinner time. Why don't we eat, have another glass of champagne, and forget all this, okay?"

Tamsyn's face fell, just for a moment, before she squared her shoulders and beamed a not-so-genuine smile. "Sure, let's do that."

Tamsyn gathered Maggie's plate and cutlery and glared when her host tried to stop her.

"You cooked most of the dinner. Let me clean up, okay?"

Maggie looked sheepish but held up her hands in surrender. "Okay, okay."

Tamsyn grinned at her. "Go sit by the fire. I won't be long."

It took a couple of trips to ferry all the used plates, dishes, and cutlery to the kitchen but only fifteen minutes to wash it all up. Contrary to what people might think, Tamsyn did know how to do washing up, and a host of other household chores. When in London and not too busy with PR and events, Tamsyn took an almost humble joy in being able to clean her own home. It was one of the few times she felt like a real person with a real life.

As she wiped the dishes dry, she thought about dinner. It had been... okay. They'd struggled for conversation topics to begin with, both clearly still unsure of themselves. But soon, as they'd filled their bellies and sipped more champagne, they'd relaxed into each other's presence again and, she was pretty sure, managed to get back to the same level of ease and relaxation they'd had before.

"Are you really okay in there?" Maggie called.

Tamsyn laughed. "Yes! Stop panicking. I do know my way around a kitchen sink. Anyway, I've actually just finished."

She washed and dried her hands, then pulled down the sleeves of her sweater before joining Maggie in the living room. Maggie was sitting in the armchair, her knees pulled up so that her chin rested on them, gazing at the fire. Gizmo was laid out, his belly turned towards the warmth, Snakey at his back. Tamsyn stopped in her tracks as a powerful wave of longing rushed over and through her. For a moment she could picture coming home to a scene like this every day and the need it engendered took her breath away. Without saying a word, she walked lightly across the room and crouched down next to Gizmo, tentatively reaching out to stroke his belly. He startled and looked over his shoulder at her, but in the next moment relaxed and stretched, offering yet more of his belly to her touch.

"Uh-oh," Maggie said softly. "You've done it now. He'll expect that from you all the time. You've doomed yourself."

Tamsyn chuckled and looked up at her. "I can think of far worse dooms than this."

She stared at Maggie, at the way the firelight danced across her hair and her face, and her breath caught in her throat. *So beautiful.* Maggie unfurled her legs and placed her feet on the floor. In the next moment she moved to a kneeling position in front of her chair, which brought her to within only a couple of feet of Tamsyn. Her fingers stilled on the dog's belly as she sat transfixed. Maggie hadn't taken her eyes off Tamsyn, and the heat in her gaze made Tamsyn's entire body tremble. Suddenly they were back here again, that place where desire was so obvious and intense it was almost tangible, buzzing between them like minute flickers of lightning. Maggie came up onto her knees and inched forward, her gaze still never leaving Tamsyn's. It was thrilling and scary all at the same time.

As Maggie reached her, Tamsyn too pushed up onto her knees to make them the same height. Gizmo stirred at the removal of her hand but Tamsyn ignored him, her attention focused on the stunning woman now only centimetres away. Before she could muster anything to say or do, Maggie's lips crashed into hers and claimed her mouth in a kiss that scorched her entire body. Maggie's hands were on her back, pulling her closer, and she let herself go there, let herself sink into the softness and warmth of Maggie's body. Maggie's tongue was insistent, and electrifying; thoughts of where else that tongue could work its magic stormed through her brain. Tamsyn kissed back with equal ferocity, running her hands up Maggie's spine to finally run her fingers into the softness of Maggie's hair and hold on tight. God, it felt even better than she could have imagined, made even more so by the delicious moan the action elicited from Maggie. Tamsyn felt that moan deep down in her belly and her clit began to throb. She trailed one hand back down Maggie's back to cup her ass, not squeezing but simply holding, luxuriating in the feel of that curve encased in tight denim, the heat from Maggie seeping into her skin.

Maggie pulled back, her eyes shining in the firelight. Her voice was a husky croak as she said, "I'm sorry, I—"

"No, nothing to be sorry about," Tamsyn rasped, leaning back in for more, capturing Maggie's mouth with a gentle kiss this time, savouring the feel of soft lips beneath hers. She licked along Maggie's bottom lip and did it again when Maggie inhaled sharply and whimpered at the touch. Her left hand was still tangled up in Maggie's hair and she used it to tug Maggie's head back a little, exposing more of her neck, which she then covered in a slow, haphazard trail of open-mouthed kisses. Tamsyn's tongue licked at the point where Maggie's neck met her shoulder and the shudder that move elicited made her groan in tandem.

"Maggie?" she whispered, her body consumed by need and ignoring any warning signals her brain might be attempting to flash her way.

"Yes?" It was tortured, that one word, and Maggie's fingers on Tamsyn's shoulder blades were frantic.

"Can we move to the bedroom?"

She didn't know if it was the sensible thing to do, or whether she'd regret it a million times over when she woke up in the morning. But here and now, she couldn't stop this tidal wave of want and desire that threatened to suffocate her unless it found an outlet.

Maggie pushed back slightly, and waited until Tamsyn met her eye before speaking.

"Are you sure?"

It was a loaded question, and Tamsyn understood completely why Maggie had to ask, but she only had one answer and she gave it quickly.

"Yes. God, yes."

Chapter 8

SOMEWHERE FAR BACK IN HER mind, in the small area that hadn't been affected by the lust-induced fog which had consumed her, Maggie wondered if they were making a mistake. The thought was blown off as fast as it arrived—if they were, she didn't care. Not now.

Leaning into Tamsyn like that, claiming that incredible kiss, had been the only thing she could do in the circumstances. The way the fire's light picked out hidden auburn highlights in Tamsyn's hair and made the brown of her eyes resemble melted chocolate had short-circuited something in Maggie.

She held Tamsyn's warm hand now as she led her into the bedroom. The single lamp by the side of the bed cast enough light to see each other by, and a quick push of the door ensured Gizmo wouldn't disturb them.

"I want to see you," Tamsyn whispered, gesturing vaguely to Maggie's clothes.

Maggie nodded but swallowed. She thought she was in reasonable shape for a woman her age, but she knew her body would be considerably softer and more rounded than Tamsyn's. She'd seen the glamour shots involving sultry gowns and designer skinny jeans, after all.

"Please," Tamsyn said, walking closer and dropping a soft kiss on Maggie's mouth. "I can't wait to touch you."

Maggie searched her eyes and saw the truth of it; the desire that burned there was fierce, and her hesitation dropped away.

She removed her jeans first, peeling them down and kicking them off with as much grace as she could manage, taking her socks with them. The thick sheepskin rug beneath her feet tickled her skin and added to the sensory overload. Her fingers fumbled at her shirt buttons.

"Can I help?"

Maggie nodded; her voice had deserted her.

Tamsyn reached out with trembling hands and Maggie's tension lessened. *Okay, I'm not the only one nervous. Thank God.*

The buttons eased out of their holes in quick succession under the ministrations of Tamsyn's slender fingers. Maggie shivered at the thought of what those fingers might do to her shortly. What she prayed they'd do.

Tamsyn pushed the shirt away from Maggie's shoulders and let it fall to her wrists, swallowing visibly at what it revealed. The blue cotton bra Maggie wore was one of her plainest, but it also cupped her breasts into what even she considered a pleasing cleavage.

"So beautiful." Tamsyn licked her lips and Maggie almost growled.

Bending her head, Tamsyn kissed the swell of one breast, then the other. Her lips were like fire on Maggie's skin and she threw out her hands to grasp Tamsyn's hips, steadying herself as she swayed into the touch.

"Sensitive?"

"Oh, yeah." Maggie looked down; Tamsyn was looking up, her mouth millimetres from Maggie's flesh, her breath warm against it. "You can spend as much time as you like there. Just so you know."

Tamsyn's throaty chuckle was sexy as hell. "Noted," she whispered before licking a long line from deep between Maggie's breasts all the way up the curve of the left one to her clavicle.

Maggie gripped Tamsyn's hips tighter, clinging on for dear life as waves of erotic sensation thrummed over her. Her clit was aching for attention, but she'd let it suffer if Tamsyn kept up those exquisite swirls of her tongue around the uncovered parts of her breasts. When Tamsyn reached behind her with a murmured, "Yes?" Maggie nodded vigorously and felt no embarrassment when Tamsyn chuckled at her enthusiasm. The bra dropped to her wrists to join the shirt; she was now nicely pinned by both items of clothing and the concept thrilled her.

"Oh, God." Tamsyn lunged in, her lips closing around one nipple and sucking hard. Maggie cried out as bolts of desire shot straight to her clit. She was wet and swollen already. "Your breasts are incredible," Tamsyn whispered as she moved from one to the other, this time biting, softly at first but increasing the pressure until she made Maggie gasp. "Like that?"

"Yes. More. Harder." If there was one thing she loved it was having her nipples bitten, and moments later she was thankful Tamsyn was happy to follow such clear instructions. Maggie was squirming and breathing heavily by the time Tamsyn lifted her head.

"I want this all off," she said, one hand plucking at the shirt around Maggie's waist. She glanced down at Maggie's underwear. "All of it."

Maggie couldn't move fast enough, despite a modicum of embarrassment still lingering about her overall body shape. Her stomach wasn't going to be as flat as Tamsyn's, and she still had a couple of stretch marks left over from the time when her weight had increased through stress some years ago. But Tamsyn was making it very clear with her lustful looks that naked was how she wanted Maggie, so naked she would be. She ripped off the shirt and bra, then eased her underwear off her hips and let them fall to the floor.

Tamsyn sucked in a breath and met Maggie's nervous gaze. "You really are beautiful, Maggie. Please don't doubt that."

"Thank you," Maggie whispered, her throat tightening a little. She inhaled and exhaled once, nice and slow, to calm her remaining nerves. "But there seems to be something wrong with this situation." She smiled as Tamsyn raised an eyebrow. "I appear to be the only one naked, and I think that needs to change."

Tamsyn chuckled. "Oh, you do, do you?"

"Uh-huh. Strip. Now." She added just a little firmness to the last word and was rewarded with a soft gasp and a shudder that seemed to sweep the full length of Tamsyn's body.

Wordlessly, Tamsyn did as she was told, and it was one of the most erotic experiences Maggie had ever had. She didn't know if it came from Tamsyn's training, but if it did, she wanted to find whichever coach had imparted this skill and shake them by the hand. Every item of clothing was eased off her body with a seductive, almost lazy motion that tantalised Maggie's senses and made her impatient for more. The shirt went first, revealing a black, lacy bra that was sheer and ridiculously sexy, never mind the breasts it contained. They looked firm and full, and Maggie's mouth watered at the prospect of touching them, and—God help her—tasting them. Leaving the bra on for the moment, Tamsyn teased her by switching to the removal of her jeans. Given these clung to every inch of her, Maggie expected a somewhat undignified wriggle would be required to remove them, but even this she managed to make look erotic, and before long the jeans were discarded alongside Maggie's in a heap on the floor. Tamsyn's legs were tanned and smooth, and perfectly toned. Her belly was flat, but to Maggie's delight, not as perfectly flat as she'd imagined, which only made her love it even more. There was a small tattoo just below Tamsyn's belly button; Maggie couldn't determine what it was right now but knew she'd have fun figuring that out later. And below the tattoo, Tamsyn's clipped and shaved pussy was already glistening in the low lamplight. The thought of putting her fingers and mouth there sent Maggie's heart rate rocketing.

She looked up and caught Tamsyn looking…uncertain? How was that possible?

"You're stunning," Maggie said with conviction, reaching out a hand and tracing a delicate line across Tamsyn's ribs with one fingertip. "You must know that."

Tamsyn trembled at the touch even as she shrugged. "Means more coming from you." The vulnerability was surprising but in the next moment Maggie knew it made sense.

"Please," Maggie said, keeping her tone low and trying to convey within it all the desire coursing through her veins, "take the rest off?"

Tamsyn's smile was tender and grateful, and she nodded even as her hands went to the front clasp of her bra and snapped it open.

Maggie's mouth went bone dry as Tamsyn's breasts tumbled out of their confines. *Good God, I might die from this.*

Maggie didn't need words. Not now. All she needed was skin, and touch, and mouths, and fingers. She reached out a hand and, when Tamsyn took it, tugged her towards the bed. She had intended to lay Tamsyn down but was beaten to it; Tamsyn's look of determination made any protest die on her lips and instead she smiled, eased back against the pillows, and opened her arms.

Tamsyn groaned softly, intoxicatingly, and warmth spread all over Maggie as Tamsyn's body finally pressed against hers. Their arms snaked easily around each other, and Tamsyn's hands slipped under Maggie's shoulder blades to hold her tight. Tamsyn's mouth found hers, kissing her hard, her tongue thrusting into Maggie's mouth. Maggie wrapped her legs around Tamsyn's thighs, bringing her closer as she did so, and they both moaned deep and low as the movement brought their pussies together.

"Jesus," Tamsyn breathed, staring at Maggie. "I'm... God, this is crazy. I'm so close already!"

Knowing she'd done that to Tamsyn, that just being with her like this had unravelled Tamsyn that much, was the biggest confidence boost Maggie could imagine.

"Uh-huh." She smiled, nodding slowly, then kissed Tamsyn's neck, just below her ear, and whispered, "Want me to do something about that?"

"Yes. No. I don't know!" Tamsyn smiled ruefully. "I don't want this to be over too soon, but at the same time I want you touching me so badly..."

"Mm, and I want to touch you. Badly. But, if it's all right with you, I'd like to take my time." She licked along Tamsyn's jawline and Tamsyn gripped her shoulders harder. "I want to enjoy every inch of you."

"Oh, yes..."

Tamsyn ground against her and Maggie's eyes closed as a wave of ecstasy swamped her. Tamsyn's body felt incredible on top of hers; their breasts touching made her nipples harden further, and the weight of Tamsyn between her legs had her clit pounding with need.

Maggie groaned, then said, "On your back. Please."

Tamsyn was quick to oblige, and waited with flushed cheeks and a hunger in her eyes that took Maggie's breath away.

It had been roughly two years since she'd last touched a woman. With Tamsyn laid out before her like this, open and wanting, it felt like a century. She wanted to do everything at once and yet she couldn't get started. She sighed, and Tamsyn gave her a questioning look.

"I think I've got stage fright," Maggie whispered. "It's...it's been a long time."

Tamsyn reached out and took her hand, entwining their fingers so that her hand was on top of Maggie's. "How about I get you started?" Without waiting for an answer, she tugged Maggie's hand, still linked so intimately with her own, towards her body. Not looking away, keeping her heated gaze locked firmly on Maggie's, Tamsyn placed their joined hands on her right breast with Maggie's palm pressing down into the soft, warm abundance of the mound.

A nipple, hard and rigid, drilled into Maggie's palm even as her fingers curled reflexively around the breast they cupped. "Oh, yeah," she murmured, and Tamsyn nodded, arching into the touch, pulling her own hand away to leave Maggie working the flesh all by herself.

"Yes," Tamsyn rasped, and all the inhibitions and hesitations that had held Maggie back fell away.

She moved then, sitting up so she could straddle one of Tamsyn's thighs.

"Oh," Tamsyn gasped and opened her eyes wide. "You're so wet."

Maggie ground against Tamsyn's leg to emphasise the point and Tamsyn's breath hitched. Then, heart pounding, Maggie bent forward and ran her tongue over Tamsyn's left nipple while her left hand continued to massage the right breast. Tamsyn rocketed upwards, a keening sound leaving her throat.

"Fuck... Yes..."

"Yours like attention too, huh?" Maggie whispered, chuckling.

Tamsyn snorted. "Um, yes, just a bit."

"Good," Maggie replied before returning all her attention to the beautiful body now at her complete mercy. She roved from breast to breast, her tongue and fingers constantly on the move. Then, when she could sense that Tamsyn's arousal was at fever pitch, decided to up the ante. She slid back a little along Tamsyn's thigh—earning another deep groan as her hot, wet pussy coated Tamsyn's skin—and let her mouth go wandering. Flicks and swirls of her tongue over Tamsyn's ribs were followed up with feathery touches down her sides and over her hips and belly. She followed those touches with her tongue, Tamsyn's moans and breathy cries urging her on as she licked a path down Tamsyn's belly towards her pussy.

"Oh, Maggie... *Please.*" There was genuine torture in Tamsyn's tone that made Maggie's own pussy throb with need.

She used her hands to push Tamsyn's thighs further apart, moving herself in between them so she could lay down, her shoulders keeping Tamsyn's legs open although Maggie didn't think she needed much encouragement in that aspect. Tamsyn's scent was filling her nostrils, and the sight of her, wet and open, sent a shiver right through Maggie. She glanced up, up over Tamsyn's belly, between her breasts, to find Tamsyn looking back at her, a whirl of emotions on her face. There was hunger, of course, and a hint of amusement, but underneath was that vulnerability again, and Maggie had to swallow hard before she could focus back on the task at hand.

Dipping her head, she licked up the inside of one thigh. Tamsyn growled, so she repeated the action on the other side, this time making sure to nudge a little closer to Tamsyn's wet pussy with the tip of her tongue. Tamsyn held her breath, then expelled it in a sudden rush as Maggie moved back to the other thigh.

"Oh, you are cruel." Tamsyn sounded equally exasperated and amused.

Maggie chuckled but didn't respond other than to lick again, this time letting the tip of her tongue run over the slickness of Tamsyn's outer lips. *God, she tastes good.* With Tamsyn's ragged breathing sounding loud in the quiet room, and one of her hands gripping Maggie's shoulder, Maggie feasted. Her tongue ran up, and in, and over, and around. Her chin and lips were coated within moments, the best dessert she could imagine at the end of their evening together. Tamsyn's clit was so hard Maggie avoided it at first—something told her it wouldn't take too many licks there to send Tamsyn into orbit, and Maggie had meant what she said; she wanted this to last. She dragged her tongue up a thigh again and this time didn't stop, burying it as deep as she could inside Tamsyn, whose hips surged off the bed as a result.

"Oh, *yes*. Fuck me, Maggie."

She did, dipping her tongue in and out, as deep and as fast as she could go. Tamsyn sounded almost in pain she was so aroused, and Maggie knew she shouldn't make her wait a second longer. Sliding her tongue upwards, keeping the pressure firm, she ran it over the hard nub of Tamsyn's clit and held on tightly to her thighs as she licked back and forth, over and over. Tamsyn was gasping for air, her free hand frantic on the duvet beside their naked bodies but Maggie maintained her pace, and the firmness of her touch, and when the shudders started in Tamsyn's thighs, she braced herself.

"Ma...ggie!" Tamsyn cried, loud and long, hips lifting off the bed as her orgasm slammed into her. It was beautiful to feel, and to watch, and to share. Maggie gazed up at her, at the ecstasy that played out on her face, the sweat beading on her chest, and held on tight as Tamsyn thrust again and again, her mouth open in a wide 'O' of pleasure.

Tamsyn's heart was thudding so sharply she was sure it must be visible from the outside and if she'd had the energy she would have glanced down at her own chest to check. However, energy was in short supply right at this moment; she was officially jelly, and it was all Maggie's fault. Not that Tamsyn was complaining, of course.

She chuckled and reached out so both her hands were on Maggie's shoulders.

"Come here, you," she murmured, and Maggie obliged, slinking her way up, pressing soft, wet kisses against Tamsyn's skin as she did so, making her shiver. Tamsyn wrapped her arms around Maggie and held her close, the touch of her along the length of Tamsyn's body stirring something more than sexual within her, something that rang a small bell of alarm in the back of her head which she tried to ignore. "That was…incredible," she whispered, kissing Maggie's hair where the side of her head was pressed against Tamsyn's cheek. Maggie's breathing was heavy in her ear.

"Mmm, I thought so too. You taste so good."

"Why, thank you."

Maggie lifted her head then, and her hot gaze and sexy smile was Tamsyn's undoing. That alarm bell fell silent as she swiftly pushed Maggie onto her back.

"My turn," she growled, cupping both of Maggie's breasts in her hands and rubbing her thumbs over the nipples, which hardened instantly, tempting her to taste them.

"Oh, yes."

Maggie was squirming already, and a heady sense of power rushed through Tamsyn. She was doing this, making this woman feel that good, and it was so much more thrilling than one of Tamsyn's usual set-ups. She'd *chosen* Maggie, even if it was just for this one night. At that thought, of it only lasting these few hours, Tamsyn's stomach squirmed; it stopped her thoughts, shut her mind down, and her body took over. She just needed to feel now, not analyse.

Leaning forward, she licked at the rigid nipples before her and smiled at Maggie's soft groan.

"Tell me, Maggie," she whispered, gazing into those hazel eyes and catching her breath at the intensity of their colour under the influence of Maggie's desire. "Do you like getting fucked? Because I really, really want to fuck you right now."

"Jesus! *Yes.*"

Maggie's laboured words sent Tamsyn's blood raging through her veins. Keeping her tongue moving over Maggie's nipples, and alternating licks with the bites she already knew Maggie loved, she ran a hand firmly down the centre of Maggie's body to her soft curls. It was refreshing to feel hair—most of the women she spent time with were models or other actresses, always fastidious about removing as much body hair as possible, as she herself did. Running her fingers through a soft bush made her smile, but she didn't linger; she had a much more interesting destination in mind and a huge desire to get there quickly. Maggie's pussy was hot, and wet, and Tamsyn could tell she was open and ready. When two fingers slid easily inside, and Maggie gasped at the sensation, Tamsyn's own pussy clenched in response; she hoped Maggie had stamina. But first, she wanted Maggie to feel as good as she had, to melt beneath her and gasp for air.

Slowly, but with intent, Tamsyn did as she'd promised. And when, a short time later, Maggie's hips bucked off the bed, and her entire body went rigid with pleasure, a warmth and satisfaction infused Tamsyn in a way she hadn't remembered feeling in such a long time. Before she could revel in it—or run from it—Maggie was kissing her fiercely, and pushing her onto her back, and letting her mouth roam once more down the length of Tamsyn's body.

Chapter 9

GIZMO'S WHINING BROUGHT MAGGIE AWAKE. Tamsyn stirred, her arms unclenching from their position around Maggie's waist. Maggie was half-lying on top of her, her back to Tamsyn's chest, her head on Tamsyn's shoulder. She wouldn't have imagined it was possible for her to drift off in such a position, but it appeared she had done so.

"What's that noise?" Tamsyn murmured against her hair.

Maggie chuckled. "That, I'm afraid, is the noise of a dog who needs to go outside." She gently pushed Tamsyn's arms away. "I'll be back, just give me five minutes."

"Mm, 'kay."

Maggie smiled and reluctantly extricated herself from Tamsyn's arms, then found her shirt and socks and pulled them on before padding out of the bedroom. Gizmo stared up at her from a few feet away, shuffling from side to side, his eyes reproachful.

"Hey, buddy. I'm sorry. I've got you now." She patted him quickly on the head then led him to the back door. By the time she had it open he was frantic, and he didn't run far down the garden before finding a useful fence post to take care of business. Maggie shivered just inside the door as she watched him, making sure he didn't get any crazy ideas about spending too long out there, but she needn't have worried; Gizmo seemed well aware of how cold and late it was and was soon scampering back up the path and into the warmth of the kitchen.

She shut and locked the door, then topped up his water and his dry food before paying her own visit to the bathroom. As she washed her hands, she smiled at her dishevelled state, reflected in the mirror above the sink.

She'd had sex—amazing sex—with Tamsyn Harris. Even though she'd tried so hard to forget Tamsyn's status in the world, it wasn't every day a woman got to spend naked, sexy time with someone famous they'd crushed on since they were a teenager. At the same time, the woman she'd been touching, and bringing to the height of ecstasy—more than once—was just Tamsyn. There'd been no acting, no need for pretence; they'd enjoyed each other as equals.

With dry hands and a buzz between her legs at the thought of returning to that hot body in her bed, she flipped off the bathroom light and walked back down the hallway. When she pushed open the door, she stopped dead. Tamsyn, caught in the act of pulling on her jeans, met her eyes briefly before looking away.

"It's getting late," she said, her voice muffled as she leaned over to yank her jeans up. "I'd better get back."

Ah. So this is how it's going to be. Well, she shouldn't be surprised, but it stung, nonetheless.

"Right. Okay. Want me to walk you back?"

Tamsyn stood and smiled, but it was weak and lacking warmth. "No, I'm good. You stay snuggled up in the warm."

"Tamsyn?"

Tamsyn walked over, kissed her quickly on the cheek, then continued past her and out the door without another word.

The coffee tasted bitter, but it was the same brand as yesterday, so Tamsyn had no idea why it stuck in her throat.

"Yeah, right," she said to the cold, empty cottage.

She tugged the blanket closer around her shoulders and glared at the logs on the fire, as if that would make them catch and burn quicker. Getting back after midnight to an icy cottage hadn't been fun, but there'd been no point lighting a fire then. Now, in the early hours of the morning, she'd built one as quickly as she could with numb fingers, but it was taking an age to get going, as if to spite her. The regular heating in the cottage was on, but the radiators weren't that effective and only took the edge off the cold. What she wanted was the deep warmth that only a fire could provide.

Or a soft body pressed up against hers.

She shook her head. No, leaving had been the right decision, even though the mix of emotions on Maggie's face had been hard to stomach. But really, what did Maggie expect? Tamsyn didn't necessarily regret their night, but she'd had to walk away. Protecting herself and her career had to come first, as always. Lingering for more would be a huge mistake, and not because of how Maggie might feel.

You wanted more, accused a voice that hadn't given her any peace all night.

Leaving the warmth of that bed, and of Maggie's arms, had torn her in ways she hadn't imagined were possible. She'd never felt like this leaving any of her other dalliances behind, so what the hell was different now?

She trembled as the answer came loud and clear.

Maggie.

Maggie was different. So very different from all the women who had come before her, and Tamsyn craved her like a drug.

But, like all addicts, she had to resist. Had to fight it. Because giving in, heading back down that path around the lake, held the risk of ruining everything she'd created for herself. And no woman was worth that. Surely.

Maggie sipped from her coffee and gazed out of the window at Gizmo exploring the back garden. It was the eighth or ninth time he'd done so since they'd arrived last week, but of course so much could have changed in that time, as far as a dog's nose was concerned. Wouldn't it be wonderful to be a dog? To have no cares other than when your next meal was arriving, and whether you were still going to get the best spot in front of the fire. Freedom to laze around all day, or go for a walk—owner permitting, of course—and cuddles whenever you played the big brown eyes card.

She sighed. Being human was so…complicated. She put down her coffee mug and rubbed at her tired eyes. There hadn't been much sleep after Tamsyn's departure, even with a warm dog laid across her feet. And she couldn't blame the little snuffling and snoring noises he made while he slumbered.

On one level, she totally understood. Tamsyn was closeted, and her levels of self-protection would therefore be sky high. Of course she didn't want to get dragged into anything that had the potential to get messy.

But Maggie hadn't asked for that, or even expected it. She knew it was completely ridiculous to think they could have anything beyond whatever it was they were finding in this secretive little corner of Norfolk. She would have liked to wake up together though, maybe have coffee and breakfast, maybe make plans to walk Gizmo together later. Just…be. No questions asked, no expectations. Tamsyn hadn't given her that opportunity. *What a waste.*

She lifted her shoulders and inhaled a deep breath. If nothing else, everything that had happened between them had only fuelled her imagination as far as that story idea went, and today she was going to test the waters and see whether words would flow. It made her nervous—what if they didn't, even when she was this excited about a story?

Gizmo yipped at the back door and she walked over to let him in. He went straight to his water bowl and lapped noisily for a minute or so, then wandered off to the living room, licking his chops. She smiled; he was so easy to please. After draining the last of her coffee, she set her shoulders once more.

Right, let's do this.

She pulled out a chair from under the small dining table, sat down, and picked up her glasses. After pushing them up her nose until they were perfectly comfy, she slowly opened her MacBook. Scrivener was open, a blank page awaiting her. She pulled her Moleskine notebook closer and opened it to the page of notes she'd scribbled so furiously the day before.

Flexing her fingers, she began to type.

Two hours later, she leaned back in her chair, an enormous smile on her face.

Bloody hell, I can still do this.

The thought gave her a glow. She glanced at the time on her screen and chuckled. When was the last time she'd immersed herself in her writing so deeply? Gizmo came padding into the kitchen and gazed at her from beside his food bowl.

"Yep, I think you're right, Giz. Time for some food. And maybe a glass of wine for the grown-up. She's earned it."

She made lunch for them both and ate hers standing up, looking out the back window again. The day was beautiful, with bright sunshine and a blue sky. The wine, a smooth Cabernet Sauvignon, gave her a warm glow.

It was tempting to sit back down at her Mac and continue, but she was happy with her progress today, and didn't want to force it. Maybe later, in front of the fire, another glass of wine by her side. Yes, she could think of far worse ways to spend her day. Although, to be honest, she could also think of far better ways. Less lonely ways.

She shook off the thought.

"Come on, you. Time for a walk," she said, looking down at Gizmo, who sat patiently beside her feet.

He leaped up, barked a couple of times, then ran between the back door and front until she'd used the bathroom, pulled on her coat and boots, and picked up his lead from the hall table.

"You're bloody crazy, dog," she muttered, clipping him in and then opening the back door. After locking it behind them she walked him down the garden, letting him sniff the same fence posts he'd already monitored that morning, before urging him to follow her out and onto the path that led to the woods. It was cold out, but not biting—spring was definitely trying to push back the winter, at last, and the plentiful woodland flowers attested to that. While the woods contained a few evergreens, there were still plenty of bare branches above that let light down to the woodland floor this time of year, and, after unclipping his lead, Maggie snapped a few photos of Gizmo romping through clumps of yellow and white low-lying blooms. It was so peaceful in here, and it soothed her. Last night had played with her mind in so many contrary ways; it was good to get grounded again by nature.

They came to the length of track that passed near the back of Tamsyn's cottage. Maggie tried not to look but couldn't resist a peek. Should she go up there? Knock on the door and have it out with Tamsyn? Or simply let her be, let her hide away from the world as she wanted. Who was Maggie to tell her how to live her life? So they'd slept together, so what? People had one-night stands all over the world, every night of the year. They were nothing special—and Tamsyn had made that abundantly clear in the way she'd left.

Except, I thought we were pretty special. At least in bed. What we did to each other was...incredible.

But since when did fantastic sex mean anything more had to happen? Maggie herself had had a couple of flings that were purely physical, so she was no stranger to no-strings couplings. She knew, though, that she was deluding herself if she thought she could just brush it off. She glanced once more at Tamsyn's cottage then followed Gizmo down the path, stepping over a couple of deep puddles left over from the rain. The trouble was, she could admit, that a part of her *had* wished for more. For much more. She wanted the fairy tale—fan meets celebrity and magic ensues.

Oh well, if I can't have it in real life, I'll just make it happen on the page. It might be torture, weaving a fantasy out of one night of blissful reality, but something told her it might be one of her best books yet.

"Thanks, Mrs French, that's plenty." Tamsyn took the huge bag of kindling and smiled, albeit a little apprehensively. Carmen's aunt was a no-nonsense woman of the country life, and it probably hadn't occurred to her that Tamsyn normally had someone to fetch and carry for her, so the rough sack she'd thrust into Tamsyn's arms was way heavier than expected. Tamsyn readjusted it until bits weren't sticking into her chest.

"Right. Just call up to the house when you're getting low next time, and I'll drop more off on my way out sometime."

"Okay, will do."

They said their goodbyes and Tamsyn staggered back off the step that led to the rear kitchen door of the big house. By the time she'd crossed half the courtyard that filled the space between the house and its outbuildings, she'd got a rhythm going that meant she was more than likely not going to drop the bag and its contents all over the track that led to the cottages. It had never occurred to her just to ring Mrs French for the kindling, but now that she was out, stumbling her way over the rutted track with a huge sack of wood in her arms, she was proud of herself doing the self-sufficient thing.

She rolled her eyes. *For Christ's sakes, it's one bag of kindling. You're not a fucking Sherpa.*

The cool day kept her face chilled while her body heated up with her exertions. It was a pleasant warmth, though, and she was glad she'd ventured out. Cooping herself up in the cottage all day really hadn't done her any favours; she'd done nothing but stew, her own actions leaving a sour feeling in the pit of her stomach. She still thought she was right to walk away—mostly—but she wasn't exactly proud of how she'd done so. Maggie deserved better.

Tomorrow. Maybe tomorrow I'll head over there and apologise.

For now, she planned on nothing more challenging for her day than a soak in the big bath that took up most of her bathroom, with another one of the books she'd brought. And a glass of champagne on the side, of course.

She'd just reached the track that encircled the lake when a brown... *something* shot out of the woods to her left, tearing its way towards her across the tufty grass alongside the driveway that led to her cottage. Fearing it was something with sharp teeth that would have no compunction about attacking her in broad daylight, Tamsyn squealed in fright and tried to quicken her pace. The creature barked, and her legs stopped moving just as her stomach flipped.

Gizmo. *Shit.*

He reached her a few seconds later and hopped around her, his front paws resting on her knees each time he did so, his barking giving way to excited little yelps and yips. Tamsyn looked up, knowing that if Gizmo was here, that could only mean one thing.

"Hi," Maggie said from a few feet away, her voice subdued but carrying on the still air around them. "Gizmo! Get down. Come here." She slapped a hand against her thigh and Gizmo immediately dropped his ears and ran back to her, sitting at her feet and gazing first at her, then at Tamsyn, then back again. "Sorry," Maggie continued. "I didn't realise you were what had got him so excited—I just assumed it was a squirrel or rat."

"Rat?" Tamsyn squeaked, cold horror washing over her.

Maggie tilted her head, a faint smile on her lips. "Yes, rat. There are rats all over the place."

"Oh, God." Tamsyn's skin crawled and she shuddered, which caused the sack of kindling to shift in her arms.

"Country rats," Maggie said, sighing. "Nice, country rats. Not the vermin that live in sewers in the city."

"Whatever." A rat was a rat as far as Tamsyn was concerned. How could Maggie be so calm about them?

Maggie bent down to attach Gizmo's lead to his collar. "Well, sorry again for startling you."

Without another word she turned and led Gizmo away. They had only gone a few paces before a wave of guilt and...something else...swamped Tamsyn, and her legs began moving almost of their own accord.

"Wait!"

Maggie glanced back over her shoulder but didn't stop walking.

"Maggie, please." Tamsyn hurried as best she could with her arms full. Bits from the top of the sack started flying out in all directions but she couldn't care less. Let the birds have them. She caught up at last with Maggie, who had finally slowed her pace. Tamsyn walked around to stand in front of her, waiting until Maggie eventually lifted her head and met her gaze. Her face was scrunched into a frown, her eyes narrowed. "Can I talk to you? Inside?" Tamsyn jerked her head towards her cottage. "Please?"

Maggie sighed. "I'd rather not. I've got things to do."

Tamsyn's stomach lurched. "Um, okay. How about—"

"I need to go," Maggie said, snapping her fingers to bring Gizmo to heel before walking away.

Shit.

"Maggie, I'm sorry! I really am." Tamsyn's words were lost in the cold air between them.

Chapter 10

TAMSYN STEPPED HER WAY CAREFULLY along the wooden dock that stretched into the lake. The boards seemed sturdy enough, but hell, if she ended up plunging into the cold water below it would at least wake her up. *What a dreadful night.*

She reached the end of the dock and gazed out over the still water. The ducks were on patrol again, but when they saw she had nothing to offer paddled away as fast as they'd approached.

The whole scene was bucolic, but her anguish over her brief and unsatisfying interaction with Maggie yesterday wasn't quelled by the beauty around her. Hurting Maggie was the last thing she'd wanted to do. And depriving herself of Maggie's company by being such an idiot pained her. She glanced over at Maggie's cottage. *Should I go over? Prostrate myself on her doorstep until she lets me in?*

She shook her head. *God, no.* The last thing she wanted was for Maggie to talk to her out of pure pity.

A bark sounded from behind her and moments later Gizmo rocketed down the boards towards her, his ears pressed back, his tongue lolling. Tamsyn had never imagined she'd be happy to see a dog bounding towards her. She looked beyond him and saw Maggie standing at the start of the dock, her hands stuffed into her coat pockets, her expression unreadable from this distance.

Gizmo jumped and yipped, and Tamsyn smiled. "Hey, dog."

"Gizmo!" Maggie called in a tired voice.

Dropping back down to all fours, Gizmo merely looked back at Maggie.

Wondering if it would work, Tamsyn said, "Come on," and walked back down the dock. Gizmo trotted along beside her, tail held high.

"Little shit," Maggie muttered, and Tamsyn couldn't help the chuckle that rumbled out of her throat.

When Tamsyn reached Maggie, Gizmo trotted over to his mum and sat down beside her. Maggie looked down at him, shaking her head.

"Hi," Tamsyn tried.

Raising her head, Maggie smiled wanly. "Hey."

"It's a cold one."

"It is." Maggie pulled her hands from her pockets and wrapped her arms around herself.

"Can we talk?" Tamsyn blurted. "I really want to talk about it. About the other night."

Maggie closed her eyes for a moment, then shrugged. "Okay."

It wasn't resounding, but it was a yes, so Tamsyn took it as a win.

"We can go to my cottage. It's ever so slightly nearer." Tamsyn risked a smile and was relieved when one corner of Maggie's mouth lifted.

"Sure. Giz, come on."

Maggie turned and took the gravel path that led left to Tamsyn's cottage. Gizmo hesitated, eyes on Tamsyn until she fell into step beside them.

Tamsyn delved into her jacket for the key to the cottage as they approached the front step. It was one of those proper old-fashioned iron keys, and every time she used it, it made her smile.

When she pushed the door open, Gizmo, now off his lead, shot into the cottage, his tail held high as he marched down the hallway like he owned the place.

"Gizmo!" Maggie sounded horrified.

"He's okay. Let him be." Tamsyn smiled at her, and was pleased when Maggie's face relaxed further. "He's kind of growing on me, so he's welcome to make himself at home."

Now Maggie's face broke out into a genuine, wide smile that was like the sun breaking through from behind a cloud, and it lifted Tamsyn's mood even more.

They stared at each other for a few moments, both smiling, before Maggie looked away and followed Gizmo into the cottage. Tamsyn walked in behind her, pushing the door shut once she was inside.

"First things first, let me get a fire going. Is that okay?" She turned to face Maggie, who had perched on an arm of the sofa, still wrapped up in her coat and scarf. Tamsyn frowned. "Would you like to take that off?" She pointed at the coat. "Make yourself at home too?"

Gizmo had flopped onto the rug in front of the armchair, clearly very happy with his surroundings and much more comfortable in them, it would seem, than his owner. Maggie's gaze flitted around the room before finally settling back on Tamsyn.

"Okay," she said, at last, shrugging. But she did at least stand and remove her coat and scarf, laying them on the back of the sofa. She cleared her throat. "Fancy a hot drink?"

Tamsyn's stomach performed a neat little backflip of joy. "That would be lovely. Peppermint tea for me, please." She smiled at Maggie, who nodded and left the room.

Okay, so far so good.

Bending to the fire, Tamsyn assessed what was needed and raked away some of the previous fire's ashes before carefully pulling out a few handfuls of kindling to start setting a fresh fire. She worked quickly, the chill in the cottage already seeping into her bones. She was aware of her audience; Gizmo watched her every move. Sounds from the kitchen told her a brew was on its way, and a minute later she heard Maggie's footfalls behind her. She glanced round and smiled as Maggie placed two steaming mugs onto coasters on the coffee table.

"Perfect. Thank you," Tamsyn said over her shoulder, smiling again as Maggie met her eye.

The fire took quickly, and well, and soon orange and yellow flames were licking all over the logs she'd placed on top of the kindling, and warmth started to creep into the room. Before sitting next to Maggie on the sofa, Tamsyn grabbed both their coats and hung them up in the hallway. When she returned, Gizmo had taken up station in front of the fire, laying on his side with his belly facing the flames.

"He's not stupid, that dog, is he?" Tamsyn chuckled, then eased onto the sofa, next to Maggie but careful to ensure there was space between them.

Maggie snorted. "Not when it comes to open fires, no. Trust me, he makes up for it in other areas."

"Thanks for the tea." Tamsyn knew she was repeating herself, but a bout of nerves crept up and she suddenly didn't know what else to say. Which was stupid, because she had so much to say. And even more stupid when she thought about all the great stages she'd spoken from in her career, in front of hundreds of people. How could an audience of one reduce her to this bumbling mess?

"So, you wanted to talk about it?" Maggie's tone was muted as she reached for her tea.

"Um. Well." *Oh classy, Tamsyn. Great start.* Metaphorically slapping herself about the head, she cleared her throat and tried again. "I wanted to apologise to you. Properly. The way I left the other night was... Well, it was beyond rude. I'm not normally so callous."

"Oh," Maggie said, her tone biting. "Lucky me."

"What? No, wait, sorry. That came out completely wrong." Tamsyn groaned and pushed her hands through her hair. "Maggie, I... That night was incredible. You and I..."

"What? You and I what?" Maggie glared, her hazel eyes a darker colour than Tamsyn remembered, her cheeks flushed. She looked...gorgeous. "We fucked, Tamsyn. That's about all it was, right? Sure, you could have been a little nicer in the way you left, but hey, you'd already made it perfectly clear nothing else was on offer, so why are we even having this conversation?"

The words were sharp, as was the tone, and Tamsyn winced even as her ire rose. "Look, I'm aware that I've made quite a mess of our interactions these last couple of days, but I haven't done that deliberately. I am trying to apologise. I believe I have upset you, and you've every right to be, but the least you could do is play nice when I'm trying to make amends for that!"

Maggie opened her mouth, then closed it again. She shook her head and looked upwards. "You're right," she murmured. "Sorry."

Tamsyn sighed. "You don't have anything to apologise for. I'm the one who's been a complete bitch."

"Not a *complete* one," Maggie said over the top of her mug, her eyes glinting.

Barking out a laugh, Tamsyn reached for her own mug. "Fair enough." She took a sip of hot tea, and revelled in the glow as it slipped down her throat. In front of the fire, Gizmo stretched and snuffled.

They sat in silence for a couple of minutes, drinking their tea, watching the fire. The light outside was fading fast, but the glow from the fire was enough that Tamsyn didn't feel the need to move from her cosy spot to flick the lamps on.

"So," Maggie said eventually, "you managed to get kindling."

Tamsyn sniggered. "Yes, went up to the main house and got handed that sack you saw me with yesterday. I nearly fell over when Mrs French shoved it into my arms."

"It wasn't that heavy, was it?"

"No, just bulky and awkward to carry. And she's a bit, um, forceful. Must be all these years living in the country."

Maggie laughed. "Not the sort of person you meet every day, I'm guessing?"

"Hah, definitely not. I'm amazed she and Carmen are related. They're poles apart."

"Carmen?"

"Oh, sorry. Carmen is my agent. Mrs French is her aunt. That's how I ended up here—Carmen knew her aunt rented out these cottages and knew how secluded they were. Luckily for me, this one was free for a couple of weeks."

"Yeah, she told me she doesn't normally open this early but when I inquired and said I'd pay for a month, I think she realised it was easy money."

"A month?" Tamsyn's voice betrayed her disbelief. "You're prepared to hide up here for a month?"

Maggie chuckled. "You make it sound like a prison sentence." She sighed. "I needed a proper break. I think I mentioned to you that I've been experiencing writer's block?" Tamsyn nodded, and she continued, "Yeah, well that's only part of it. I've become...disillusioned with the whole thing. I've been lucky to write full time for a while now, which I thought would be my dream life, but it hasn't turned out that way." She shook her head. "After being so successful with my first two books, the pressure to write more of equal quality has been way more intense than I anticipated. I sort of burned out, earlier this year, and agreed with my publisher that a break might do me good." She shrugged. "So here I am."

"Wow. I don't mean this to sound condescending at all, but I had no idea an author's life could be so stressful."

Maggie's smile was wan. "I suppose it's like any creative life—if things are flowing everything's wonderful. When they're not..."

"True. I've had a few times in my career when I've sat down at the end of a long shoot and wondered just what the hell I'm doing. I mean, I spend my entire life pretending to be someone I'm not, and sometimes it all just seems so...daft."

"Oh, but come on, some of the roles you've played have been so important! Samantha in *Blue Lights* sent such an important message about women in power, about their capabilities and strength. You didn't get the BAFTA for nothing, you know." Maggie nudged her with a shoulder, sparking a glow inside Tamsyn.

"Thank you," she said quietly, unable to stop herself from gazing at Maggie, drinking in her beauty, the serious expression on her face that lent such a thrilling intensity to her features.

"Well," Maggie said, her voice husky. "It's true."

Don't kiss her. No matter how bloody gorgeous she looks right now, do not—

Maggie's lips were warm from her tea, her tongue even more so. She moaned softly as Tamsyn's tongue traced over her top lip before plunging back inside her mouth. Then, in the next moment, Maggie pulled back, her eyes wide.

"What the—? What are you doing?" She didn't look as outraged as she sounded, but even so, Tamsyn sat back, her own shock careening around her brain.

Yes, Tamsyn, what are *you doing?*

"I'm... I was going to say I'm sorry, but actually, do you know what? I'm not." She inched closer, and noted that Maggie didn't pull away. "I was an idiot to walk away from you the other night. A complete and utter idiot."

"So?" Maggie's voice was only just above a whisper. "I'm pretty sure everything you've said still holds true. You can't offer anything more than a fling, right?"

Tamsyn sighed but knew that she had to be honest. "Yes, true." She paused. "How would you feel if that's what we did?"

Maggie blinked. "You mean, just say right now that that's all we're doing? Do this for however long you're here and when you leave, that's it—goodbye?"

Tamsyn's stomach dropped. It sounded like she'd pushed things too far again, that her honesty, despite being well-intentioned, had shot her in the foot. Oh, well, she'd tried and—

"Okay." Maggie swallowed. "Okay. No strings. No expectations. Right?"

"Er, right. Yes." She stared. "Seriously?"

Maggie shrugged. "I have no clue where *I'm* going to be in a month's time, never mind you. I have no clue how our lives would fit together even if we did try to have anything more, and it's very clear that's not something you would consider anyway. So yeah, why not? I mean," she said, with a gentle smirk, "have you *seen* you? I'd be the craziest lesbian on the planet to turn down the chance of more of what we did to each other."

Tamsyn guffawed, and rocked in her seat. "Well," she said, reaching for Maggie, "when you put it *that* way."

Maggie's mouth on hers undid her in so many ways. Her limbs trembled; her stomach filled with butterflies. There was heat, and softness mixed with a hunger that took her breath away. She was naked faster than she could have imagined, with Maggie's still fully-clothed body pressing her into the sofa even as her fingers slid up the inside of Tamsyn's thigh and slipped into her pussy. Tamsyn gasped as each thrust sent a myriad of pleasurable sensations thrumming through her. Maggie's mouth left hers and her tongue swirled around Tamsyn's left nipple, teasing it to hardness, then nipping and sucking to send exquisite pulses down to Tamsyn's clit.

"Maggie, please, I need to come."

Maggie's only response was to bite down on the nipple; her fingers kept up their steady pace, moving in and out of Tamsyn with a rhythm that ensured her pleasure kept rolling on without finding a peak.

"Oh, Maggie. *Please...*" She wasn't above begging, not when she felt this good, this owned.

Raising her head, her eyes as dark as burnished walnut, Maggie whispered, "Touch yourself. I want to watch."

The words were nearly enough on their own. Tamsyn's arousal leaped, and she couldn't slink her hand quick enough between her own legs. Not surprisingly, her clit was rock hard, and she groaned as she rubbed two fingers over its peak. Maggie, head down now as she watched the show, was breathing heavily, each exhalation accompanied by a soft moan.

It was too much, all of it—the feel of Maggie inside her, the sounds she was making, the heat between their bodies, and the fast circles Tamsyn was making against her own clit. Her orgasm wrenched a long, guttural cry from her throat as her hips thrust upwards, taking more of Maggie inside her as wave after wave of intense pleasure lit her up from the inside out.

"Okay, bath is ready!" Tamsyn called from the other side of the cottage.

Maggie smiled, yet groaned as she knew that meant she had to get her butt off the sofa. She was rather comfy here, wrapped up in a soft fleece throw, the material sensuous against her naked skin. She raised her arms above her head and stretched languidly. Damn, she felt good. It was amazing what a couple of hours of sofa sex could do to a woman.

"Come on, where are you?" Tamsyn sounded impatient and it had Maggie chuckling as she finally hauled herself upright.

"All right, diva, give me a minute."

Tamsyn's bark of a laugh told Maggie her cheeky nickname had hit its mark. She wandered into the kitchen, Gizmo at her heels. She let him out the back door to take care of business, then opened the fridge. Just as she'd hoped—and expected—there was a bottle of champagne in there. Actually, there were three. She shook her head. *Oh, how the other half lives.*

She poured out two glasses, stoppered the bottle, and returned it to the fridge. Gizmo barked, and she let him back in, then found a shallow bowl that could be filled with water for him. Once he seemed happy with her care for his welfare, she picked up the glasses and walked through to the bathroom.

"I thought it was about this time," she said, nudging the door closed behind her. Then she stopped, taking in the sight before her.

Tamsyn had already climbed into the bath. The bubbles, of which there were many, frothed up to her chest and that cute, sexy view made Maggie's breath catch in her throat. Tamsyn's arms were draped on the sides of the bath, her slender fingers hanging loosely, her head leaning back against the rim of the tub. Her eyes were closed and a small, relaxed smile played across her lips. Maggie's heart—and other parts of her anatomy—thumped in response to the visual.

Tamsyn opened her eyes and widened her smile. "Ooh, I like your thinking," she said as her gaze alighted on the glasses in Maggie's hands.

Maggie smiled and sauntered over to the bath. She placed a glass at each end, then carefully stepped into the huge tub, sitting opposite Tamsyn and wriggling until her legs were lined up on the outside of Tamsyn's.

"Comfy?" Tamsyn arched one eyebrow, smirking.

Maggie wriggled a little more, simply for effect. "Yes. Thank you." The hot, bubbly water was divine against her skin. She grinned and reached for her champagne. "To hedonistic times," she said, reaching forward with her glass.

"Indeed." Tamsyn raised her glass and met her toast.

They sipped, then simultaneously placed their glasses back on the side of the bath.

"You're a long way away." Tamsyn rolled her bottom lip. "How can I kiss you if you're over there?"

"I would have thought you needed a rest from all that," Maggie said, grinning. "We did rather out-do ourselves this afternoon."

Tamsyn laughed, the sound rich and musical. "Well, that's true. But it's also true that I can't seem to get enough of you today." Without warning she stood, sloshing water over the sides of the tub but not giving the spillage a single glance as she knelt before Maggie, pushing Maggie's legs apart with her knees, which triggered another rush of wetness from Maggie's pussy. Her mouth was on Maggie's before she could comment or protest, not that she wanted to do either. The kiss started slow, but moments later Maggie was moaning, her arms wrapped around Tamsyn's shoulders as Tamsyn's tongue, deep in her mouth, brought her to a height of arousal she would have thought was gone for the day. Tamsyn slipped one hand beneath the water, letting her fingertips trail over the swollen lips of Maggie's pussy. The touch jerked her hips, sending yet more water sloshing up the sides of the bath and causing Maggie to slump down into the bath from where she'd been braced against its end. A small tidal wave of water hit the opposite end of the bath before ricocheting back at twice the height and swamping over Tamsyn's lower back, splashing into Maggie's stomach and up into her chin. She spluttered; Tamsyn looked horrified.

"Shit, I'm sorry!" Tamsyn said, sitting back and removing her hand from between Maggie's legs before stretching out her legs again, wrapping them around Maggie's thighs.

Maggie laughed, shaking her head. "It always looks so easy in the movies, doesn't it?"

Tamsyn dropped her head, sighing. "Yes, but actually, you'd think I'd have known better. I've done a couple of these scenes and they're a bloody nightmare. And cold too."

"Really?"

"Oh, yes—they keep topping up the hot water, but just sitting around in a tub, half-naked, while you wait for the director to have the scene set just as they want it, you soon get chilled on the, um, exposed parts."

Maggie snorted, carefully wriggled forwards, and reached out her hands to cup Tamsyn's damp breasts, which were centred with deliciously hard, deep pink nipples. "Would these be the exposed parts you are referring to?" She ran her thumbs over the nipples, revelling in the sharp intake of Tamsyn's breath, the way her teeth bit down slowly on her bottom lip. God, this woman was sexy all over.

"Uh-huh." Tamsyn seemed to be struggling to speak, and the tightness in Maggie's pussy increased at the thought that she was responsible for that. She pinched Tamsyn's nipples between her thumbs and forefingers, then pulled them, which was something she remembered engendering a lovely reaction earlier; she wasn't disappointed now. Tamsyn's head dropped back, her chest pushed forward so that even more of her breasts were cupped in Maggie's hands and she moaned, long and low. Maggie carefully sat up until her mouth could replace her fingers, then licked and teased at the full breasts as if her life depended on it. Her own pussy was throbbing, aching to be filled, simply from what she was doing to Tamsyn. This was what had happened between them all afternoon—a constant, never-ending cycle of cause and effect.

She lifted her head for just a moment, long enough to see where Tamsyn's right hand was and pull it from its position on her own hip to under the water.

"Go inside me," she murmured, and Tamsyn gasped as Maggie guided her hand to where she needed it.

Tamsyn obeyed, slipping two fingers inside, the action slow and gentle, sending another shockwave of pleasure up and down Maggie's spine. This time she controlled her hips—just—and simply pushed slowly forward onto Tamsyn's fingers, making sure they were buried as deep as they could go. As Tamsyn filled her, Maggie returned her mouth to Tamsyn's breasts, licking between the two in a random pattern that had Tamsyn gasping above her. At the same time, Tamsyn was doing an extraordinary job of maintaining a perfect pace with her thrusts. The warm water around them rocked in gentle waves that added to the sensation across Maggie's thighs. She continued her ministrations on Tamsyn's breasts but now brought her own hand between Tamsyn's legs, and didn't hesitate, when she discovered thick slickness there, to push inside with a single finger.

"Yes!" Tamsyn hissed, and Maggie added another digit.

How long they rocked each other like that Maggie couldn't say. It seemed endless and yet it also seemed that within moments her pleasure was increasing to the point of climax. Everywhere throbbed and pulsed. With her mouth full of breasts and nipples, her fingers wrapped in Tamsyn's hot pussy, it didn't actually take much stimulation from Tamsyn's fingers inside her to bring her to the edge. As if reading her mind, Tamsyn twisted her hand slightly so that her thumb could glide over Maggie's wet and swollen clit. Maggie tried to concentrate on still setting a good rhythm for Tamsyn, but it was impossible as her orgasm neared and then tipped her over into that place where she was falling and floating all at the same time. She cried out and clung to Tamsyn with her spare hand, her face now pressed tight against Tamsyn's chest, Tamsyn's heartbeat thumping in her ear.

It took a couple of minutes for her own heart to slow to a manageable rate, and for her to be able to lift her head and gaze up at Tamsyn. She was flushed but looked rather proud of herself, and Maggie smirked.

"Feeling good about something?"

Tamsyn nodded, but her voice, when it came, was husky and shy, which startled Maggie. "I've…I've always wanted to do that. It was as delicious as I thought it would be."

"Sex in a bath?"

"Yes." Tamsyn seemed to shake herself out of her momentary wistful place, and now grinned. "Tick that off the list."

Maggie chuckled, but somewhere down inside a speck of hurt made itself known. She pushed it away; she'd agreed to the terms, and she'd stick with them. But it niggled, she had to admit.

Tamsyn leaned down to kiss her, and it was easy then to banish those darker thoughts and simply focus on that hot mouth. Which reminded her of somewhere else hot and warm, and she wiggled her fingers inside Tamsyn, who shuddered and tore her mouth away.

"Maggie, please…don't play…I'm…"

"Shhh. I've got you."

She lost herself then, in wetness and warmth, and breathy cries and a hard clit that begged for her attention. Lost herself in Tamsyn's climax, in the stunning beauty it presented to her: Tamsyn spread open before her, her back arched, her head thrown back as her pussy clenched tight around Maggie's fingers. Lost herself in this moment, right now, where everything was perfect and there were no deals and no tomorrow.

Chapter 11

MAGGIE CLOSED THE LID OF her Mac and arched her arms above her head, easing out her spine. Three hours, with only one pause to use the bathroom and freshen up her tea, and five thousand words written. The total now was over sixteen thousand in only four days; she couldn't remember the last time she'd written at that pace.

Must be something about the inspiration for these characters.

She smirked. Was it wrong to be using hers and Tamsyn's story as the basis for this book, especially as they were still 'living' that story? Although, she really was only using the basis—the fundamental premise was there, but she'd mapped out a completely different pathway for the imaginary Maggie and Tamsyn to follow compared to the reality. Which wasn't to say she wasn't having a good time. A great time, in fact. Tamsyn was wonderful company, for the few hours a day they spent together.

It was just that most of that time was spent in bed, and as much as that was satisfying Maggie in so many ways, there was an emptiness about it, a void of knowledge that left her feeling jaded every night they said goodbye. Tamsyn still wouldn't stay the night, and Maggie had stopped asking. She had wondered, last night, if Tamsyn's resolve might be crumbling. She'd taken longer to pull away, dressed a little slower, and there had been a long look back before she'd finally pulled the bedroom door open and departed. But was that just wishful thinking on Maggie's part? Was her yearning for more a real thing, a real need, or was she merely letting the romance of the story she was writing colour her judgement?

She stood up from the table, did some stretches to ease out the ache in her left hip, and walked into the living room. Gizmo, with Snakey, was asleep in front of the fire, which had died down to a red glow. Maggie banked it up and added some more logs. Her woodpile was dwindling so she'd need to either call up to the main house or take the car down to load up. Given she needed some groceries soon, perhaps a day of domesticity should be planned. And, if the weather held up the way the forecasters were anticipating, perhaps she could combine that with a drive up to the coast and a long walk on a beach. She gazed down at Gizmo. He'd love that.

I wonder if Tamsyn would too.

Maggie shook her head. If she wasn't careful, she was going to get herself hurt before Tamsyn's two weeks were up. They only had a few days left, so she just needed to stick with the deal and make the most of the incredible sex they were having. And definitely try to stop wishing it was more than just sex.

After lunch, Maggie pulled on her coat and boots and led Gizmo out of the house. She and Tamsyn had agreed to dinner at Tamsyn's cottage later, so they had plenty of time for a romp in the woods. Gizmo trotted along the path in front of her, tail held high, nose sniffing the air, and she smiled. While meeting Tamsyn had unblocked her writing flow, it was being tucked away in this beautiful spot with her beloved Gizmo that had really started the calming process that she'd needed so badly. So yes, saying goodbye to Tamsyn later in the week probably would hurt, and she'd probably be a bit of a mess for a few days after, but she'd still be here, and so would Gizmo, and with a new book that had her mind so excited to work on, she would be fine. More than fine.

Tamsyn threw the Maddie Jones book down on the sofa beside her; even something that good couldn't soothe her mood. Sure, it was one she'd read before, but it was one of her favourites, and it *always* calmed her down, so why wasn't it working today?

She snorted as the answer came quickly and far too easily: Maggie.

Leaving her the night before had been a wrench stronger than Tamsyn was willing to acknowledge until this morning, when she'd woken after a fitful sleep with an aching head and her mind whirling. A light breakfast and a long yoga session hadn't had the effect she'd wanted, and now reading wasn't working either.

"This is ridiculous. We said it was just a fling. Just sex." She stood and moved to build up the fire. "So why can't I stop bloody thinking about her?"

Because she couldn't. Thoughts and images of Maggie seemed to have taken up permanent residence in her brain. She found herself wondering what Maggie was doing at any given moment of a day, and—much to her disbelief—had begun counting down the hours until they'd see each other again.

Maybe the problem was seeing each other every day. Perhaps they shouldn't be so...regular with their liaisons. If they only saw each other haphazardly, then the dependency would ease, yes? Except... The thought of not seeing Maggie, touching and kissing her, as much as possible in the little time they had left, sat like lead in Tamsyn's stomach. She *wanted* to see her that much, wanted to make the most of this extraordinary connection. She'd even caught herself pondering the logistics of them seeing each other after this trip, of somehow carrying this on whenever Tamsyn was in London. But then the fears she'd been carrying for the last three decades would rear their ugly heads and she'd shake her head and return to contemplating only what pleasure she could bring Maggie in the next few days.

After making a large mug of coffee, she hauled her laptop out of its bag and propped it on her legs, which were stretched out along the length of the sofa. She sipped her drink as her emails loaded, and continued to sip as she deleted all the ones that didn't need her attention or response. Two or three she read and marked for follow-up after next week, but Carmen's she opened and read fully.

Hi Tamsyn,

So, how's it going? Has the break done you good? Have you been doing that thinking we were talking about? I'm still fielding calls from the production company, and still maintaining you'll be back with them on the 20th, so I need to know if you think that's unrealistic. Let me know as soon as you can so that if damage control is needed, Tony and I can get on it sooner rather than later. I hope it isn't, but I meant what I said when I saw you last: I want what is best for you, not that film. If working with Don really isn't something you want to pursue, we'll deal with that. But you do need to think what it will cost, and I'm not just talking about money.

Call me, or reply to this, when you can.

Carmen

Tamsyn closed the lid of the laptop, placed it on the coffee table, and sighed. Had she been doing that thinking? No, not really. She'd buried herself in books, yoga, and fantastic sex. Don Speed hadn't entered her thoughts once, and while on the one hand that was good, Tamsyn knew it wasn't sustainable. She had to think about this, and make some decisions.

Her phone pinged as a text message was received. Lesley.

Hey you! Long time no speak. I called the house but no answer. Thought you were done filming? Where are you? We need to get together. I have news!

Tamsyn grimaced. She didn't want to have to talk to anyone while she was here on retreat, but Lesley was her closest friend and would see through any half-hearted excuse to explain her absence from London. Sucking in a deep breath, she stood, walked over to the window where the signal strength bars moved up a notch, and dialled Lesley's number.

"Well, hello stranger!" Lesley's voice boomed down the surprisingly clear line. She had one of those voices that always caught people's attention, loud but not shouting, beautifully enunciated with more than a hint of her public-school background, and random words emphasised in nearly every sentence.

In spite of herself, Tamsyn smiled. She missed Lesley.

"Hello you. How's things?"

"Oh, I'm *fine*! But where the hell are you? You sound like you're at the end of a long tunnel."

Tamsyn chuckled. "I'm not in London, as you may have guessed." She sighed. If there was anyone she could trust with this secret, it was Lesley. God knew Lesley had kept Tamsyn's biggest secret all these years. "How long have you got?"

"*Ages*. Tell me everything."

Slowly, Tamsyn recounted the events that had led to her hiding out in the wilds of Norfolk.

"That filthy *bastard*!" Lesley roared. "How *dare* he talk to you like that? And with no bloody apology either! You should sue him or something."

Grinning, Tamsyn leaned against the window sill, idly gazing out at the lake as Lesley's warm support washed over her. "I knew I could count on you to get up in arms on my behalf."

"Too bloody right! If I *ever* come across the little shit at an event, I'll be sure to spike his drink with a *big* dose of laxative. Sounds like he needs a good cleansing. Mind you, I would have loved to have seen him wearing that orange juice!" She laughed. "Shame there weren't any pictures."

"Oh, I'm quite happy about that. Definitely not the sort of publicity I'm seeking."

"Hmm, I suppose so," Lesley mused. "But us women have got to stick together against these twats. Maybe if it *had* become public it might make a few people sit up and take notice."

The thought made Tamsyn shudder, and a sneaky little doubt about Lesley's secret-keeping ability made an unwitting appearance in her mind. There was something in Lesley's tone, something that made Tamsyn very nervous. "You *will* keep this to yourself, won't you?"

Lesley gasped. "Of *course*! Oh, Tamsyn, I would never do that to *you*."

There was a strange emphasis on the final word that Tamsyn couldn't quite understand, but before she could consider a response, Lesley changed the subject.

"So, can I tell you *my* news now?"

"Of course." Tamsyn chuckled at Lesley's eagerness.

"Well, remember that LGBT activist group I told you about, SHOUT, the one that contacted me and asked if I'd be willing to be the very *public* face of their new campaigns?"

Tamsyn only vaguely remembered, but she made a sound that suggested it was a more solid memory.

"Well, I've met with them a few times, and Tamsyn, honestly, they are *such* an amazing bunch of people! So focused, so driven, and so *ambitious* about what they want to achieve. They all said some lovely things about me, and vented freely about how awful it was that my career was affected so much by my coming out. I did try to tell them it wasn't entirely that, as you and I both know—let's face it, I was never in *your* league, was I?" She laughed, but there was an edge to it that told Tamsyn she'd never quite got past her unspoken jealousy. It was a wonder their friendship had survived, but she supposed that's because they went through so much together in the first ten years; that foundation was hard to break. Before she could respond in some mollifying way, Lesley continued. "Anyway, they've asked me to a top-secret meeting next week with another group that's visiting from America. They're working on something *big*, and they want me to be the spokesperson for it."

"Wow! That sounds great." Tamsyn hoped she was expressing the correct level of enthusiasm; Lesley's love of LGBT politics had always made her uncomfortable. By closeting herself, she felt she had no right to have an opinion on what should or shouldn't be done in the LGBT community and its interactions with the non-LGBT world. But Lesley's impassioned speeches about human rights and respect and equality always struck a nerve, and made Tamsyn feel as if, by living her lie, she was somehow turning her back on other men and women who didn't conform to society's view of what 'normal' should be. And that made her feel all sorts of things she really wasn't ready to face up to yet—if ever.

"It really is. I feel, whatever it is, I'll be able to *really* make a difference. Put a famous face in front of a cause and you up the value of that cause. I'll be so proud to be able to do this for the community."

There it was again: the community. The one Tamsyn played no part in, even though she did anonymously donate to many of the campaigns Lesley told her about. Her guilt money, she always called it.

"Well," she said, mustering herself, knowing her own issues needed to be set aside right now to support her friend, "I am thrilled for you. I know how much this all means to you, and being such a key part of it will be perfect for you."

"It really will. Thank you, Tamsyn. I know sometimes this stuff makes you a tad uncomfortable."

She supposed she should have realised Lesley would have picked up on that—you couldn't be friends for over thirty years and not become adept at reading each other.

She sighed. "Sometimes, yes. But that won't stop me supporting you as best I can."

"And I really appreciate that. So, how is Norfolk? Probably deadly dull, yes?"

Tamsyn nearly laughed out loud. Hardly dull... But something in her held back from telling Lesley about Maggie. Mainly because she was scared to talk about it out loud, and about how it was affecting her.

"It's beautiful, actually. I'm going for long walks, and reading lots, and generally trying to stay as mellow as I can."

"When do you have to go back?"

"Carmen was able to get me two weeks' grace, so not long, not really." Her stomach flopped at the thought. "I know I have to face up to it when I get back, but at the same time I'm hoping we can all just move on. I love this film, even if I don't love its director, so I just need to find a way to deal with him—or, at least, not let him get to me."

"It annoys me *intensely* that you're the one having to do the soul-searching. I bet they haven't told that asshole to take even five minutes to think about his behaviour."

"You're probably right," Tamsyn agreed ruefully. "But hey, let's not talk about that anymore. What else are you up to?"

They chatted on for a few more minutes, arranging to meet for dinner once Tamsyn had finished filming *Great Plains*, and said their goodbyes.

When Tamsyn slumped back onto the sofa, depositing the phone beside her, her mind was whirling. Lately, everything Lesley shared about her work in the LGBT activist community gave rise to a confusion and discomfort in Tamsyn that followed her like a dark cloud for days afterwards. She didn't want that here in Norfolk; she had enough to deal with as it was.

She finished her lukewarm coffee and set the empty mug back on the table. It was another gorgeous day and suddenly fresh air sounded like a really good idea. Maybe in amongst the trees she could free her mind up to focus on this hiccup in her career, and what to do about it.

In next to no time she was pulling on her jacket, wrapping a thin scarf around her neck, and slipping into her ankle boots. As expected, after a few dry days, the track was easy to walk on and she could wander without having to look out for puddles and boggy patches. This allowed her to spend some time gazing up into the trees, catching brief, flitting movements from the birds up in the higher branches, all while her lungs pulled in the rich, scented air.

Carmen's email came back to her, and with it, the recollection of why she was really here. The insult from Don Speed, taken in isolation and in the grand scheme of things, wasn't actually that offensive. Well, no more offensive than plenty of other insults she read in the gossip rags, or the sniping she had to put up with from Melinda on an almost daily basis. She'd demanded a personal apology, but it seemed that would never materialise. The studio had apologised, later that day, but not Don. That stuck in her craw, definitely, but what really troubled her was the nugget of truth in his insulting words, and what that meant for the rest of her career.

She lifted her shoulders and sighed, stepping carefully over a fallen log and briefly admiring the array of fungi that had taken up residence in its decrepit bark.

At fifty-two, she was now in that 'dead zone' for actresses. Considered too old to play the love interest, but too young to start taking the sorts of roles reserved for the likes of Judi Dench, Helen Mirren, and Maggie Smith. It was unfair, and she wasn't the only one complaining about it, but nothing in the industry seemed to be changing. She despaired at some of the scripts that came her way now; she seemed doomed to play the mothers of the new bright young things, or variations of her role from *Blue Lights*. As much as she'd loved playing that part, she'd walked away after five series for a reason: not to get typecast. And yet, that seemed to be what was happening to her anyway. It was why what had occurred on the *Great Plains* set was even more galling—for once she'd been given a role that was out of the norm with a story that genuinely excited her. She'd be an idiot not to go back, but it would rankle daily to be working with that…dick.

Carmen was right: if Tamsyn walked away from this film now, the damage to her reputation would be immense, and she really would be left in the dead zone. As much as it galled her, deep down she knew she only had one choice. And yes, Lesley was right too—having to be the one who went crawling back knowing that he hadn't been censured at all was utterly unfair. But that was the way the business worked, and she for one wasn't brave enough to stick her head above the parapet and challenge it. A knot of something gripped her stomach at the acknowledgement; she *wished* she was braver, sometimes, but old habits, she'd found, died very hard.

A blackbird whizzed across the path in front of her, squawking loudly, and she jumped. She gazed around; she'd walked for ages without any awareness of her surroundings, and just now realised just how far she'd come. Oh well, the walk was doing her good, so she may as well keep going. If she remembered correctly, there was a side path that led to the far side of the paddock, and she could cut back across there to the cottage. Her mood brightened as she remembered she also had a dinner date later. Her body warmed at the thought. Yes, that could be just what she needed to shake away the gloom of her afternoon musings.

Good food, good wine, good—make that *great*—sex. Perfect. *In denial much?* a nagging little voice asked at the back of her mind, but she shook it off as she strode down the trail.

Chapter 12

GIZMO'S TONGUE WAS HANGING OUT, his breath expelling in little pants.

"You tired, Giz?" Maggie asked, roughing the top of his head.

He barked but didn't jump, a clear sign that he'd run his legs off. She wasn't surprised; for every yard she walked, he ran about ten, back and forth, side to side, always on the move.

"Okay, let's go home." She clipped him back onto the lead and headed back down the path. There was a side track not too far up ahead that cut across the paddock near Tamsyn's cottage. It had been fun, walking from the opposite direction she normally took; it gave the woods a whole different look, somehow. While it had taken longer, and it wasn't only Gizmo's legs that were feeling it, she'd loved not only the exercise but also the story-planning time it had granted her. She'd scribbled quite a few ideas down in her Moleskine, which was now tucked safely back in her coat pocket.

Gizmo barked again, and Maggie looked ahead to see what had captured his attention; she couldn't help the little leap of her heart when she saw Tamsyn about twenty yards ahead, leaning nonchalantly against a large tree, her hands tucked into her jacket pockets. She smiled, and Maggie's heart leaped again.

With Gizmo straining at his lead, Maggie half-walked, half-trotted after him, chuckling at his eagerness, a feeling she could well understand. She let him go once they reached Tamsyn, and he jumped up a few times until Tamsyn deigned to bend and look down at him, keeping her hands tucked in her pockets but telling Gizmo what a good boy he was until he spun in circles on the spot, the picture of joy.

"Fancy meeting you here," Tamsyn said when she stood upright again, her voice low and husky, which sent a delicious spike of arousal throbbing between Maggie's legs.

"Of all the gin joints, in all the towns..." Maggie laughed as Tamsyn rolled her eyes. "Oh, come on, it's a classic!"

"I suppose so." Tamsyn leaned forward and kissed her, a soft, lingering kiss that only served to stoke the fire between her legs.

Maggie shuddered, and when Tamsyn pulled back, her expression quizzical, Maggie grinned even as she blushed.

"Ah," was all Tamsyn said, before pulling her hands out of her pockets and wrapping her arms around Maggie, tugging her close and kissing her again. This kiss wasn't soft; it was Tamsyn crushing her lips to Maggie's, her tongue thrusting deep into Maggie's mouth and stroking forcefully. It was fire and lust and hunger all personified in the meeting of wet mouths and hands grabbing for purchase on coats and jeans.

"Maggie..." Tamsyn breathed as their mouths parted for a moment.

"Yes?"

But Tamsyn didn't answer with words; instead, she turned them around, pinning Maggie's back against the tree, her hands reaching for the zip on Maggie's jacket. Maggie stared into her eyes, wondering just what the hell Tamsyn had in mind but knowing whatever it was, she'd agree to it. She couldn't *not*. Everything about Tamsyn consumed her with an irresistible intensity.

Tamsyn pushed the jacket open and immediately bent to kiss and lick at Maggie's neck even as her hands began working the zipper on Maggie's jeans. Moments later Tamsyn's warm fingers inched their way inside Maggie's silken underwear and slipped through the copious wetness between her legs.

"*Jesus...*" Maggie arched into Tamsyn, needing more, and Tamsyn went with her, pushing first one, then two fingers inside her and thrusting as well as she could within the confines of the jeans. It was enough given the extra thrill Maggie got from doing this out in the open. Sure, it was a private estate, but that didn't mean this was totally risk-free. At any moment, any of the people who worked for Mrs French could step onto this portion of the track, and the thought of that set free an exhibitionist side that Maggie hadn't known she possessed. Tamsyn's palm was pressed against Maggie's clit as she continued to work her fingers in and out of Maggie in short but fulfilling thrusts, and the secondary rhythm was delicious in a whole different way.

Tamsyn kissed her again, softer this time, a tenderness in her lips that belied the raw passion lower down between their bodies. The contrast was compelling, and exciting, and Maggie was so close, faster than she would have imagined, but it all added up to a maelstrom of sensation that was pulling her in, taking her under. She came hard, bright lights spinning across the inside of her eyelids, a low, keening sound escaping her throat as she fought hard not to cry out loud. Tamsyn held her, fingers locked inside her, until her breathing returned to near normal and a small chuckle from Maggie broke the silence between them.

"Wow. Can't say that I've ever done *that* before," she whispered, opening her eyes and staring into the depths of Tamsyn's.

"Me neither." Tamsyn pulled back slightly to stare intently at her. "Was that okay? I mean, I didn't stop to ask, I just—"

Maggie shushed her, then kissed her. "Trust me, it was more than okay. Although, I must confess, I'm a little surprised." She tilted her head. "That was rather public from a famous actress who wants to keep her lesbian side hidden."

Tamsyn blinked, and swallowed. "Yes," she said, carefully extracting her fingers, and kissing Maggie with a lingering tenderness once she had done so. "I think you are bad for me," she said, smirking, but Maggie saw something flit across her eyes, and wondered what it was. Tamsyn stepped back and slowly wiped her fingers on a tissue she pulled from her pocket. "Do you think he'll be traumatised?" she asked, gesturing to Gizmo, who lay on the ground a couple of feet away, head on his paws, brown eyes gazing up at them.

Maggie snorted. "That's not the first time he's witnessed Sapphic love in all its glory, trust me."

"Oh, really?" Tamsyn waggled her eyebrows and the tension that had marred her features a few moments before was gone. "Do tell."

Laughing, Maggie adjusted her underwear and zipped up her jeans. She was still throbbing, a dull beat somewhere in the background, and it wasn't unpleasant—it simply made her hungry for more, but perhaps with a soft bed or sofa at her back instead of a gnarled tree. She stepped away from it, rubbing at a couple of sore spots that she hadn't noticed so much while in the throes of passion.

"Oh, sorry!" Tamsyn moved closer, wrapping her arms around Maggie inside her jacket and rubbing slow circles on her back with her hands. "Are you sore?"

Maggie breathed in Tamsyn's scent as she kissed her neck. "I'll live," she murmured. "And it was very much worth it."

"I'm pleased," Tamsyn said against her hair. "I couldn't stop myself."

Maggie tried to pull back to look at her, but Tamsyn clung on, and continued speaking to Maggie's head. "The sight of you, looking so content, so carefree, and with those jeans hugging your thighs the way they do... And when I kissed you, and you were obviously already so turned on, suddenly all I wanted to do was touch you. To feel your energy, to share it. To... I don't know, to just connect with you in the most intimate way I could imagine. There wasn't even a conscious thought to it, it was just... I needed..." She fell silent, her breath warm against Maggie's scalp.

Maggie swallowed. What was Tamsyn trying to say? They were supposed to be just having sex, weren't they? Feelings and emotions weren't supposed to come into it. But Tamsyn sounded awfully emotional, and Maggie didn't know what to do with that.

Tamsyn gave her a squeeze then stepped back, dropping her arms. Her gaze was anywhere but on Maggie, and there was a faint blush to her cheeks. "Sorry, don't know what all that was about," she said, shrugging and grinning half-heartedly. "So, still on for dinner at six?"

Maggie had to blink a couple of times to allow her brain to catch up with the change in Tamsyn's demeanour and direction. "Um, sure. Yes."

"Great. I'll see you then." And with that, Tamsyn turned and walked quickly towards the side path, her strides long, her arms swinging.

Maggie wanted to call her back, yet at the same time wondered what she would say if she did. *Hey, I know you're closeted and not looking for anything more than a fling but you're confusing the shit out of me with your words and actions and...*

And what? What did Maggie want or, alternatively, what did she think she could ask for? What she was starting to want she knew was impossible, and asking for anything less would only lead to heartache, of that she was sure.

So she clamped her mouth shut, zipped up her jacket, and walked over to Gizmo. He got to his feet, tongue lolling, and she ruffled his ears before picking up his lead. When they reached the side track she could see Tamsyn in the distance, a bright-coloured speck against the dark green of the paddock.

"This chicken is amazing," Maggie said, reaching for another piece, and Tamsyn glowed at the praise. She was a nervous chef as she rarely cooked for others. If she entertained at home, which wasn't that often, it was usually for a houseful of people so she'd have a catering company do all the hard work. She did, however, love to cook, and often experimented with dishes for herself. Over the years she'd built up a small but trusted repertoire of favourites, and she was trying one of them out tonight on Maggie. It was clearly going well, and that gave her a buzz that made her smile widely.

"I'm very glad to hear that. It's one of my favourites."

Maggie made delightful humming noises as she ate, and Tamsyn sniggered.

"A satisfied customer, this is good."

After swallowing and taking a drink of her champagne, Maggie grinned. "Completely," she replied, "and in more ways than one after this afternoon's little shenanigans."

Tamsyn blushed. "Ah, yes. That was rather spectacular, wasn't it?"

"I'll say." Maggie blew her a kiss.

She was positively sparkling tonight, and as much as Tamsyn would have liked to take all the credit, something told her there was more to it than a great orgasm and melt-in-your-mouth lemon chicken.

"You're buzzing tonight. Care to share?"

Maggie blushed. "I'm feeling good. I… Well, what we did in the woods obviously helped." She smirked. "But I also had a really good writing session after I got home." She looked away for a moment. "This new book is really flowing, and I almost can't write it quick enough." She turned her head back to meet Tamsyn's gaze. "It's been a very long time since that happened and it feels wonderful."

"I bet it does! Good for you." She didn't know whether to ask about the story, given that she'd inadvertently insulted Maggie's writing before. The last thing she wanted to do was put her foot in it again, so she decided to stay silent on the book's content, at least. "How long can you write for in one session?"

"Depends," Maggie said, taking another sip of her champagne. "If I'm tired it doesn't work, no matter what I do. But if not, then I can probably keep going for two or three hours in one sitting, and on a really good day, do two of those, one in the morning and one in the afternoon or evening."

"And what sort of word count would that generate?"

Maggie paused to eat another mouthful of chicken, then said, "Again, totally depends on what sort of scene or chapter I'm writing. But I guess anywhere between seven and ten thousand words."

Tamsyn nearly choked on her champagne. "Bloody hell! But that means, on a good week, you could write probably a whole book, surely?"

Maggie smiled and shook her head. "Yeah, but I can't sustain days like that, day after day, and if the chapters I'm writing are heavy on historical detail there's a lot of stopping to check things, et cetera. But, having said that, most of my books have been written in four to six weeks. And that *is* good going. I know that much from talking to other authors."

"Well, *I'm* impressed, I can tell you that. I couldn't write a letter, never mind a book."

There was mirth in Maggie's tone as she asked, "No plans to write your memoirs then? All the sordid details of your career laid bare?"

Laughing, Tamsyn playfully slapped Maggie's forearm. "Given how many details I'd have to leave out, it would be a pretty thin book." She swallowed. That wasn't a revelation she'd planned on ejecting into the evening.

Maggie's eyes were wide. "Have you..." she began, then shut her mouth.

Wondering if she'd regret it, Tamsyn said, "No, it's okay. Ask."

"Well," Maggie continued, her hand twirling her champagne glass, "I suppose I was wondering how long it's been since you came out. Well, to yourself, that is. I mean, as someone who's followed your career closely, I've never picked up on a single rumour about you being anything other than straight. Is this a...recent thing?"

Okay, so we're going to go there. Well, she had kind of opened the door, so she couldn't blame Maggie for asking.

"If I told you the first time I slept with a woman was when I was nineteen, would you be shocked?"

Maggie's eyes went wide but then she chuckled. "Wow, how has this not made it into the public domain?"

Tamsyn sighed. Despite being sure that what she'd done was absolutely right for her career, she knew what she'd say next wouldn't paint her in the most LGBT-positive light.

"I made an arrangement with the woman involved that we would keep each other's secret. She was married, and her husband had no idea that she regularly had affairs with other men and also with women. I felt a bit of an idiot for not realising I was just one more notch on her bedpost, so to speak, and it had me running scared of the whole 'let's be a lesbian' thing." Of course, having a best friend who then came out as lesbian and lost her acting career over it hadn't helped. "Especially as shortly afterwards I got my first big break, with the lead in *Danger Zone*. I...I basically threw myself into my work, desperate to do whatever it took to become the next big star. And that meant keeping my sexuality hidden from the world." She drank down the last of her champagne. "Silly me thought I could hide it from myself too. That if I didn't do anything about it, it would gradually just go away."

"But it didn't." Maggie's tone was soft and understanding and Tamsyn met her gaze. "It's part of who you are, isn't it? Not something you can ignore at all."

Tamsyn shook her head. "No, I couldn't. So, then I had a new dilemma. Here I was, ten, maybe twelve years later, a big name, face everywhere, offers coming out of my backside, and desperately unhappy. I was dating male actors but never quite managing to, er, consummate things. I freely admit, I mainly did it for the publicity. Anyway, I'd got the house in LA by then, was going to all the right parties, and I soon realised, if you were smart enough, and listened carefully, you could pick up hints that you weren't the only woman with the same plight."

Maggie's eyebrows shot up and Tamsyn couldn't help but laugh. "I'm not going to give you any other names. It took a while, but soon I was able to set up the occasional evening to, um, let off some steam, shall we say." She glanced away from Maggie's shocked face. "I'm not exactly proud of it, you know. But I couldn't see any other way around the problem. Coming out would have ruined me. I believe it still would."

Tamsyn shrugged and waited for Maggie's response, her insides churning a little the longer the silence held.

After a minute or so, Maggie sat back in her chair, draining the last of her champagne. "I think," she said, putting down her glass and getting up from the table, "we need some more of this."

Tamsyn barked out a laugh. It was the last thing she'd expected Maggie to say—she'd thought she'd be judged, or vilified for not providing an outstanding role model for the LGBT community.

"Yes, I think we do," she agreed, her voice husky with emotion. She'd taken a bit of a gamble on spilling out her story to Maggie. Only three other people in the world knew it—Lesley, obviously, but also Carmen and Tony, and the latter two only in case it ever did hit the front pages, so they could be prepared with a career-rescuing plan. But Maggie's calm reaction, plus the fact that, deep down, Tamsyn knew she could trust her, had made the confession easier on her nerves than she would have imagined.

They took their full glasses of champagne into the living room, threw another log on the fire and sat close together on the sofa, smiling as Gizmo walked up to them and promptly flopped down between their feet to sleep.

Maggie's hand rubbed soothing lines on Tamsyn's thigh, back and forth but never venturing too far up towards other, more sensitive areas.

"Thank you for telling me," she said quietly, after a few minutes. "Obviously, speaking personally, it's nice to know my teenage crush wasn't entirely off the mark."

Tamsyn snorted, champagne dribbling down her chin. As she wiped at it with the back of her hand, she said, "Teenage? Just how old are you?"

Maggie grinned. "I'm forty-nine, so yeah, the eighteen-year-old Maggie thought the twenty-one-year-old Tamsyn Harris was red hot. Especially in *Days Like These*. Of course, the topless scene helped enormously."

Tamsyn dug her in the ribs and Maggie yelped even as she laughed and pulled away.

"Hey, come on!" Maggie protested, "I'm just telling it like it was. I told you before, I've been a fan of yours for years. Learning now that my celebrity crush might have had an actual chance of being fulfilled is thrilling." She laughed again. "I mean, obviously not really, because when would my eighteen-year-old self have ever had the chance to meet you? But you know what I mean."

Tamsyn dipped her head in acknowledgement, then smirked. "Hey, you should try being me, having celebrity crushes on women you then *do* go and meet or work with." She shook her head. "Pure bloody torture, let me tell you."

Maggie laughed, her shoulders shaking. "Oh, God, I can imagine! Poor you," she said, patting Tamsyn's cheek.

"Patronising little shit," Tamsyn muttered and smiled when it was Maggie's turn to dig *her* in the ribs.

Maggie's expression turned serious. "I can't lie to you, though, it is... disappointing that you haven't come out publicly." Tamsyn bristled but held her tongue when Maggie raised her hands. "I respect your decision, for you. I do. But...yeah, given how high-profile you are, I do think it's a shame that the business being what it was and still is, you feel you are not in a position where making such a statement, which could help so many young people, can be done without harming your career." She stroked Tamsyn's hand, where it had come to lay on Maggie's warm thigh. "And I feel really sorry for you, because the chance to be in a fulfilling relationship hasn't been possible. Assuming, of course," she said, her eyes widening again, "that that's something you'd ever want anyway. Maybe you wouldn't; not everyone does."

"Do you?" The question escaped Tamsyn's lips before she could stop it.

Maggie sighed, then shrugged. "I haven't been that good at it so far. My last serious relationship just kind of petered out when I got so successful with the writing. We never saw each other—I was way too busy with writing and researching and doing interviews. But..." She looked away. "Yeah, deep down, I do want that. One day. If I can ever get the balance right in my life again."

"Is that what this trip is about?"

Maggie nodded, finally looking at Tamsyn. Her serious expression had softened, and Maggie managed a small smile. "Yes. And it's working, I think. It's certainly given me thinking time, and I really needed that. Some decisions are starting to form, and I'm sure by the end of my stay I'll have a much better idea of what I want to do next."

Other than returning to the set of *Great Plains*, Tamsyn had no idea what she would do next with her life. Much the same as she'd done for the last ten years, she imagined: fight for roles, fight to keep working, have the occasional one-night or few-night fling with another woman seeking total discretion from her temporary partner. The thought of it suddenly depressed her. She needed a distraction from such thoughts. Throwing back the last of her drink, she placed the glass on the coffee table with some force.

"Well," Tamsyn said, gazing at Maggie before running a finger gently down the line of her jaw. "I know what I want to do next." She leaned in and brushed Maggie's lips with her own. "And it involves you and me naked in my bed." She kept her voice low, knowing how much that drop in tone tended to unravel Maggie.

The reaction played out on Maggie's features, sending a throb to Tamsyn's clit. Maggie's eyes widened, then darkened as her cheeks flushed a little. She stood, reaching for Tamsyn's hand.

Tamsyn grinned and allowed herself to be pulled upright. "I'm so glad you agree," she whispered, and Maggie's soft laughter led them to the bedroom.

Chapter 13

"So, I wanted to ask you something." Maggie trailed a finger across Tamsyn's bare stomach and smiled as the muscles contracted beneath the skin. The tattoo—which, she'd discovered a couple of days ago, was the Chinese symbol for strength—rippled along with the muscles, an intriguing effect.

"Ask away," Tamsyn murmured, mellow in the aftermath of her orgasm. She was flat on her back, legs and arms akimbo, and looked utterly glorious. "I have no more secrets to tell you, though."

Maggie chuckled. "Nope, not that sort of question." She let her fingertips wander over Tamsyn's ribs. "God, you are so gorgeous."

Tamsyn smiled, and opened one eye. "That's not a question."

"Ha ha, smart ass." Maggie stilled her hand. "Totally okay for you to say no, but I was going to have a day out tomorrow. I need to get groceries, but I thought I'd make a full day of it and take Gizmo to the coast. He loves beaches but we rarely get to go. Would you like to come with us?"

Tamsyn's eyes were like saucers. "Out? Like, in public?"

Maggie rubbed her chin. "Well, that's the thing. I don't think it would be that public. I mean the supermarket, yes, but you could always stay in the car for that bit. But the beach will be dead quiet at this time of year, and if you, I don't know, wore sunglasses and a hat, maybe no make-up—"

"No make-up?" Tamsyn squawked, and Maggie rolled her eyes.

"Think about it. You'd be totally anonymous. You'd get some fresh sea air. You could play fetch with Gizmo."

Now it was Tamsyn rolling her eyes. "I may pet him on the head occasionally, but I think playing fetch might be a step too far in our relationship."

"Aw, come on, you love him. You know you do," Maggie cajoled, knowing that Tamsyn *did* have a very soft spot for her dog, even if she'd never admit it. Many times during the last week Maggie had caught the two of them having a woman-to-dog moment that was full of affection on both sides.

"Maybe," Tamsyn admitted. She folded her arms across her chest. "And what do you get out of this?"

Maggie shrugged and tried to act as nonchalant as she could. "Just a fun day out with another adult to talk to. God knows Gizmo tries but our conversations do tend to be a bit one-sided."

Tamsyn snorted and pulled Maggie on top of her. "You're a funny woman, you know that?" She kissed Maggie, her lips soft and plump, her tongue teasing. "Let me think about it, okay? Can I tell you in the morning?"

"Sure." Maggie kissed her. "I need to leave by ten, though, so if you want to join us, be at the cottage before then."

Tamsyn saluted. "Ma'am, yes ma'am."

"Whatever," Maggie muttered, and hauled herself out of Tamsyn's arms. Of course, she wanted to stay, but that wasn't part of their arrangement, and Gizmo more than likely needed a toilet stop anyway, so now was as good a time as any to say goodbye for the night.

Tamsyn chuckled, then propped herself on one arm and watched as Maggie got dressed.

"Maybe see you tomorrow," Maggie said quietly, once she was at the bedroom door.

"Maybe," Tamsyn replied, her smile tentative, her eyes impossible to read.

Tamsyn paused at the end of the driveway. *This is your last chance to back out of this crazy idea.* She looked at Maggie's cottage, at the glow of the light coming from the living room, and saw Maggie pass in front of the window, a notebook in her hand. That simple sight was all it took to propel her forwards once more. It was as if Maggie was some kind of magnet, pulling Tamsyn in, and that was why she'd woken up after a restless night with thoughts of spending just one more day together. One more day and then she'd have to seriously think about getting ready to go back to the set of *Great Plains*. And away from the temptation that was Maggie and yes, even little Gizmo, who was his own special attraction. It was getting harder each day not to dream of something more. Something that might last. They kept telling each other it was just a holiday fling, but Tamsyn's words sounded hollow to her own ears—and Maggie's did too. Which made it particularly stupid that she was now walking up the path to the front door, smiling as Gizmo announced her approach from inside the cottage.

She literally couldn't help herself, though, and when Maggie opened the door, that incredible smile splitting her face, her blonde hair tossing in the breeze, Tamsyn's sensible side took a hike and the inner Tamsyn, the one that no one ever got to see, leaped to the fore.

"Good morning," Maggie said, as Gizmo jumped between them.

Maggie's smile became a knowing smirk, and Tamsyn chuckled before leaning in and kissing her, lingering in the warmth of it as their tongues gently, sensuously stroked one another's, then moaning softly as Maggie's hands cupped her face, pulling her in closer.

"Good morning to you too," Tamsyn murmured as she pulled back. "And to you, young man." She gazed down at Gizmo, laughing as he spun in circles at their feet. "Don't you dare throw up on my boots after that," she said, wagging a finger at him.

Maggie laughed and stepped back into the cottage. "No worries on that score. He's got a cast-iron constitution."

"I don't doubt it." Tamsyn followed her into the warmth of the living room. "Now, other than an instruction to be here by ten," she paused to glance at her watch and then fist-pumped dramatically, which elicited a snort from Maggie, "which I have managed with six minutes to spare, I might add, you didn't ask me to bring or prepare anything for the day."

"That's okay, there's nothing needed. I thought we could head to the coast first, have a romp on the sand, then see if we can find somewhere to sell us some sinful takeaway food like fish and chips for lunch, and hit the supermarket on the way home." Maggie looked at Tamsyn with a hesitant expression. "How does that sound?"

Like my diet coach would have a heart attack. "Bloody perfect."

Maggie's pleased grin was totally worth the calories.

After settling Gizmo into the back seat, strapped in to his own doggy seatbelt, Maggie climbed into the driver's side. "Ready?"

Tamsyn turned to look at her. She'd by lying if she said she wasn't nervous, but when Maggie gently squeezed her thigh, she knew she didn't have to say anything about the turmoil raging through her. "Okay, let's go," she said quietly, and jammed on her sunglasses.

The drive was an hour of uneventful normalcy. Tamsyn found herself relaxing and chatting as they cruised up the main road towards the coast. Things slowed down a little when they hit the small towns and villages that dotted the north part of Norfolk, and twice they lumbered along behind tractors until Maggie could find a decent stretch to pass them. Maggie was right; it was dead quiet out here in the middle of April, and that extended to the beach car park they pulled into a little after eleven. Only three other spaces were occupied, and none of the vehicles contained people. Tamsyn pulled her thick beanie hat on before exiting the car anyway; her hair was already tied and clipped back in a tight bun, and with the hat on, barely a strand was on display. With that, the big sunglasses, and as Maggie had advised, no make-up, she would only be recognisable by someone who was a keen fan and standing within a couple of feet. As they had no intention of letting anyone get that close, she was as anonymous as she was ever going to be.

"Here, can you take him for a minute while I just get my bag?" Maggie handed her Gizmo's lead and walked away before Tamsyn could protest.

She held on tightly, staring down at Gizmo, who simply stared back up at her. He didn't try to run away, or dance circles around her until she was tied up in his lead. He just...stared.

"He trusts you," Maggie said quietly, and Tamsyn looked up, startled. Maggie was leaning against the side of the car, watching the interaction between Tamsyn and her dog. "And he, well, he really likes you, so he's being on his best behaviour for you."

Tamsyn looked back down at him, and this time he shuffled just a couple of steps nearer, then sat down slowly, right by her feet. The affection she felt in that moment was not an emotion she was sure she'd ever experienced. She'd never had pets growing up, and had never allowed herself to get even vaguely this close to another human being, never mind a dog. Well, until this week, of course. It wasn't just the dog who had her experiencing a new range of emotions.

She raised her head and met Maggie's gaze. What she saw there made her stomach flip in a way that was not entirely unpleasant. She couldn't look away, even if she wanted to. Her mouth suddenly dry, she searched for the words that would make something of this moment, something more than it already was, but they wouldn't come. What exactly did she want to say? *Maggie, I have to leave soon but I don't want to. Can we...?* Could they what?

"Well," she said at last, her voice croaking until she cleared her throat. "I'm honoured." Tearing her gaze away from Maggie's hazel eyes, she crouched down and ruffled Gizmo's ears. "Thank you, Gizmo. The feeling is mutual." She glanced up at Maggie with those last words, and just at the moment when she wondered if Maggie could read the double-meaning, she knew she did. There was warmth in Maggie's eyes coupled with resignation. Yes, she knew. And she, too, knew it was for the best. Tamsyn's stomach flipped again, only this time it left her feeling queasy.

"So," Maggie said, pushing away from the car, looking away from Tamsyn and towards the path that must lead to the beach. "Shall we?" She held out her hand and Tamsyn dropped Gizmo's lead into it. Maggie chuckled. "Actually, it was your hand I wanted to take, but hey..." She shrugged.

"You...you want to hold my hand?" The thought was strangely thrilling, and before Tamsyn could second-guess herself, she took back Gizmo's lead with one hand and entwined the fingers of the other with Maggie's. It wasn't that warm a morning, but the mere occasion of standing in a public space holding another woman's hand spread a remarkable heat throughout Tamsyn's entire being.

"You okay?" Maggie tilted her head, looking quizzical.

Tamsyn chuckled. "I...I've never done this before." She shook her head. "This appears to be a week of many firsts for me."

Maggie visibly swallowed. "You've never held hands before?"

"With a woman in public, no." She smiled, and leaned forward to give Maggie a brief kiss. "Never done that, either," she said with a smirk, feeling about ten feet tall all of a sudden. Maggie's sharp bark of a laugh made her grin from ear-to-ear. Between them, Gizmo let out a little yip.

"Well, I think we should get you on that beach before you get completely out of control." Maggie laughed again and tugged on Tamsyn's hand. "Come on."

"Will he... I mean, should I...?" Tamsyn glanced down at Gizmo, then at the lead in her other hand.

"Like I said, he trusts you. He'll let you walk him."

Tamsyn shook her head but walked on anyway, fully prepared to hand the lead over to Maggie when Gizmo completely ignored her tug on the leather. To her utter bafflement, not only did he start walking, but he positioned himself directly along her outer side, trotting at a pace that kept him even with her.

She caught Maggie's smirk and muttered, "Smart ass," under her breath—but loud enough for Maggie to hear, and laugh loudly in response.

They trotted down a half-rotten kind of boardwalk, in between tufts of sturdy coastal grass, and then the beach was before them. Tamsyn emitted a low whistle of amazement. It was so huge, she couldn't even see the sea. Level, damp sand stretched as far as the eye could see, both left and right as well as in front of her. Here and there, channels cut by the retreating tide glistened in the sun as the slivers of water reflected the bright light. At various points in the distance, flocks of unidentifiable birds dabbled in or around the channels, their beaks digging deep before emerging with who knew what tasty morsel. It was like something out of a watercolour painting, and it brought a deep smile to Tamsyn's face.

"Tide's out," Maggie proffered. "We've got about an hour before it comes back in, but that should be plenty of time for this one to run his legs off." She pointed at Gizmo, who was now straining at his lead, his nose twitching crazily. "You can let him off now. It's a dog-friendly stretch of beach."

Still gazing in wonder at their surroundings, Tamsyn did as she was told, unclipping the lead and pocketing it as Gizmo raced away, his excited barks carrying back to them on the stiff offshore breeze. The wind whipped at Tamsyn's face and she relished it. Maggie had been right—a dose of sea air would indeed do her good. She found herself wishing she was as fit as Gizmo and could tear up and down the sand with the same abandon.

Maggie laughed at something Gizmo did, and Tamsyn turned to face her. Her smile was radiant, and even though her eyes were hidden by sunglasses, the crinkles around them were still visible, and her joy was obvious. Gizmo was racing away from them before skidding to a halt, his claws spraying up clouds of sand into the air around him, then turning on a sixpence and sprinting back to them, his tongue flapping at the side of his mouth. As soon as he reached them, he'd swerve around them and start the process again.

"Your dog is insane," Tamsyn said, laughing as she watched.

"I know! Isn't it great?"

"It really is." Tamsyn shook her head—the simple joy of watching a dog go slightly loopy on an empty beach, with no one to pester her, or demand something from her, was wonderful.

Maggie caught her eye and tilted her head. "What?"

Tamsyn strolled over to her, pulling her hands out of her pockets so she could cup Maggie's face, and draw her in, and kiss her. It wasn't passionate, or particularly long-lasting, but it made her quiver from head to toe. God help her, she was falling for this woman, and in the next couple of days she'd have to say goodbye to her.

"You okay?" Maggie murmured. "Not that I didn't enjoy that, but you seem…" She waved a hand in the air, clearly searching for the right word. "Wistful."

Tamsyn nodded, not trusting her voice given the size of the lump in her throat.

"Want to just walk on the beach?"

To answer, Tamsyn merely reached for Maggie's hand, tugged her round, and led them off at a strolling pace across the sand. Gizmo had calmed down a tad, and was now trying to sniff out some of the creatures who had buried themselves in the wet sand as the tide retreated. Luckily for them, he was crap at digging them up.

Tamsyn and Maggie walked, hand in hand, in a meandering path towards him, not speaking, simply…being. It was enough. Tamsyn still didn't trust herself to speak, worried about what she'd blurt out if she did. There'd be nothing to gain from letting Maggie know just how much trouble she was having knowing their parting was rapidly approaching. She ought to back off, spend the last couple of days of her break on her own, make sure she'd done all of that thinking she'd promised everyone. But the thought depressed her too much, whereas the alternative—spending as much of that time with Maggie as possible—made her steps feel lighter, and her face break out into an involuntary smile. Screw it; if she was going to crash and burn, she might as well make the most of it.

"So," Maggie said a few minutes later, "do you think this break has done what you needed it to? You mentioned having trouble on the set of a film, and needing some space to think."

Tamsyn swallowed. She didn't want to lie to Maggie, but neither did she want to reveal more than was sensible. "Yes, I think it has. I mean, I've pretty much decided I just have to grit my teeth and get back on set. Learn to work with the person with whom I had the…spat. It's not like he's the first asshole I've worked with," she said with a tight grin.

Maggie chuckled. "I can imagine. You don't have to give me details, but what made him such an asshole?"

"Oh, the usual. Ageism. I'm battling it more and more these days and it's so tiresome. This is the twenty-first century and yet there are still dinosaurs behind the camera on way too many films. And in the top positions in the production companies."

"Really? I thought with all the new women directors coming in, things would have improved somewhat?"

"Sure, if you're lucky enough to work on a film or TV programme directed by one of them. But they're still so thin on the ground, which means it's the men you generally have to deal with. And they have *very* different ideas about the value of a woman in her fifties, and what roles she should play."

"Seriously?"

"Oh, yes. Did you ever watch *The First Wives Club*?"

"Yes, of course. I love that movie!"

"Remember the scene where Goldie Hawn's character is in the chair, begging her doctor to pump her lips full of God knows what?"

Maggie laughed. "Yes!"

"I always remember the key line she had in that scene. 'There are only three ages for women in Hollywood. Babe, district attorney, and *Driving Miss Daisy*.'" Tamsyn sighed. "That was over twenty years ago and it's still true today. I'm way too old for babe, allegedly too old for district attorney, and thankfully, still years away from *Driving Miss Daisy*. The trouble is, there is nothing else in between, or not very much anyway, and most male directors only want to work with the babes and young DAs."

"Shit."

"Yes. Shit indeed."

Gizmo ran up to them, panting heavily, and stood with them looking out over the wet expanse of the beach.

"I take it you still want to do this. Acting, I mean. Never thought of taking a seat behind the camera? Give up on the stress of fighting for your roles all the time and do something different?"

Maggie was clearly asking the question in all seriousness, the frown marring her forehead emphasising that, so Tamsyn held back her snort. Her, direct?

She shook her head. "No, I belong in front of the camera. Yes, it is stressful, but it's always been fairly cut-throat." She chuckled, but even she heard how lacking in warmth the sound was. "I'm a big girl. I can look after myself."

"I wasn't suggesting you couldn't," Maggie said, a little sharply. "I was thinking more that you could possibly achieve more…good, *behind* the camera. If not as a director, then maybe as a producer. If more women like you, with your status and reputation, started running things, maybe change could come quicker." She stared at Tamsyn, then swallowed when Tamsyn remained quiet. "Sorry, just my opinion."

"I…I'm not mad at you. I just never thought of it that way." Tamsyn shrugged, feeling helpless. "Maybe I'm too selfish."

Maggie shook her head. "Not selfish. Just…used to this life, to the battles. It's what you've always done, so perhaps it hasn't occurred to you that you could follow an alternative path." She sighed, waving her free hand in the air. "Look, it's none of my business. Ignore me." Before Tamsyn could interject, she plunged on. "I'm getting hungry for those fish and chips. What do you say?"

Maggie was probably right to end the conversation, to return them to fun and frivolity. But her words, her ideas, were still ricocheting around Tamsyn's brain, and she knew that when she had some quiet time to herself again, they would return.

"Okay," she said, forcing into her voice some cheerfulness she wasn't really feeling, "take me to fish and chips." She grinned. "God, I haven't had them for years. This is going to be *great*."

Laughing, Maggie tugged on her hand and quickened their pace as they strode back up the beach, Gizmo trotting along between them.

Chapter 14

TAMSYN WIPED THE GREASE OFF her fingers with a paper napkin and sighed happily.

"That," she said, pointing at the decimated remains of her lunch, "was *perfect.*"

Maggie grinned, then tucked the last of her chips into her mouth and chewed while humming in what Tamsyn could only assume was contentment, given the way her eyes sparkled.

Scrunching up the paper wrappings that had until only minutes ago held a large piece of cod in batter and a ridiculous portion of chips, she shook her head. If someone had told her two weeks ago she'd be sitting on a hard, worn out wooden bench overlooking a Norfolk beach with a fish and chips lunch filling her belly, she'd have thought they were crazy. Never mind the fact that she was doing so with a beautiful, thoughtful woman next to her, and a crazy cute dog at her feet. She stood up quickly, her emotions spinning all over the place again. It was as if something was unravelling inside her, she thought as she headed for the nearest rubbish bin to deposit the ball of greasy paper. Something that until very recently had seemed super-strong and immune to anything remotely resembling genuine feeling.

"Hey, what about mine?" Maggie called, looking affronted until she smiled while pointing at her own screwed up ball of rubbish.

"Forgive me, your ladyship," Tamsyn said, with a flourish of a bow, "I was not aware that you were incapable of walking the, oh, three yards to this receptacle."

Maggie stuck out her tongue and threw the ball at Tamsyn, who only managed to catch it on the third attempt, much to her embarrassment. Gizmo, thinking this was a new game, leaped up and tried to snag the ball with his way-too-small mouth just as Tamsyn finally took hold of it.

"Let go, you little bugger," she muttered, laughing when he stepped back, looking peeved. She slam-dunked the bag into the bin, then returned to sit beside Maggie, snuggling up to her in the face of the cool breeze.

"Tide's turning," Maggie said. "Look." She pointed, and sure enough, in the distance, a line of wavelets was now progressing slowly up the sand towards them, scattering the feeding birds into small flocks that swept away from the edge and then landed again two feet further up the beach from where they'd started. It was mesmerising, and watching it in silence with Maggie close beside her brought all those emotions swimming back to the surface.

God, what is this? Why am I being so…mushy all of a sudden? For a brief moment she pondered if it was her menopause to blame, but knew that was the easy target. No, it was nothing to do with hormones and everything to do with what their time together had meant to her. She cast a quick glance at Maggie. What this woman meant to her.

The trilling of her phone made all three of them jump. Gizmo, who until then had been snoozing on the sandy boardwalk at their feet, sat up and barked. Maggie pressed a hand to her chest, half grinning, half scowling as she said, "Jesus, that scared the shit out of me."

Tamsyn murmured an apology and stood up; the caller ID showed Carmen's office number.

"Hey."

"Well, hello stranger." Carmen's tone was warm despite the sarcastic address.

Walking away from the bench, Tamsyn chuckled. "Now, you can't tell me to shut myself away for thinking time and then complain when you don't hear from me."

Carmen snorted. "I suppose that's true." She paused. "So, how are you? Really?"

"I'm…good." Which was true, so why did it make her feel so sad? "The break has definitely done me good. So, thank you for being right about that."

"Yes!" Carmen exclaimed, and Tamsyn rolled her eyes, imagining Carmen fist-pumping at her desk.

"Okay, okay. Yes, you were right."

Carmen's laugh was gentle. "Well, that's good. But, dare I ask, have you come to any decisions?"

"Yes, I have." It was easier to say than she'd thought it would be; but after all, this was who she was and what she did. "I know I was wrong to storm off that set. I know he's an asshole, but I also know this film is a great opportunity, and I'd be stupid not to finish it. I'm ready to get back, and soon." Well, she was and she wasn't, but Carmen didn't need to know that.

Carmen let out an audible sigh. "Well, that is perfect timing because there was another reason I called, not just as a general touch base kind of thing."

"Yes?"

"Uh-huh. I got a call from the studio this morning. While he's not outright apologised, Don has accepted that he offended you. The studio has extracted a promise from him to be more...civilised in his dealings with you and is keen for you to return to work ASAP. They know what a name you are, and having that name on all the publicity is going to put more bums on seats. So," she cleared her throat, a classic indicator that she was about to say something Tamsyn may not completely enjoy, "they'd like to send a car to collect you. Tomorrow morning."

Tamsyn's stomach fell to her knees. "That...that soon?" Her voice broke but she didn't care.

"I know, I know. I mean, if you're desperate for more time, I can maybe push that back by twenty-four hours but..."

Tamsyn knew why Carmen didn't feel she could finish the sentence— any more diva-like behaviour from Tamsyn and the studio might decide her name wasn't worth as much trouble as she caused. She glanced back at Maggie and Gizmo, who were having a love-in on the bench, Gizmo sitting beside her while Maggie ruffled his head and ears. The thought of walking away from them, from this, wrenched at Tamsyn's insides but she knew it had to be done.

"No," she said, finding a firmness in her tone that surprised her. "It's time. I understand. What time will the car be there?"

"Around eleven. Tamsyn, are you sure—"

"That's fine. I'll be ready. Thanks for the call." She hung up before Carmen could complete her goodbye because her throat was tightening and tears were pricking at the corners of her eyes, and she'd be damned if she was going to blub on the phone to her agent. Or even in front of Maggie, so she kept her head turned away, gazing unseeing up the beach, while she fought to get her rampaging emotions under control.

A couple of minutes later she'd managed it—she sincerely hoped—and turned back towards the bench.

———— ❧ ————

Tamsyn looked so serious that for one moment, Maggie thought someone had died. Then that trademark glamour smile split her face, and Maggie knew whatever it was, it wasn't *that* dramatic. Still, as Tamsyn approached the bench, she braced herself. Something told her their time was coming to an end, and Tamsyn didn't know how to break the news.

"That was Carmen. My agent," Tamsyn began, shuffling from foot to foot.

"You're leaving," Maggie said, with as little emotion as she could manage, even though, as she said the words, her stomach churned.

Tamsyn opened her mouth to speak, then closed it again and merely nodded.

"Now?"

"No. Tomorrow morning." Tamsyn's voice was gruff, but not with anger.

"Right." Maggie looked away, out to sea, her fingers curling and uncurling around Gizmo's ears as she tried so hard to keep her emotions in check. She'd known, of course, that Tamsyn would depart at some point and their fun would come to an end. But now, when it was so imminent, she realised how much she'd been hoping for more, and the reality that there wouldn't *be* more was crashing down around her. Tamsyn, despite sounding as emotional as Maggie felt, wouldn't allow them to talk about a possible future. And Maggie wanted that; the force of her desire for a future with Tamsyn was overwhelming. Angrily, she brushed at the tears that threatened to fall.

She cleared her throat before speaking, and was vaguely pleased that she sounded close to normal as she said, "Shall we head back now? I still need to get my groceries so the sooner we get on the road, the sooner I can do that and get you back home to pack."

"Maggie," Tamsyn breathed, stepping forward, her hand reaching out.

Maggie shook her head. "Please. I...can't. Not now."

Tamsyn dropped her hand. Maggie dared to look at her and was rewarded with a pained face, a deep frown marring that otherwise perfect brow.

"It's... Maggie, you know I can't. I know that makes me sound like a coward and—"

Maggie held up a hand and smiled wanly. "You don't have to explain. I get it. I don't agree, but I get it, and don't worry, I'm not going to go all Glenn Close on you."

Tamsyn chuckled, shoving her hands in her pockets. "Good to know."

Maggie reached for Gizmo's lead and stood up, encouraging him to hop down to the pavement before she turned back to Tamsyn. "Come on, then. Let's get back."

Nodding, Tamsyn fell in beside her and they walked slowly to the car. Gizmo glanced up at them numerous times, and Maggie wondered yet again just how her dog could know. Because he always did.

The drive to the supermarket was mostly silent, but not uncomfortable. Leaving Tamsyn in the car, still wrapped up in her sunglasses-and-hat disguise, Maggie grabbed her handbag from behind her seat and told Gizmo to stay before heading into the large shop. It was a struggle to find the enthusiasm for decent food when all she wanted to do was eat biscuits and wallow in self-pity for the next few days, but she restrained herself to one packet of chocolate digestives and ensured she added plenty of fruit and vegetables to the basket. Two bottles of red wine were also added; she had some sorrows to drown.

Tamsyn was scrolling through something on her phone when Maggie returned. After loading the bags of groceries in the boot, she climbed into the front seat, accepted Gizmo's little yips and whines of greeting with a ruffle of his ears, then slipped her seatbelt on.

"Get everything you need?" Tamsyn's voice was quiet, and Maggie glanced over at her before starting the car. She looked tired.

"Yes, thanks. You okay?"

"Yes. No. Sort of." Tamsyn shrugged and looked out of the front window.

Maggie waited, trying to tamp down a sudden upwelling of anger. It was Tamsyn's decision to end this, to walk away. If she was sad about it now, that was her own damn fault.

"Sorry," Tamsyn whispered. "Whether you believe me or not, I really wish I could be braver. But I'm not that person."

Maggie huffed out a sigh. "Well, maybe one day you will be. And whoever gets to benefit from that will be one lucky woman. But more than that, *you* will be better for it, whether you believe *me* or not."

Tamsyn said nothing, and Maggie started the car.

When Maggie swung the car down the track that led to the lake, Tamsyn's stomach tied itself into knots. Maggie hadn't spoken again since their…discussion in the car park, and Tamsyn had had no idea how to break the heavy silence that had enveloped them on the drive back. Even Gizmo seemed to know something was up, whining softly from the back seat at regular intervals.

Now, here they were, less than two minutes away from the cottages, and Tamsyn did not want to leave things like this. She didn't know if Maggie wanted to hear it, but she would miss her, of that she was certain, and she wanted their last memory of each other to be at least nice, if not happy.

Maggie pulled them up at the end of the short drive that led to Tamsyn's cottage. She engaged the handbrake, turned off the engine, and then sat very still, head straight forward and hands clasped in her lap.

Tamsyn swallowed, undid her seatbelt, then reached out a hand and laid it across Maggie's joined ones. At the touch, Maggie's head bowed, and moments later, cold drops fell on the back of Tamsyn's hand. Tamsyn's heart stuttered.

"I'm sorry," Maggie said. "I promised myself I wouldn't cry, but…"

"Please," Tamsyn pleaded, "can we still have the rest of today together? I don't want to say goodbye like this."

"You want one last tumble in the sheets for the road, huh?" Maggie's voice was so cold it was a wonder the air around them didn't freeze.

Tamsyn resisted yanking her hand back and instead took a deep breath before saying, "Actually, that was the last thing on my mind." She dared to reach out her other hand, twisting in her seat so she had room to reach Maggie's chin and turn her head to face her. Maggie's eyes brimmed with tears, and her expression was a mixture of sadness and frustration. "I just wanted more time with you. To talk to you, and share a meal with you, and one last drink to toast what we've had, what we've been. Because as much as I'm a shit for walking away from you like this," her voice cracked, "this past week with you has been one of the happiest times in my entire life. And I would just like to extend that for as long as I can before I fuck it all up by leaving."

"Not fair," Maggie sniffed, and moments later a small smile crossed her lips. "Now you've made it all right again and I can't say no." She playfully slapped at Tamsyn's arm with her free hand.

The relief Tamsyn experienced was palpable, and she exhaled a long breath.

"Just…give me a little time. I want to put the shopping away, and make myself a bit more presentable after this." Maggie waved a hand at her own face. "Come to mine in about an hour, okay? That way you can decide when you leave and it won't get awkward."

It was the matter-of-fact way she said the last words that really got to Tamsyn. Maggie was resigned now—to losing what they had, and to the knowledge that Tamsyn wouldn't do anything to change it. That hurt more than the anger had.

"Okay. An hour." She forced the words out past a tightened throat, then reached for the door handle. After pushing the door open and swinging her legs out, she ducked her head back inside. "Want me to bring anything?"

Maggie shook her head, her smile weak. "Just your beautiful self."

Tamsyn tried to smile back, but wasn't sure it was successful. Her feet were like lead as she walked down her driveway, and when she stepped into her cold cottage, she knew that no amount of heating or fire would warm the deep cold that had settled into her heart.

Maybe I should have stuck to my guns, told her to stay away. Said a crappy goodbye in the car and been done with it.

Maggie flopped onto the sofa and sighed. Yeah, as if she could have done that. Despite her harsh words to Tamsyn, Maggie herself wanted more time, to put off the moment of farewell to the last possible minute. She glanced at her phone to check the time; Tamsyn would be here in about five minutes.

And I want one more evening of nakedness with her. A few more hours of feeling that closeness, that connection that has been so strong since the first time we touched each other. It had been incredible, how quickly they'd learned each other, and how well they'd pleasured each other as a result. She'd be a fool not to want that one more time.

The fire popped and Gizmo, in his customary position in front of it, twitched in his sleep.

A muted knock at the front door stirred him from his slumber and he raced to the door, an excited yelp passing his lips. Maggie slowly followed behind him, heart pounding, palms dampening. When she swung the door open and Tamsyn smiled at her, it tugged at Maggie's already fragile heart. It wasn't the flashy actress smile, the fake one that hid everything. It was the real one, tinged with sadness and melancholy for the person Tamsyn wished she could be but for some reason didn't believe she was deserving of.

It wasn't what Maggie would have planned, or anticipated, until she saw her standing there. But in the next moment she reached for Tamsyn, pulled her close, and kissed her. Her tongue dove deep immediately, arms encircling Tamsyn and walking them into the cottage without breaking the contact between their mouths. Tamsyn groaned, low and powerful, and kicked the door shut behind them. Maggie kept moving backwards, still holding Tamsyn close, stumbling them down the hallway and into the bedroom. She broke the kiss only to close the door, barring Gizmo from entering, then turned to the gorgeous woman facing her in the centre of the room.

It was slow, and tender, their touches both assured and somehow hesitant, as if their hands were scared to believe that this was the last time they would be able to do this. Everything they'd learned about each other's bodies was used to maximum effect but without calculation or planning. When Tamsyn slipped two fingers inside Maggie, she in turn reached for Tamsyn's breasts, rubbing the nipples with her thumbs, cupping the delicious flesh in her palms, knowing that Tamsyn loved the combination of being inside Maggie while being touched herself. Tamsyn kissed Maggie then, knowing that Maggie loved to be kissed while being fucked, loved the action of Tamsyn's tongue in her mouth mirroring what her fingers were doing deep inside. It was a perfect choreography—unscripted yet known by heart. Their first orgasms were their strongest; hot skin, slicked with perspiration, met at multiple points as their bodies arched, and writhed, and then collapsed back onto the bed. They rested only for moments before hands again reached for breasts, and thighs, and mouths met over and over again as their arousal rapidly rose.

"Lay on your front," Maggie whispered hoarsely, and Tamsyn instantly obliged, flipping herself over and laying with her arms outstretched and her legs parted. She was wet. Very wet, and Maggie relished the sensation of the slickness that coated her fingers as she trailed through softness and plunged inside Tamsyn. Tamsyn's gasp evolved into a tortured, wrenching groan that turned Maggie on so much she feared she'd come without any manipulation at all. "Up on your knees," she rasped, and Tamsyn couldn't move fast enough, it seemed, pushing back against Maggie's fingers and crying out as Maggie pressed deeper, her free hand on Tamsyn's ass, spreading her open even more.

"God, yes!" Tamsyn said, her voice a ragged shadow of its usual self.

Maggie's arm was burning with the effort, but she didn't care. Her knees were complaining, but she didn't care. All she cared about, all that she could see and feel and hear, was Tamsyn, open before her, hot wetness pulling Maggie even further in, joining them so deeply, so profoundly that tears spilled out of Maggie's eyes and tracked down her cheeks to fall onto Tamsyn's ass below her. If Tamsyn noticed she said nothing, but she braced herself on one arm and reached back with the other, grabbing Maggie's wrist and clinging on just as her orgasm crested and her back bowed with its release. Her low, long cry tore through Maggie like a hurricane.

Later, much later, after they had paused for water and something to eat, they lay naked under a blanket on the sofa, watching the fire and holding each other close. Maggie's back was pressed up against Tamsyn's front; their legs were entwined and Tamsyn's breasts were soft cushions against Maggie's shoulder blades. Tamsyn was kissing Maggie's ear, and neck, her hands squeezing where they were joined with Maggie's in front of Maggie's chest.

"God, you're beautiful," Tamsyn whispered before licking a soft line from Maggie's ear lobe up to the top of her ear and back down again. "So beautiful."

"Thank you," Maggie murmured, her skin on fire again, her clit throbbing with need again. This time in front of the fire was bittersweet; it was already midnight, and Tamsyn would need to go soon, but Maggie didn't want to be the one to remind her. They felt so right like this, cuddled up together, no need for words.

Tamsyn tucked her head into Maggie's hair and inhaled deeply. "And you smell bloody divine," she said, chuckling.

Maggie snorted. "It's just regular shampoo. Nothing fancy."

"Well, it suits you." Tamsyn yawned, snuggling in further against Maggie's back.

"You okay?"

"Uh-huh." Tamsyn yawned again. "Someone wore me out."

Maggie smiled and squeezed Tamsyn's hands. She traced a haphazard pattern with one fingertip across the back of one of them, keen to keep contact wherever she could, for as long as she could. Her own eyes were heavy with fatigue, and she closed them briefly, soothed by the sound of Tamsyn's breathing in her ear. Her fingertip slowed its pattern as lethargy took over, and she sighed. This was nice. This wasn't something they'd really done before, and she fully intended to make the most of it. Tamsyn's breathing deepened, and her hold on Maggie loosened but didn't break. Maggie relaxed too, wondering briefly if she was too heavy, pressed up against Tamsyn like this, then discounting the notion in the next moment. If Tamsyn didn't like it, she'd say. She'd get up soon, Maggie knew that, but for now, Maggie would keep quiet, and lay with her, soaking up these feelings for the lonely nights ahead.

———✦⟨✕⟩✦———

Tamsyn didn't understand how Maggie failed to stir when she eased herself away at four in the morning, but she was grateful for whatever force made it so. Gizmo stood at once, cocking his head to stare at her, but she put her finger on her lips and he miraculously kept quiet. She tucked the blanket carefully around Maggie, her heart aching as she did so; Maggie looked so peaceful asleep, her eyelids flickering as she dreamed.

"I'm so sorry," Tamsyn whispered into the cold, quiet room. "I wish it could be different. If it could, I'd give you the whole fucking world, Maggie." Her throat constricted, and she swallowed hard before turning away from the sleeping form.

She crept to the bedroom to retrieve her clothes, but didn't put on her boots until she'd slowly inched the front door open enough to slide out onto the front porch. Was she yet more of a chicken for running off without saying goodbye? Possibly—but they'd been saying goodbye all evening, with their bodies, their mouths, their fingers. Somehow, she thought Maggie would understand. She looked back when she reached the path that would lead to her own cottage, and her heart wrenched. Maggie had shown Tamsyn what might have been possible, if she'd made different choices. She knew she was too old to make them now, but it was nice to have experienced that, even just for a couple of weeks. She'd always have that, at least—warm memories to fall back on whenever things got too lonely or too crazy to deal with. They wouldn't be anywhere near as perfect as the real thing, but they would be enough.

She hoped.

Part Two

Chapter 15

"Perfect timing," Maggie said as she opened the door. Her sister shot into the house out of the rain. "Kettle's just boiled."

"Hurrah." Ruth stamped her feet on the mat. "It's dreadful out there." She peeled off her coat and hung it on the rack, then slid her boots off. Gizmo, who had come running into the hallway when the doorbell rang, now sniffed at Ruth's discarded boots with some interest.

Ruth laughed. "Went for a walk in Richmond Park yesterday. I'm sure there's lots of interesting scents on there, eh, Giz?"

Maggie smiled as her dog paid her sister absolutely no attention, his nose glued to the boots. "Tea or coffee?" she asked over her shoulder as she set off back down the hallway, Ruth following.

"Tea, please. A very large mug of it too."

"Coming right up."

The kitchen at the back of the house, an extended room topped with a sloping glass roof, was bright and welcoming in spite of the gloomy weather. Maggie motioned her sister into the snug area that formed the farthest part of the room, near the doors that led to the small courtyard garden. Ruth flopped onto the small leather sofa that faced the garden and sighed.

"You okay?" Maggie asked, reaching for two large mugs from the cupboard.

"Yes, just tired. The girls ran me ragged yesterday, and we had to be up early this morning as Will has some conference thing in Birmingham today." She sighed again. "I love my family, I really do, but sometimes I wish I could just abandon them for about a month. Do something like that retreat you had back in April."

Maggie's hands trembled as she reached for the tin that held the tea bags. She didn't think of that trip so much these days; it had proved better not to, in the long run. So when something did trigger a reminder, it still surprised her how much it affected her.

She finished making the tea, not trusting her voice just yet, then carried the steaming mugs over to the small table beside the sofa. Sitting next to Ruth, she stretched out her legs and let her feet rub back and forth on the wooden floor. The soothing warmth of the underfloor heating she'd installed a couple of years ago was so worth it on days like this.

"Thanks," Ruth said, reaching for her mug.

"You're welcome. So, apart from running you ragged, how are my nieces?"

Ruth chuckled. "They're good. Really. Just so full of energy I sometimes struggle to keep up. Twins are a handful, believe me."

"Oh, I do." Maggie smirked. "If it's this bad at eight, just imagine what they'll be like when they're thirteen."

Ruth glared at her. "Well, that's just *mean*."

They both laughed, and Ruth shoved Maggie with her elbow.

"So, what's the latest with you?"

Maggie's heart thudded hard against her ribs and she sat up a little straighter. While this had been her plan all along, now that the time was here, her nerves and doubts reappeared tenfold.

"Maggie?" Ruth placed her mug back on the table and stared. "Why do you look like you're about to have some kind of panic attack?"

Maggie snorted, and it helped. "No, it's not that bad." She ran her fingers through her hair. "I...I've made some decisions about some things and I wanted to share them with you. But now that I am sharing, I'm scared of what you'll think."

Ruth's eyes went wide. "You're not shaving all your hair off and joining some crazy religious sect, are you?"

"What? No, of course not!"

"Then," Ruth said, patting Maggie's leg, "whatever you have to tell me can't possibly be scary. So, spill."

"You're bonkers." Maggie shook her head, but smiled when Ruth grinned. She sucked in a big breath. "Okay, here goes. So, firstly, Jessica Stewart is going to retire."

Ruth's mouth dropped open, but she waited a beat before speaking. "Okay." She dragged the word out. "And this is because...?"

"Because," Maggie said firmly, "I have no more ideas for that genre, and no appetite for the research anymore. I can't say it bores me, that's not really it. I'm just...tired of sitting in dusty libraries and trawling around academic buildings. Of arranging interviews, trying to find reliable sources, and everything else that goes with trying to make a historical romance as authentic as possible."

Ruth nodded slowly, reaching for her tea again. She took a few sips before saying, "Okay, that makes sense. You have been doing that for quite a while now."

"I have." Maggie sighed. "It kind of stopped being fun about three books ago, but I was so wrapped up in bringing out the next bestseller I ignored the little voice inside me that was telling me that."

"So, I'm sure you know what my next question will be. If you aren't Jessica Stewart anymore, does that mean you won't be writing at all?"

And now we come to the big revelation. Yikes.

"Well, there's something I need to tell you, and I want to apologise up front for not telling you before. I had my reasons, and they seemed right at the time for where I was in my career and life, but now, well, now they don't."

"Well, I'm certainly intrigued, Mags. Come on then, hit with me it." If Ruth was annoyed at her for keeping secrets, she wasn't showing it. They'd been close their whole lives but not to the point where Maggie had felt the need to share everything, and she was pretty sure that went both ways; she was convinced there were significant things in Ruth's life that she wasn't privy to and she was okay with that.

"Okay. So, as well as writing Jessica Stewart books all these years, I've actually had another pen name, in an entirely different genre."

"Wow." Ruth was staring at her.

"Yeah. I'm also Maddie Jones, writing lesbian fiction."

"What, dirty stuff?" Ruth actually looked shocked.

Maggie rolled her eyes. "And *that* is one of the reasons why I never told you or anyone about it. No, not dirty stuff—lesbian fiction is *not* just erotica, but for some reason that's the reputation it's got. Yes, part of the market is erotica, and trust me, some of it is very good. But actually, the bulk of the market is romance in one form or another. And I've been writing romances in that genre pretty much the same amount of time I've been publishing Jessica Stewart in the mainstream."

"For the same publisher?" Ruth's tone made her confusion evident.

"No, not at all. I have a specialised lesbian publisher for those books. They don't know I'm Jessica Stewart, and vice versa. I've kept both identities completely separate. You're the only person who knows I'm both."

Ruth slumped back against the sofa, her head shaking and a wicked smile on her face. "My sister, the clandestine lesbian author." She laughed when Maggie rolled her eyes again. "This is amazing. So, are you as successful writing as Maddie Jones?"

"In terms of being a big name in that genre, yes. In terms of the money I earn, not really. The market is so much smaller. But I don't care about that. Jessica Stewart has been my bankroll. Maddie Jones writes purely for the love of it."

"Now I'm even more confused. Why would you give up your bankroll if the money you make from Maddie Jones won't support you? Of course, I'm assuming you're telling me all this because it's as Maddie Jones that you want to continue?"

"Yes and no. I'll have royalties for years yet from Jessica Stewart, and the earnings from my Maddie Jones writing will just top that up. But I also have plans to write other things too, in other genres. I have no idea if I'll be any good at it, but I've always fancied crime."

"As a lifestyle or a writing genre?" Ruth asked with a cheeky grin.

"Ha bloody ha." Maggie downed the rest of her tea. "I needed something to give, something to make way for my brain to be able to focus on giving other types of writing a go. And when I weighed it all up, I knew I wouldn't miss being Jessica Stewart nearly as much as I would miss being Maddie Jones. She's the real me, really, despite the pen name. I mean, what I write as her comes from my heart, and I don't ever want to give that up. I have to be realistic and know that I won't necessarily do as well in the future as I have done in the past, but..." She swallowed, knowing she was going to open up a can of worms with her next statement but suddenly feeling a strong need to tell Ruth all of it. "I met someone on that retreat, someone who wasn't living her true self, and it pained me to see her doing that. It pained me even more when I realised after she left that, in a way, I was doing the same thing. The last two Jessica Stewarts have only been written because the market and my publishing contract demanded them. I didn't enjoy doing them at all. And I don't want my writing to be that way. I want to write what I want, what I feel, what makes me *want* to write."

Ruth glanced at her watch. "It's beyond noon," she said. "Got any wine? I think we need it for my next round of questions."

Maggie grinned, relief washing over her. Not that she'd seriously doubted Ruth would be there for her, but her level-headed acceptance was soothing, nonetheless.

Maggie served up a platter of bread, cheese, salami, and olives to go with the generous glasses of red wine she plonked on the table in front of them a few minutes later.

"Cheers," Ruth said, chinking her glass against Maggie's.

"Thanks."

"For what?"

"For not calling me an idiot. At least, not yet anyway."

Ruth snorted, then sipped her wine. "I trust your judgement on what will work, both for you in a sense of soul and self, and on the business side. You know your market, your business, far better than I do. If you think the numbers work for you, even if that does mean perhaps an adjustment in lifestyle, then go for it. All I'm ever going to want is my sister to be happy." She popped an olive into her mouth, her gaze unfocused as she chewed. "And talking of that," she said after swallowing, "given that, to my knowledge at least, you haven't had a girlfriend in about four years now, do any of your future plans for a happier life include one of those?"

Maggie sighed. "Maybe one day. I… The woman I met in April, on the retreat, she…we…"

"What?"

"Well, we sort of had a fling."

Ruth gulped her wine, then leaned across the table. "A fling?"

"Yes. She was in…hiding, shall we say. She's quite famous, so I won't give you her name, but she had a need to be off radar for a while. We were the only two people using the cottages on the estate. I knew who she was, of course, but had no idea she was a lesbian. She's kept herself in the closet her whole life, and it just made me so sad to watch her denying such a fundamental part of herself."

"And the fling?"

Maggie smiled even as her heart faltered. "It was lovely. Wonderful. Heart-breaking."

"Oh, no. You wanted more?"

"I did. I would have loved to have seen what we could make of it, even as I knew it would be impossible since she was adamant she needed to stay in the closet. But I genuinely was more upset about what she was denying herself than what she was denying *us* as a result. She's so lonely, and yet has such a capacity for love, and warmth, and…passion."

"I don't understand—why did you get together with her if you knew it couldn't have a future?"

"Because, like so many of the love-crazy heroines I write about, I simply couldn't resist her. I would have much rather had one week with her knowing it was going to end than have nothing at all and always wonder 'what if.' And trust me, as much as it hurt when she left, I didn't regret it."

"And there's been no contact since? Nothing at all?"

Maggie shook her head, the sadness she'd kept at bay for so long now swamping her. "No. We didn't swap phone numbers or emails, and I never even told her my last name. She really has no idea who I am, other than that I write as Jessica Stewart."

"Okay, so she could technically contact you that way, if she was so inclined."

"Yes."

"But she hasn't?" Ruth's voice was quiet.

"No."

"Oh, Maggie. I'm so sorry."

Maggie shrugged. "It is what it is. I knew that, going into it, and I knew it when I woke up alone the morning she had to leave."

Ruth topped up their glasses and they drank in silence for long moments.

"So," Ruth said eventually, "I guess you're not exactly ready to be with someone else again. It's obvious you're still smarting from that ending the way it did."

"I am. So yes, not looking yet, but being with her also did me a favour because as a result I understand that I need to be with someone who knows themselves and is living authentically. I also know I need to be with someone who understands my life, my work-life balance, and is willing to support me in that. Not like Kate." Ruth snorted in agreement. "I have to live as me, completely me, and that doesn't mean I won't compromise a little—I know all relationships need that. But at my age I'm not going to be giving up all that's important to me for a partner who can't accept me and my life. I'd rather be alone."

"Good for you." Ruth raised her glass and waited for Maggie to follow suit. "To my marvellous sister, who has always known what she wants but seems to be finally making sure she gets it. I'm very proud of you."

The lump in her throat prevented Maggie from speaking, but she nodded, tapped her glass against Ruth's, and swallowed another delicious mouthful of wine.

It seemed rather fitting that the proof copy of Maggie's latest Maddie Jones novel was delivered the next morning. She and her publisher had worked unbelievably hard to get this one ready for pre-Christmas release, both recognising its potential to top the lesfic charts over the holidays, when book sales peaked.

She had finished it at the cottage. That first day after Tamsyn had left, she'd allowed herself to indulge in a few hours of emotional wallowing, but then channelled all she was feeling into her writing. The result—put together at a rate of five to six thousand words a day, sometimes even ten thousand when she couldn't seem to stop her fingers flying across the keyboard—was the book she now held in her hands. In the story, unlike the reality that had inspired it, the actress forged herself a new kind of future and she and the writer lived happily ever after.

Flicking through the pages, Maggie experienced that same thrill she always did when holding one of her own books. That feeling never lessened, and she hoped it never would.

Gizmo strolled into the room from the kitchen and hopped onto the sofa next to her, nudging her arm with his head.

"Oh, let me guess. It's walk time, is it?"

He barked, and she would swear he was grinning.

"Come on then."

An hour of fresh air, even if it was going to be in the drizzle that hadn't stopped since she'd first got out of bed, would be the perfect precursor to sitting down with the proof copy. She had no other commitments this week and was relishing her freedom. Gizmo was in for some treats, too—she'd planned a day down at the south coast at the end of the week.

For now, though, they wandered through the almost-deserted landscape of Putney Common. The trees were already mostly stripped of their leaves, and a thick carpet of them squished under her boots. Gizmo was in his element, snuffling around in the undergrowth, chasing squirrels, and rolling in the damp grass.

Maggie trailed after him, lost in her own thoughts. It had been hard talking about her time with Tamsyn, but actually no harder than occasionally seeing her in the newspaper or on TV. Maggie had deliberately not watched anything in which Tamsyn starred, which meant she'd missed a one-off UK drama series that had, of course, won high acclaim. Maybe she'd catch it on repeat sometime next year. Maybe by then she'd be able to cope better with seeing that beautiful face, remembering how that incredible body felt under her hands; her mouth, how easy they'd been with each other, both in and out of bed.

Gizmo had missed her too. He'd wandered around the cottage looking in all the rooms for two days after she'd left, and every time he thought someone was approaching the front door he'd bark excitedly, only to switch to whining when he realised he'd imagined it.

"We both wanted her to stay, didn't we?" Maggie said, looking down at her dog as he lay on his back in the wet grass, all four paws sticking up in the air, tongue lolling to one side of his mouth. "Gizmo, you're weird, you know that, right?"

Gizmo barked and rolled to his feet.

"Come on, you. Home time. Mummy needs to get back to work." If only to halt the flow of memories of a certain famous actress, which would of course be impossible given how much of Tamsyn she'd written into her book. *Yeah, maybe not the smartest idea I ever had.*

She pulled Gizmo's lead out of her coat pocket and clipped him in. He gave her face a quick lick while she was bent over, and once again, she wondered if he knew more than should be possible for a dog. His brown eyes stared at her, his head tilted.

"I'm okay, Giz. Promise."

He whined, but obediently followed her when she tugged on the lead and walked him to the path that led back to the car park.

Chapter 16

"Tamsyn, give us a smile!" "Tamsyn, over here, darling!" Tamsyn!" "Tamsyn, this way!"

Her face ached from the forced smiles, and a myriad of white splotches spun across her eyelids each time she blinked. The press were out in force, which wasn't unexpected, of course, but her weary reaction was. Tamsyn was sick of this. Sick of putting on a show, dressing to the nines in an admittedly glorious gown, posing for the swarm of photographers. *It'll be a miracle if I don't have a headache before the end of the showing.*

Zane—*what the hell kind of name was that?*—tugged discreetly at her hand, and although she resented being pulled around like a puppy dog, Tamsyn followed because Zane *did* know how to work a crowd. His hand was slightly clammy; in the year since they'd worked together on *Midnight Escape*, the premiere of which they were now attending, she had forgotten that little snippet about him. Always with the damp hands. The rescue scene they'd filmed, with her in nothing but a flimsy camisole and shorts, had been particularly uncomfortable as a result.

"You're doing great," Zane whispered, and she rankled at how patronising it sounded, even while she maintained her perfect smile and poise.

Of course she was. She'd been doing this since he was in nappies, the little shit.

She inhaled slowly, a technique she'd learned years ago to fill her lungs without it looking like she was desperate for breath. The intake of oxygen helped, and she mentally shook herself out. *You've got this. Come on, you are Tamsyn Harris. This is just a walk in the park.*

Minutes later, the relative calmness of the foyer of the Odeon cinema in Leicester Square wrapped her in its embrace. There were still people everywhere, of course, but at least the clamour of the press and fans had muted and she could hope her head wouldn't pound any harder than it was already. She made the rounds, greeting co-stars and all the right people, but was grateful when they were finally led into the auditorium and could take their seats. As the room plunged into darkness, she sighed in relief and relaxed back into her seat. Two hours where she didn't have to talk to anyone, or pose for anything, or even think about the film playing out on the big screen in front of her if she didn't want to. Bliss.

Later that night, after she'd kicked off her shoes and groaned in sweet relief, she looked around at her empty home and a shiver of something she couldn't identify caused goose bumps to break out over her arms. Another solo appearance in public, another solo ride home, another solo night in a house that used to feel like her sanctuary and now felt more like a prison.

She'd not drunk all evening; she never did at public events, keeping her head straight so that nothing bad could ever hit the front pages the next day. But now she opened a bottle of her favourite champagne and took a glass to the living room, her favourite room in the house. The mock fire under the impressive mantle was a modern concession to London building regulations but at least gave her the illusion of the fires she'd shared with Maggie. She'd had it fitted soon after she'd finished filming *Great Plains* and sat in front of it every night she was home since the weather had turned cool enough to justify it. And every time she did, the flicker of the flames, even if they were artificial, immediately took her back to that heady few days where she'd found, for a moment, someone who made her feel... human.

The champagne was cold but delicious, and she sipped slowly in the quiet room.

When her phone rang, she was tempted to ignore it, but Lesley's name appeared in the caller display and she smiled as she answered.

"Hey, you."

"Hello! How was it?"

"Ugh, okay. You know I hate those things sometimes."

"Yes, I know, but I saw some of the photos online and you looked *gorgeous*, as always."

"You're very sweet."

"Are you okay, Tam? You sound awfully low."

Tamsyn sighed. "I'm fine. Just tired. You know how it is." The lie slipped out easily. Although she and Lesley had managed to meet a couple of times for lunch over the last few months, she still hadn't told her about Norfolk, and she wasn't ready to do so yet.

"Oh, you poor thing! Maybe you need to go on another retreat, take some time for yourself."

"Well, funny you should mention that," she replied, pushing thoughts of Norfolk out of her mind, "because I've got Jennifer's villa on Sardinia booked next week."

"Oh, *lovely*! How is she? Still as bitchy as ever?"

Tamsyn chuckled. "Totally. But the villa's to die for so…"

"Do you want some company? I have a few things on but I could—"

Alarm flooded her and she cut Lesley off quickly. "Oh, no, it's fine! Honestly, I'm so tired I'd be rubbish company. I just need a quiet week to myself and I'll be right as rain again."

"Sure. I understand. But call me whenever, okay?"

She was a good friend, and Tamsyn's guilt at not making more time for her since Norfolk twisted in her gut. "You know, we really should do something more than lunch soon. How about we get something in the diary now?"

"*Super*! Just a sec."

When Lesley came back on the line, they found an evening that worked for both of them, and Tamsyn offered to cook.

"That's perfect, Tam. Listen, I'll let you go now because I know you need some rest. See you in a couple of weeks, darling!"

Tamsyn placed the phone back on the sofa and sipped at her drink. The call had lifted her for a moment, Lesley's natural cheeriness easing the gloom while they talked, but as soon as they were done, she was back to her own thoughts, alone in her big house.

She sighed. The melancholy that had gripped her the minute she'd finished filming *Great Plains* back in July had never loosened its hold. In fact, she could admit it was becoming stronger, and she'd briefly entertained the idea that she might need to talk to someone. But what could a therapist tell her that she didn't already understand herself? She knew what was wrong, knew why she was feeling the way she was.

Maggie.

Memories tortured Tamsyn, kept her awake at night, and caused her to suddenly find herself standing in a room with no recollection of when she'd entered it or how long she'd stood there daydreaming before snapping out of it. Even bloody Gizmo invaded her thoughts on a way-too-regular basis. Every time she saw a Border terrier her heart did a little lurch. Ridiculous.

It wasn't ridiculous to think of Maggie though, she knew that. What they'd had, what she'd walked away from, had been the most real thing Tamsyn had experienced in years. So of course she would keep remembering it with fondness and longing, wouldn't she? That was fine. What wasn't fine was that it was now starting to impact her whole life; she wanted to hide away from the world and wallow in it. She didn't want to work, didn't want to read scripts, or meet with Carmen or any other contact from the industry.

She relaxed into the mellow buzz of the champagne, grateful for the lassitude it imparted. Maybe tonight she'd sleep, for once. God knew she was tired enough after a whirlwind couple of days performing the mandatory interviews for the release of *Midnight Escape*. A few more tomorrow and then she was done for this cycle. The week in Sardinia would hopefully be the break she needed, and by sheer luck, coincided with the release of a new Maddie Jones book which she had on pre-order and express delivery; it was guaranteed to arrive sometime Friday, ready for her to pack for the trip. By Saturday evening she would be curled up on a sofa with a view of the ocean, Maddie Jones in one hand—so to speak—and a champagne glass in the other.

Her smile was, for the first time that day, genuine.

"Carmen, I'm fine." Tamsyn wedged the phone under her chin and pulled the suitcase off the carousel. She stood it next to her while she rearranged her outfit, making sure the beanie was firmly on her head, the tinted glasses securely on her nose.

"I can't help worrying." Carmen's soft tones definitely held a hint of that worry. "You really haven't been yourself lately, and now you're hiding away on your own." She sighed. "I could easily have arranged a companion for you, you know. Alexandra is back in town and you always tell me you enjoy seeing her."

Tamsyn grimaced. The thought of hooking up with someone else, even someone as distracting as Alexandra, had lost all appeal.

"Thanks, but no. Trust me, that sort of thing… Well, it's just not what I want anymore. Alone time is exactly what I want, actually."

She pulled the suitcase after her as she stepped away from the carousel and made for the exit. No one cast her a second look; the disguise was either doing its job well or the people of Sardinia were so used to a regular flow of celebrities that her arrival didn't warrant any particular attention. It was a relief.

"Okay." Carmen sound dubious. "Do we need to talk about anything in particular? I mean, you've turned down the last three scripts I sent you, and—"

"They were all crap, Carmen. And you know it."

Carmen sighed. "I know. I'm… I am trying, okay?"

"I know you are," Tamsyn said with some force. "This isn't your fault. You know that too."

"Yeah," Carmen breathed. "I do. So, is your driver there?"

Tamsyn walked out of the automatic doors and smiled when a suited gentleman with a sign that read "Mrs Mavis Wood" met her eye.

"Yes, he is. I'll talk to you later in the week, okay?"

"Take care."

She snapped the phone shut and slipped it into her handbag. The driver stepped forward and took her suitcase from her.

"Just this one?" he asked.

She smirked. "Yes, that's it."

He smiled and turned away, pulling the case behind him. Tamsyn followed, keeping her eyes on his back, not wanting to risk engaging with anyone else in the airport as they made their way to the car. It was, thankfully, a regular sedan, not a limo and she sent a silent thanks to Carmen for the subtlety.

The drive to the villa took just under an hour. As the driver swung the car up a steep driveway and through a security gate, Tamsyn's entire body relaxed. A housekeeper met them on the front step. Her posture was as starched as her uniform, but her smile was warm and she welcomed Tamsyn into the house with alacrity, her English superb and sounding even more wonderful with the Italian accent.

After murmuring a goodbye to the driver, who merely tapped his hat in response, Tamsyn followed the housekeeper on a brief tour of the villa and its facilities. It was beautiful—the perfect spot, as she'd been assured, for a quiet getaway.

"All of the food and drink you requested has been stored in the kitchen, Mrs Wood." Tamsyn smiled; the housekeeper undoubtedly knew who she really was. "I will clean as much or as little as you like during your stay. Merely leave a message on the service line there," she pointed to a phone on the kitchen wall, "and tell me when."

"Sounds perfect, *signora. Grazie.*"

"*Prego.*"

The housekeeper nodded once and then left. Moments later, Tamsyn heard a car start up. When the security gate clanged shut a few moments after that, she let out a happy chuckle.

Alone at last.

Humming contentedly to herself, she set about unpacking her suitcase. She really had packed light, intending to do nothing more than lounge around the beautiful villa or perhaps take a stroll along the rugged coastal path. After unpacking, she wandered into the bathroom attached to the master bedroom. The shower cubicle—such a minuscule word for the enclosure that faced her—was luxury personified, and its mere presence invited her to instantly disrobe and lose herself in the multiple jets of steaming hot water.

Twenty minutes later, refreshed and with her skin tingling from the pounding it had taken, she dressed in her softest yoga pants and a loose T-shirt, with a sweater thrown over her shoulders. It was past five in the afternoon, a perfectly acceptable hour for a glass of champagne to celebrate her first real week of freedom since April.

Since Norfolk and Maggie.

A wave of sadness had her pulling on the sweater in a vain attempt to fight off the chill that consumed her body. No amount of warm clothing could combat that sort of chill, though; it came from too deep within.

Come on, you can't spend the whole week wallowing in memories.

She poured herself a drink and took it through to the large, open room that served as both living and dining area. A long sofa faced the enormous windows that looked out over the deck, the pool, and beyond to the sea. The villa was up on a promontory, so although she couldn't see the waves breaking against the rocks immediately below, she could see the surf pounding the cliff across the bay. She watched for a while, mesmerised by the action of the waves, and slowly some of the sadness drifted away, crawling back into the hole in her heart where it usually resided.

It still shocked her, just how much pain had stayed with her. She'd assumed it would fade over time as she forgot Maggie. The problem was, she couldn't forget her, and that hadn't factored into her plan at all. Throwing herself into her work afterwards should have been the perfect tonic for recovery, for moving on. Except, she couldn't move on. Memories of Maggie, and what they'd been for each other that week, haunted her.

Briefly, the day after wrapping *Great Plains*, she had considered trying to contact Maggie via her publisher. She'd fantasised about it for one whole day, then found herself right back at square one: what was the point? They couldn't date, not openly anyway, and something told her that Maggie would hate to be someone's dirty little secret. And Tamsyn wouldn't ask her to do that anyway—Maggie was far too special to be treated that way.

She finished her champagne and set the empty glass down on the sleek, glass-topped coffee table in front of her. Food was next on her list, and in ten minutes she had a plate piled high with olives, prosciutto, artichokes, assorted crudités, and a dip she couldn't identify but which smelled heavenly. Before making her way back to the sofa with her haul, she trotted into the bedroom to retrieve her book. The new Maddie Jones was still in its Amazon packaging. She ripped off the brown cardboard and turned the book over in her hands. The cover startled her somewhat—a photo of a woman, her back to the camera, her arms shielding her face as she faced a barrage of photographers. Tamsyn's skin prickled, the image stirring up memories of the premiere she'd just attended. She turned the book over as she wandered back to the kitchen. She'd not read the blurb before ordering—for authors like Maddie Jones she never did, not caring what the story was, just knowing that she wanted their latest offering.

Her footsteps faltered as she read, until she came to a standstill in the hallway between the bedrooms and the living area.

What the—?

She turned the book back over to look at the cover photo, then read the blurb again, only much slower. Key phrases leaped out at her, making her heartbeat quicken and her confusion intensify.

"Writer on retreat." "Actress in hiding." "Holiday romance." "Actress in the closet." "Is she willing to risk all for love?"

Food forgotten, she stumbled through to the sofa and sat down, staring at the book in her hands.

Well, this was…weird. How could she be holding a book that promised a story so much like the one she'd shared with Maggie only a few months ago?

I mean, obviously it's pure coincidence, but how bizarre is that?

She put the book on the coffee table and sat back. *Do I even want to read this now? Isn't it going to strike a bit too close to home?* Her sigh was exasperated. And she'd been so looking forward to losing herself in another one of Maddie Jones's wonderful stories of love triumphing against the odds.

Knowing it was rather irrational but doing it anyway, she shoved the book under a cushion, then stood and walked back to her bedroom. Choosing one of the other three books she'd brought—checking carefully that its storyline wasn't something likely to mess with her head—she finally retrieved her food and returned to the sofa.

An hour later, half her food still on her plate and her second glass of champagne beside it on the coffee table, she closed the book and threw it on the sofa beside her. Two chapters. That was all she'd managed to read, and she'd read each of them twice because she simply couldn't focus. The Maddie Jones book, even out of sight, niggled at her. How similar would it be to her own story? How *would* it make her feel to read something that close to home?

"Oh, for crying out loud," she said into the empty room, and stood. Ten minutes later, she'd returned the food to the fridge, topped up her champagne, and wrapped a soft throw over her legs as she stretched out lengthwise on the sofa, the Maddie Jones book in her hand. With trembling fingers, she turned to page one and began to read.

By the time she reached the end of chapter two, her champagne was forgotten. Two more chapters in, her hands were shaking as her heart pounded. And after reading—and re-reading—chapter five, she was a mess of conflicting emotions that were almost making it hard for her to breathe.

Confusion. Disbelief. Anger. Sadness.

Maddie Jones was Maggie.

Of that one fact she had no doubt, not after reading five chapters that described, almost word-for-word, how she and Maggie had met and begun their fling. Everything was there—every meeting prior to their first kiss, the description of the estate in Norfolk, even the writer having a pet dog, although the one in the book wasn't nearly as adorable as Gizmo.

She reached for her phone and Googled Maddie Jones's website. No author photo, and only the briefest of biographies which illuminated nothing. Next she tried the publisher's website; nothing extra. Similar searches of Jessica Stewart's website and her mainstream publisher's website also drew a blank. None of them gave Tamsyn any hint that Maggie was either writer, but she knew Maggie was Jessica Stewart, and she was convinced she had to be Maddie Jones too. It was all too close to the truth. And although Maddie—Maggie—had used poetic licence to fill in the scenes that were written from the actress's point of view, she'd done so with alarming accuracy. Tamsyn hadn't realised she'd revealed that much of herself to Maggie—or was she just that easy to read?

A sour taste filled Tamsyn's mouth. Maggie had been reading her all along, simply using her and what they shared as material for her next bestseller. The idea sat like lead in her stomach. She'd thought she meant more than that to Maggie; that their time together had meant something. Clearly not, if Maggie had been so quick to turn their experience into this. The one thing she was thankful for was that the actress wasn't identifiable as her—Maggie hadn't been that cruel. Or, at least, Tamsyn wasn't identifiable from the first five chapters alone.

Shit. I have to read the whole thing now, just to check.

Grimly picking up the book again, she turned to chapter six.

Chapter 17

"Tamsyn, how lovely to hear from you." Carmen sounded far too jolly for a Sunday morning and Tamsyn scowled, even though she knew Carmen couldn't see it. "How is—?"

"Carmen, I need you to do something for me." Tamsyn paced in front of the big windows; the grey sky and rough sea perfectly suited her mood.

"Er, sure. What's wrong?"

Tamsyn blew out a breath. "Maybe nothing. Maybe something." She ran her free hand over her face, rubbing at her tired eyes. Only three hours of sleep had taken a toll. "I need you to read a book and tell me if you think... Well, look, just read it and then call me back."

"What? Tamsyn, what the hell are you talking about?"

Tamsyn growled. "Just trust me, Carmen, please. I emailed you the link to it on Amazon, and I want you to buy it and read it as soon as you can, okay?"

"Are you okay?" Carmen asked softly.

"Yes. Mostly." She didn't feel the need to elaborate, and she certainly didn't want to give Carmen any clues as to what the book contained. She'd read it through last night and although she wasn't named in it, and nor were any of her films, she couldn't help but worry that people would know it was her. And the last thing she needed was a bunch of lesbians talking about a lesbian romance where she was the lead character.

"Right." Carmen sounded dubious. "Well, okay. Send me the link and I'll give it a read. It's not some sick horror story, though, is it, because I really can't—"

Tamsyn chuckled, but it lacked warmth. "No, it's not that."

"Phew. All right, I'll talk to you soon, okay?"

"Thanks, Carmen."

They hung up and Tamsyn shoved her phone in her pocket. She folded her arms across her chest and gazed, unseeing, out at the view before her. Once again, the same thought that had been careering around her brain most of the night came back to her: how could Maggie do this? How could she take what they'd had and...abuse it so?

She didn't know how long it would take Carmen to get hold of the book, so there was no point just sitting around waiting for her to read it. Tamsyn needed to move, to do something with the nervous energy that had built up inside her. Although tired from her sleepless night, she needed exercise, and yoga wouldn't quite cut it, not today. No, right now she needed wind in her hair and the taste of the sea on her tongue.

Her walk took her out of the house for nearly four hours. Jennifer had recommended this route for "blowing away any cobwebs you might have" and she was proved right. The coastal path was rugged but manageable in Tamsyn's walking boots, and she actually relished the challenge of picking her way over some of the trickier sections. The wind was cool but not biting, and she left her hair untied and free to blow in any direction the wind fancied taking it.

Halfway along the track, she came to a point where the path overlooked another small bay; there was a trail down to the beach below but she stayed up top, soaking in the view, trying hard not to think about how the Maggie she thought she knew would have loved this, and how Gizmo would have loved it even more. *That* Maggie, as far as she could tell, had been an illusion. *Probably couldn't believe her luck, having a famous actress to shag for the week and then write about.* Although... The book wasn't quite like that. It was much more romantic than they'd been—or let themselves be. In the story, Maggie had them spending several weeks together, not nine days, and knowing by the end of it that they were falling for each other. The two characters—she tried hard not think of them as herself and Maggie—made plans to continue their relationship back in London, despite the actress being so closeted. Gradually, in the weeks and months that followed, the actress realised she had a key choice to make or risk losing the love of her life. Several times, Tamsyn forgot she was supposed to be angry with Maggie and her flagrant misuse of their secret, because the story Maggie had woven pulled her in and had her rooting for them to get that happy ever after.

She sighed, swallowing hard against the sudden lump in her throat. No, the book didn't reconcile at all with Maggie being so conniving, and Maggie being so conniving didn't reconcile at all with the Maggie she had made love with back in Norfolk.

Whoa. Made love? Since when was she calling it that?

A strong gust of wind whipped her hair over her face, and with her vision obscured, her mind threw her an image of their last night together, of the connection, the passion, the tenderness they'd shared. She shivered, not from the chill of the wind but from memories of how incredible Maggie had felt inside her, and she in turn inside Maggie. How beautiful Maggie had looked, gazing down at her in the charged moment before their lips touched for yet another searing kiss.

She wrapped her arms around herself and faced into the wind, letting it buffet her. Yes, those last couple of days, they hadn't been having sex. At least, not as far as Tamsyn was concerned. And if she allowed herself to really think back on it, on Maggie's expressions and the look in her eyes, it wasn't sex for Maggie either. They'd made love.

And then Maggie had written all about it in a book.

Tamsyn shook her head. She still couldn't reconcile the two things in her brain, and was tired of trying. She turned around and headed back to the villa.

———

Carmen called her at lunchtime on Monday, an amused tone to her voice that rankled Tamsyn as soon as she heard it.

"Well, that was a first for me. I always assumed lesbian fiction was just porn for men to get off on. Thank you for re-educating me."

"And?" Tamsyn asked, trying not to snap as her impatience threatened to get the better of her. She stood up from the breakfast bar where she'd been preparing her food and walked to the big windows. It was sunnier today; maybe she'd do another, shorter walk later.

"And what?" Carmen sounded bemused.

Tamsyn almost growled. "And what did you think? Was it obvious?"

"I… Tamsyn, what are you talking about? I read the book, I enjoyed it. More than I thought I would once I realised what I was going to be reading. I mean, it would make a cute film, but I can't see any major studio going for it, and if you wanted this to be your big coming out, well, I can think of better—"

"No! God, I'm not planning on getting it made into a film, for crying out loud. That's the last thing I want to do with it." She took a deep breath. Either Carmen hadn't seen the main character as a representation of Tamsyn, or she was deliberately winding Tamsyn up. "Did the actress character remind you of anyone?"

Carmen was silent for a few moments. "No, not really. Why?" Then, before Tamsyn could actually reply, Carmen said, "Wait, are you trying to say that she was based on you?" Carmen laughed. "Oh, Tamsyn, get a grip. I mean, I love you and you're my favourite client but please, don't be getting all egocentric on me now. You've done very well at avoiding that all these years."

Tamsyn didn't know whether to be affronted or relieved. "You mean it didn't seem like me?"

"God, no! Is this why you were so adamant that I read this? You thought someone had written some kind of fanfic about you and you object to being 'outed' in it?"

"Fan what?"

Carmen sighed. "Another time," she murmured. "Look, Tamsyn, I think you are totally overreacting. That character, even if she was based on you, bears no resemblance to you. At least not to any part of you the public knows about. Yes, it's kind of a coincidence that it's all set in Norfolk where you were earlier this year but she's a UK author, so why wouldn't she set a book there?" She paused. "I admit, now you've said it, there are some things in there that do remind me of you, but that's only because I see sides to you the general public doesn't and because you've now made me think about it." She chuckled. "Of course, there are plenty of things in there that aren't like you at all, so clearly the author used poetic licence even if she did start with you in mind."

Tamsyn was scared to ask, but did it anyway, her free hand pressing against the cool window as she braced herself for Carmen's response. "What things weren't like me?"

"Oh, um…" Carmen sighed again. "Please don't make me do this."

"No, I really want to know. I won't bite your head off."

"What is it about this book that's got you so in a tizzy?"

"Carmen, please. Just tell me." Tamsyn rolled her eyes.

"Well," Carmen began cautiously, "you know, the, um, touchy-feely stuff. That's not really your style, is it? You know, being all romantic and getting squishy about a dog. You hate dogs."

"Not that one." Tamsyn started as she realised she'd said the words out loud.

"What one?"

"Nothing. Doesn't matter."

"Tamsyn, are you okay? I'm really getting worried about you. You haven't been yourself for ages, since the trip to Norfolk finished actually, and—"

Tamsyn could almost hear the penny drop inside Carmen's brain.

"Oh. My. *God*." Carmen's voice was an octave higher than normal. "Are you serious? It *was* you? It's based on reality?"

Tamsyn groaned and pushed away from the window, then paced a circuit that took her round the dining table and chairs, along the back of the sofa, and back round to the windows again.

"Tamsyn?" Carmen was more insistent this time. "Talk to me."

Tamsyn huffed out a long breath. "Yes. It *is* me. It is based on reality. Her name is actually Maggie." Saying her name out loud brought a stab of pain somewhere low in Tamsyn's belly.

Carmen exhaled loudly in Tamsyn's ear. "I'm coming out there."

"What? No, Carmen, this is not a problem my agent needs to fix, I—"

"I'm not coming as your agent," Carmen said softly. "I'm coming as your friend."

Tamsyn managed to squeak an "Oh" around her closed up throat.

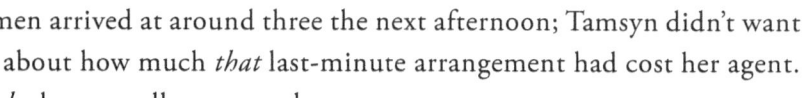

Carmen arrived at around three the next afternoon; Tamsyn didn't want to think about how much *that* last-minute arrangement had cost her agent. *My friend*, she mentally corrected.

"This place is amazing." Carmen was standing in front of the windows, soaking up the view. She turned back to face Tamsyn. "I can see why you jumped at the chance when Jennifer mentioned it was free this week."

"I still can't believe you dropped everything to come here." Tamsyn shook her head. "That's above and beyond. And probably unnecessary, you realise."

Carmen shrugged. "I don't think so." She stepped closer, tilting her head. "Something isn't right with you. As your agent that concerns me, but as someone who considers herself your friend beyond that, it worries me." Carmen's brown eyes narrowed.

Once again that lump threatened to close Tamsyn's throat. She and Carmen had never done this, and it was unsettling as much as it was warming. Something told her she'd be shedding a few tears before the day ended.

She cleared her throat. "Want some fizz?"

Carmen smiled. "Why the hell not. Tell you what, let me grab a quick shower and get into some really comfy clothes. I'll be back in fifteen, okay?"

"Perfect." By then, Tamsyn might have found a way to compose herself ahead of the interrogation, which she knew would be gentle and come from a place of care, so that helped. A little.

When Carmen returned, looking fresh and happy in a baggy pair of holey jeans and a hoodie, Tamsyn chuckled. "I can honestly say I've never seen you looking so casual. Even when we've met for dinner or lunch as friends, you've always dressed up."

Carmen's laugh was rich, her curly blonde hair bouncing on her shoulders. "I happen to like dressing up. Always have. But every now and then, the occasion demands something much more...shabby."

"You pull off shabby very well," Tamsyn said with a smirk, walking across the living area to hand Carmen a perfectly chilled glass of champagne.

They clinked glasses, smiling at each other.

"This never gets boring," Tamsyn said, tilting her glass.

"Diva," Carmen muttered, rolling her eyes.

Tamsyn snorted with laughter.

They settled onto the sofa, both facing the big windows. The late afternoon sun cast a beautiful orange glow across the cliffs facing the villa, highlighting nooks and crannies in the rocks, and making the scraggly bushes that clung to them look as if they were tipped with flame.

"So," Carmen said eventually, shuffling so she sat at a right angle to Tamsyn. "What *is* the story behind the book and the trip to Norfolk?"

"I'll need a top up of this before we get into that," Tamsyn said, pointing at her glass.

Carmen nodded and Tamsyn retrieved the bottle from the kitchen. She refilled their glasses, stood the bottle on the coffee table, and sat back down, turning to face Carmen. A strange tingle of anticipation skittered down her spine.

She started slowly but was soon stumbling over her words as she rushed into it, until Carmen's raised hand cut her off.

"Take deep breaths, Tamsyn. We have all evening, and all of tomorrow. I want to hear everything, but you don't have tell it all tonight. And you certainly don't need to skip over the good parts," she finished with a smirk.

Tamsyn lifted one eyebrow. "I never kiss and tell," she said, her tone as haughty as she could manage while trying not to laugh.

"You will. You're itching to, I can tell."

Sighing, Tamsyn shook her head. "I hate how you can see right through me."

Carmen chuckled. "Okay, from the garbled beginning, I understand that Maggie, who is also Maddie Jones *and* also Jessica Stewart, was staying in the other cottage on my aunt's estate, yes?"

"Yes, she and her dog, Gizmo." Tamsyn smiled, wondering how Snakey was faring.

"Gizmo?" Carmen's eyebrows had met her hairline.

Tamsyn laughed. "He's the most gorgeous dog, probably ever."

"That's not saying much, given how much you hate them."

"No, trust me. Totally adorable."

"Okay, okay. As much I want to hear about the dog who won your heart, I'd rather hear about the woman who achieved it."

Tamsyn nearly choked on her champagne, wiping at dribbles of it on her chin as she sat bolt upright. "She didn't win my heart!"

"Right," Carmen said, nodding, her eyes narrowed, lips quirked in a half-smile. "My mistake. Please do continue with the tale."

Huffing, Tamsyn leaned back against the sofa once more, and, slowly this time, told Carmen the entire story. She did manage it over the course of the evening, with many interruptions for questions or observations from Carmen, and over the remains of the first bottle of champagne and well into another, too. At some point they remembered they needed food and broke off for fifteen minutes to rummage in the fridge and put together a strange assortment of ready-to-eat nibbles coupled with a rich tomato soup. They took it all back to the sofa and ate off their laps while Tamsyn continued to talk.

It was cathartic, but also brought to the surface a level of emotion she hadn't acknowledged up to this point. Memories of Maggie, of the way they had been with each other, rocked her. By the time she'd finished, ending with her discovery of Maggie's other identity by reading the book, and her fear that Maggie had been using her just for a story, she had her arms wrapped around her knees where they were folded up into her chest.

"You see," Carmen said, slumping back on the sofa, "that's where I tend to disagree with you, now that I've heard the whole story. I honestly can't see how this is anything other than her using a bit of reality to write a good story." She paused, shifting in her seat. "And... Well, if I am totally honest, I also think the book was her way of getting the resolution she wanted to happen in reality."

It took a moment for Carmen's words to sink in, but when they did, Tamsyn whipped her head up to stare at her.

"What?" Her voice was strangled, her heart thumping wildly.

"Tamsyn, she's written the love story she wishes she'd had with you. The happy ending. The pair of you riding off into the sunset." Tamsyn snorted but Carmen ploughed on. "Yes, I know, that's the last thing you want. But she did, I think." She paused and took a deep breath. "And I also think she wrote the happy ending she wanted for you in your own right. Out of the closet, free to be you, free to live the life you've been denying yourself all these years."

Tamsyn couldn't listen to it; there was a rushing in her ears, and her blood suddenly felt as if it were molten lava coursing through her veins. She stood up, stomping away from the sofa over to the big windows. It was long dark by now, so all she saw was her own reflection, and the reflection of Carmen sitting on the sofa behind her, unmoved.

"That's...ridiculous," Tamsyn said, almost to herself.

"Not to me it isn't," Carmen said firmly. "And I think, deep down, it isn't to you either."

"But..."

"But what?"

"We...we had a deal," Tamsyn asserted, even as, way down deep in her soul, she knew she didn't believe it herself. "No strings. That's what we said."

Carmen's laugh was more like a sharp bark. In the dark mirror of the window, Tamsyn could see her stand and walk slowly over until they stood shoulder to shoulder. "Look at me, Tamsyn."

She didn't want to. It was all going to unravel if she did. But Carmen's hand tugged her arm, and her feet willingly moved even as her brain tried to stop them.

"Tamsyn," Carmen said softly, once Tamsyn was facing her. "Stop lying. To me, to yourself, and to the memory of Maggie. Admit it: that no-strings deal went out the window after about day three, didn't it? When you left her that last night, a part of you broke, didn't it?"

It hurt. She'd buried it so deep all these months, living only on the surface of herself, that it was a yawning chasm once it sprang open. She didn't have to speak to answer—the tears falling down her face said it all.

Tamsyn slept fitfully, and when dawn broke, she gave up and quietly made her way to the kitchen in her pyjamas. Carmen's bedroom was farther down the hall than Tamsyn's own master suite, but even so, she kept her movements light while she made coffee, thankful that the machine didn't spit and scream like some she'd used.

She cupped the warm mug in her hands and sat at the dining table, her gaze on the sea, which was calm and grey this early in the morning. After stumbling into bed beyond midnight, Tamsyn had merely lain in the dark, eyes wide open, a confusing welter of thoughts and emotions spinning through her mind and body. Her rational, self-preserving brain told her to ignore Carmen's theories, but the rest of her, the part that had cried at the thought of all she'd missed by not continuing to see Maggie, had held the upper hand in the darkness.

And it was doing so now, even in the cold light of day.

Could she do it? Start dating women, publicly, and to hell with the consequences? Fear and temptation mixed in a strange cocktail in her stomach. As Carmen had rightly pointed out last night, it wasn't as if Tamsyn was short of money, so even if by some chance work did dry up completely, she'd still be okay. And she had to admit that Carmen was also right when she said it was highly unlikely the work would dry up. She'd lived with that fear for so long that she'd almost not realised just how successful she was, how lauded her skills were. Of course the work wouldn't dry up *completely*. Yes, it might tail off for a while as people reconfigured who Tamsyn Harris was by this one nugget of her personal life changing, but she would always work, as long as she perhaps made a few compromises on the kinds of role she played.

"Any more of that in the pot for me?" Carmen croaked from behind her.

Tamsyn turned and smiled at her. "I'll pour you a cup."

Carmen flopped onto the sofa, her cream towelling robe pulled tight around her as she snuggled back into the cushions.

"Did I wake you?" Tamsyn asked, contrite.

"No, not at all." Carmen waved a hand in the air. "Just my brain wouldn't quite shut off all night."

"I know what you mean," Tamsyn murmured, walking to the coffee pot and filling a large cup for Carmen before retrieving her own half-empty drink from the dining table.

"I bet. Did you sleep at all?" Carmen managed through a loud yawn.

"A little." Tamsyn passed Carmen her cup, then joined her on the sofa.

"Thanks, honey," Carmen said, clinging to the cup as if it held all the answers to the universe. She moaned after her first sip. "Oh, yeah, I needed that."

Tamsyn smiled and slowly drained the last of her own drink.

"So," Carmen said after a while, her voice tentative. "How are you feeling?"

"I...I'm not sure, to be honest." Tamsyn sighed. "Confused. Scared. Tired. And I don't just mean physically." She met Carmen's eyes. "Tired of working so hard to protect myself when maybe I don't need to worry so much about that anymore." She blinked a couple of times. "I think a lot of what you said last night was right, about how I've become so obsessed with not ruining my career. Maybe I need to start thinking about how much happier I might be if I could be free to live my personal life exactly how I want to, believing that my career is probably only going to take a small hit and if it does, it's not the end of the world."

Carmen smiled widely. "Does that mean I need to talk to Tony about setting up a coming out interview?"

Tamsyn stared at her. "Already?" she squeaked.

Laughing, Carmen patted her on the thigh. "Not today, no. Look, when you're back in London, let's meet with Tony and think about the timing, the strategy. I mean, I guess it partly depends on how soon you want to get in touch with Maggie again."

Tamsyn's breath caught in her throat. "What?"

Carmen stared at her. "What?"

"What do you mean, 'get in touch with Maggie again'?"

Carmen's eyes went wide. "Well, you have to, don't you? Tamsyn, you can't *not* try to see if you two can have something. Look how much she meant to you in the space of a few days. You'd be a class A idiot to not even *try* to find her and see if she still feels the same way about you as you do about her."

"What the fuck are you talking about?" Tamsyn exclaimed, but even as she said it she knew. It was one of the reasons the tears had fallen last night and why she hadn't been able to sleep properly afterwards. It was why her hands were trembling now while her heart thumped so hard it was a wonder Carmen couldn't hear it.

"What did I say last night about stopping lying to yourself?" Carmen said, her voice gruff. "God, lots of people would give their right arm to have the kind of connection you talked about having with Maggie. Me included," she said, jamming a finger into her own chest. Her cheeks were flushed, and her eyes glistened in the weak morning light, and suddenly Tamsyn knew that all Carmen's talk over the years of being happy to be single and having the entire playing field at her mercy was a load of crap.

"Carmen, I—"

"Don't. It's okay." Carmen took a deep breath. "But it's not okay for you to give up on this so easily. She wrote a whole fucking book about how much you meant to her, for crying out loud."

"You don't know that!" Why was it so much easier to think of Maggie as a gold-digger who'd only used their story to make a few bucks?

"Tamsyn, get real," Carmen said, exasperated. "If that isn't the most romantic gesture in the world, I don't know what is. And you don't think that's worth pursuing, given how you feel about her too? And don't tell me you don't—it's written all over your face even now."

Knowing it was silly, Tamsyn pressed her fingers to her face, as if she could feel the evidence of what Carmen was talking about. Because having to admit it out loud, saying the actual words, seemed too momentous. She'd never let herself feel what she was experiencing now, and if she kept it inside she'd be able to...what? Protect herself?

Or, more likely, keep living a lonely life that didn't make her happy.

She exhaled slowly. "I... This has never happened to me." Her voice was barely above a whisper.

"I know." Carmen shuffled closer to her. "And I know that's scary, but please, don't walk away from Maggie before you find out what you two might have."

"But how?" Tamsyn threw her arms up in frustration. "How the hell would I find her even if I wanted to?"

Carmen glared at her.

"Okay, okay," she mumbled. "I want to."

"Yes!" Carmen fist-pumped and grinned before squeezing Tamsyn's arm. "Well, the only contact we have for her is her publisher, right?"

Tamsyn nodded, watching in amusement as Carmen tapped her chin, her eyes narrowing, her cog wheels apparently turning at full speed now despite the early hour.

"So," Carmen said, a small smile forming at the corners of her mouth, "I'm sure an author would be very keen to meet with a film production company who were interested in dramatising one of her books, wouldn't they?"

"Film prod—"

"Mickey over at FilmLight owes me a huge favour. *Huge.*" Carmen's grin was positively feral.

Chapter 18

"I DO LIKE THIS TRADITION we've started," Ruth said as the waitress held her chair back for her. She slipped into her seat, murmured a "thank you" to the young woman, then smiled at Maggie. "So much better as a Christmas present than a gift box of Oil of Olay."

"Definitely." Maggie grinned as she glanced around. The restaurant, one of the hip places to be seen at these days, was packed, as she would have expected two weeks before Christmas. "And I am *so* glad we thought of this back when we did, otherwise I don't think we would have got a table."

"Oh, yes." Ruth took the menu the waitress handed her and flipped it open.

They ordered champagne to drink before their meal, and Maggie's heart did that little flip it seemed unable to stop itself from doing every time the subject came up. Tamsyn. She wondered where she was right now, what she was working on, who she was with. Maggie was still avoiding any coverage of her on the internet or in the press—every picture she saw left her weak with memories and sad for what had never been.

"You okay?" Ruth asked.

"Yes, why?"

"You drifted off for a moment."

Maggie shrugged and smiled. "Just soaking up the atmosphere."

Ruth looked as if she was about to say something, but then seemed to think better of it. She raised her glass and they toasted a "Merry Christmas" to each other.

"Yum," Ruth said, placing her glass carefully on the table before picking up her menu again. "So, what are we having?"

Once they'd placed their orders, they chatted easily. Maggie had always loved a night out with her sister, especially as they happened so rarely. Their tradition of a posh meal out together rather than buying each other things they really didn't need had started two years previously and was an instant success they'd promptly repeated for their respective birthdays. Each time they picked a new fabulous restaurant to try, and each one had been amazing. This one already looked like it was going to outclass them all.

"Is it true lots of famous people come here?" Ruth was trying hard not to look too eager, but Maggie chuckled as she craned her neck to look around the room. Her observations were brought to an abrupt end by the arrival of their starters. "Oh, yes," she breathed, reaching for her cutlery.

Maggie grinned but tucked into her own food with equal alacrity. When they'd finished, after each sampling the other's dish, of course, Maggie excused herself to the ladies, leaving Ruth to resume her search for famous people. When Maggie returned, Ruth's eyes were wide and she motioned Maggie down into her chair with an excited hand.

"Do not look round until I tell you," she hissed. "But Tamsyn bloody Harris just walked in and is sitting..."

The rest of whatever Ruth said was lost in the rushing sound that filled Maggie's head, the pounding of her heartbeat in her ears, the sudden dampness of her palms.

"Didn't you used to have the biggest crush on her when we were teenagers?"

"Um—"

"I always remember you having posters of her on your wall, and Mum looking at them in horror every time she came in." Ruth laughed. "She knew back then, didn't she?"

"Knew what?" Maggie was distracted, trying so hard not to look over to where Ruth had surreptitiously pointed out Tamsyn's location.

"That you were gay. Hey, Earth to Maggie?"

Maggie blinked. "Sorry, what?"

Ruth tilted her head. "Are you sure you're okay?" She stared at Maggie for a moment, then laughed. "Oh, God, you still have a crush on her, don't you? And I've completely freaked you out by telling you she's in this room, right now."

Relieved at being given an easy 'out', Maggie smiled. "Yes," she said, hoping she wouldn't blush, "you have." It wasn't a lie; Maggie *was* utterly freaked out knowing Tamsyn was sitting not more than fifty feet away. She wanted to look, was desperate to look, but at the same time was terrified. What if she looked, and Tamsyn acted like she didn't know her? Or worse, looked like she didn't even remember her?

"Aw, my big sister with the big crush." Ruth smiled gently.

Maggie chuckled. "Yeah, yeah, okay, you can stop laughing at me now."

Ruth smirked. "Why? Takes all the fun out of things."

Rolling her eyes, Maggie reached for her wine and was relieved that her hand was steady as she grasped the glass and brought it to her lips.

"Are you seriously not going to look?" Ruth looked confused, her forehead creased into a small frown.

Maggie swallowed the smooth Chardonnay and was thankful she didn't choke on it. "No, I'm not. I can see her on TV any time I like." God, could they not just talk about something else?

Ruth snorted. "Not the same! Come on, how many chances in life do you get to see someone that famous in the flesh?"

Maggie's chest pounded, and now she knew she was blushing. Tamsyn in the flesh was something she remembered all too well. How her skin felt beneath Maggie's exploring fingers, how her lips and tongue fit so perfectly with Maggie's when they kissed. How she tasted.

She shifted in her seat and took another gulp of wine. Ruth lifted her head, craning for another long look across the room, over Maggie's head.

"Will you stop?" Maggie hissed, now seriously agitated at her sister's behaviour. If Tamsyn spotted her...

"Relax," Ruth muttered before looking back at Maggie. "She's deep in conversation with some woman. I can't tell if they're someone famous too because they've got their back to me."

Okay, maybe one look then, if Tamsyn was that focused on her dinner companion. Slowly, Maggie turned her head, as if needing to rub at the back of her neck, and glanced over her shoulder. Tamsyn looked stunning, fully glammed up for the evening. She was wearing something in a rich cream fabric, dress or top Maggie couldn't tell from here, with gold jewellery shining in the lights of the restaurant. Her hair was coiffured into a high pile on top of her head, with elegant loose strands framing her face. Her make-up was flawless and her skin was practically glowing. She looked nothing like the woman Maggie knew, the woman who wore a beanie jammed onto her head when she went for a walk, the woman who turned up for dinner with zero make-up or jewellery and looked so much more a real person as a result. As much as Maggie had crushed on this glamorous version of Tamsyn all these years, it did nothing for her now. Not compared to the *real* Tamsyn.

Maggie looked back round at her sister, having seen all she needed to see. She schooled her features as Ruth grinned at her.

"Yes, she is just as beautiful in real life as she is on the screen," Maggie said to her sister's questioning look.

"I'll say. I wonder how much work she's had done though, to still look that good at her age?"

Maggie bristled, itching to leap to Tamsyn's defence but knowing she couldn't. To her relief, the waitress saved her by delivering their main courses, and it was easy to switch the conversation to their food, and plans for Christmas, until Tamsyn Harris was forgotten, and Maggie's heart could return to its normal rhythm.

"Are you okay, Tamsyn?" Jennifer asked, a small frown marring her otherwise perfect face.

"Hmm?" Tamsyn pulled her gaze away from the woman on the other side of the restaurant, the woman she had been convinced, for a moment at least, was Maggie. "Sorry, yes, I'm fine. What were you saying about Christmas?"

Jennifer rattled off her oh-so-dull sounding plans and Tamsyn pretended to listen, injecting the appropriate 'oohs' and 'ahs' in the right places. Her mind, however, was still on that glimpse from a minute ago. The woman had been scratching her neck, her head turned in profile but for such a short span of time that Tamsyn's brain hadn't quite connected all the dots before she turned away again. Now all Tamsyn could see was the back of her head, blonde hair pulled up in an elegant style that showed off a delicious line of neck. But was it Maggie's neck? And if it was, what the hell did Tamsyn think she'd do about that? Whoever the woman was, she was having what looked like an intimate dinner with someone she was very familiar with.

Still pretending to listen to Jennifer, Tamsyn cast furtive glances at the women. They were friendly, that much was obvious. But was it a date? It had been eight months since Tamsyn had seen Maggie; there was every chance Maggie had started seeing someone in that time. Tamsyn's stomach churned, her appetite diminishing as the seconds ticked by. Wouldn't this just be the biggest kick in the teeth—finally deciding to contact Maggie to see if they could resurrect what had happened between them, and then facing up to all that would mean for herself, but discovering Maggie had moved on? Of course, she had every right to; it wasn't as if Tamsyn had given her any reason not to.

She wanted to scream but did what she was world-class at—masked her features, kept herself professional, and left her turmoil to seethe beneath her calm exterior. She managed to finish her food—even though it sat like uncooked dough in her stomach afterwards—and graciously accepted Jennifer's thanks for the evening out.

"My pleasure," Tamsyn said, "and the least I could do after you loaned me the villa last month. It's a wonderful place."

"Any time, Tamsyn, darling."

They stood and walked to the door to retrieve their coats. Jennifer's car was already waiting out front, her driver/bodyguard standing before it, arms held loose at his side, eyes scanning the area. Tamsyn wanted to glance back one more time, to see if that woman was still there, to see if she could get a proper look at her, but she was distracted by an excited shout from a few paces away.

"Oh, my God, you're Tamsyn Harris!"

The wide-eyed woman was already scrabbling for her phone. She snapped off a couple of shots as Tamsyn plastered on her best superstar smile.

Jennifer turned to her, one foot already in her car. "Want a lift, darling?"

"Yes, thank you." Tamsyn slid gratefully into the seat alongside Jennifer. "Life-saver," she muttered as she closed the door, shutting out the glare of the flash from the woman's phone.

"Parasites, every last one of them," Jennifer said, her tone scathing. "But I suppose they do pay the bills."

Tamsyn faked a laugh but said nothing. No, she didn't particularly like having a camera rammed in her face every time she left her house, but she'd never considered her fans parasites. She'd forgotten how little she and Jennifer had in common. Thank God they didn't see each other that often.

After being dropped at her door, which she was genuinely grateful for, and air-kissing Jennifer the obligatory three times, Tamsyn could finally shut the evening away. It took her only fifteen minutes to strip off the outer, glamorous layer and let her hair down. The evening had been necessary, but it had frazzled her—from having to listen to Jennifer prattle on right through being haunted by memories of Maggie, and finally being pounced on by an enthusiastic fan. Each one on their own would have been manageable, but as a combination they were deadly to the calm state she'd been attempting to maintain. It was a fragile calm, she knew that; considering contacting Maggie, and knowing that if it went the way she wanted that would more than likely mean coming out, was a pretty big thing to stay calm about.

She poured herself a glass of fizz, having steadfastly refused alcohol in the restaurant, then flopped down on the sofa in front of the fake fire. For the umpteenth time in the last couple of weeks, she wondered where Maggie was, what she was doing, if she ever thought of Tamsyn. Although that last question had pretty much been answered by the publication of the book. She was more and more inclined to believe Carmen's theory about that, rather than her own pessimistic version, but at the same time wondered if it was all just wishful thinking.

As she sipped, she scrolled through emails on her phone, then sat bolt upright, nearly spilling her drink, when she spotted one from Carmen sent while she was at dinner. The subject read 'Operation Maggie is a GO!' and she scrambled to open it.

Hi hon, we're all set. Mickey came through with the email, and it was sent out earlier this evening. Her publisher should see it tomorrow morning at the latest, so fingers crossed!

Carmen had signed off with a smiley face, which made Tamsyn roll her eyes, but at the same time, a tingle of excitement ran through her. She just hoped the bait was big enough to hook the publisher and, in turn, Maggie.

"And this is legit?" Maggie stared at the email from her publisher for the fifth time.

"Well, yes." Polly sounded peeved. "While it is unusual for them to ask to meet with the author, it's not entirely unheard of."

"I wasn't suggesting they were hoodwinking you, Polly." Maggie rolled her eyes. Polly had always been a tad on the sensitive side, but she had been efficient as Maggie's main contact at the publishing house, so she couldn't complain. Moving the phone to her other ear, Maggie used her mouse to scroll down to the original email Polly had received the day before. "I'm just more than a little surprised a Jessica Stewart book would be worthy of dramatisation."

"Don't underestimate yourself," Polly said. "You know how well you sell, and God knows the British public loves a costume drama."

"True," Maggie mused, a small flush of pleasure rushing over her at Polly's words. "So you think I should do it?"

"I don't think it would hurt to have this preliminary meeting with them next week. Don't sign anything, obviously—if there's a contract to be made it will be with us. But I certainly don't have an issue with you having a chat with them. Feel them out, so to speak. I could come with you, but we'd have to reschedule for after Christmas."

"Well, I don't think I want to leave it that long."

"Indeed."

"Okay," Maggie said, her tone decisive even as her insides churned. "Tell them I'll be there."

She heard the sound of keys being tapped. "There, sent," Polly said. "Just listen to what they have to say, and don't—"

"Yes, I know, don't commit to anything. Got it."

They said their goodbyes and Maggie popped the appointment in her phone calendar. She sat back in her chair and gazed out of the window. The small garden at the back of her house was bare, winter having stripped it, and although Gizmo was outside, sniffing at his favourite spots, even he looked despondent in the cold. It wouldn't be long before he was whining to be let back into the house. They'd take a walk a little later, build up an appetite for lunch.

A film company. It was…ridiculous. She refused to get overexcited; chances were, they'd have some stupid idea about how to convert her book to the screen to make it far more glamorous or over-the-top than she'd written it, and although she cared more about the Maddie Jones books than the Jessica Stewart ones, she wasn't going to let anyone mess with her work.

As expected, within minutes Gizmo was scratching at the back door. He shook himself down when she let him in, accepted a ruffling of his cold ears, and then went straight to his water bowl. His noisy lapping made her smile—it had been a few days since she'd properly managed one of those. She knew why: Tamsyn. Seeing her at the restaurant had unsettled Maggie to a degree that she still couldn't quite fathom. Yes, it made her think of Norfolk, and of the wonderful time they'd shared. Yes, it made her wonder for the thousandth time since that trip just what might have been, if Tamsyn had been open to more. But that was eight months ago now, and Maggie really ought to be past the…craving. Only she wasn't—even a brief view of Tamsyn had emphasised that.

I need to get out. Meet someone. Try again.

She snorted. Like she was even remotely interested.

Looking down at Gizmo, who was now staring up at her, licking his chops, she sighed.

"Come on, you. Let's get out. I need some air."

The offices of FilmLight were just off Soho Square, in a modern building that stuck out like a gargoyle amongst the finery of the older structures that surrounded it. Maggie winced at the contrast, bemoaning the crazy planning ideals of the sixties and seventies that had allowed such insults to architecture to be brought to fruition. She hopped up the front step and pushed through the glass doors into a bland lobby enlivened only by large posters on the walls depicting, she presumed, the latest films the company had been involved in.

She had to admit, their résumé was impressive, and a sudden jolt of nerves hit her somewhere low in her belly.

"Hi, can I help you?"

The receptionist was young and chirpy, and Maggie tried her utmost to match her energy, even as she felt more and more out of her depth.

"Jessica Stewart to see Michael Kirby."

"You have an appointment?"

Maggie nodded and waited while the receptionist tapped a few keys and seemed satisfied with what her screen showed her.

"Perfect. Please take a seat and I'll let his assistant know you're here."

Easing herself into the strange-looking chairs that formed a semi-circle across from the receptionist's desk, Maggie braced herself to be flipped backwards, or eaten alive by the layers of fabric slats that made up the seat element, but was surprised to find the chair stable and comfortable. *Although*, she thought, as the slats moved beneath her bottom with each movement she made, *getting up could be another matter*.

She tried to breathe evenly and compose herself.

Just a preliminary meeting. Nothing to worry about. Just listen to what they have to say.

"Ms Stewart?"

She looked up to see a statuesque brunette walking her way, her heels clicking on the tiled floor of the lobby.

"Yes." Maggie rose from the chair, thankful beyond measure she managed it in one smooth action, and shook the proffered hand.

"I'm Scarlett, Mickey's assistant. Please, follow me."

Without waiting for a response, the woman turned on a sixpence and marched off towards a pair of lifts just beyond the reception desk. She punched the 'Up' button and smiled at Maggie as she caught up. The doors opened with a loud ping and Maggie followed Scarlett into the small car.

"How has your day been so far?" Scarlett asked as the doors closed.

"Oh, fine." Maggie's voice croaked, and she winced.

Scarlett smiled but said nothing more. The lift was slow and rumbled as it made its way up to the third floor, which only added to Maggie's nerves. She was relieved when they finally reached their destination and Scarlett led her out of the lift and down a carpeted corridor to a small conference room. It had frosted internal windows that separated it from the harsh lighting of the corridor, and contained only a small round table with six ordinary office chairs circling it.

"Please take a seat. Can I get you anything to drink?"

Maggie smiled in gratitude. "Some water would be perfect, thanks."

"Super. I'll be right back." Scarlett swished round and exited the room.

Maggie breathed out slowly and slipped into one of the chairs, dropping her bag onto the floor beside her and undoing, but not removing, her coat.

It was cold outside and she still hadn't warmed up, and she was too old to worry about impressing this Michael Kirby with the way she dressed.

Scarlett returned a minute later with a bottle of water and a glass, placing them on the table with a wide smile.

"They'll be with you shortly," she said and left, closing the door behind her, before Maggie could do anything more than murmur her thanks and wonder who 'they' were.

She poured herself a half-glass of the water and took a few sips. There wasn't much to see in the room, not even posters like those that lined the reception area, and that told her this was a room normally used for internal meetings, not showing off to clients. If she'd thought about the meeting at all in advance, which she had tried hard not to, she would have assumed they'd be out to impress her, not tuck her away in this pokey little room deep in the building.

It all seemed a little odd, until the door creaked open, and instead of Michael Kirby, she came face-to-face with Tamsyn Harris.

Chapter 19

MAGGIE LOOKED SO SHOCKED, TAMSYN feared for one moment that she might have a stroke of some sort. Her eyes popped wide open, and her mouth followed a moment later. Then she blinked rapidly and swallowed hard.

Closing the door behind her with a soft click, her gaze locked on Maggie's, Tamsyn said, "Hi."

It was all she could manage, now that they were face-to-face again, and she knew it was probably the most idiotic and simplistic start she could have offered to this meeting. Maggie looked incredible, even more beautiful than Tamsyn remembered, and it was as if a mini movie played out in Tamsyn's mind as she looked at her. All the memories of that wonderful time they spent together whizzed by on a high-speed roll through her brain, and heat spread all over her body at the remembrance of how Maggie had felt in her arms, how it felt to kiss that mouth that was still open in shock as Maggie stared at her.

Maggie finally closed her mouth but still said nothing, her gaze darting to the door and back to Tamsyn's face. Then she frowned, and sat slowly back in her chair, confusion writ large all over her features.

"I don't understand," she said, eventually. There was something else in her eyes now, and Tamsyn flinched as she recognised it.

Anger.

"You're Maddie Jones, aren't you?" Tamsyn blurted out, her well-rehearsed lines forgotten in the glare of that anger.

Maggie reeled in her chair. "What?"

"You're Maddie Jones, and you wrote a book about us, about our time in Norfolk." Tamsyn's heart was racing and her words came out in a rush. "I read it. I've read all of your books. I love them." *Oh God, now you sound like a besotted teenager. Get a grip!*

"Wait. Just...wait. You read the Maddie Jones books?" Maggie's eyes were so wide Tamsyn worried they'd never regain their normal shape.

Tamsyn nodded, and inhaled deeply to try to calm her heart rate.

"And you figured Maddie Jones was me?"

Tamsyn's breath caught in her throat. "You... Am I wrong?" Surely not. Surely she hadn't gone to all this trouble only for—

"No, you're not wrong." Maggie spoke in a whisper, shaking her head, then dropped her gaze to the table. She brought her hands up to rest on the wood, and they were trembling. When she looked back up, the confused hurt on her face cut through Tamsyn like a knife. "Tamsyn, what the hell is going on? Why am I here? Why are you?"

"Can...can I sit down? I'll explain everything, I promise. I just need to sit."

Maggie shrugged and motioned with one hand to the chair opposite her own. Tamsyn sank into it, grateful her quaking knees could finally have some rest. She too rested her hands on the table, and tried again to gather her thoughts before speaking.

"I'm sorry, Maggie, for confusing you and..." Why had the power of words escaped her? Maggie stared at her. "Well, here's the thing. I read your latest book and it was us. Or, at least, the first half of it was. And I was so shocked. Shocked that you were her, and, to be honest, shocked you would use our story in one of your books."

"Use?" Maggie arched one eyebrow, her nostrils flaring.

"Wait, no, wrong choice of word." Tamsyn sighed. "Actually, no, I have to be honest. That was my first reaction, that you'd merely used our story to make some money." She winced, waiting for the reaction.

Maggie simply shook her head and looked away, biting at her bottom lip in a move that spoke of her frustration but was also ridiculously sexy, and Tamsyn admonished her libido for going *there*, right now.

"But then a very good friend of mine made me rethink that. She... she had a couple of theories as to why you'd written it, and knowing what I know of you, her theories were vastly superior to my own pathetic take on things." It still staggered her how quickly she'd thought the worst of Maggie. "I'm really not proud of my initial reaction. I was scared of being outed"— Maggie snorted but Tamsyn plunged on—"and I had my usual knee-jerk reaction to that. Luckily for me, Carmen has a better head on her shoulders and made me see sense."

Maggie still wouldn't look at her, and it was causing a pain the likes of which Tamsyn had never experienced.

"Maggie, please. I'm so sorry for thinking that way. I've…I've missed you."

At that, Maggie's head whipped round, and her eyes locked on Tamsyn's. There was a mixture of disbelief and wonder in them, and Tamsyn's heart leaped at the sight.

All or nothing, Tamsyn. She's here, and you're probably only going to get this one chance, so bloody well take it.

"I haven't been able to stop thinking about you ever since I left Norfolk. You…" She chuckled softly, shaking her head at the words she was about to offer up, words she'd never imagined saying in her life. "You torment me. In the nicest way possible of course. And I have no experience of that, and I've been fighting so hard against it, trying to keep the facade maintained. But when I read your book, read our story again, and the ending you imagined for us, something broke in me." She kept her gaze on Maggie, willed her to hear and see the truth of her words. "I wondered what it would be like to have that ending. I wondered if that was what you really wanted, and if I could find you and ask you." She was shaking now but didn't bother trying to hide it. "Maybe this is out of line. Perhaps you're seeing someone. But I couldn't continue asking the 'what ifs', so Carmen helped me set up this elaborate way of getting your attention. I…I didn't have a way to contact you directly, and I couldn't be sure you'd respond if I did, so I apologise for the subterfuge, but I just wanted to be able to sit down with you and, well, spill my guts."

At that, the faintest of smiles did breach Maggie's defences, and then she exhaled slowly, her fingers twisting together in front of her.

"Ever the diva, huh?" she said, but her smile was warm.

"Well, I could have hired a skywriter, I suppose."

They were joking; that had to be a good sign, right?

Maggie's smile widened but she shook her head again. "God, Tamsyn. I...I need a minute to take this all in." She shuffled in her chair and eased her coat off her shoulders. The simple green jumper she wore underneath only set off her hazel eyes more, and they shone in the glare of the overhead lights.

Tamsyn had to swallow hard to fight back the urge to walk around the table and kiss Maggie senseless.

After taking a couple of deep breaths, Maggie said, "I've missed you too. And no, I'm not seeing anyone."

Tamsyn's stomach flipped.

"And yes," Maggie continued, "I did write that book with an ending that I fantasised about us having." She blushed deep pink. "But I never, for one minute, thought it was possible. It was just that, pure fantasy." She sighed. "And now, out of the blue, you track me down and make this declaration and, well, I don't know what to think."

"Sorry, I have rather blindsided you, haven't I?" Tamsyn's stomach rolled in a much more unpleasant way. Maggie looked confused, and unsure, and like she wanted to run.

"Yes, you have." Maggie's voice softened. "And as much as it is wonderful to see you again, I'm just in shock. I can't quite take it all in."

Don't force this. Give her space, no matter how badly you want to be with her right now.

"Okay." Tamsyn swallowed hard. "Then why don't you take some time to think about what I've said, and... Well, about how you feel."

Gratitude swept across Maggie's entire demeanour. She nodded, flexing her fingers against the edge of the table. "I think that's what I need. I..." She looked round the room, her bottom lip trembling. When she turned back, it was clear she was struggling. Her voice croaked as she murmured, "It's all too much."

Tamsyn felt awful, and knew she had to back off. "I understand, and I'm so sorry. Look, can I...can I give you my number? And you can call me any time, whenever you want to talk?"

Maggie nodded, and Tamsyn scrabbled in her handbag for a pen and a piece of paper. The only thing she could find was the receipt from the restaurant the other night, stuffed into an inner pocket. She turned it over and wrote her number in clear, large numerals; the last thing she wanted was for Maggie not to be able to read it.

Upon handing over the receipt, she was intrigued when Maggie turned it over to the printed side and laughed, the sound of it loud in this small room.

"How bizarre," she said.

"What?"

"I was there that night. I...saw you. It's kind of funny that—"

"It *was* you!" Tamsyn didn't know whether to laugh or cry. What a missed opportunity.

"Huh?"

"I saw you. Well, no, that's not true because if I had I would have come over and said something. But I caught a glimpse of someone I thought was you, but I couldn't be sure."

"I was having dinner with my sister. She spotted you and pointed you out. I...I almost didn't want to look. I wasn't sure I could handle the memories resurfacing." Maggie's voice was heavy with longing and it sent shivers down Tamsyn's body.

They stared at each other in silence for a few moments.

"Maggie—"

"Tamsyn—"

They both chuckled.

"You first," Tamsyn said.

Maggie shrugged. "I don't actually know what I want to say." She pushed her hands through her hair and slumped in her chair. "I think I need to go." She snorted. "I assume there is no film deal for my Jessica Stewart book?"

Tamsyn blushed. "No, I'm sorry. That was all just a ruse on my part. Please don't think badly of Mickey. He was just helping me out."

Maggie waved off the apology. "It's fine. I probably would have been too anal about keeping the script true to the book anyway and it would never have got off the ground."

Tamsyn smiled in relief, then struggled to maintain her smile as Maggie began pulling on her coat.

She really is leaving. Shit.

When Maggie was wrapped up again, she tucked Tamsyn's number deep into her handbag and closed it. She looked up, eventually, and gave Tamsyn a wan smile.

"I will call you. I just don't know when."

"Okay." She stood as Maggie did. "Please do. I... God, Maggie, I really want to see you again."

Maggie walked round the table until she stood a foot or so in front of Tamsyn. She gazed into Tamsyn's eyes; Tamsyn held her breath. It was as if Maggie was searching for something and Tamsyn had no clue what it was, so she held her ground and gazed back, drinking in the view, storing up this new memory of Maggie to dwell on later.

"Okay," was all Maggie said before sidestepping around Tamsyn, opening the door, and leaving the room.

———————◆◇◆———————

Tamsyn's phone number burned a hole in her handbag the entire journey back to Putney. When she walked into the house, where she was greeted, as usual, by an exuberant Gizmo, Maggie hastened out of her coat and boots and headed straight for the kitchen. It was only three in the afternoon, but this was a drastic time and called for drastic measures. The first sip of red wine sent an immediate glow into her chest and after another four or five mouthfuls she could actually breathe properly for the first time since walking into FilmLight's offices three hours earlier. She fished the paper with the phone number on it out of her handbag and laid it out on the kitchen table before her.

Gizmo was prowling around her ankles, whining softly, and she realised that in her distraction, she had been remiss in meeting his needs. She let him out into the garden and then back in again a few minutes later. A quick glance out the window told her she had no little packages to clean up and she was grateful for that.

The paper, still sitting benignly where she'd left it on the table, drew her gaze.

Tamsyn bloody Harris.

Of all the things that could have happened in a meeting with a film company, having Tamsyn walk into that grubby conference room was the last thing she would have imagined. Of course, Tamsyn had looked incredible—barest hint of make-up, hair falling in soft waves that caressed the tops of her shoulders. Although, there'd been a tightness about her eyes, and faint dark circles beneath them. She'd looked…troubled, and sad, even as she'd gushed out her jaw-dropping declaration of…what, exactly?

Maggie flopped onto a chair, and let her fingertips scroll across the top of Gizmo's head when he pressed near. It was soothing to her as she tried to sift through her multitude of thoughts. What had Tamsyn actually confessed, and what was she offering? She'd made it quite clear back in Norfolk that she was firmly in the closet, practically in Narnia, and had never dared peep so much as a toe out from its safety in all the years she'd been secretly sleeping with women. There was a difference, though, Maggie had to admit, between what Tamsyn had described her previous…excursions as, and what they had shared in Norfolk. And she knew that wasn't just wishful thinking on her part. The fact that Tamsyn had gone out of her way to set up this elaborate scheme for them to meet was testament to that.

Still, the issue of Tamsyn's closeted status troubled Maggie. She'd never force anyone out if they didn't want to be, but at the same time, there was no way she could get into a relationship with someone who needed to keep her as their dirty little secret.

Yes, but the woman asking you to do that is Tamsyn bloody Harris, for God's sake! You're insane if you're considering turning this down.

Was she? Yes, of course Tamsyn was amazing, and beautiful, and sexy, and Maggie had lusted after her for years. Many people would sacrifice a limb to take what Maggie was being offered right now. Wouldn't they? So why was she holding back? Why wasn't she picking up her phone and calling Tamsyn and simply getting on with being her…?

And that's where the hesitation came from, because what the hell *would* she be to Tamsyn?

The next twenty-four hours passed in a blur, her mind churning it over and over. Finally, sick of her own indecision, she realised she couldn't do this alone. Gizmo whimpered at her side as she sat at the kitchen table again, a cup of tea forgotten in front of her. He knew something was up and had been following her around the house while she ruminated.

"I need help on this, Gizmo. And as you can't talk back, that means it has to be your Aunty Ruth."

He stared up at her, blinked once, then wandered out of the room.

Turning her back on the phone number that continued to flirt with her from its position on the table, she grabbed her mobile from her handbag and dialled her sister.

"Maggie! How are—oh, hang on." Her voice went muffled but Maggie could still hear her next words. "Anna. Anna! Put that down, right now, young lady. Ellie, it's not funny. Both of you, it's time for some TV. Go into the living room and let Mummy talk to Aunty Maggie, okay?"

Maggie chortled as two sweet young voices cried out, "We want to speak to Aunty Maggie!" and Ruth grumbled, "Later. Go on, off to the living room, please."

There were some disgruntled sounds and then, mercifully, silence.

Ruth huffed out a breath. "I bloody hate Christmas."

"No, you don't. It's just the first day since school broke up. You know tomorrow it'll be better."

Ruth grunted. "I suppose so. Anyway, how are you?"

"Um, I'm okay. Sort of."

"What?"

"Well, I could do with a friendly ear to listen to something that's troubling me, but I must admit I forgot the schools had broken up already so you're up to your neck."

"Today I am, and only really because Will's out this evening for his office Christmas party. Ugh. But I'm free tomorrow night, if it can keep until then?"

"Sure. Just text me when you're on your way and I'll get the wine open."

Ruth chuckled. "Perfect. I'll see you tomorrow."

Maggie hung up, a smile on her face. Ruth never let her down. She hadn't even asked what Maggie needed to talk about—just the fact that Maggie needed it was enough.

"You really are earning your bonus this year," Tamsyn said with a rueful smile as she let Carmen into the house.

Carmen laughed. "There's a gorgeous Rolex I've got my eye on. Just saying."

In the living room, a bottle of champagne was already open and sitting in an ice bucket on the coffee table, two glasses beside it. Carmen flopped onto one of the small sofas, at right angles to Tamsyn's seat on the other one, and kicked off her shoes.

"Oh, that's better."

Tamsyn poured them each a glass and handed one over.

"Marvellous, thanks," Carmen murmured. "It's been a long day, which started with a hangover, and this is just the ticket."

They sipped, then Carmen set her glass down and rubbed her hands together.

"So, yesterday's meeting—tell me *everything*."

Tamsyn sighed. "It feels rather pathetic, you know. I'm fifty-two years old. I should be able to work my way through this situation on my own."

Carmen stared at her. "What the hell does age have to do with this? You're attempting something you've never done before. Of course you're allowed to ask for help." She shook her head. "Tamsyn, there's no shame in reaching out. It's all part of losing that armour you've been wearing for so long."

Once again Carmen's wisdom and care brought a lump to Tamsyn's throat. "Thank you," she squeaked out, before clearing her throat and telling Carmen all about the meeting with Maggie.

"How did you feel as she left?" Carmen asked, her tone careful and gentle.

"Terrified," Tamsyn whispered.

"Of?"

"Of her never calling, of her not wanting me, not wanting to take a chance on me. I know," she held up her hands, "I haven't exactly given her a lot to work with on that, with my big 'oh, let's do no strings, I don't do relationships' groundwork, but I'm trying to show her I've changed, that I know now what I've been missing out on. So if she turns me down after hearing that, I'll know it's because she doesn't want me as much as I want her. And the thought of that hurts so much."

"I'm sort of glad."

Tamsyn sat up straight and glared at her. "Care to explain that?"

Carmen shrugged. "It tells me you're still very much invested in her, not just the *idea* of her. I worried for a while that, having found someone who you thought you could have something more meaningful with, you were pursuing it just because it was the first one, not because it was actually

176

her. And hey, you know, it might not have been bad to pursue it anyway, even if it just was the *idea* of being in love that appealed to you."

Tamsyn spluttered champagne at the words 'in love' and Carmen snorted.

"Get over it, Tamsyn." She edged closer and reached out to take Tamsyn's hand. "I will feel terrible for you if Maggie doesn't call, I truly will. But either way I will thank her for showing you what the possibilities are. I'm so proud of you for finally taking this step, however it turns out."

"Thank you." Tamsyn sighed. "And what about the other side of the equation? Me coming out. Have you given any more thought to that and the implications?"

"Well, actually I have. I've chatted to Tony a few times, and I've also been putting out some very subtle feelers with various people in the industry, from producers to directors to casting directors."

Tamsyn's heart dropped to her stomach. "Carmen! What have you said? Who have you talked to? How could you—"

Carmen held up her free hand. "Stop! Calm down. I mentioned no names. Like I said, I was very subtle. Please, trust me."

Exhaling slowly, Tamsyn nodded. "Okay. So?"

Carmen blinked a couple of times. "Well, yes, unfortunately, the consensus of opinion was that it would, for a little while at least, affect the number of roles being sent your way. It's stupid and a waste of acting talent, but it's the reality. However, I did get told by one very prominent director—male, I hasten to point out—that if Helen Mirren suddenly announced she was a dyke, he wouldn't bat an eyelid and would still want her in his next movie. It's about the reputation, not the personal life. For many in the industry, you have that good a reputation. So, we'd have to work a little harder, and I'd have to earn next year's bonus with a certain amount of elbow grease, but I don't think coming out would end your career. Not someone of your calibre."

Tamsyn breathed deeply and pondered Carmen's words. It was slightly better than she'd been expecting, actually. And Carmen was right, she did have calibre. Two BAFTAs and an Emmy weren't to be sniffed at. Of course, it would be nice to have an Oscar to complete the set, but she was no closer to that now by being in the closet anyway. She sat up a little straighter as another thought, even more crystal clear, jumped into her brain: being in the closet wouldn't bring her any closer to Maggie either, or to the chance of happiness with someone else, even if Maggie did turn her down, and she ever got over the loss.

"You okay?" Carmen asked, squeezing Tamsyn's hand.

Tamsyn searched within herself. Was she okay? She still didn't know if Maggie would come back to her, had no idea whether she would be working beyond next March after her current TV project wrapped up but strangely, yes, she was.

"You know what?" she said, letting go of Carmen's hand and reaching for the bottle to top up their glasses, "I am very much okay."

Carmen grinned.

"And," Tamsyn continued, "whatever happens with Maggie, even though it might kill me more than a tad if she doesn't call, I would like to have a meeting with you and Tony to discuss how and when I come out to the public."

Carmen's eyes went wide. "Are you serious?"

Tamsyn nodded, and chinked her glass against Carmen's. "As a heart attack. Which I might have on the day we do it, but let's worry about that later."

Chapter 20

I SHOULD HAVE CANCELLED. TAMSYN sighed as she looked round her kitchen. The dinner she was preparing for herself and Lesley was only halfway to completion and yet the room resembled the aftermath of an explosion in a food factory. *I'm really not in the mood.*

It was obvious why—waiting impatiently to see if Maggie would call was killing her. But she and Lesley had made this arrangement weeks ago, so here she was, in the carnage of her kitchen, desperately trying to summon the enthusiasm to finish making the Moroccan chicken and butternut squash stew that had sounded so delicious when it had popped up in her search for 'easy chicken recipes, low calorie'.

A quick glance at the large clock on the wall told her she needed to move her backside if she was ever going to be ready by the time her guest arrived. *Come on, if nothing else, an evening with Lesley will take your mind off everything.*

She was just pulling on a pair of jeans when the doorbell rang. After hurrying to zip up, she trotted down the stairs. The video intercom in the hallway showed her Lesley's beaming face and she smiled as she opened the door.

"Well, hello stranger," Lesley said, pulling Tamsyn into a bone-crushing hug. "You look *fantastic*, as always."

Tamsyn could barely squeak out a reply. "Thanks. It's good to see you."

Lesley chuckled and finally let go. Tamsyn grinned at her. "You're stronger than ever! What on earth is that personal trainer doing with you?" She shut the door behind them and led Lesley down the hallway.

"Oh, all sorts of things. I *love* it! Feel so energised."

"Good for you." They entered the kitchen and Lesley hummed appreciatively.

"Wow, whatever it is, it smells *amazing*!"

"Yes, it may turn out well. You're being guinea pig tonight for a new recipe."

"I am completely up to the task," Lesley said with a smirk.

Tamsyn pulled a bottle of Perrier from the fridge and dangled it in the air. "Your usual?" Lesley had been teetotal for some years now, and even though she always said she didn't mind if Tamsyn drank in front of her, Tamsyn was more than happy to have an alcohol-free evening.

"Perfect."

Feeling significantly cheerier than she had an hour earlier—Lesley's mere presence could often do that for her—Tamsyn poured them each a glass over ice with a slice of lemon, and they sat at the small bistro style table in the corner of the room.

"Cheers!" Lesley said as they clinked glasses.

They sipped quietly for a moment, Tamsyn's shoulders finally relaxing the tension they'd been carrying around for the last two days. Since she'd met with Maggie...

"You okay, Tamsyn?"

"What? Oh, yes, I'm fine." She sat a little more upright in her chair. "Just tired, you know how it is."

Lesley tilted her head and stared at her. "Are you looking after yourself properly? You seem to have been working an awful lot this year."

Tamsyn sighed before sipping once more at her drink. "It's been a tough year, I can't lie. Although, as Carmen would tell you, most of it's self-inflicted." She chuckled ruefully. "I'm so scared of being a has-been that I'm taking on probably more than I should to prove a point."

"And it's wearing you out."

"Exactly."

"I hardly think *you* could ever be a has-been," Lesley said, a wistful look in her eyes. "Look what you've achieved. Look at the never-ending accolades you receive both here *and* in the US." There was an edge to her tone, warning Tamsyn that, deep down, Lesley did resent her success.

"Yes, well. Enough of that," Tamsyn said brightly, trying to steer them onto a different course. "How's things with Georgie?"

As Tamsyn had anticipated, mention of Lesley's wife made her eyes soften and her smile reappear. "Oh, still in that *blissful* post-wedding state that we hope never comes to an end."

"Good for you!" They had married a year ago. Tamsyn hadn't gone, claiming a work conflict when actually, to her inner shame, she was scared to be seen at something so overtly gay as a same-sex wedding. She'd regretted it on the morning of their big day, but by then it had been too late to make the journey to Georgie's native New York from Berlin, where Tamsyn had been filming, albeit on a short break in between the days that needed her attendance. She'd spent the day locked away in her hotel room in a melancholy state. It was the first time she'd started to question just what her life was all about.

"And how about *you*?" Lesley peered at her over the rim of her glass. "Any joy for you on the romance front?"

Shit, I should have realised that's where she'd head next. Do I tell her?

The answer came surprisingly quickly: yes. She was so tired of keeping everything a secret from everyone. And if Carmen knew about Maggie, then Lesley had every right to, too.

"Well," she said, slowly drawing out the word, "there might be."

Lesley sat up and leaned forward, her eyes bright. "Oh? *Do* tell!"

And so she did. Over the rest of their drinks, on through dinner—which turned out surprisingly tasty—and beyond into coffee on the big couch in the living room.

"She sounds *amazing*, Tamsyn! I'm *so* happy for you." Lesley pulled her into a quick hug. "But, now you're waiting to see if she'll ever call? Oh my God, I don't think I could *bear* the suspense!"

Tamsyn chuckled but it lacked mirth. "I know. It's awful, I can't lie." She shook her head. "I finally seem to have found someone who can take my heart and I don't know if she's willing to take a chance on me."

"Well," Lesley said quickly, "you *could* make that an awful lot easier on yourself if you came out. Hiding her from the world won't make her feel very *special*, will it?"

Sometimes Lesley could be blunt to the point of trauma.

"I am well aware of that," Tamsyn said icily, her hackles rising. She'd thought that after all these years, Lesley would have realised this was no easy matter for her.

"Honestly, Tam." Lesley shook her head, her mouth pinching into a tight line. "Even after all this time, you are *still* hanging on to the back of that large closet you've been hiding in? Aren't you *tired* of it?" Before Tamsyn could answer, Lesley ploughed on. "And just think what you could do for the community if someone as stellar as you came out! You'd have so much support. So much *love*!"

"So much unemployment?" Tamsyn bit back, shifting in her seat, instinctively putting space between them.

Lesley scoffed. "Really, I find it hard to believe, given your stature, that anyone would give two hoots about *your* sexuality."

"If no one gives two hoots, why should I risk it all and make a big public declaration?"

"Because of the message it would send!" Lesley huffed out an extended breath. "Honestly, it's bad enough when these high up politicians hide behind a straight veneer, but closeted movie stars and pop stars are almost as bad." There was a venom in her voice that had Tamsyn reeling as if she'd been struck.

"That's what you really think of me?" she asked in a smaller voice than she would have liked.

Lesley sighed, her gaze somewhere on her own knees. "Honestly? Sometimes, yes." She took a moment to meet Tamsyn's eyes, and they shared a look that told Tamsyn their friendship had been affected by this issue all along, and more deeply than she'd realised.

"What about *me* in all of this?" Tamsyn asked quietly. "What about my feelings, my privacy, *my* life? Does that not count in the scheme for the greater good? The needs of the many outweigh the needs of the few, is that it? It's okay for everyone to know everything about who I'm sleeping with, or spending time with, even though that means I probably can't actually *spend* time with them because of the damn media constantly in our faces, but that's okay if it's 'for the community'?"

"Yes, actually! Because *you* coming out might just make the difference to that *one* teenager, feeling terribly alone in their bedroom late one night, wondering if it's *okay* to be gay. Because seeing you plastered all over the press, being *happy* being gay, could just make the difference between *them* being happy with life or on the edge of suicide!" Lesley's words were more impassioned than they'd ever been, and her hands were clenched into tight fists on her lap.

Tamsyn didn't know what to say. Yes, a lot of what she said struck a chord, but Tamsyn had never felt the need to be a trailblazer for any cause. Hell, she was only just coming to terms with what it might mean to be in a real relationship for the first time in her life—the last thing she wanted was to put that under the microscope of the vicious outside world before she'd become comfortable with it herself.

"I'm sorry," Lesley said quietly, staring at Tamsyn. "I'm not singling you out, but it has been *hard* to watch you all these years, presenting one thing to the world when I knew something different. It's hit a sore spot, with some other things that are in the works right now."

"What things?"

Lesley waved a hand. "I can't really say. Nothing for you to worry about."

She sounded suspiciously vague, but it was obvious she wasn't going to elaborate.

Tamsyn inhaled deeply. "Here's the thing, Lesley. This thing with Maggie, it could be the best thing that's ever happened to me. Don't you think I deserve to see what it might be before I risk it all in front of the world? I do get where you're coming from, really I do. But if I'm going to come out, I want to do it when *I'm* ready, and on my terms. I don't need anyone, even you, telling me I should do it before then, or, God forbid, someone finding out about Maggie and I and spilling it all to the press."

Lesley startled. "*I* wouldn't leak it. I may feel *very* strongly about this subject, but you are still my friend and I don't do that to friends." Her tone was stiff, as was her posture.

Tamsyn reached out and touched her forearm. "I wasn't suggesting you would." *Or was I? Is that what I'm really scared of?* Do *I trust her?*

An uneasy silence fell between them. Tamsyn couldn't believe how the evening had derailed—she'd actually been rather excited to tell Lesley all about Maggie, but now the telling had left a sourness that would take some time to dissipate.

"Well," Lesley said after a moment. "Perhaps I'd better get home. Georgie wants to plan our next holiday. God help me, there'll be brochures spread all over the kitchen table by now and the credit card is about to take a fair beating."

Tamsyn appreciated Lesley's attempt to lighten the atmosphere, and smiled in return. "Oh, come on, she deserves it, doesn't she?"

Lesley's eyes took on that dreamy look again. "Yes, she really does."

Their hug at the door wasn't as close as usual, but Lesley gave her a quick squeeze before letting go and sighing.

"I am *very* happy for you about Maggie. I really hope she calls. Please do let me know how it goes, won't you?"

"I will. And Lesley, I know things were tough in there tonight," she gestured back towards the living room, "but this doesn't change us, okay?"

"God *no*! Of course not. Made of stronger stuff than that, you and me," Lesley said with a lopsided grin, and departed.

Tamsyn locked the door behind her and returned to the living room. She slumped on the couch and switched on the TV, desperately searching for anything that would take her mind off what a car crash of an evening that had turned out to be.

Chapter 21

"Oooh, give me that," Ruth said, reaching for the full glass of wine Maggie had just poured. She gulped down a long mouthful, smacked her lips, and flopped back into the sofa. "Much better."

"Anyone would think you didn't love your children," Maggie said, grinning.

"You know, sometimes I really don't," Ruth deadpanned.

Gizmo trotted into the room and made a beeline for Ruth, laying down across her feet and wriggling until he was comfortable.

Ruth chuckled. "Knows what he wants, doesn't he?"

"Always. I'm so envious of him and his life." Maggie hadn't meant to sound so wistful, but her sister caught the tone immediately.

"So? What's going on?"

Maggie stalled by chomping on a salted almond from the selection of snacks she'd laid out on the coffee table between them, until Ruth's glare made her swallow hard and clear her throat.

"So, remember I told you about the woman I had the fling with back in April?"

"The mysterious uber-famous one in the closet?"

Maggie laughed. "Yes, that's the one." She shook her head. "Well, she made contact with me."

Ruth's eyes went wide. "How? When?"

"Through my publisher. She set up a meeting with a film company to ostensibly talk about dramatising one of the Jessica Stewart books, but actually it was all a smoke screen for her to meet with me."

"Wow! She must like you a *lot*."

"You think?"

"Oh, come *on*! It's so romantic! And think how much work that must have taken. A-plus for effort, I say." Ruth stared at her. "Wait, so you've already met with her?"

Maggie nodded. "Two days ago."

Ruth's frown was deeply etched into her forehead. "So why the hell are you here with me at home when you should be with her?"

"See, therein lies the problem." Maggie shuffled in her seat and tried to relax. "She told me she hadn't stopped thinking about me—that she wanted to see me again, to see what we could have together."

"And? So far I'm not hearing anything that would mean you wouldn't have leaped into her arms in an instant."

Maggie sighed. "She made such a big point of being in the closet when we were together back in April. I can't be someone's secret bit on the side, Ruth. That's not me at all." Ruth nodded. "I mean, I'm not all rainbow T-shirts and going topless at Pride, but I *am* out. To my family, to my friends, hell, even to my neighbours. How can I truly be with T—her, when we wouldn't be able to just go out for a coffee together, or her come to my place without having to be in disguise, or whatever?"

"Okay, fair point. But what did she say about that, about the closeted thing, when you saw her?"

"Well, nothing, that's the problem."

"And you didn't ask?"

"I was in shock!" Maggie snapped. "Tamsyn bloody Harris had just told me she missed me and—" Horror coursed through her as she realised what she'd said, and Ruth's spluttering only made it worse.

"Tamsyn Harris?" Ruth whispered, her hand on her chest. "*Tamsyn Harris?*"

"Shit, I wasn't going to tell you that bit yet. Not until I figured out what—"

"You're actively considering turning down a relationship with Tamsyn bloody Harris?" Ruth was almost shouting.

"I don't care how famous she is—I won't be her dirty little secret. I won't do that for anyone." Maggie's body was hot with her anger. "I know I'm nobody in comparison to her, but I still have pride in myself, you know."

Ruth swallowed, and reached out to touch Maggie's arm. "You're right. God, I'm sorry. I was just thrown by the fact that it's *her*. Your big crush and one of the biggest stars we Brits have produced in ages. I got a bit star-struck. Sorry." She squeezed Maggie's arm. "And trust me, you're not nobody. You're Jessica bloody Stewart. *And* Maddie bloody Jones. I looked you up—you're consistently one of the top sellers in lesbian fiction, and the reviews of your books there are incredible. You are not nobody, Maggie."

Maggie's eyes filled with tears. "Thank you," she squeaked.

Ruth squeezed her arm once more then reached for her wine, taking a couple of slow sips before turning back to face Maggie.

"Okay, so is the closeted thing the only thing stopping you? I mean, we all know she's gorgeous but is she a nice person too?"

"She's wonderful," Maggie said, blushing. "Without all that glamorous stuff, she's really down to earth, very funny, smart, and when she lets herself, she's got a big heart. She's just got so used to keeping it locked tight it takes her a while to shake off the whole famous person outer shell for someone to see what's underneath."

"So, if we forget that she's famous and all that, she's a woman you could see yourself being with? Someone you'd curl up with on a Sunday afternoon on the sofa with a cup of tea and a DVD?"

The image that presented to Maggie spread warmth all the way through her body. "Definitely."

"And how did this one take to her?" Ruth pointed at the still-sleeping Gizmo. "Because we know what a good judge of character he is, after all. Remember how he pretty much chased off that woman who tried to hit on you that time in the brasserie?"

Maggie laughed. "I do remember that. And yes, he loved Tamsyn. And she professed to hating dogs, but within a couple of days he'd totally won her over. She was giving him belly rubs and everything."

"Always was a charmer, this one." Ruth leaned down to scratch the top of Gizmo's head; he twitched but didn't wake. "Well," she said, straightening up, "it sounds like you have just one question to ask her. I admit, it's a pretty big one, but until you get the answer to that, you're never going to know what could happen, are you?"

"I know." Maggie smiled, feeling calmer than she had done for the last forty-eight hours. "You see, I just needed someone to talk me down from the state of panic I'd got myself into."

"Always happy to help, you know that. Especially if there's wine." Ruth reached for the bottle and topped up their glasses.

She stayed for another hour or so, and they chatted about everything except Tamsyn. Maggie could tell her sister was bursting with questions about the actress and the time Maggie had spent with her, but she was grateful Ruth kept them to herself.

"So, are you going to call her?" Ruth pushed her arms into her coat and buttoned it up tight.

Maggie exhaled slowly. "Probably."

"When?" Ruth's gaze was intense.

"Jesus, pressure much? Okay, now. If I don't do it soon, I guess I'll chicken out."

Ruth tilted her head as she stared at Maggie. "You won't do that. You'd torture yourself with the 'what ifs' if you did that. But yes, call her tonight. Invite her over here to talk sometime—you'll feel more comfortable doing it under your terms in your house."

"That's a good idea." Maggie pulled her sister into a hug. "Thank you. For everything."

Ruth looked embarrassed at the overt affection; they were not normally huggers. "You're welcome. I just hope you get the answer you're looking for because I can see you really do feel something for her beyond hero worship."

"I really do."

"But, look out for number one, okay?" Ruth prodded Maggie in the arm. "You definitely don't deserve to be someone's secret, hidden away from the world. If she can't move beyond that, you walk away, you hear?"

Maggie nodded, then said, loudly, "Yes!" when Ruth scowled at her.

"Good," Ruth replied with a nod, then stepped through the doorway and waved as she headed down the short path to the street.

Gizmo's claws tapped on the wooden floor of the hallway behind her, and she turned to face him.

"Right, boy," she said, after sucking in and exhaling a deep breath. "It's time to do this. Stick with me, I may need your support."

He cocked his head, gave one short, sharp bark, then trotted off to the kitchen. Laughing and shaking her head, Maggie followed him. After she'd collected the receipt with Tamsyn's number on it, she walked back to the living room, her knees trembling and her stomach churning. If Tamsyn couldn't make the commitment Maggie needed, this call would all be for nothing and she would be left nursing a wounded heart.

She made herself comfy on the sofa, and Gizmo waited until she was settled before jumping up beside her and snuggling down along the length of her thigh.

Maggie whispered, "You're a mind reader, Giz."

She planted a quick kiss on the top of his head, then closed her eyes for a moment before picking up her phone. It took three attempts to tap in the number, as her trembling forefinger kept missing the correct digits on the tiny keypad. Why did they make the damn things so small anyway?

Eventually she got it, and hesitated only a moment before pressing the icon to dial. With the phone against her ear, she tried to breathe evenly as the call connected, and then rang.

"Hello?" Tamsyn sounded tentative.

"Hi," Maggie croaked, then cleared her throat before saying in a much clearer voice, "It's Maggie."

Tamsyn exhaled. "Maggie." It was only one word, but it carried a weight far beyond its six letters. "I'm so happy to hear from you."

"I... That's good to know." Maggie swallowed. "So, um, I was wondering if we could maybe meet up sometime. I have questions, things I need to know before... Well, before anything more happens."

"I understand." Tamsyn's voice was like soft velvet in her ear. "When are you free? I'm not required on set until after Christmas, so for the next few days, I can make myself available any time that suits you."

There was an earnestness to her tone that warmed Maggie. Already Tamsyn was making an effort, trying to prove herself. It helped.

"Well, I'm free tomorrow from the afternoon onwards, if that's not too soon?"

"Not at all. I...I can't wait to see you again, Maggie."

"Um, how would you feel about coming to my house?"

"I would feel very positively about that." There was a smile in Tamsyn's voice and Maggie chuckled in response. "Will Gizmo be there? I'd love to see his cute little face again."

"Yes, he will. He's right beside me now, in fact."

"Keeping you company?"

"Something like that." Maggie gazed down at him and he stared back, unblinking. "I think...I think he'd like to see you too."

"And you, Maggie," Tamsyn breathed, "would you?"

Maggie swallowed. "Yes, of course. It's just..."

There was a small silence. "I know. Sorry, I shouldn't push. I..." Tamsyn inhaled deeply, then said, "God, I've missed you." Her voice ached with something Maggie didn't dare think about. Not yet.

They didn't speak for a few moments more, then Maggie gathered herself, and cleared her throat again, pushing the words out. "Would two o'clock work for you? We can have some coffee, perhaps a mince pie."

"Well, that's sold it. Bring on the mince pie."

Maggie couldn't help the snort of laughter, relieved that Tamsyn had eased them away from the intensity of the previous moments with her dry humour.

"I'll text you my address. It's, um, it's a quiet street and you should be able to arrive without a mob of people working out who you are, or—"

"Maggie, that's fine, don't worry. I'll see you tomorrow at two, yes?"

"Yes. Perfect. Thanks, Tamsyn."

"No, thank *you*. Thank you so much for calling, I can't tell you how happy that's made me."

"I... You're welcome. See you tomorrow."

They hung up, and with fingers that trembled even more than before she'd called, Maggie tapped her address into a text message and hit send. The three roving dots indicating that Tamsyn was typing a reply popped onto her screen immediately, and she waited, teeth worrying at her bottom lip.

Got it. Thanks again, it means the world to me that you at least want to meet. We'll talk, I promise. Don't hold back, Maggie, ask me anything and everything. I will answer. T x

Maggie slumped back against the sofa cushions, and accepted Gizmo's snuffles against her neck as he stood and stretched on his hind legs to reach her.

Tamsyn sounded deadly serious about this. Did that mean...?

God, I hope so. I don't think I could take losing this before it's got started. Again.

———————◦✕◦———————

Gizmo went supersonic moments before the doorbell rang. Maggie watched in wonder as he sprinted out of the kitchen, claws scrabbling for purchase on the wood floor of the hallway, ears pinned back, and what could only be described as delirious barks issuing out of him.

Guess I'm not the only one who missed her.

She followed him at a more sedate pace, breathing evenly, and held him back by his collar as she opened the door.

Tamsyn smiled radiantly as soon as they came face-to-face, which did nothing to settle the beat of Maggie's heart.

"Hi," Tamsyn said, before looking down at the quivering dog. "And hello to you too, Gizmo."

He yipped, and jumped up at her.

"Come on in." Maggie stepped aside. "If you can get past this one, of course." She pointed at Gizmo, and Tamsyn laughed before stepping carefully around him and into the house.

Maggie closed the door and turned back to see Tamsyn lavishing love and ear ruffles on Gizmo, who stood stock still, almost in a trance. His eyes had glazed over, and Maggie didn't think she'd ever seen him look so contented. She couldn't be affronted; she kind of understood how he felt.

When Tamsyn stood again, her smile was even wider. "Well, that was some welcome."

"He missed you," Maggie said quietly. "After you left Norfolk, he kept waiting by the door for you to come back."

Tamsyn blinked. "Aww, that's..." She swallowed and looked down at Gizmo, who was now sitting at her feet, gazing up at her. "I missed you too, buddy."

"So, shall I take your coat?"

"Thank you, yes. Sorry, I got so distracted by Gizmo I didn't even really say hello to you properly." Tamsyn frowned as she undid the buttons on her cream, woollen coat.

Maggie waved the apology off. "He's good at distracting. I get it."

Tamsyn chuckled, and nodded her thanks when Maggie took the coat from her. "Your house is gorgeous," she said, her gaze moving down the hallway, and then up the staircase. "Well, what I can see of it so far."

"I'll give you the quick tour, shall I, and then we can sit down?"

"Whatever you prefer, Maggie. We can do the tour later or another time or…" Tamsyn's hands were clutched in front of her, and her forehead kept creasing into a frown, as if she were totally unsure about whether she should speak, and if so, what she should say.

"Actually," Maggie said, relaxing as she realised she wasn't the only one who was a mess today, "how about a coffee?"

"Perfect," Tamsyn replied on an exhale.

"Okay, why don't you take a seat in there," Maggie pointed to the living room, "and I'll bring it through in a minute."

Tamsyn nodded and followed Maggie's pointing finger to the living room. Gizmo followed her, his head and tail held high.

Oh, dear—more than one heart could get broken today if we can't work this out.

Maggie sighed and walked slowly to the kitchen. She could have invited Tamsyn into the back of the house to chat while she made the coffee, but she needed a moment, time to collect herself and martial her thoughts. Tamsyn's beauty had, as always, stopped her in her tracks. The thought of taking the 'what the hell' route, and simply marching Tamsyn up to her bedroom was way too tempting, and she'd had to step away. She knew she had to do this right, *if* they were going to do it.

The coffee machine spluttered and gurgled and reminded her yet again that she needed to replace it. However, it did manage to produce two steaming cups of rich, black coffee, and she placed those on a small tray with a little jug of milk, and then took a deep breath before leaving the kitchen.

Tamsyn was sitting on the sofa, not quite at one end, with a dozing Gizmo at her feet. Her hands were on her knees, clenched tight, and again the signs of her nervousness calmed Maggie.

She set the tray on the coffee table and sat down a couple of feet away from Tamsyn, who smiled at her.

"Thank you," Tamsyn said, freeing one white-knuckled hand to gesture at the coffee.

"You're welcome."

There was an awkward moment of silence, then Tamsyn exhaled.

"And thank you for seeing me. For inviting me here. This is a lovely room."

"Mm, my favourite in the house." *Come on, you can't talk about bloody decor the whole afternoon. Just spit it out, that's why she's here after all.* "So, um, I did a lot of thinking after we met the other day."

Tamsyn immediately tensed, her posture rigid, both hands back to clasping her knees through the material of her black, skinny jeans.

"And I realised," Maggie continued, determination now flooding her body, giving her strength. "That I actually only have one question about what you said. I mean," she smiled, unable to help herself, "attraction between us is not the issue, is it?"

Tamsyn's smile was tight, but it did relax her frown lines somewhat.

"And even your exalted status as one of Britain's best-loved actresses isn't even really an issue," Maggie said, chuckling as Tamsyn rolled her eyes. "Although I have no idea how that would feel being the partner of it, if you see what I mean." She locked gazes with Tamsyn. "The biggest issue I have about contemplating a relationship with you, is you not being out. I will never force anyone out, but I live my life very openly as a lesbian and I can't, no matter how strongly I feel about you, get involved with you when I am just going to be your secret thing on the side. I'm sorry if that's—"

Tamsyn held up a hand. "I'm coming out." Her voice was ragged, her eyes shining.

Maggie stared at her. Had she heard correctly? "You... You're what?"

"My PR manager, Tony, and I, plus my agent Carmen, have plans to meet after Christmas to discuss how best to manage it and when to do it. Carmen has laid my mind to rest about my career prospects once I'm out, but, more importantly, I have accepted that it is the right thing to do for *me*, whatever the impact on my career. And," she shuffled in her seat, but didn't take her eyes off Maggie, "I decided all of that before I decided to track you down. I'm doing this for me, not for us, first and foremost. Not to negate what you mean to me, or what I hope you can mean to me, but coming out is separate from that, and it's an important distinction for me to make."

Tamsyn was trembling, and she was blinking back tears, and it was the simplest of instincts that propelled Maggie forward to wrap her arms around the shaking woman, and pull her close, and whisper, "I am so proud of you, and so pleased for you."

Tamsyn sobbed against Maggie's hair, and her arms clutched tight at Maggie's body. There was nothing sexual about the contact, nothing but friendship and support and care.

"I realised," Tamsyn gasped between sobs, "that even if I couldn't be with you, I wanted something like we had. I was lonely, and so tired of being so." She lifted her head, her face blotchy and her eyes still watery. "But just to be clear, I would very much prefer that I *am* with you."

Maggie gazed into those wet, brown eyes and smiled, her heart thumping and joy coursing through her veins.

"Then," she said, her voice croaking with the weight of her emotions, "we'd better make sure that happens, yes?"

Tamsyn's eyes went wide. "Are you... Do you mean that?"

Maggie nodded, and made to speak, to affirm all that she was feeling, but whatever she was going to say was lost in the warmth of Tamsyn's lips pressing against hers, and Tamsyn's arms encircling her back. She let herself sink into the kiss, into the feeling of that mouth on hers, and all the sensations that engendered throughout her whole body. God, she'd missed this. Tamsyn's tongue was tentatively seeking entrance, and Maggie opened to it willingly, moaning at the sweet feel of it stroking against her own, at the increased pressure of Tamsyn's lips, the ragged breathing that told her just how badly Tamsyn wanted her.

When they emerged from the kiss a couple of minutes later, Tamsyn's eyes were damp again, but her smile was wide.

"You just made me so happy, Maggie."

Maggie ran the fingertips of one hand down Tamsyn's cheek. "Myself too."

Tamsyn laughed gently. "I have no idea what happens now." She shrugged. "I've never been in a relationship before."

Maggie laughed, and kissed her. "Don't worry, I'll teach you all you need to know."

Raising her eyebrows, Tamsyn said, "Sounds interesting."

Maggie rolled her eyes, but her heart was doing cartwheels and her skin tingled.

Then Tamsyn's face turned serious. "It's true though. I really don't know. I'm worried I'll make mistakes, or ruin things before they've even got started, or—"

Taking Tamsyn's face in both hands, Maggie said, "Relax. Breathe." Tamsyn grinned and nodded. "We'll both make mistakes as we navigate this. But we'll just keep talking to each other, and being honest with each other, and if it's meant to be, it will work."

"If?" Tamsyn's eyes looked haunted.

"I… Look, we're both too old for games and false promises. And you're not even out yet, so you've got a whole minefield waiting for you with that." Maggie rubbed a thumb across Tamsyn's soft lips. "At the risk of sounding far too practical, we don't really know each other that well. Not yet. Yes," she said, rushing on as Tamsyn made to interrupt, "we had an amazing nine days together. But that was eight months ago. We need to take our time to learn each other. Reconnect. See if what we had back then is as amazing as we both remember."

Tamsyn smiled then. "I think it will be."

"And I love your optimism. Don't get me wrong, I'm optimistic too, but I'm also a realist."

"Fair point." Tamsyn dropped a gentle kiss on Maggie's lips. "So, in the spirit of learning each other, how about I get that tour of the house now? And I believe someone promised me a mince pie?"

Maggie laughed, and reached for Tamsyn's hand, which was warm within her own. "I did indeed. Right this way, ma'am."

Maggie's house was lovely, and everything about it spoke of the woman who led her by the hand through each room. There was a warmth here, in the colours Maggie had chosen to paint each of the rooms, in the furnishings she'd used—rich-coloured woods, soft but thick fabrics for the curtains, the cushions, the bedding. And there were books. Everywhere.

Tamsyn smiled as Maggie blushed while showing off her own 'honour' shelf in the living room, where hardback copies of all the Jessica Stewart novels were flanked by the awards she'd won for them.

"Don't blush. You *should* be proud of this."

"Have you got something similar, for your BAFTAs and the Emmy?"

"I'm flattered you know exactly what I've won." Maggie blushed again, and Tamsyn raised one eyebrow. "What?"

"Well, you know I've had a lifelong crush on you, since I was a teenager."

"Ah, yes." Tamsyn grinned.

"So, you know, I've followed your career quite closely."

Tamsyn's grin widened. "'Quite closely'," she said, smirking.

"Don't let it swell your head." Maggie dug Tamsyn in the ribs.

"Ouch!"

"Serves your big diva head right." Maggie chuckled, and Tamsyn stole a kiss. God, being able to kiss Maggie again was heavenly. Underneath their interactions was a simmering of the passion they'd shared all those months ago, but Tamsyn was content to let it do just that, simmer. For now, they needed closeness rather than nakedness, and being in Maggie's home like this, joking and teasing, and learning things about each other, was perfectly satisfying. And being with Maggie had helped Tamsyn forget the worries that her evening with Lesley had stirred up. She *was* determined to come out—mostly—but she really did want to do it in her own time and ease herself into what would be a stunning change in the public's perception of her.

"Fair enough," Tamsyn said, still holding Maggie close. "And yes, I do have a shelf with my awards. Not the first thing you see when you walk in my house, but certainly on show. We worked hard for these things," she pointed at Maggie's trophies, "so we have every right to show them off."

"Hear, hear." Maggie pulled back. "And now I'm going to show you something no one else has seen."

Intrigued, Tamsyn let Maggie pull her into her study. This was the cutest room in the house, a small space tucked next to the kitchen at the back of the house, with a window looking out to the small garden, and furnished with only a simple, small desk, a well-worn chair, and two small bookcases overflowing with tomes of all sizes.

Maggie pointed to a shelf above the desk, and Tamsyn smiled.

"Maddie Jones," she breathed, her eyes taking in the spines of all nine books Maggie had published under that name. Dotted in amongst the books were awards for these too. "But why is this hidden in here and not on display in the living room with the Jessica Stewarts?"

"Maddie Jones is my deep secret." Maggie sighed. "When I was such an instant success as Jessica Stewart, I didn't want to run the risk of the two personas crossing over. I couldn't imagine my lesbian readers being that impressed that I wrote bodice-ripping straight romances, and vice versa." She shrugged. "It became a habit to keep those two aspects of myself so far apart, but now... Well, now I wonder if that was a mistake. One of the things I came to terms with in Norfolk was that I, too, was not living the life I truly wanted. And keeping Maddie Jones a secret was part of that."

"So, no one knows?"

"You. And I told my sister, Ruth, only recently."

Tamsyn slowly ran a hand up Maggie's arm. "Yes, I think you're right. I think Maddie Jones also needs to come out now."

Maggie laughed, and leaned in to give her a kiss, which, even though it was gentle and brief, still sent sparks of something much deeper than lust pinging along Tamsyn's spine.

"Very true." Maggie glanced up at the shelf, then back to her. "Mince pie time?"

Tamsyn rubbed her hands together and grinned. "Hell yes."

The afternoon passed in a delicious haze of conversation, mince pies—two each—and coffee. They talked about what they had each been up to in the intervening months, and fascinated each other with background info about their professional lives.

"Maybe one day," Tamsyn said, reaching for Maggie's hand across the table, "when I'm fully out and the dust has settled, you could come to a set, and watch me at work."

Maggie's eyebrows shot up. "Seriously? That's possible?"

"Hey, I'm not one of Britain's best-loved actresses for nothing, you know." She grinned.

"I'd love that," Maggie said, for once sounding amusingly like the star-struck fan.

Into the silence that suddenly fell between them, a loud ping from the hallway announced a reminder on Tamsyn's phone, and her memory jerked awake.

"Oh, damn." She groaned. "I'm so sorry, I completely forgot I have to be somewhere tonight. In all the excitement and nerves it totally slipped my mind, but that ping has just told me I have a rather boring dinner tonight with the producer of the show I'm filming right now." She smiled at Maggie. "But don't ever tell her I think she's boring if you meet her, okay?"

Maggie laughed, and it lit up her face. Tamsyn drank in the sight, storing up every feature, every molecule of smooth, lightly tanned skin until whenever they could see each other next.

"Your secret is safe with me." Maggie pushed back her chair and stood.

"Maggie, if I could get out of it, I would, I—"

"Tamsyn, it's fine. Honestly. We both have commitments like that. Everybody does. Relax."

Every time Maggie said that word it had the intended effect. Tamsyn's shoulders loosened, her breathing eased, and a smile broke out across her face.

"You're very good at doing that, you know."

"What?"

"Calming me down." Tamsyn walked around the table to pull Maggie into her arms. It felt so good to hold her this close, to inhale the scent of her hair, have the warmth of her invade Tamsyn's body.

"Mmm," Maggie murmured, her mouth close to Tamsyn's neck, her lips a teasing breath away from touching it.

"I might need that from you in the next few weeks," Tamsyn admitted, only slightly worried about being so honest. "It's not going to be easy."

Maggie eased away to look at her. "I know. And I'll be here for you. Promise."

A rush of heat that had nothing to do with the proximity of their bodies swept through Tamsyn, and she glanced once at Maggie's lips before pressing her own against them once more. Maggie felt so perfect in her arms, and her mouth transported Tamsyn to somewhere everything else was forgotten. Maggie's tongue pushed deeper into Tamsyn's mouth as her arms tightened, and between Tamsyn's legs a throbbing started that was so intense it was almost painful.

"What are you doing tomorrow evening?" Tamsyn asked, breathless.

"Babysitting my two nieces," Maggie replied with a grimace. "Saturday? I know it's the twenty-third, and pretty close to Christmas, but—"

"Saturday is perfect," Tamsyn jumped in. "Come to my place? Dinner?"

Maggie's eyes shone. "I'd love that."

"Wonderful." She stole another kiss, then reluctantly pulled away. "Okay, I need to call my car firm to get a ride home but as soon as I've done that, can we have some more of this," she kissed Maggie again, "while we wait?"

Maggie grinned. "Oh, yes. Definitely."

Chapter 22

"WHERE THE HELL ARE THE napkins?" Tamsyn said to no one as she rushed from one side of the kitchen to the other. *Great, senility can only be a whisker away.*

She pulled open drawer after drawer, slamming the last one shut in frustration when the napkins failed to appear. Maggie was due to arrive in less than fifteen minutes and the perfect table Tamsyn had hoped to display was far from it. Abandoning the napkin quest for now, she concentrated on lining up the cutlery, the glasses, and the antique silver salt and pepper shakers that had been a gift from her mother before she'd died. Next the champagne was placed in its cooler on a mat in the centre of the table, with two elegant crystal flute glasses next to their sister water glasses. None of these fancy accoutrements had seen the light of day in months, possibly years. But she wanted everything to be perfect tonight and had sent her own head into a tailspin.

The timer on the oven pinged and she dashed over to stare through its window. The bubbling around the edges of the dish told her the fish pie was done, so she dialled the temperature knob back to a 'keep me warm but don't cook me any more' level and huffed out a breath to blow a stray strand of hair out of her eyes. A quick glance over her shoulder at the clock on the wall told her she now had less than five minutes to find the bloody napkins.

After ripping off the apron she'd worn to protect her little black dress, and stowing it in the washing machine out of sight, she trotted down the hallway—there was only one place left the pesky napkins could be hiding. She let out a whoop of triumph when they revealed themselves in the middle drawer of the sideboard where she stored all that stuff you only ever needed to use once a year.

She had just finished folding the second of the two napkins when the doorbell rang, and her heart, which had been beating a fairly rapid pace for the last twenty minutes or so, jumped up to fifth gear.

"Come on, it's Maggie. It's okay," she muttered to herself as she used the reflective qualities of the oven door to check her hair one more time.

Breathing in and out a few times, she walked down the hallway to check the video intercom. There was Maggie. Her stomach flip-flopped. She took a deep breath and pulled open the front door. Her heart calmed, as did her breathing, and a smile broke out on her face.

"Hi, come on in. You're right on time."

Maggie returned the smile. "I always am. My mother was a stickler for punctuality when we were growing up and I've never shaken it off." She looked Tamsyn up and down, not bothering to hide that she was doing so. "You look incredible in that dress," she whispered.

Tamsyn swallowed, her body sizzling under the intensity of Maggie's gaze.

Her smile widening, Maggie stepped into the house and Tamsyn, her hands trembling, helped her out of her coat, hanging it in the cupboard in the hallway. When she turned back, Maggie was gazing around her at what Tamsyn knew was an impressive entryway.

"Wow," Maggie whispered, her eyes wide. "You've done all right for yourself, haven't you?"

Tamsyn snorted. She loved that Maggie had gone for a joke rather than politeness. "Well, you know, it's not much but I like to call it home."

Maggie stuck out her tongue and Tamsyn roared with laughter. *God, this woman...* She looked amazing tonight—the deep red silky shirt and black dress trousers showed off every subtle curve of Maggie's body, and she was wearing heeled boots that made her a tad taller than Tamsyn. Being shorter was a new feeling for her, and she liked it.

"Want the tour before we eat? And would you like a glass of something while we do that?"

"Oh, two marvellous ideas rolled into one. Love it."

With glasses of champagne in their hands, Tamsyn led Maggie on a strolling tour of the house. With three reception rooms, one of which doubled as a formal dining room, and four bedrooms, the house wasn't small and the tour wasn't short, but it was fun. Maggie seemed genuinely impressed with Tamsyn's taste in decor—"At least you haven't gone totally diva with gold everywhere"—and squeezed Tamsyn's hand when she confessed to buying the fake fire in the living room based on her memories of their time in front of real ones in Norfolk.

"Yes, those fires were wonderful, weren't they?" Maggie's gaze softened, and her hand held Tamsyn's tightly. "Maybe one day we could go somewhere like that again."

Tamsyn swallowed down the emotion that clawed at her throat. "I'd like that. Very much."

Maggie kissed her then, good and proper kissed her, and it left her breathless and aching and unable to remember her own name.

"We... There's... Dinner?" Tamsyn stammered, aware of every cell in her body, all of them throbbing with need in the face of the expression Maggie wore. There was tenderness, and hope, and affection, and...desire. It was an intoxicating cocktail, but Tamsyn had promised herself she wouldn't rush things, wouldn't sprint them back to the physical side of their connection while they got used to the idea that they had much more than that. It was mighty difficult to remember that at the moment.

Shaking her head slightly, Maggie murmured, "Sure. Dinner sounds good."

Over the starter of gravlax, they caught each other up on their previous couple of days. Tamsyn's dinner with the boring producer took all of two sentences to describe but Maggie still laughed in all the right places. Then it was Tamsyn's turn to guffaw as Maggie regaled her with stories of Anna and Ellie, her precocious eight-year-old nieces.

"The thing is, neither Ruth nor Will are up themselves, so none of us have a clue where the girls are getting this from," Maggie said, after swallowing the last bite of her salmon. "And before you ask, no, they haven't been sent to some posh private school. It's as if they've come to this princess-like state all by themselves."

"I love that they think Cheddar is no longer appropriate for their lunch boxes, and only chèvre will do."

"I know, right? I mean, when I was eight I just thought cheese was cheese. No idea it came in so many different varieties."

"Oh, me neither. As you know from online stalking me." She chuckled as Maggie tutted. "I came from a nice, ordinary background too. Hell, I didn't even eat my first olive until I was twenty-three."

Maggie clutched at her chest. "*Quelle horreur.*"

Tamsyn threw a small piece of bread at her, which Maggie caught more deftly than she would have imagined, before popping it in her mouth and chewing it.

"Hey, that was mine!"

"What's yours is mine." Maggie's grin was wide and her eyes sparkled with mirth.

"Right," Tamsyn said, sitting back and folding her arms. "Now I see how it's going to be."

"Oh yeah, get used to it." Maggie matched Tamsyn's pose and her grin widened.

Tamsyn leaned forward, dropped her voice an octave, and said, "You know, I think I'll enjoy doing just that." She smiled as Maggie mimed sliding off her chair.

"So not fair," Maggie muttered. "Bringing out the Tamsyn bloody Harris seductive thingy."

"Thingy?" Tamsyn arched her eyebrows, trying—and failing—not to smirk.

Maggie waved a hand. "That thing you do with your voice lowering, and your eyes narrowing, and, you know, the breathing."

"Breathing?" Tamsyn was now genuinely mystified.

"Yeah, you do this thing with your breath. It's like, all in and out and sexy." Maggie was blushing but smiling.

"'In and out and sexy'. Wow, that's, um…"

"Yeah, yeah, I know, it makes *no* sense at all. But it's a thing, okay? And you're very good at it."

Tamsyn stood and walked round the table. Just before her lips met Maggie's, she said, "I bloody well hope so."

The kiss was fireworks and explosions and heat. Their tongues stroked together and they both groaned. Maggie's hands clutched at Tamsyn's hips, and even through the fabric of her dress she could feel the heat from Maggie's fingers and wanted that heat in other places, inside and out.

They pulled back, panting heavily.

"How hungry are you?" Maggie whispered raggedly.

"Not," Tamsyn rasped.

She grabbed Maggie's hands and tugged her up out of her chair. She didn't ask, because she knew she didn't need to. Nor did she even look back, simply pulled Maggie along with her.

The master bedroom was cool, the way Tamsyn liked it, but when she offered to turn the heating on Maggie smiled and shook her head before walking into Tamsyn's arms. This kiss was deep, and slow, and long. The spark that had been lit down in the kitchen flared into full-blown flames. Tamsyn was throbbing, and although aching for Maggie's touch, she wanted to instead do everything to Maggie that she'd been fantasising about since they'd parted eight long months ago.

She broke their kiss only to nudge Maggie back towards the bed. When they reached it, she started undoing the buttons on Maggie's silk shirt, delighting in the texture of the material beneath her fingers, the way it shimmered as it parted to reveal Maggie's pale skin beneath.

"I can't wait to touch you," Tamsyn whispered as she pushed Maggie's shirt back from her shoulders. It dropped to the floor in a gentle swish of sound and she gazed at Maggie's breasts, enclosed—barely—in a lacy half-cup bra that made Tamsyn's mouth go dry.

"Good God," she said, before reaching out and cupping a breast in each hand. The weight of them was just as she remembered: perfect. As was the tiny gasp that left Maggie's throat. Using her thumbs, she eased the lace down on each cup until Maggie's hard nipples were revealed, then she dipped her head and licked each one in turn. Maggie pushed against her, moaning.

"More," she murmured. "Please."

"Yes." She fumbled for the zip on Maggie's trousers and pulled it down as fast as she could once she'd finally got a decent hold on it. The trousers, too, fell to the floor, and she stepped back for a moment to allow Maggie to kick them off properly, and ease off her boots and socks with them. Then Maggie stood in her underwear, the bra still pulled down over her nipples, the matching lacy bikinis highlighting the width of Maggie's hips. Tamsyn instantly reached out to place her hands on those hips and pull Maggie nearer.

"You are so beautiful. And I have missed you so much." Tamsyn's voice was thick with the emotion that was swamping her.

"Oh, God, I've missed you too." Maggie pulled her close and kissed her, thrusting her tongue deep into Tamsyn's mouth, her hands frantic on Tamsyn's still-clothed body.

"Lay down," Tamsyn panted. "I need to touch you."

Maggie rapidly complied, easing herself back on top of the duvet. She looked wanton in a way that was so sexy it robbed Tamsyn of breath. Her arms were thrown up over her head, her legs slightly parted, and her eyes were heavy with need. Tamsyn scrambled out of her dress and shoes, smiling at Maggie's appreciative groan when her own sexy black underwear was revealed. The plunge bra was one of her favourites, and she'd rather hoped one day Maggie would get to appreciate it.

"Come here," Maggie commanded, and Tamsyn went willingly.

As she bent over Maggie, her legs straddling Maggie's thighs, Maggie reached for her breasts, cupping them inside the bra, making them both moan. She tugged Tamsyn down, and laved her breasts with her tongue, licking and sucking until Tamsyn was groaning at an octave lower than she'd thought possible. She ran her fingers over Maggie's skin, from her breasts to her belly, then over Maggie's pussy, teasing with her nails as she dragged them up over the fabric of the bikinis. Maggie gasped, pushing her head back against the pillow and arching her back.

"Oh, God, Tamsyn. Please."

Tamsyn didn't respond, merely moved so that she could lie beside Maggie. She slipped one arm under Maggie's shoulders and pulled her close, leaning down to kiss her, savouring the sweet taste of Maggie's mouth, licking at her top lip before slowly dragging her tongue along her bottom lip, then plunging back into her mouth. Maggie was in constant motion beneath her, pushing her hips upwards, seeking more contact. Tamsyn obliged, running her free hand back down Maggie's body, sliding beneath the waistband of the bikinis, and, not wanting to drag this out for either of them—there'd be plenty of time for that later—ran two fingers down through Maggie's hot, wet, pussy, skimming her clit and finishing pressed against her entrance.

"Oh, Jesus!" Maggie's voice was ragged, the words shredded as they left her lips, and Tamsyn's own pussy pounded painfully in response.

The constriction caused by the bikinis was now a massive hindrance, and Tamsyn pulled her fingers out again, stifling Maggie's complaints with a kiss as her hand yanked at the fabric of the underwear. Maggie immediately understood what she was trying to do and helped with her free hand, the one that was not clasped to Tamsyn's back. Between them they wrestled the bikinis down beyond Maggie's knees so she could kick them away, and as soon as she had done so, Tamsyn pushed Maggie's legs apart.

"Let me look at you," she said as she broke their kiss.

Maggie gazed up at her, eyes so heavy they were almost closed, breathing chopped and warm on Tamsyn's face. She opened her legs even wider and Tamsyn lifted herself a few inches to gaze down at the wetness that was revealed. She turned back to kiss Maggie again, mouths ravenous, lips bruising in their passion. Running her hand up the inside of Maggie's thigh, the warm skin like soft butter beneath her touch, she groaned into Maggie's mouth. Then she reached Maggie's pussy, and once again didn't hesitate, slipping through her wet warmth, pushing a single finger deep inside her in one smooth stroke.

Maggie cried out and clutched at Tamsyn with both hands, pulling her down, and closer, and into another searing kiss while Tamsyn worked her finger in and out, keeping her thrusts slow, yet deep. The sounds Maggie made against her mouth, the feel of her hot skin pressed up against so much of Tamsyn's, the beautiful wet warmth that enveloped her finger, had Tamsyn on the edge of her own orgasm faster than she would have thought possible. She dragged her finger out of Maggie and ran it up between the folds of her pussy to her clit. Maggie bucked and moaned, and so she repeated the action, dipping into Maggie then dragging back up to her clit. Over and over, all the time thrusting her hips, desperate for some sort of friction that would ease the ache between her own legs. They rocked together, and Maggie got tighter and tighter around her finger until Tamsyn simply concentrated on stroking her hard clit. She used long, slow movements, back and forth, never increasing her pace, keeping it steady until Maggie arched completely off the bed and gasped into Tamsyn's mouth, her nails digging into Tamsyn's biceps.

"So beautiful," Tamsyn whispered, placing soft kisses all over Maggie's face as she quivered in her arms. "God, so beautiful."

Maggie's fingers, still gripping her biceps, twitched convulsively along with her hips. Tamsyn had stopped moving her finger, but it was still captured within the swollen folds of Maggie's pussy and it seemed Maggie had no intention of letting it go. Tamsyn was still undulating her hips against Maggie, her own pleasure at a plateau that could simmer for a while longer before she would need Maggie to do something about it. Even as she had that thought, Maggie was opening her eyes, and smiling up at her, and moving her free hand down from Tamsyn's arm to her hip.

"How close are you?" Maggie rasped.

"Oh, God, *so* close."

"Give me...a little...room." Maggie squirmed her free arm between them and Tamsyn rolled slightly so her hips opened up, pulling her hand away from Maggie's pussy but allowing Maggie to easily slip her hand onto Tamsyn's belly and down inside the wisp of a G-string Tamsyn was wearing.

"Oh, Maggie...*yes*."

Tamsyn thought for a moment she might come from just that first touch upon her clit but then Maggie moved down, into her wetness, and thrust inside her. White light splashed across Tamsyn's closed eyelids, and pleasure rippled through her body. Maggie stroked her much the same way she herself had been stroked moments before, and it was wonderful, experiencing what her lover must have felt. Tamsyn rocked against Maggie's hand, making sounds that might have been words; she couldn't be sure. Maggie's fingers were firm in their touch, and perfect in their rhythm, and oh dear God this wasn't going to take long. In the next moment, all thought stopped, her brain shut down, and pleasure took over. The orgasm rolled over her and through her like a tidal wave. She pressed against Maggie, holding that warm body close, as pulse after pulse of intense sensation thrummed through her entire body, centred on her clit but throbbing over every inch of her. She stopped breathing for a few moments, her mouth open in a silent cry as even the power of sound deserted her.

When it had finally run its course, finally let her loose from its grip, she flopped back on the bed beside Maggie, her heart pounding, her breathing a mess, her eyes shut tight. Maggie wrapped her arms around her and held her, kissing her shoulder, her neck, then nuzzling her nose into that soft spot below Tamsyn's ear.

"That was…" Tamsyn gasped out, her mind still lost behind a wall of white noise.

"Yes," Maggie replied, "it was." She snuggled even closer, and Tamsyn wrapped her arms around Maggie, and they lay quietly, listening to each other breathe.

They were eating fish pie, naked, in bed. Maggie was sure there was dirty joke in there somewhere, but she didn't have the energy to conjure it up. Instead she concentrated on forking more of the delicious food into her waiting mouth, humming in happiness every time she did so.

"You okay there?" Tamsyn asked, in between mouthfuls.

"This," Maggie said, pointing at the plate she held in her left hand with the fork she held in her right, "is bloody amazing."

"Why, thank you." Tamsyn made a small bow of acknowledgement with her head.

"Seriously, you're a fabulous cook. I sort of knew that from Norfolk but this just vindicates it." She loaded up her fork again with the seafood and potato mix, its deliciously rich sauce coating the entire little package, and popped it into her mouth. The flavours exploded on her tongue and she closed her eyes, knowing that right now, eating this food, sitting in this bed with this woman beside her, having just spent two hours making spectacular love to each other, she was as close to heaven on Earth as she was likely to get. Who'd have thought that would ever happen with the woman she'd crushed on all these years? Life sure was strange.

"I'm just so glad it didn't burn or dry out in the time it sat in the oven waiting for us," Tamsyn said with a grin. "Because, I mean, we did rather keep it waiting."

"Oh, yeah," Maggie murmured. "And it was *so* worth it."

"I'll say!"

They munched on in comfortable silence until both their plates were clear. Maggie was tempted to literally lick hers clean but wasn't sure if Tamsyn was ready to see that side of her yet, then laughed out loud as Tamsyn cast her a sly glance and promptly ran her tongue over her own plate. Maggie picked up hers and they raced each other to see who could lick her plate clean the fastest. By the time they'd finished, they were laughing so hard there were tears running down their faces and remnants of fish pie smearing their lips and chins.

"You're insane," Maggie said, using her thumb to divest Tamsyn's chin of a piece of potato.

"Huh, like you're not." Tamsyn grinned and dived forward to lick Maggie's chin clean too.

"Ugh, that reminds me of one of Gizmo's tongue baths." Maggie dragged the back of her hand across her face to wipe away the wetness Tamsyn had left behind.

"Talking of my favourite dog, where is he tonight? Not home alone, surely?"

Maggie shook her head. "No, he's at his favourite dog-sitting service." She grinned. "Anna and Ellie. He *loves* them, and they adore him. Ruth loves it too because she says it's the only time the two girls are in total agreement about something, spending the whole evening laid out in their play room with Gizmo between them. It's completely adorable to watch."

"Aw, I bet it is."

Maggie startled herself with a crazy thought that popped into her head. It was too soon, wasn't it? But what if...

She cleared her throat. "So, um, here's a question."

"Hmm?" Tamsyn snuggled closer, dropping a trail of small kisses on Maggie's shoulder.

"Well, I was wondering. What are your plans for Christmas Day?" Maggie's heart was beating a rapid tattoo.

Tamsyn raised her head, her eyes wide. "Christmas Day?"

Maggie's stomach flipped. "Yeah, you're right, it's too soon. It was just—"

"No, wait! Why were you asking?" Tamsyn looked earnest, and she reached out to hold Maggie's hand, squeezing tight.

"Well, you know, I was wondering if you wanted to join me and my family." Maggie's cheeks were blazing, but she carried on, given that Tamsyn was still looking at her, somewhat expectantly. "I'm hosting this year. And, you know, if nothing else I could use the help in the kitchen. You seem to know your way around one, if that was any indication." Maggie pointed at her empty plate, abandoned on the bed beside her, and painted a smile on her face in an attempt to quell the nerves that were dancing a frenzy in her belly.

Tamsyn affected a haughty tone. "Oh, really? I'm good for helping out in the kitchen?" Her eyebrows rose but there was a glimmer in her eyes that immediately told Maggie this was all for show. "Do you know who I am?" Tamsyn said, in a remarkably good impression of Maggie Smith in *Downton Abbey*. "Double BAFTA winner, Emmy winner, numerous other awards from organisations around the *entire* world, and *you* want *me* to scrub your pots on Christmas Day?"

"Well," Maggie said, heart thudding but determined to play along until she got a straight answer, "when you put it like that, I suppose it was a tad presumptuous of me. All right, you win—you can chop vegetables, not clean pots."

Tamsyn burst out laughing, her plate nearly toppling off the bed as her body shook with mirth. "I am so glad," she said, pressing closer, "that you don't let me get away with that crap."

Maggie shrugged and kissed her. "I don't because I know it's not the real you."

"That is very true." Tamsyn's mood shifted to sombre. "And, my gorgeous woman, I would love to spend Christmas Day with you. Thank you very much for asking."

She gazed at Maggie, and there was heat there, yes, but underneath was tenderness and affection that set Maggie's heart pounding with a new kind of joy: excitement for the future.

Chapter 23

TAMSYN WAS HUMMING TO HERSELF as she made them a morning cup of tea, when her phone pinged from inside her handbag which was hanging from one of the chairs at the bistro table. She smiled ruefully as she realised just how distracted her time with Maggie had made her; she hadn't once thought to check her phone for messages or emails. It had been wonderful waking up next to her—not like before, when Maggie would have to get up at midnight and do the walk of shame back to her own cottage. Instead, Tamsyn had pulled Maggie into her arms in the early hours and kissed her lovingly goodnight. Maggie had sleepily mumbled, "Are you sure?" which had earned her another kiss, and then they'd fallen into a deep sleep together. Maggie's smile this morning had been a sight to behold.

She retrieved her phone while the kettle boiled. A message from Carmen made her blood run cold.

Have you seen the news? Looks like your friend Lesley is back in the limelight, and not for the best of reasons in my opinion. Outing someone? Really? We may need to do some distancing here. Call me

Tamsyn closed her eyes briefly. *Oh, Jesus, what has she done?*

Scrolling quickly to her news app, her stomach plummeted to the floor as she read the main headline and the first few sentences of the article beneath it:

CABINET MINISTER FACING CALLS TO RESIGN

After the shocked revelation that he is gay and living a secret life with a man ten years younger than himself, Duncan Harewood, MP for Manchester South and married to wife Ingrid for fifteen years, is facing calls this morning to resign from the government. In a surprise move last night, the LGBT rights group SHOUT made public the details of Mr Harewood's private life, saying it was for the good of the gay community, and the general public. Spokeswoman Lesley Jenkins-Garcia told reporters, "It's time that the men and women who make the decisions that affect all of us do so with nothing to hide. It is no shame to be gay, not in the 21st century, yet Mr Harewood's continued campaign to hide his sexuality undermines so many of the advances we in the LGBT community have made in recent decades. I call on all public faces in politics and the arts to make a stand, and to live proudly out!"

Tamsyn gripped the phone so tightly she wondered vaguely if it might crack under the pressure.

Oh, my God, is this the special campaign she was so excited about? Is this what she was hinting at the last time we spoke?

Tamsyn scrolled down further.

The outing of Mr Harewood has divided public opinion, with many claiming this is an unforgivable breach of Mr Harewood's privacy, while others support what Ms Jenkins-Garcia's group are trying to achieve.

She switched to Twitter, where it took less than thirty seconds to see evidence of that divided opinion. Many out politicians, actors, and musicians were lambasting the move, and criticism of Lesley, in particular, was running at vitriolic levels, even while many others were applauding what she had done.

No wonder Carmen thinks I might have to distance myself from her. Shit.

Tamsyn slumped into the chair and dropped the phone on the table with a loud clatter.

Fuck. What am I going to do?

Putting the phone on speaker mode, she dialled Carmen's number.

"Did you know?" was all Carmen said when she answered.

"*No!* God, no. Trust me, if I had I would have done everything I could to talk her out of it!"

Carmen sighed. "I know. Shit, I don't know why I even asked you that. What is she thinking?"

"I have no idea. I mean, I've known for ages that she's annoyed at famous people living closeted lives. In fact, when I saw her a few days ago she pretty much told me she's always resented that I've never come out."

"Ouch."

"Indeed." Tamsyn exhaled slowly. "But I never imagined she'd go this far."

"So, what do you want to do? I mean, she's your friend, and that's well known. Do you want to step back from her until this all dies down? Or see if you can talk her out of doing anything more? I'll be honest, Tamsyn, I'm worried she's going to ambush *you* now."

Tamsyn hesitated, but then the answer came from her gut. "No, she wouldn't do that," she said firmly, realising in that moment that despite their disagreement the other night, it was true. "Whatever else is going on in her brain, our friendship means far too much to her for her to do something like that." Carmen made a disbelieving sound. "No, I trust her. I really do." She glanced, unseeing, around her kitchen. "And I don't want to step back. Not obviously, at least. I'll call her, see if I can get her to see sense."

"Okay. If you're sure. And I'll talk to Tony. We'll get a statement ready for you to sign off on in case anyone comes sniffing trying to link her views with you, okay?"

"Sure." She sighed loudly. "God, what a mess. Merry Christmas everyone."

Carmen chuckled, but it was a hollow sound.

———— ✦✧✦ ————

"Are you okay?" Maggie asked when Tamsyn finally walked back into the bedroom with the two mugs of tea in her hands. She'd been gone ages—to the point where Maggie was just thinking she should go hunting for her.

"Not really, if I'm honest," Tamsyn said, her voice sounding tired as she set Maggie's mug down on her bedside table, then walked round to deposit her own.

She clambered back into the bed and pulled Maggie close.

"You know Lesley Jenkins-Garcia, the activist that I'm friends with?" she said quietly, her mouth close to Maggie's forehead.

Maggie nodded gently. "I do."

Tamsyn sighed. "She's become the spokesperson for a new LGBT activist group and last night they outed Duncan Harewood, the MP."

Maggie blinked rapidly, trying to process the news. Outing someone was high on her shit list—but this was Tamsyn's friend.

"Well, I can honestly say that's not something I can condone," she said cautiously.

"Oh, God, me neither, obviously! I'm *so* mad at her. I don't know what she thought would come of it!" Tamsyn sounded exasperated. "She's in all the news, of course, and getting slammed on Twitter and Facebook." Tamsyn rubbed at her face. "I need to call her but I'm so angry I can't do it now, otherwise I'll just end up screaming at her."

The thought rose up, and she had to ask, even if it upset Tamsyn. "Would she ever do that to you? Out you?"

Tamsyn swallowed. "No, I really don't think she would. But it's bad enough pondering the whole how-to-come-out situation without finding out your best friend thinks this is a great way for it to happen." Tamsyn's eyes widened in shock. "God, is *that* why she was so irritated the other night? Does it annoy her that she knows this about me and can't use it?"

Maggie had never seen her so riled up. Before she could respond, however, a ringing phone interrupted them. The sound came from the pocket of Tamsyn's robe and she grimaced as she pulled it out and looked at the caller display.

"It's her," she whispered, holding the phone as if it were a live snake.

"You don't have to answer. You said yourself you're too angry right now."

Tamsyn pursed her lips as the phone continued to ring, then hit the 'Decline' icon and exhaled heavily.

Maggie had no idea what to say. She wanted to support Tamsyn in whatever she chose to do, and yes, she wanted Tamsyn to be out publicly because she couldn't see how their relationship would work otherwise. But never in a million years would she want Tamsyn to be outed, or to feel pressured to come out before someone *could* out her.

"Can I be honest?" Maggie asked quietly.

"Of course!" Tamsyn looked puzzled. "Always."

"Okay." Maggie took a deep breath. "I'm worried if you confront her about this, it will go bad for you. That she'll out you. And as much as I want you to be out and free, I don't want her doing it for you. I'll wait, Tamsyn, is what I'm saying. Not forever, but for as long as it takes for you to feel truly comfortable. So don't rock the boat on my behalf, okay?"

"Oh, Maggie." Tamsyn gently cupped Maggie's face in her hands. "Don't you see? I *do* feel comfortable. I *do* feel ready. This crap has nothing to do with my own decision, and it won't sway me one way or another. I promise." She kissed the end of Maggie's nose. "I see why you're worried about what Lesley might do, but despite all of this, despite her bad judgement on this, I trust her. She won't do this to me. What she has done may damage our friendship, I can't deny that. But it won't make her do something *that* stupid."

Maggie wished she had the same conviction, but she didn't know this Lesley woman at all. Tamsyn did, though, and Maggie would have to trust her judgement.

"I'm very happy to hear you talk so strongly about all this, you know. You seem to have worked through your concerns about being openly gay, and it's lovely to see. Not for me, although that's a nice side effect, but for you, in yourself."

Tamsyn's smile lit up her face. "I have worked it all through, and yes, I am very happy with what I've decided." She chuckled. "Doesn't necessarily mean it will be easy or that I'll enjoy it, but I will do it. I can't live the life I want now *without* doing it."

She kissed Maggie then, properly, and sweetly, and Maggie knew their tea was going to go cold.

"We still on for tomorrow?" Maggie asked, and Tamsyn hated seeing the doubt in her eyes.

She pulled Maggie close, wrapped her arms around her, and kissed her chin. "We are. Nothing would keep me away."

"Good." Maggie's voice was muffled against her cheek where her warm breath teased at Tamsyn's skin. "I hope everything goes okay."

Tamsyn had decided she couldn't put Lesley off beyond today. She'd already called once more, and again Tamsyn had sent it to voicemail. Lesley hadn't left a message.

"It will be fine. Messy, but fine. Don't worry, please. Although it's lovely that you do."

Maggie smiled and kissed Tamsyn softly on the lips. "See you tomorrow."

She pulled away and Tamsyn opened the door for her. Maggie slipped out, gave her a cute wave, and then was gone.

Tamsyn shut the door behind her, inhaled slowly, and exhaled even slower.

Now or never. I can't, and don't want to, put this off any longer.

She made herself a coffee first, feeling lethargic from the morning in bed with Maggie.

With the hot mug in hand, she walked through to the living room, switched on the fake fire, and folded herself into the armchair. What she wouldn't give for Gizmo's warm little body and cute face beside her right now; something about that dog's presence always calmed her. *Much like his owner's.*

Lesley answered on the third ring.

"You're mad, aren't you?"

"Yes." Tamsyn had decided she wouldn't sugar coat it. They'd been friends too long for her not to be brutally honest now. "For God's sake, Lesley, what were you thinking?"

"Tamsyn, it *has* to be done!" Her passion and excitement were palpable, and Tamsyn knew in an instant that they were never going to agree on this matter. "This sort of stuff has gone on for *far* too long. This is the twenty-first century. A man should be free to be openly gay no matter what his job or position in society, and the longer these people keep perpetuating these ridiculous situations, the worse it is for all of us. Surely you can see that? I mean, look at *you*, having to hide who you really are because you fear what it would do to your career? Wouldn't your world, *our* world, be a better place if coming out *wasn't* a big deal? If everyone was out and *no one cared*?"

Tamsyn closed her eyes and pressed a hand to her forehead. Her heart raced as anger bubbled up. "But Lesley, don't you see? His situation is exactly the same as mine—as in, I assume he had very good reasons for keeping it quiet. You don't know him, you don't know what those reasons are. So what gives you the right to ride roughshod over his whole life like that? Have you seen what some of the more right-wing press are doing to him? It's awful, Lesley. Absolutely *awful*."

"He'll survive," Lesley said bitterly. "His type *always* do."

"For fuck's sake, Lesley, what's happened to you?" Tamsyn was genuinely mystified; this uncharacteristic heartlessness cut her to the bone. "Since when did you stop caring about people?"

"*Caring* about people?" Lesley was practically shouting now. "Have you *seen* how many teenagers still kill themselves because they're scared to tell their families they're gay? Have you seen how many kids get kicked out of their family homes when they do finally pluck up courage to come out? Don't you *get* it?"

Tamsyn was breathing heavily, and Lesley's inhalations were loud in her ear. "Lesley, I understand all that, I really do. But how is ruining one man's life going to change any of that? How is ruining the lives of the people he loves going to change it?"

The latest headlines were all focused on his wife, and how the news must have devastated her. The boyfriend, too, had been harassed all morning by the paparazzi, and was allegedly fleeing the country to get away from the attention.

"They'll all *deal* with it." Lesley didn't sound quite so sure of herself now, and Tamsyn seized her chance.

"What if this was *me*, Lesley? Hmm? What if someone had suddenly outed me and I was being hounded by the press? How would you feel then?" It was a cheap shot, but something told her nothing else would break through.

Lesley was silent for a minute. When she finally spoke, her words carried no conviction. "That's different, and you know it. He's a *politician*. He shouldn't lie."

Tamsyn snorted. "For crying out loud, they make a living from lying! Don't be so fucking naive." She shook her head, even though she knew Lesley couldn't see her. "I honestly don't know what else to say to you. I thought I knew you, but now..."

"I didn't expect you to be *happy* about this," Lesley replied, her voice tight. "But I thought you'd understand, if you thought it through. If you thought about the example that needs to be set for the LGBT youngsters who are still struggling to live in this world."

"Lesley, I don't think you have the faintest idea what LGBT youngsters are feeling." It was hard not to be scathing. "I don't think this is about them at all. And I think you need to go away and have a long, *long* think about that before you do anything else with this group."

The empty sound of a call that had been ended was her only answer.

Chapter 24

"I think we should make a concerted effort not to mention anything about who Tamsyn is in front of the kids, right?" Maggie passed Ruth a glass of champagne.

"Agreed. They're far too sharp for their own good and it'll spread round their school in no time." Ruth nodded before taking a loud slurp.

"Hey, you make our children sound positively vicious!" Will objected, frowning. He was handsome, in a rugged kind of way—years of playing rugby had ensured his face would never be entirely symmetrical again— with thick black hair and piercing blue eyes, and he looked good dressed up for Christmas Day. Both he and Ruth had made a bit more of an effort than they normally would, and Maggie had smiled but not commented.

Ruth patted him on the hand. "No, my love, that is not what I'm suggesting. They won't understand why it needs to be a secret, that's all."

Will harrumphed but a small smile crossed his features. "Okay, I agree with that." He accepted the glass Maggie handed him, then grinned. "To my sister-in-law and her new, rather famous, girlfriend."

Maggie blushed but accepted his toast with a smile. They all chinked glasses and drank, although Ruth was frowning as she took her first sip.

"Something wrong with the fizz?" Maggie asked, thinking it tasted fine to her.

"Oh, er, no. It's nothing," Ruth replied with a quick sideways glance at Will, whose face creased with confusion. Ruth sighed, then spoke to her husband. "I know you said I shouldn't, but I have to."

Will tutted and shook his head. "I'll see how the girls are," he threw over his shoulder as he left the room.

"What's going on?" Maggie was mystified; Will had looked positively pissed off.

Ruth set her glass firmly down on the small kitchen table and motioned for Maggie to take a seat.

"Ruth, you're scaring me. Is something wrong?"

Ruth's eyes widened as she slipped into her own chair. "Oh! God, no. Nothing like that. I just want to talk to you about something and, well, Will thinks it's not my place and…"

Maggie instantly went on alert. If Will thought that, then Ruth was about to stick her nose in Maggie's business in a big way. She folded her arms across her chest and glared at her sister. "What? Go on, spit it out."

"You saw the news, yes? About Duncan Harewood."

Maggie nodded sharply, pretty sure she knew where this was going.

Ruth straightened in her chair, her tone mildly defensive as she said, "Look, I know you and Tamsyn have only just reconnected and are probably still working out what the two of you are or could be. And granted, her coming to Christmas lunch is a pretty big statement on that—meeting the family so quickly and everything. But when is she going to come out? You said she was thinking about it, but discovering what Harewood made his boyfriend do all those years has—"

"Whoa, wait!" Maggie held up a hand, trying to get her irritation under control before she continued. "You have no idea if Harewood made his boyfriend do anything. For all we know, it was the boyfriend who wanted them to keep it a secret. Or he was perfectly happy living a secret life. Why does everyone always assume the worst of the person being outed?"

"But Tamsyn told you before that she wouldn't be able to live a publicly out life, and therefore by definition she would expect you to keep everything secret!"

"Back *then*, yes. But not now. She's made it quite clear she does want to come out. In fact, yesterday's news only seemed to bolster her on that. The last thing she wants is to be outed like that. She wants it done on her terms."

"But *when*? It's all well and good saying you *want* to do it, but then you actually have to do it," Ruth said adamantly.

Maggie inhaled deeply before responding. "Look, I get where this is coming from. You're worried about me having to creep around pretending I'm not with her, yes?"

Ruth nodded. "Of course. I don't think it would be healthy for you or the relationship."

"But what makes you think I would agree to that? Do you think I have so little backbone that I'd just capitulate like that?"

They stared at each other for a moment, before Ruth sighed and shook her head. "No, I don't. I... Maggie, I'm sorry. I'm just concerned that the woman you've had a mighty crush on all these years is going to give you the run-around." She sipped her drink. "Maybe it'll be easier for me once I see the two of you together. At the moment all I have is what you're telling me."

Maggie snorted derisively. "And that's not enough to trust me?"

"Maggie, of course I trust *you*. But I don't know *her*. And until I do, I reserve the right to be sceptical. I'm your sister. I love you and care about what happens to you, so don't blame me for being unsure about someone I've never bloody met, okay?"

Exhaling, Maggie unfolded her arms and reached for her glass. "Okay," she said before she took a sip. "I can accept that."

"I didn't mean to come across so heavy-handed," Ruth said, her tone contrite. "I do just care—"

Maggie reached across and patted her sister's hand where it rested on the gnarled wood of the tabletop. "I know. It's okay. Just try not to be too judgemental too quickly, okay?"

Ruth sighed. "I'll try."

By unspoken agreement they stood and began preparing vegetables, gradually relaxing again, and chatting about inconsequential things.

Will reappeared a few minutes later. "Everything all right?" he asked, looking at his wife.

"It's all fine, Will," Maggie said, feeling it was important it came from her.

"Well, okay then. So, when does Tamsyn get here?" Will asked.

Maggie glanced at the clock "About half an hour. She's visiting her father in the nursing home this morning, then her car will bring her direct to here."

"Her car," Ruth said, rolling her eyes. "Imagine being that privileged."

Wondering if they were about to start another heated discussion, Maggie shrugged to make light of it. "She has money, she uses it. Trust me, there's nothing pretentious about it."

"Oh, no! Sorry, I didn't mean it like that. I'm just, you know, a little bit jealous." Ruth looked sheepish.

"Of what?" Will asked, turning to face her.

"Oh, I don't know. Just the ease of it all, when you have that much money."

"Hey, we do all right, don't we?" Will looked genuinely upset.

Ruth's face was contrite as she leaned forward to kiss her husband. "Oh, God, of course! Honey, I didn't mean anything by it. Promise," she said, kissing him again.

Mollified, Will kissed her back, turning it into something far more passionate than Maggie needed to witness; she scurried back across the kitchen and pretended to fix some small thing with the vegetables. Laughter from across the room told her it was safe to turn back round.

"Sorry, did we embarrass you?"

Ruth didn't look sorry at all, and Maggie stuck her tongue out at her sister.

"Aunty Maggie, you're not supposed to do that," came a small, shocked voice from the doorway.

Maggie looked over at her niece and smiled. "Different rules for grown-ups, Ellie. Sorry."

"So not fair." Ellie pouted.

"What do you want, missy? You can't be bored with your presents already." Ruth gazed down at her daughter.

Ellie grinned and skipped into the room. "No, I'm just thirsty. Can I have some juice?"

"Please," Ruth said, pinning Ellie with a glare.

The youngster rolled her eyes. "Pleeeeeease."

Trying hard not to snort, Maggie poured her a small glass of juice, plus one for her twin, then ushered her out of the room. She followed Ellie back to the living room and stuck her head round the door to make sure all was well. It still looked like a small tornado had blown through, but was no worse than before. She laughed out loud when she spotted Gizmo in amongst the wreckage, his head adorned with a hat fashioned out of used wrapping paper.

"Nice hat, Giz."

He looked up at her and wagged his tail.

"He's our prince," Anna said, glancing up from the colouring book she was scribbling in.

"Right. Of course." Maggie had no idea what that meant but all three of them were quiet and busy and that was what counted.

She returned to the kitchen where Ruth and Will were busy canoodling again. They broke apart with silly grins and Maggie shook her head.

"You two are like teenagers."

"Hah, as if you won't be doing the same with Tamsyn when she gets here," Ruth said, her eyes gleaming.

"If I do I'm not going to do it in front of you." Maggie grinned. "You'd never watch any of her films in the same away again."

Ruth laughed. "Trust me, I won't anyway knowing she's shagging my sister."

"So crude," Maggie muttered, but she chuckled along, happy that they seemed to be back on even ground.

When the doorbell rang fifteen minutes later, Maggie left the kitchen, silently admonishing herself for her trembling hands and thumping heart. She found two inquisitive young girls and one very excited dog waiting in the hall.

"Calm down," she muttered to Gizmo, but also to herself.

When she pulled open the door, she and Tamsyn exchanged smiles, their gazes saying everything without the need for words.

"Merry Christmas," Tamsyn said softly.

"Merry Christmas." Maggie stepped to one side to allow Gizmo to lavish his own Christmas greetings on their guest, which Tamsyn lapped up with all the appropriate gooey noises, as well as compliments on his hat.

When she'd managed to prise him off her legs, she stepped into the house properly and removed her coat. She'd dressed down, as Maggie had advised, and looked good in her black jeans and jade green turtleneck jumper. Her hair was in a loose ponytail, and Maggie itched to undo it and run her fingers through the lush thickness of it all.

Swallowing down a sudden burst of arousal, Maggie watched as Tamsyn's gaze drifted and a wide smile lit up her face.

"Well, hello. You must be Anna and Ellie."

Maggie turned to see her nieces shyly nod. "Say hello, girls. This is Tamsyn."

They whispered a hello in unison, then broke into giggles and scampered back into the living room, Gizmo trotting after them.

"They're shy around strangers," Maggie offered.

"Perfectly sensible." Tamsyn passed a large bag to Maggie. "Some extras for the day. I couldn't turn up empty-handed, even though you said not to bring anything."

Maggie grinned. "Somehow I thought you'd ignore me." She glanced in the bag and saw champagne, smoked salmon, two small teddy bears, and a large box of chocolates. "You're naughty, but nice."

"I can live with that." Tamsyn leaned in. "So, hello." She kissed Maggie, her lips cool from the cold day outside, her tongue warm as it dipped into Maggie's mouth.

"Mm, hello back." Maggie smiled, her heart full. "I'm so happy you're here."

Tamsyn nodded, her smile equally wide.

"Come on, come and meet my sister and her hubby." Maggie took Tamsyn's hand and tugged her through to the kitchen.

When they walked into the room, Ruth was pulling the open bottle of champagne from the fridge, and Will was reaching for a fresh glass from the dresser.

"Ruth, Will, I'd like you to meet Tamsyn."

They turned, big smiles on their faces even as their eyes betrayed how star-struck they were. To Maggie's delight, Ruth was first to walk over, hand extended.

Tamsyn shook it. "Lovely to meet you."

"And you." Ruth inhaled deeply. "Okay, I'm just going to get this out of the way right off and then not bother you with it again. You're *amazing*! I've loved almost everything you've done and *Blue Lights* is one of my favourite TV shows *ever*," she gushed.

Tamsyn chuckled. "That's lovely to hear. And hey, if you feel the need to boost my ego at any other time during the day, you go right ahead."

"No, don't," Maggie chimed in. "Her head's big enough as it is."

Tamsyn gasped, and clutched at her chest. "Such betrayal."

Ruth looked between them, her mouth open. "Oh, boy," she said after a moment, "this is going to take some getting used to."

Shaking his head and smirking, Will stepped forward. "Hi, Tamsyn. It's lovely to meet you."

Tamsyn shook his hand.

"Champagne?" he asked, gesturing to the empty glass.

"Did you prep him?" Tamsyn asked, turning to Maggie.

"Nope, he's just that kind of guy."

"You and I are going to get along just fine," Tamsyn whispered, and Will laughed.

The four adults sat around the kitchen table, sipping champagne and chatting. Maggie was thrilled at how easily Tamsyn assimilated into the situation—not that she'd really had any doubts. Ruth and Will were both easy-going, and they seemed to quickly forget who Tamsyn was out in the wide world. Tamsyn, for her part, was clearly revelling in the ordinariness of Christmas with Maggie's family. She'd told Maggie her alternative plans would have been to accept an open invitation from a fellow actress to join an assorted selection of 'misfits', as Tamsyn had called them, for lunch at one of the swanky hotels in Mayfair. Watching her now, laughing and joking with Will and Ruth, Maggie knew she'd never regret turning that invite down.

They ate their traditional turkey meal around the same table, making use of its extending leaves to ensure it was big enough for all six of them to fit. Anna and Ellie gradually relaxed around Tamsyn and chattered away about everything and anything as they ate. Gizmo, his loyalties on display for all to see, sat by Tamsyn's chair for the entire meal—not begging, just sitting, clearly happy just to be close to her.

When they'd finished eating, the girls sprinted back to the living room to watch *Shrek*, and the adults opened a bottle of Sancerre dessert wine to accompany the *tarte au citron* that Maggie had made the night before.

"This is sinful," Tamsyn said as she polished off her last mouthful.

"Mmm," Ruth managed around her own last bite, and Will chuckled.

"Ruth's favourite," he said. "Which I'm sure is deliberate on this one's part." He pointed at Maggie.

Maggie shrugged and grinned. "I have to keep everyone happy. You got the traditional turkey, she gets the dessert."

"What about me?" Tamsyn demanded, a mock-offended look on her face.

"You get Maggie," Ruth quipped before Maggie could respond.

Maggie blushed deep pink and Tamsyn roared with laughter.

"Perfect. I get the best of what's on offer," she said, smiling warmly.

Maggie wanted to kiss her, but they had yet to have the discussion on public displays of affection, so she settled for smiling back just as warmly, and hoping her eyes were conveying everything she was feeling in the moment. Tamsyn's soft blush told her she might have been successful.

"You don't have to do this, you know," Ruth said as Tamsyn carried in the tray of empty coffee cups from the living room. Ruth had her hands in the sink, washing the crystal-cut wine glasses they'd used over dinner. "It's my job to clean up if she's cooked, and vice versa if we're at my house."

"I don't mind." Tamsyn put the tray on the counter, pulled open the dishwasher, and started loading the cups into the top drawer. "I like to help, and many hands make light work, as my mum used to say."

"Don't you have staff to do that sort of thing normally?" Ruth asked, and Tamsyn wasn't sure what she heard in her tone. Resentment? Accusation?

"Er, no, actually. I live alone. I have a cleaner who comes in once a week and a driver on call but that's it." She tilted her head at Ruth's sceptical expression. "Contrary to what you might think, I'm not quite that rich—or pretentious." She leaned in and whispered conspiratorially, trying to lighten the moment, "Don't believe everything you see in those trashy newspapers and magazines."

Ruth's eyes blazed, and Tamsyn knew her attempt to be frivolous had backfired. "I don't actually read *any* of that crap. But you have to admit you are in a significantly better position in life than my sister, aren't you?"

What? Where was this coming from? Knowing she had to ride out this storm, whatever its origins or purpose, Tamsyn took a deep breath and said, "Ruth, do you have concerns about me being involved with Maggie?"

Ruth seemed taken aback by Tamsyn's directness and blinked rapidly a few times before replying. "Well, yes, actually, I do." She peeled off her washing up gloves and turned to face Tamsyn properly, her stance rigid, almost aggressive.

Tamsyn willed herself to present as relaxed, even though she was anything but on the inside. "Then please, ask me anything. It's very important to me that I be accepted by Maggie's family. I need you to believe that. And that I have only the best intentions where your sister is concerned."

"Then why aren't you out yet?"

"Oh." She might have guessed. "That."

"Yes, *that*. Maggie trusts you when you say you're going to do it, but when exactly is this in your plan? A few months, a year?"

"I don't know when exactly." She rushed on, raising a hand when Ruth made to interrupt. "I have a meeting soon with my PR manager and my agent to discuss the best strategy and timing. But please," she leaned forward slightly, infusing her words with as much sincerity as possible, "believe me when I say that I want to do this sooner rather than later. I will not have Maggie hiding who she is, who we are."

"I can't help worrying about her," Ruth said, although her tone was slightly softer now. "You've waltzed into her life with all your fame and money, and I don't want her to get hauled through the mud for being your partner."

"Trust me, that is the very last thing I want. That's why I'm working as fast as I can to get the story out my way. I want to protect Maggie from the worst of the circus that surrounded Harewood's outing yesterday. She's far too special to me to risk ruining her life for it all. I want a life with her, a long life, if she'll have me," Tamsyn said, her passion leaking into her voice, "and so I will do everything I can, spend every last penny I have if needs be, making sure she is not damaged by her association with me in any way. I also want her to be a part of the decision and process of me coming out, every step of the way, because it affects her so much too." She took a deep breath as her voice wobbled. "I will never, ever intentionally hurt her, Ruth. You have my word on that."

"Ruth, what's going on?"

Tamsyn turned to face Maggie, and Ruth shifted beside her.

"We're just—" Tamsyn started, but Ruth cut her off.

"I'm being an over-protective mother hen," she said, and placed a hand on Tamsyn's forearm.

Tamsyn turned to face her, smiling at Ruth's rueful grin. "I think you're allowed," she said quietly.

Ruth sighed. "Thanks. But I'm sorry if I overdid it."

Maggie walked over and slipped her arm around Tamsyn's waist. It felt wonderful, natural, something Tamsyn didn't think she'd ever tire of.

"Did you kick her ass?" Maggie asked.

Tamsyn snorted, and Ruth chuckled. "Nah, I thought I'd save that for later."

"Hah," Ruth said, her eyes sparkling, "like *you* could take *me*."

Tamsyn eyed Ruth up and down, took in the slightly sturdier frame, the defined arms—*How did she get those and how can I do the same?*—and grinned. "You know what, you're right. Let's just drink more champagne, okay?"

Laughing, Ruth patted Tamsyn's arm again, then turned back to her washing up. "Let me finish this and then you are on, Ms Harris."

Maggie pulled Tamsyn gently away.

"You sure everything's okay?" she asked quietly as they neared the door.

"Totally." Tamsyn smiled at her. "She really does just care so much about you. It wasn't even personal, not really. More about my situation and position in the world. She doesn't want you dragged through the mud, but now, hopefully, she realises that's the last thing I want too." She glanced back; Ruth was focused on her work. Dropping a quick kiss on Maggie's warm lips, Tamsyn breathed in the scent of her and her senses flooded with calm. "And I realised something, in talking to Ruth. I'd like you to be involved in the decisions I make with Tony and Carmen about when and how to come out, okay? This affects you just as much as it does me."

"You sure? I mean, I trust you to do the right thing but—"

"Please, I want us to do this together. I think it's important. For now and for, you know, any future we have." She swallowed hard.

Maggie's smile made her heart lighten and her stomach turn cartwheels.

"Thank you," Maggie whispered, and laid a proper kiss on her that made Tamsyn swoon.

Much later, curled up in each other's arms in Maggie's bed, their heart rates finally slowing after the thumping, simultaneous orgasms they'd just given each other, Tamsyn glanced down at Maggie and smiled.

"I had the most wonderful day today." She kissed Maggie's nose. "Probably the best Christmas I've had in about twenty-five years."

Maggie's face registered her shock. "Seriously?"

"Oh, yes," Tamsyn mused. "As soon as my career took off, my life changed so much. Then Mum died, and although Dad and I tried to keep it as normal as possible, things just started getting in the way." And now, of course, her dad could barely remember who she was. "So, thank you."

She kissed Maggie again, never tiring of the feel of that mouth on hers. Maggie held her tight, and returned the kiss with vigour.

"Now," Tamsyn said when they parted, "I have a crazy idea about New Year's Eve, if you don't already have plans?"

"Nope, no plans."

"Good. How do you fancy Paris?"

Maggie's eyes went wide. "Paris?" she squeaked.

"Uh-huh. I booked this ages ago, for myself, as a little escape at the end of the year that didn't take me too far away from where I'll be shooting. I have a rather lovely room booked at Le Meurice from the thirtieth through to the second of Jan. If you could get a flight sorted that quickly for yourself, would you like to join me?"

Maggie's eyes brimmed with tears. "I would love that, Tamsyn."

Tamsyn's heart swelled. "I've never shared New Year's Eve with anyone other than friends. This will be a secret fantasy come true." Her throat was tight. "We can have dinner somewhere, watch fireworks somewhere else, drink champagne, do whatever you like."

Maggie lunged up and kissed Tamsyn, hard and deep, and Tamsyn's entire body throbbed in response. Then they were off again, into the space that contained only the two of them, the space that was all about heat, and lust, and tenderness. The space that filled Tamsyn with deep emotion, with...love. The word should have terrified her, should have made her want to slam her shields back into place, but it didn't. Now it excited her, made her want to laugh and cry all at the same time because for the first time in her life she knew what all the fuss was about. And she was so glad she'd figured it out. *Better late than never.* And then she stopped thinking altogether as Maggie's tongue swept a hot trail down her belly.

Chapter 25

MAGGIE SAT BACK AND STRETCHED her arms upwards, easing out the stiffness in her back. A glance at the clock made her chuckle.

No wonder I feel like I've been put under a press. I've been writing for three hours solid.

She stood and did some more extensive stretching, using the edge of her desk. She couldn't wipe the smile off her face, even if she wanted to. The new book was roaring along—she'd started it about ten minutes after Tamsyn had left on Boxing Day, suddenly itching to be sat in front of her MacBook, a blank Scrivener page in front of her, waiting to be filled with words. The idea for the book had been building for a while, characters forming themselves into solidity in her mind, settings popping in to be scribbled in her Moleskine. As soon as she'd had the house to herself again, she'd made a large pot of coffee and headed for her study. She hadn't resurfaced for four hours, until Gizmo's almost frantic whining for an outdoors visit finally pulled her out of her zone. She'd never been so absorbed in a story; something about working in a new genre, perhaps, or even just crime drama, where all the connections between events and the clues that should be laid down like a trail of breadcrumbs had to be thought through so carefully.

Since then, her days had been following a set pattern: three to four hours writing in the morning, long walk with Gizmo in the afternoon, and in the evening, a long phone call with Tamsyn—who was out in the middle of the very cold Cotswolds, filming a segment for the TV drama she was starring in. They wouldn't actually see each other again until they met in Paris.

In the kitchen, she found Gizmo curled up in his basket in the corner, Snakey wrapped around him like a shield. He'd been out of sorts since Boxing Day, and Maggie couldn't help but wonder if he missed Tamsyn as much as she did. Her bed was awfully lonely without that beautiful woman wrapped up beside her. As much as their long calls in the evenings delighted her, they didn't compare to actually being in Tamsyn's presence, and being able to hold her, and kiss her.

Tomorrow, she reminded herself. Tamsyn would arrive first, and had promised to have the champagne chilling and room service ordered so they could simply enjoy each other that first night. Maggie couldn't wait.

She took Gizmo for a long romp in Richmond Park that afternoon, then dropped him round at Ruth's for his extended stay while she was away.

"Everything ready for your weekend?" Ruth asked as they sipped tea in her kitchen, the sounds of Anna and Ellie arguing over who was going to cuddle Gizmo first coming to them from the living room.

"Pretty much. I'll pack in the morning. My flight's not until three, but I want to write again in the morning too."

"Oh, yeah, the new genre! How's it going?"

"It's going amazing," Maggie whispered, scared to say it too loudly in case she jinxed it.

"I'm so pleased for you. When can I read it?"

Maggie was surprised; as far as she was aware, Ruth didn't read a lot and certainly hadn't ever mentioned reading any of Maggie's previous works.

"I know, I don't read much, but that's not for a lack of wanting to. Those two," she thumbed in the direction of her children's giggles, "run me ragged most days. The book I've got by the bed I started two months ago and I'm only halfway through." She snorted. "I get into bed, read three pages, and then Will's waking me up taking the book off my face and switching out the light. But, when I do read, I read a lot of crime, so, you know…" She shrugged and inhaled a deep breath. "If you'd like someone who knows a bit about the genre to cast an eye over it and give you an honest opinion, I'd be more than happy to do that. In fact, I'd be honoured." She blushed, and her hands twitched on the table in front of her.

A rush of affection swept over Maggie, and she reached across and clasped Ruth's arm. "No, I'd be honoured to have you read it. I would love that. I'll email you the first three chapters I've written when I get home later. They're rough draft, remember, but maybe you could at least see if I've got the right 'feel' going, yes?"

Ruth nodded, her smile wide. "Definitely. I'm really looking forward to it. And I will make time for it—maybe I need to get better at letting those two fend for themselves more when I need 'me' time."

Warmth spread through Maggie. It seemed as if her recent decisions were having some rather lovely, if unexpected, consequences, and not only for herself.

The next day, as she sat on the plane waiting to taxi to the runway, she thought back on those moments with her sister, and a big smile broke out over her face. Her phone pinged with a text message from Tamsyn:

Room 504! Can't wait to see you. T x

Maggie grinned, and quickly fired off a "Me neither" response before she got told to switch her phone off.

The flight was uneventful, the taxi ride less so. She exited the cab in front of the hotel and gazed in awe at the grand building. The opulent lobby left her speechless and she barely resisted the temptation to stop and gawp.

Jesus, I am so glad I dressed up a little for this trip.

It had been an issue, deciding what to wear to make sure she didn't embarrass herself—or Tamsyn—during their stay at the five-star palace. In the end she'd foregone her usual comfy travelling jeans and worn dressy black trousers instead, with her leather coat, rather than her bright red hiking jacket, over a smart shirt. On the one hand, it was nice to dress up for something this special, but on the other, she was distinctly out of her comfort zone, and very glad when she found the lift. She pressed the button for floor five and exhaled a long, slow breath.

Tamsyn couldn't relax, despite the luxury of her surroundings. She was tired from the long hours they'd put in this week, and still smarting from the way things had unfolded with Lesley, who had tried to contact her again, once. Tamsyn had ignored the call, not ready to get into it again.

Underneath that fatigue, too, was the dull ache of feeling that a big part of her was missing and would be put back together the minute Maggie walked through that door. She'd texted from the airport to say she was in the queue for a cab, so she couldn't be too far away.

Tamsyn busied herself checking that the champagne was still crisply cold—it was—and that the food platters that had been delivered a few minutes previously still looked delicious—they did—and told herself for the tenth time to just bloody relax.

It was so hard. She'd missed Maggie so much, and wanted to spend so much more time with her, especially now her shooting schedule would ease off soon. She'd be required in the studio for most of January, but that was always far easier on her middle-aged body than the location days. God, the Cotswolds had been bloody freezing!

A knock at the door made her heart leap into her throat, then chuckle at herself. *Teenager.*

She swung open the door and there she was, her beautiful Maggie, looking simply stunning in a long leather coat that Tamsyn hadn't seen before.

"Hi," Maggie whispered, her smile huge.

"Hi back."

Tamsyn reached for her, pulling Maggie in by the lapels of her coat, and casting a quick glance up and down the corridor to make sure they had no audience.

Once Maggie was past her, she shut the door and turned round, ready to swoop this glorious woman into her arms and kiss her until—

Maggie was glaring at her, hands clenched at her sides, mouth set in a tight line.

"Maggie?" Her voice cracked with worry.

"What the hell was that?" Maggie said through gritted teeth.

Tamsyn scrambled through her memories of the last minute and came up empty. "What?" She kept her tone soft, not wanting to antagonise Maggie any more than she already—clearly—had.

"Checking behind me as I came in," Maggie snapped. "Way to make me feel like your dirty little secret."

Tamsyn blinked, then realised what Maggie was referring to, and implying. *Oh shit.*

"Maggie, I'm so sorry. I... It's...necessary. Just for now," she added quickly, holding up her hands as Maggie's eyes went wide and her cheeks flushed. "Please, come in, sit down, and let me explain."

Her heart was thumping, and her palms were sweating. Maggie looked ready to walk right back out the door and Tamsyn willed her with every fibre of her being not to.

Maggie stared at her for one moment, then abruptly turned on her heel, leaving her suitcase standing in the entryway, and walked over to one of the small antique sofas that encircled the informal, low table in the middle of the room. She sat rigid in its seat, her hands clasped in her lap.

Knowing it probably looked dramatic but doing it because it felt right, Tamsyn dropped to her knees next to the sofa, took Maggie's hands in her own, and looked deep into her eyes.

"You and I have flown this new relationship under the radar up until now, mainly because we haven't been anywhere that public." She took a deep breath. "And until I am able to come out publicly, we still need to do that." She held one hand up when Maggie made to interrupt. "And not, contrary to what you might be thinking, to protect my precious reputation. That is part of it, yes, of course, but I don't think you have any idea what the press are going to do to you, and your family, once they find out you are my girlfriend. And as I said at Christmas, I would much rather they do all that at a pace that *we* can control, rather than by being...incautious and having to deal with unwanted attention when we're not ready."

She leaned a little closer, rubbing her thumbs across the back of Maggie's hands, which had, much to her relief, relaxed a little.

"Maggie, I should have talked to you about this before we got here, but I have been so wrapped up in the wonder of being with you, of spending time with you, that I allowed myself to forget the reality. And you standing on the doorstep of my hotel room, which only has my name on the booking, suddenly brought that reality crashing back down on me, and I acted on autopilot. Protection mode is all I have known for so many years, and it has served me well. I can't, and won't, switch it off, especially when it can be used to protect *you* too."

Reaching up, she cupped Maggie's cheek, and the next words flowed out of her without rhyme or reason, though she didn't regret them for even a nanosecond.

"Maggie, I am falling in love with you, and I will do anything to keep you safe from anyone who wishes you harm. And I won't apologise for doing it."

Maggie's mouth opened in a small 'O' of shock, and in the next moment she covered Tamsyn's hand on her cheek and smiled, her eyes damp with tears.

"You're falling in love with me?" she whispered.

"Oh, yes. Good God, yes." It felt incredible to say it and to witness the joy that spread across Maggie's face as she did so.

"Oh, Tamsyn."

The words left Maggie's throat an instant before she pressed her lips to Tamsyn's and pulled her close. Tamsyn shivered from the connection, the heat of Maggie's mouth on hers, the intensity of the moment they were sharing. So many new experiences, so many more she wanted to share with this woman.

When they broke for air, Maggie was smiling so widely it looked painful. "I'm a little ahead of you, I'm afraid."

Unsure of her meaning, Tamsyn raised an eyebrow in question.

Maggie blushed. "I'm already in love with you. Not just falling."

Oh. Wow.

"Trust me, I suspect I'm not that far behind," Tamsyn said, her heart racing at a mile a minute. "You'll have to forgive me, I'm new at this game and it might take me a little while to acknowledge where—"

Maggie pressed a finger against her lips. "Trust me, you're doing just fine." She swallowed. "I'm so sorry for flaring up at you about the door thing."

Tamsyn shook her head. "No, no, you have nothing to apologise for. I realise how it looked, and I'm sorry."

"Okay, apology and explanation accepted." Maggie's eyes were shining and her arm still held Tamsyn close, despite the awkwardness of Tamsyn's posture.

"Good." The relief was intense. "God, I'm so glad. I thought you were about to sprint out of here."

Maggie held her thumb and forefinger close together and Tamsyn laughed.

"Okay, I need to get up off the floor." She eased out of Maggie's arm and stood, rubbing her knees through the material of her skinny jeans. "And you and I, my darling, need to drink champagne."

Maggie glanced over at the table. "And eat some of that incredible-looking food."

Tamsyn laughed, pulling Maggie to her feet. "Absolutely. Whatever you want. My love." She said the last words on a whisper, as the magnitude of them hit her full force.

Maggie melted in her arms, and Tamsyn pulled her close, and kissed her with everything she had.

Chapter 26

THEIR NEW YEAR PASSED IN a blur of fine wine, fine dining in their hotel—lying low, which Maggie could fully accept and enjoy as it gave her ample opportunity to lay hands on the woman she loved—and walks along the Seine, and through various parks, wrapped up in beanie hats and scarves that kept their faces obscured. They avoided the temptation to hold hands, or link arms, instead presenting themselves as two friends who were enjoying some outdoor time together. Cafés were avoided, unless they were quiet, unassuming places with outdoor seating, where Tamsyn could remain in disguise while sipping her coffee.

Strangely, it was returning to the hotel that seemed to cause Tamsyn the most concern. While she said she trusted such a high-class hotel to be respectful of its patrons' privacy, she never seemed fully relaxed walking back in with Maggie at her side, as if waiting for someone to leap out from behind one of the ornate chairs in the lobby with a large camera and an evil grin. Maggie did her best to make that easier, always lagging a couple of paces behind Tamsyn to make it less obvious they were truly together. It was discomforting, but she absolutely understood the need for it.

When they returned to London, they managed a quick Skype meeting with Tony and Carmen to talk through initial ideas about Tamsyn coming out before Tamsyn had to get back to filming. However, as she was now based at the BBC studios, she could at least manage some evenings at home or at Maggie's. When she did, they spent much of their time exploring each other's bodies, whispering words of love and desire as their hands and tongues elicited intense pleasure from each other.

Maggie couldn't remember ever being this happy in a relationship. Tamsyn's absences, while painful to her heart, meant that she finally had the balance in a partnership she'd always been looking for. There was plenty of time to write, and spend time with her dog—who, of course, was delighted that Tamsyn was back in their lives now—and with her sister. At least once a week, she'd started taking the girls to school and picking them up again, to give Ruth a bit more of that 'me' time she'd been talking about. In return, Ruth was proving to be an invaluable and brilliant beta reader of Maggie's first foray into crime.

"It's all about atmosphere," Ruth said one evening over wine. Will was in the living room playing with the girls before bedtime. "You've really got to make me want to turn that next page and not give a shit about being late to work the next day. You're almost there, but here," she jabbed at the pages on the table in front of her, "for example, in the middle of chapter six, it kind of drifts into this domesticity that slows it down. If you skipped that, and jumped straight to the meeting the next day between our main suspect and the woman we fear is next on his list, *that* would make me cringe in fear and read quickly to see what the hell happens next."

"God, you are so good at this!" Maggie said, scribbling frantically across the page Ruth had pointed out.

"I love helping you like this."

"Me too."

They smiled at each other across the table.

The following day, when Tamsyn called her at nine in the evening, she sounded more weary than usual.

"You okay?" Maggie asked, concerned.

"Yes, long day. I…I met with Tony and Carmen this evening."

"Oh? Was that planned? You didn't mention it."

"No, it was all a bit rushed. They'd talked, come up with a final plan, and wanted to run it by me as soon as they could. Sorry, I know I said I wanted you involved but they were adamant about meeting that quickly. I've just got home."

Maggie settled back on the sofa and sipped her tea. "It's okay, I understand. So, how was it?"

Tamsyn sighed. "You know, it's actually a good plan. And I had an idea that we've added to it, and so now I want to tell you all about it and make sure you're okay with it."

"That's great, but you sound awfully tired. Want to leave it until morning? Or want me to come over?"

"Oh, God, you coming over sounds wonderful but it's rather late."

"It's only nine, Tamsyn. We're not eighty."

Tamsyn laughed. "Well, okay. It could work nicely actually, as I'm not required on set tomorrow until noon, so we at least wouldn't have to get up at the crack of dawn."

"Then I will call a cab and be there as soon as I can, okay?"

"You're perfect. You know that, right?"

Maggie chuckled. "No, I'm just in love and want to be with you."

She heard Tamsyn's sharp intake of breath and knew she'd be blushing. Tamsyn was still getting used to Maggie professing her love, and the effect it had on her was adorable.

Maggie, Gizmo, and Snakey arrived at Tamsyn's place a little before ten. Her dog, seeming to pick up on Tamsyn's weariness, simply walked up to her and waited for her to rub him rather than leaping all over her.

"Good boy, Giz," Tamsyn murmured as she patted his head, and he shuddered under her touch.

I know how you feel, boy, Maggie thought.

"Okay," Tamsyn said as she stood up straight. "Tea?"

"Yes, please. But first." Maggie stepped closer and dropped a soft kiss on Tamsyn's lips. "Never forget that bit."

Tamsyn looked sheepish. "Sorry, I'm a little distracted. Did I just lose girlfriend points for that?"

"Meh, only a couple. You'll make up for them soon, I'm sure."

Tamsyn smiled and led them down to the kitchen.

"Okay," she said, once they had sat, cups of camomile tea before them. "Here's the plan. Please be honest if you are not happy with any aspect of it, yes?"

Maggie nodded and gestured for her to continue. She could see how tense Tamsyn was, and just wanted her to be able to get this off her chest.

"Tony's plan is for me to sit down with someone from *The Guardian* for an exclusive. There will then be a press release that goes out that morning to everyone else, but no other interviews will be granted to anyone. Your name will not be anywhere, but I will say that I am in a relationship and ridiculously happy."

Maggie smiled at that, and reached out to stroke Tamsyn's free hand.

"Of course," Tamsyn said, with a grimace, "just because your name isn't anywhere doesn't mean they won't be camped out on my doorstep trying to get a glimpse of you. Tony's going to get me some security until the fuss dies down, and we'll do our best to sneak around a little in terms of you coming here, just to keep them off your back as much as we can for as long as we can." Tamsyn shrugged. "They'll find out who you are, eventually. They always do, those shits."

"I'm sure they will. But it sounds like what you've got planned will mitigate some of that."

"I hope so." She sighed wearily. "Anyway, that's when I had my idea, and this is the other bit I want to run past you. I wrap up filming on the twenty-third. Tony wants the interview to go to print on the twenty-sixth, so he's going to have me sit down with them the day after I finish filming. Now, as a way of perhaps lessening the scent for the bloodhounds, how would you feel if we skipped out of the UK the day before the interview is published, and spent a week at a gorgeous villa on Sardinia that I know of? That way, without me around to spy on, they might get a bit bored and move on to the next big story while we're away. When we come back, it might all have died down and we can sneak on in without anyone noticing and get back to some semblance of normal life from then on."

Maggie was smiling before Tamsyn had even finished speaking. A week away sounded blissful, whatever the reason for it. And it did make sense in the grand scheme of things, although she wasn't sure she shared Tamsyn's optimism that it would only take a week for the fuss to die down.

"I love it. Count me in. But, honey, at the risk of sounding pessimistic, please do keep in mind that you coming out is a huge story, and it might take a little more than a week for that to drop off the front pages, okay?"

Tamsyn sighed. "Yes. I wish you weren't right, but you probably are."

They travelled separately to Heathrow, ignored each other at the gate, and sat in different rows on the plane, although both were in business class.

If anyone wanted to delve into the airline records, they'd discover that the same PR firm had paid for both Ms Tamsyn Harris's ticket and that of a Ms Maggie Cooper, but that small detail was unlikely to see the light of day.

When they landed on Sardinia, as agreed, Maggie left the terminal and wandered along the front of the concourse towards the exit where the pre-booked cars or limos picked up their passengers. Tamsyn spared her one surreptitious glance before she flagged down her driver, who clutched a sign reading Mrs Mavis Woods, and followed him out to the waiting car. After ensuring no one had paid her too much attention, she gave him the signal to pull away from the kerb, and he rolled to a stop alongside Maggie a few moments later. Maggie scrambled in, and as soon as they looked at each other, they burst out laughing.

"I feel like a bloody spy," Maggie said, her eyes bright.

The driver pulled away from the kerb again, raised the privacy screen between his seat and theirs, and then they were off, away from the airport, heading for a place where they could really relax.

"I know," Tamsyn replied, squeezing Maggie's hand. "It's completely ridiculous, but hey, welcome to my world, my love."

Maggie smiled and tugged her close. It was a brief kiss, but even that settled Tamsyn.

When they drove through the gates of the villa, Maggie's wide-eyed expression was a delight.

"It's beautiful, isn't it?" Tamsyn said. "But wait until you see the view over the ocean."

"I'm still getting used to this." Maggie's voice was a tad wobbly.

"To what?"

"All of this." Maggie swept her arm out to encompass the villa beyond the confines of the car. "You having money and connections and, you know, all of this."

"You must tell me if it's too much. I don't do it to show off. I'm fortunate to have things like this at my disposal so I want to make use of them. But if you find it overwhelming, I can do low-key too."

"I'm sure I'll be fine, eventually. And yes, I know you can do low-key." She nuzzled closer just as the driver brought them to a stop at the foot of the steps leading to the front door. "And I kind of like you when you get low." She kissed beneath Tamsyn's left ear, and shivers plummeted down her spine.

"Uh-huh," she managed, her clit wide awake now and happily anticipating the moment they'd be alone.

The housekeeper was there to greet them, and was gone just as quickly as the last time Tamsyn was here, leaving them, finally, alone together. They gazed at each other, then at the suitcases scattered across the entryway around them.

"Let me show you around," Tamsyn offered.

Maggie nodded, and Tamsyn led her first to the master suite, where they left their cases and coats, and then back to the living area.

"Wow, this is gorgeous!" Maggie enthused, gazing around the huge room.

"Check that out," Tamsyn said, pointing to the large windows overlooking the deck and pool.

Maggie wandered over, gasping loudly when she caught sight of the view. "Good grief, that's stunning."

She turned back to Tamsyn, her face alight with wonder, and Tamsyn's breath caught in her throat.

"No," she whispered, stepping closer, "*you* are stunning."

Maggie's cheeks flushed, and her tongue slipped out of her mouth to wet her lips, which made a low moan rumble up out of Tamsyn's chest.

"I'll check out more of that view later," Maggie rasped, "but right now I'd much rather lay my eyes on you. Naked."

The bold statement shot a bolt of heat straight to Tamsyn's pussy, swiftly followed by wetness. Any concerns she had over the impending announcement of her sexuality were forgotten as she closed the distance between them and pulled Maggie into her arms.

The next morning was cloudy, so Maggie didn't get to see much of the view, but she didn't care. Since they'd arrived at the villa less than twenty-four hours before, they had barely left each other's side. There was a need in both of them to stay close, to touch often, to share kisses. They'd had breakfast, neither of them mentioning the fact that today was the day.

Today, everyone who knew of Tamsyn Harris would know she was a lesbian.

"More coffee?" Tamsyn asked, her voice shaky.

"Switch your phone on, Tamsyn," Maggie said gently. "At least to see if Carmen's messaged. You can ignore all the other stuff, if you want."

"What are you, a mind reader now?" Tamsyn muttered, but she was smiling.

Maggie stuck her tongue out.

Tamsyn walked over to flop down on the sofa beside Maggie, her phone in hand. She powered it up and waited. Within seconds her screen went crazy, the pings and beeps that came from the device seeming endless.

"I guess they ran the article, then." Tamsyn's grin was wry, but her eyes spoke of her trepidation.

She activated the main screen, cleared all notifications, and then opened the message app. After a few silent moments, which tortured Maggie, Tamsyn turned with a huge grin on her face.

"Carmen says it's amazing! Vast majority of people really positive." She stopped, suddenly choking up, her hand going to her mouth.

Maggie carefully removed the phone from Tamsyn's hand, wrapped her arms around her, and pulled her close. As Tamsyn cried, Maggie kissed her hair, smoothed it away from her face, and simply held her.

When Tamsyn had stopped sniffling, she eased herself back from Maggie's arms, blew her nose, then reached for her phone again.

"Let me just read one more," she said quietly.

Maggie watched as she scrolled to it, read it, then passed the phone to Maggie.

Proud of you x

The name at the top of the message said *Lesley*.

"How does that make you feel?" Maggie asked.

Tamsyn sighed. "I honestly don't know. I still can't forgive her for her role in Harewood's outing, but I have known her for nearly three decades. That's a lot of friendship to throw away over one disagreement." She shrugged. "I'll probably contact her again, sometime in the next couple of months, and see if we can rebuild. I'm not sure though…"

Tamsyn stood up, walked to the big windows and stood staring out for some time. Maggie left her to it, understanding the need to be with her own thoughts.

Much later, they popped open some champagne.

"To my beautiful girlfriend," Maggie said, holding up her glass. "Who I couldn't be more proud of today. Welcome to your coming out, my love."

"Thank you," Tamsyn whispered, her eyes still puffy and red from crying. "It's a pleasure to be here."

"I'll drink to that!"

They sipped and laughed and sipped some more. Soon, hunger set in again and they worked together to make a risotto for a late lunch, accompanied by more champagne. By the time the sun set they were hysterically drunk, but even in her inebriated state, Maggie knew this was just what Tamsyn had needed. When they collapsed into bed at only nine o'clock that night, neither of them complained. It had been one heck of a day.

Tamsyn's phone rang as she popped the last of the croissants on the plate and she sighed. While the calls had diminished since Saturday, there was still a steady stream of them. She saw Carmen's name in the caller display and winced. She'd already left three voicemails, each more annoyed than the last. Maybe this time she should just answer.

"Hi, Carmen."

"Well, it's about time! You can't seriously have been shagging the *entire* time you've been there?"

"Maybe we have," Tamsyn said, snippily.

"Uh-huh, whatever."

"Sorry I haven't called you back."

"I'll forgive you. Seriously, Tamsyn, I get it. Of course you want to hide away. But I'm not actually ringing about all that now, at least not directly."

"No?"

"No. I mean, if you want to hear what an overnight legend you've become in LGBT circles, then sure, I can chew your ear off for hours on that score."

Tamsyn laughed. "That's okay, that can wait, I'm sure. But has it really been that positive?"

"God, *yes*! Even Tony's a bit taken aback. I mean, you've probably lost the entire readership of the *Daily Mail*, but I'm quite sure that's something you can live with."

"Hell, yes."

"Good. So, anyway, I have something rather juicy to share with you. Are you sitting down?"

"Uh-oh."

"Trust me, this is a good one."

Tamsyn moved to the sofa, sweeping up her glass of water en route. Maggie strolled into the room, a quizzical look on her face when she saw Tamsyn on the phone.

"Carmen" she mouthed, and Maggie nodded before heading off to the kitchen.

"So, comfy yet?" Carmen said impatiently.

"Yes, yes. Go on, spill."

"Well, I know it's only January, but I just earned my bonus for this year already."

"That's quite the brag."

Carmen laughed. "Trust me, I own it. I got a call early this morning from a producer in LA. Guess who they're keen to talk to about a starring role in *Ocean's 9*?"

Tamsyn blinked. A few times.

"Are you kidding me? Please, Carmen, don't kid about—"

"I'm not. I'd never do that to you. He said they'd been thinking about casting for a while and your name kept popping up. I kind of knew this through some of my contacts, so I'd let it be known that you would be *very* keen to talk to them about this."

"And they called today? A few days after my big news broke?"

"They did. I even went so far as to check that he'd heard and he just said, 'Yeah, so what?'"

Tamsyn flopped back against the sofa cushions, her heart pounding. "Oh, my God, Carmen. This is *incredible*! A film that big, in that franchise..."

"I know," Carmen said quietly. "Now, I know it isn't in the bag yet, but when we get you this, if there's any doubters out there questioning your career prospects, this should shut them up forever."

Tamsyn's laugh started small but within moments it consumed her, until tears were rolling down her cheeks.

"Tamsyn, you okay?" Carmen said between guffaws.

Maggie strode over from the kitchen, her face a picture of confusion and amusement wrapped into one.

"I'm...I'm fine," Tamsyn stammered. "I need to tell Maggie. I'll call you later, okay?"

"Sure."

The line went dead and Tamsyn threw the phone onto the end of the sofa. She patted the seat beside her and Maggie promptly sat.

"What the hell is going on?" she asked, then laughed as Tamsyn grabbed her and squeezed her tight.

"Remember how I worried about how being out would hurt my career?"

"Yes," Maggie said slowly, staring at her.

"*Ocean's 9*, baby. *Ocean's 9*."

Maggie's eyebrows shot up, her eyes went wide, and her hands convulsively squeezed Tamsyn's hips.

"Serious?"

Tamsyn nodded. "Serious."

Maggie squealed and Tamsyn laughed, pulling her back in for one of those all-encompassing hugs she'd grown to love so much.

"I think that calls for more champagne," Maggie whispered against her skin. "Don't you?"

"As if you need to ask me twice." Tamsyn rolled her eyes.

Maggie threw her head back and laughed out loud.

<hr/>

As they headed for the exit, the porter wheeling their luggage behind them, a sharp tug on Tamsyn's arm brought her up short. She turned to face Maggie, whose expression was unreadable.

"What?" Tamsyn asked, another nervous tremor juddering through her body to add to the pile of nerves already in residence. They were about to face the waiting crowd at Heathrow. Tony had surreptitiously leaked her arrival time to the more friendly papers as a sop to them missing out on interviews. The idea was that they could run photos of a smiling Tamsyn returning from her break; she'd answer just a couple of questions and then be whisked away by her new security detail to the car that, by then, would already have collected Maggie. It was a good plan, one that they'd both endorsed, but now that it was here, Tamsyn was nauseous. What if people shouted horrible things? Or asked completely insensitive questions? When facing the press before, none of this had bothered her, or even entered her mind.

Somehow, this was entirely different.

"I've changed my mind." Maggie's voice was quiet, and she bit her bottom lip as soon as she'd spoken.

Tamsyn's heart faltered and her breath caught in her throat. "What?" Terror filled her—was Maggie about to leave her? To change her mind about everything they'd planned and dreamed about together?

Her fear must have been evident on her face; Maggie's eyes widened and she rushed to say, "Oh no! I don't mean about *us*. I mean about this." She waved towards the exit. "About the plan for me to sneak out and you to face the press on your own."

"What do you mean?" Tamsyn was thoroughly confused.

"I mean, we're together now," Maggie said, stepping closer. "We're in this *together*. I'm your partner. And we need to get used to this—*I* need to get used to this, our new reality. That you are who you are, and the press are always going to be interested in you. And interested in us." She took Tamsyn's hand. "So, we should do this together. Hand in hand."

Tamsyn was lighter, all of a sudden. Almost as if she were floating.

"Have you *any* idea how much I love you?" she said, pulling Maggie close.

Maggie chuckled. "I have a pretty good idea, yes, but, you know, you can show me later."

"Oh, I plan to," Tamsyn whispered. She sucked in a breath. "Are you sure?"

Maggie nodded. "Absolutely."

"Okay," Tamsyn said, inhaling deeply again. "Then let's do it."

She squeezed Maggie's hand, holding onto it as they walked to the exit.

As the automatic doors opened before them, they were met with a wall of flashing lights, shouts, applause, and cheering, and a plethora of rainbow flags waving back and forth over the heads of the bank of photographers.

Maggie glanced over at Tamsyn and grinned, even though her eyes were wide.

Tamsyn grinned back, clasped tightly to Maggie's hand, and together they turned back to face the waiting crowd.

About A. L. Brooks

A.L. Brooks was born in the UK but currently resides in Frankfurt, Germany, and over the years she has lived in places as far afield as Aberdeen and Australia. She works 9–5 in corporate financial systems and her dream is to take early retirement. Like, tomorrow, please. She loves her gym membership, and is very grateful for it as she also loves dark chocolate. She enjoys drinking good wine and craft beer, trying out new recipes to cook, and learning German. Travelling around the world and reading lots and lots (and lots) of books are also things that fight for time with her writing. Yep, she really needs that early retirement.

CONNECT WITH A.L. BROOKS
Website: www.albrookswriter.com
Twitter: @albrookswriter1
E-Mail: albrookswriter@gmail.com

Other Books from
Ylva Publishing

www.ylva-publishing.com

One Way or Another

A.L. Brooks

ISBN: 978-3-96324-094-2
Length: 186 pages (63,000 words)

Corporate lawyer Sarah is living a simple life: No ties, no hassles, no love.

Demure teacher Bethany just wants to be swept off her feet.

A chance meeting outside a London sex shop draws the unlikely pair together. But how can two people so different even connect, let alone fall in love? Can Ms. Wrong ever be right?

A fun, sexy, lesbian romance about finding not what we want, but what we need.

Breaking Character

Lee Winter

ISBN: 978-3-96324-113-0
Length: 315 pages (106,000 words)

Life becomes a farcical mess when icy British A-lister Elizabeth and bright LA star Summer try to persuade an eccentric director they're in love to win Elizabeth her dream role—while convincing a gossiping Hollywood they're not. Worse, they're closeted lesbians who don't even know the other is gay. A lesbian celebrity romance about gaining love, losing masks, and trying to stick to the script.

Damage Control

(The Hollywood Series – Book 2)
Jae

ISBN: 978-3-95533-372-0
Length: 347 pages (140,000 words)

When actress Grace Durand is photographed in a compromising situation with a woman, she fears for her career. She hires PR agent Lauren Pearce to do damage control, not knowing that she's a lesbian. As they run the gauntlet of the paparazzi together, Lauren realizes how different Grace is from her TV persona. Getting involved would ruin their careers, but the attraction between them is growing.

Scissor Link

(The Scissor Link Series – Book 1)
Georgette Kaplan

ISBN: 978-3-95533-678-3
Length: 197 pages (72,000 words)

Wendy is in love with Janet Lace. Janet is beautiful, she's intelligent, and she is also Wendy's boss.

Still, a little fantasy never hurt anyone. Or so Wendy thought until Janet got a look at the e-mail she sent. The one about exactly what Wendy would like to do to Janet.

But when Wendy gets called into the boss's office, it might just be her fantasy coming true. If it doesn't get her fired first.

Write Your Own Script
© 2019 by A.L. Brooks

ISBN: 978-3-96324-156-7

Also available as e-book.

Published by Ylva Publishing, legal entity of Ylva Verlag, e.Kfr.

Ylva Verlag, e.Kfr.
Owner: Astrid Ohletz
Am Kirschgarten 2
65830 Kriftel
Germany

www.ylva-publishing.com

First edition: 2019

Credits
Edited by Alissa McGowan
Cover Design and Print Layout by Streetlight Graphics